I0740791

Robert Herbert Story

William Carstares

A Character and Career of the Revolutionary Epoch (1649-1715)

Robert Herbert Story

William Carstares
A Character and Career of the Revolutionary Epoch (1649-1715)

ISBN/EAN: 9783337032234

Printed in Europe, USA, Canada, Australia, Japan

Cover: Foto ©Raphael Reischuk / pixelio.de

More available books at **www.hansebooks.com**

A Character and Career

OF

THE REVOLUTIONARY EPOCH.

(1649–1715.)

BY

ROBERT HERBERT STORY,

MINISTER OF ROSNEATH.

"Res gestas majorum nostrorum a fabularum vanitate liberare, et ab oblivionis injuria vindicare."—GEO. BUCHANAN, *History, Book I.*

London:

MACMILLAN AND CO.

1874.

TO

HER ROYAL HIGHNESS THE PRINCESS LOUISE,

MARCHIONESS OF LORNE.

MADAM,

IN dedicating this volume to your Royal Highness, I venture to hope that you will recognise, in the history which it traces, two claims to your Royal Highness's consideration.

The principles which animated Carstares, in his conflict with political misrule and ecclesiastical oppression, were identical with those which placed the Elector of Hanover upon the British throne. Throughout the long struggle which secured their ascendency, those principles found no more faithful champions and martyrs than the chiefs of the House of Argyll.

In writing this book I have discharged a duty to a kinsman's memory; in connecting it with the name of your Royal Highness I indulge a wish of my own, which your great kindness has permitted me to gratify.

I have the honour to be,

Madam,

Your Royal Highness's most faithful and obedient servant,

ROBERT HERBERT STORY.

"The good and great Mr. WILLIAM CARSTARES, high favourite of King William and of his Cabinet Council for Scots' affairs: the Jacobites and ill-affected lords for this called him the Cardinal. He surely was one of the greatest clergymen ever embellished any Church; often Moderator of General Assemblies; full of piety and Christian charity."

COLTNESS COLLECTIONS, p. 78.

PREFACE.

By way of preface to this book, I have only to mention my sources of information, and to acknowledge my obligations to the gentlemen from whom I have received help.

Carstares's sister Sarah married her cousin William Dunlop, who was my great-great-great-grandfather, on the mother's side. By Sarah, who possessed a mass of her brother's letters and papers, a large collection of these was bequeathed to her son Alexander, and is now the property of my cousin Alexander Graham Dunlop, of Gairbraid. He did me the favour of selecting from this collection all the MSS. in Carstares's handwriting or directly connected with his affairs, and entrusting them to me. They form the basis of this biography.

Another set of papers, consisting almost wholly of letters addressed to Carstares, is in the possession of my aunt Mrs. Murray Dunlop, of Corsock; and to this also, through her kindness, I have had full access.

I found several letters of Carstares' among the MSS. of the University Library in Glasgow, and a few embedded in the unwieldy mass of the Wodrow MSS., in the Advocates' Library.

Next in importance to these, and of the same value as original sources, are the 'State Papers' edited by M'Cormick, to which a sketch of Carstares's life, of no great historical worth, is prefixed. These State Papers consist, with but one or two exceptions, of letters addressed to Carstares by the leading public men of his time.

Besides these primary authorities, I have found much that illustrates Carstares's character and career, in the 'Correspondence' and 'Analecta' of Wodrow; in the 'Coltness Collections'; the 'Caldwell Papers'; the 'Marchmont Papers'; the 'Lockhart Papers'; the 'Leven and Melville Papers'; 'Fountainhall's Historical Notices,' and some of the minor publications of those clubs which have thrown the light of their valuable memoirs upon Scottish history. For the narrative of the general events, political and ecclesiastical, in which Carstares was concerned, I have had recourse, mainly, to the 'History of the Sufferings,' by Wodrow; the 'History of his own Time,' by Burnet; the admirable 'Memoirs' and Appendices, of Dalrymple; and to the recent histories of Mr. Hill Burton, Dr. Cunningham, and Mr. Grub. The work of these three gentlemen has appeared to me so accurate and trustworthy that, at several points, I have thought it best to append to a statement in the text nothing more than a reference to one, or another, or all, of them, when recourse to their original authorities would be troublesome or impossible to the general reader.

I have derived great help from the collection of pamphlets in the Advocates' Library (which, I may be permitted to remark, would be rendered much more available to the student by a good catalogue).

In recording my thanks to the gentlemen who have been so good as to aid me in my work, I wish to name along with them the Very Reverend the Dean of Westminster, who—when it was scarce begun, and when I was inclined to doubt whether I should be able to accomplish it—encouraged me with more than one very kind expression of his interest in its success. To David Laing, Esq., the patriarch of Scottish historical research, I, in common with every one, whether beginner or veteran, who ventures into the field which is peculiarly his own, owe the heartiest thanks for advice and information which no one else could have supplied; to say nothing, in my case, of the loan of books and pamphlets from his own library, and from that of which he is—and long may he be—the curator.

I am also much indebted to Mr. Jamieson, the curator of the Advocates' Library; and to the Rev. Professor Dickson and Professor Edward Caird, of the University of Glasgow, to whom I owe the privilege of unrestricted access to its rich and admirably arranged collection.

Mr. Marwick, formerly town-clerk of Edinburgh, and now of Glasgow, was most courteous in letting me examine the city records, and in allowing the experts in his office to decipher and transcribe for me some peculiarly puzzling letters among the Graham Dunlop MSS.

The Rev. William Ferrie, the biographer of John Carstares, and who is now settled in the State of New York, is a descendant of Mrs. Drew, one of Carstares's sisters. A box full of MSS. was lost in crossing the Atlantic; but he still has several letters and papers which belonged to Carstares, from which he has communicated to me some important extracts. For these, as for several of his own interesting letters, I beg to offer him my sincere thanks.

To those of my own kindred, who placed at my disposal the documents without which I should not have attempted to write this book at all, I need not say my very hearty acknowledgments are due, and will, I know, be accepted without further asseveration.

R. H. S.

Rosneath, *February* 1874.

TABLE OF CONTENTS.

WILLIAM CARSTARES.

CHAPTER 1.

" WILLIAM had one Scottish adviser, who deserved and possessed more influence than any of the ostensible ministers. This was Carstares, one of the most remarkable men of that age. He united great scholastic attainments with great aptitude for civil business, and the firm faith and ardent zeal of a martyr, with the shrewdness and suppleness of a consummate politician. In courage and fidelity he resembled Burnet; but he had what Burnet wanted—judgment, self-command, and a singular power of keeping secrets."[*]

It is thus that the most recent, and most copious, historian of the Revolution in England describes the position and character of William Carstares.

Mr. Hill Burton's sketch of him is traced in similar lines. " Carstares had scarcely the rhetorical and literary talents of his rival Burnet, but he was entirely free of that prelate's foppish love of consequence, and dangerous incontinence of tongue. He exhibited the rare phenomenon of a powerful churchman, who could look beyond his order, and use his influence not solely for the advancement of the Church, but

---

[*] Macaulay's 'History of England,' vol. iii. chap. xiii.

for the State too. . . . . Except Bentinck, it would be difficult to point out any one whom William so entirely esteemed and trusted as Carstares. . . . . Carstares' integrity has been unquestioned; and among the many dubious and treacherous men of this restless age, he remained firm and honest."[*] Other names, of less account than his, occur much more frequently in the books, pamphlets, and letters of the reigns of James VII., William, and Anne; but, with hardly an exception whenever William Carstares is named in these, it is with the respect accorded, even by his opponents, to a man of acknowledged power, influence, and integrity. No one passes with less scathe through the controversies, slanders, scurrilities, of an age when rival factions used poisoned weapons, and gave no quarter. Of many references to him that I have discovered, almost the only one which has a bitter flavour, as of personal dislike, is in the spy Macky's "Characters of the Nobility of Scotland," where he is described as "a fat sanguine-complexioned fair man, always smiling where he designs most mischief." "The cunningest subtle dissembler in the world."[†] Yet often and honourably as Carstares is mentioned among the political characters of the second half of the 17th century, the notices of him are so scattered and so incidental, that it is difficult to form from them a complete idea of his character and life. The memoir, which is prefixed to the 'Carstares State Papers,'[‡] is the only attempt that has been made to relate his history as a whole; and the narrative there given, well-intentioned as it is, is rather confused, and lacks many details which are now

---

[*] 'History of Scotland from 1688.' J. H. Burton, vol. i. p. 30–2.

[†] 'Memoirs of the Secret Services of John Macky.' London, 1733, p. 209. Swift's note appended to Macky's text is "A good character, but not strong enough by a fiftieth part." See annotated edition (in the Advocate's Library).

[‡] 'State Papers and Letters, addressed to William Carstares, &c., to which is prefixed the Life of Mr. Carstares, published from the originals by Joseph McCormick, D.D., Minister at Prestonpans.' Edinburgh, 1774. McCormick, afterwards Principal of St. Andrews, was Carstares' grand-nephew.

ascertained, though apparently unknown to the author; nor is it altogether successful in giving a clear picture of the events of the epoch of the Revolution and of the Union, and of Carstares' relation to them. The principles, which governed the statesmen and churchmen of that epoch, are now better understood; and the acts, in which those principles were embodied have been more thoroughly examined, than when the biographer of Carstares wrote. The materials for the construction of a memoir of his life are ampler and more accessible than they could then be. It seems legitimate to attempt, with these advantages, to depict anew the character and career of a man whose place is second to none in the long and honourable roll of Scottish worthies.

In the 15th century a certain William Carstares* was a substantial burgess of St. Andrews. In October, 1483, he obtained from John Lok, Canon of Brechin, a charter " of a tenement on the north side of the South Street of St. Andrews, and that in consideration of a certain sum of money paid to him by the said William Carstares, in his urgent necessity." Besides this tenement, he possessed property in the " Kirk Vennel" of the same city. The house in South Street was assigned, in 1503, to his daughter Beatrix; and, after one or two other transfers, appears to have come in the year 1518 into the hands of "Sir Henry Carstares, son and heir of William Carstares;" who in his turn made it over to another William Carstares, " citizen of St. Andrews." This William, who also held " lands on the west side of the Brig of Crail," granted a new charter of this tenement in South Street to Sir William Myrtoun, Vicar of Lathrisk, on the 23rd of July, 1521.†

In 1573 we find Thomas Carstares, of the same family, in possession of New Grange, near St. Andrews. He died in

---

* The name was spelled, indifferently, Carstaris, Carstairs, Carstaires, Carstaers, and Carstares, until the subject of this memoir adopted and adhered to Carstares.

† These documents are in the Charter Chest of Crail. See ' Fifiana,' by M. F. Conolly. Glasgow, 1869.

1615, and appears to have left several children.* John Carstares, who succeeded him as proprietor of New Grange, had a nephew and son-in-law in a certain James Carstares, resident in St. Andrews.

In February, 1625, this Mr. James Carstares makes his will, and appoints his father-in-law, " John Carstares, merchant," and John Carstares, jun., his brother-in-law, his executors. John Carstares, merchant, was Provost of St. Andrews, as well as laird of New Grange. His son became afterwards Sir John Carstares, Knight, of Kilconquhar. James Carstares, who made his will in 1625, names as his eldest lawful son John Carstares. John was born on the 6th of January, 1623, and inherited the Carstares blood both from father and mother, the latter being, as his father's will proves, the daughter of Carstares of New Grange. He married, in 1647, or 1648, Janet, fourth daughter of William Mure of Glanderston, in Renfrewshire, a cadet of the family of Caldwell and ancestor of the present representative of the Mures.† Of that marriage was born, on the 11th of February, 1649, William Carstares, his parents' eldest son. They had three other sons and five daughters, of whom two sons and one daughter died early.

John Carstares was a man of no small mark among the Scottish Churchmen of the days of the Commonwealth and the Persecution. He entered the University of St. Andrews in 1638, and studied there till the close of his *curriculum*, his teacher in theology being the learned and pious Samuel Rutherford. Having been for a short time parish minister of Cathcart, near Glasgow,—where he married, and where his son William was born,—he became, in 1650, minister of the Cathedral, or High Church, of Glasgow. His first conspicuous engagement in the public turmoils of his time was on the 3rd of September, 1650, at the Battle of Dunbar. He was there, rather unnecessarily, one should say, along with other

* Information partly supplied by Mr. Ferrie.

† 'Notices of the Life of the Rev. John Carstaires,' by Rev. Wm. Ferrie, A.M. Edinburgh, 1843. See pp. 3, 6, 54.

ministers, who thronged the camp of General Leslie, and strove not only to stimulate the fervour, but to direct the tactics, of the Scottish host. Some of the warlike clergy were slain; Carstares and Waugh (the minister of Borrowstonness) were taken prisoners, and carried to Edinburgh.* Amidst the dissolution of parties and forces which followed the battle of Dunbar, a so-called "Western Army," numbering about 5000 men, and professing Covenanting principles of an extreme sort, was organized by Colonel Ker and Colonel Strachan—well-known soldiers of the time. Cromwell kept his eye upon this body, with a special hope of being able to bring its leaders to peaceable treaty, or to consent to act along with him; and he tried to come to terms of agreement through the intervention of his prisoners, John Carstares and Provost Jaffray of Aberdeen,† who were liberated on parole for the purposes of this negociation. Although the "Remonstrance" issued by Ker and Strachan, while they awaited, at Dumfries, the course of events, expressed but scant loyalty to Charles, the "Covenanted King," its sentiments were nowise friendly to the "English Sectaries." Cromwell's well-chosen envoys effected nothing; and his hopes of conciliation were disappointed. Where he could not conciliate, he must needs quell; and the differences between him and the "Remonstrants" being put to the arbitrament of the sword, the decision was, as usual in those days, in favour of the English invader.‡ After this bootless mission John Carstares returned to confinement in Edinburgh. Several of his letters to his wife, during his imprisonment, are extant, and may be read in Mr. Ferrie's volume; but they are so entirely filled with pious reflections on the course of Providence, and on his own spiritual condition, and with the religious

* Carlyle's 'Oliver Cromwell,' vol. ii. p. 41. Mr. Ferrie, in his 'Life of John Carstares,' misapprehends his situation at this time, and erroneously represents him as flying from Dunbar to Edinburgh Castle and remaining there till its surrender. He was Cromwell's prisoner till after that time.

† Baillie's 'Letters,' Bannatyne Club, iii. 120.

‡ Carlyle, vol. ii. p. 85.

"improvement" of his troubles, that they throw little light on the history of the events that were passing around him.

In one dated the 4th of October, he says, "I may cry out 'Woe is me, my leanness! my leanness!' It's a wonder to me, at least it may be, how it has not been obvious and palpable—feasible to all his people, standing by and looking on, that my nakedness has not been long ere now discovered; that the peinture upon this tomb has not been rubbed off, and the rottenness within seen; that the vizorine and cover has not been pulled off this face, which has long, even very long, deceived a world. . . . What have I done—as a husband—a father and head of a family? What as a minister, a pastor, a watchman, a steward, a servant of Jesus Christ, a friend of the Bridegroom? What as a member of judicatories? . . . It cannot be told how empty and worn in all these I have been."* Again, he writes on the 24th of December, on the very day on which the Castle was surrendered by Colonel Walter Dundas; and the only reference he makes to external circumstances does not extend, although the letter is a long one, beyond two short sentences: "I am somewhat weary of this place. . . . I have as yet made no application to these men for liberty, but purpose to do so shortly."† And yet we know that he was personally concerned in the negociations for the surrender. On the 14th of December, Cromwell wrote to the Governor of the Castle: "If you please to name any you would speak with, now in Town, they shall have liberty to come and speak with you for one hour;" and Dundas asks that Provost Jaffray and Mr. Carstares should be sent to him. They, in their turn, write a note which Cromwell forwards, wherein they decline the conference: "In such an important trust we dare not," they say, "take upon us to meddle." How the capitulation was managed without their help may be read in the pages of Mr. Carlyle.‡ After a lenient captivity (for he tells his wife in another undated letter that he is like to forget he is a prisoner through the

---

* Ferrie, p. 63.   † Ibid. p. 72.   ‡ Carlyle, vol. ii. p. 91-2.

"abundant ease of his accommodation," and that he has liberty to walk abroad),* he was exchanged, along with Waugh and Jaffray, for some prisoners in Leslie's hands; and returned to Glasgow, where his wife awaited him with her son, and with a daughter that had been born during his imprisonment.

"Here," says his biographer, "he began to preach against the times." The meaning of this phrase is only too notoriously illustrated in the records that remain of many of the preachings in those confused and excited days. The ministers constantly thundered from their pulpits against the backslidings of the party to which they were opposed, or of the person who happened to be obnoxious to them.† Baillie tells us how General Leslie, amidst "the shame and discouragement" of his overthrow at Dunbar, was "irritate with Mr. James Guthrie's public invectives against him from the pulpit."‡ When Cromwell and his troopers came to Glasgow in October, 1650, at the time of the Ker and Strachan Remonstrance, and went soberly to church, "Mr. Zachary Boyd railed on them all to their face"§ from the pulpit of the Cathedral. On the great sectary's next visit, in April, 1651, he again betook himself to church both in the forenoon and afternoon, and had from Mr. Robert Ramsay "a very good honest sermon, pertinent for his case;" and heard Mr. John Carstares lecture, and Mr. James Durham (his colleague), "preach graciously and well to the times, as could have been desired."§ "Generally all who preached that day in the town gave a fair enough testimony against the sectaries."‖ "Bearing testimony" supplanted the simple gospel in those days; and the clergy's influence too often tended rather to intensify the

* Ferrie, Letters vii. and viii.

† "In their sermons, and chiefly in their prayers, all that passed in the state was canvassed: men were as good as named, and either recommended or complained of to God, as they were acceptable or odious to them. . . . The pulpit was a scene of news and passion." 'Burnet's History of his own Time.' Oxford (2nd) edition, vol. i. p. 60.

‡ Baillie's 'Letters,' Bannatyne Club, vol. iii. p. 111.

§ Ibid. vol. iii. p. 119.   ‖ Ibid. vol. iii. p. 165.

divisive fervour of contention, than to promote moderation and wise forbearance. Profound personal piety of the God-fearing and self-condemning sort, such as marked strongly the character of John Carstares, seemed to be in nowise incompatible with the keenest partizanship, and an extreme contentiousness of spirit. That this piety in his case was deep and sincere no one who reads the letters published by Ferrie can doubt. His " savouriness and the exceeding grace of God in him ;" his wonderful power in prayer ; * his strange prophetic " rapture " in preaching—are all borne witness to with admiration by his contemporaries.† Nor was this accompanied by narrow or fanatical doctrinal convictions. He appears to have understood the gospel of God's goodwill to men in its fulness and freedom. " His thoughts," he writes to his wife, " are the same for ever for love and goodwill. Whatever changes there be of dispensations he is never indeed . . . an enemy. When he is as an enemy, it is still peace that is in His thoughts : there is never ill in his mind—never an ill turn, so to speak. None of his thoughts are thoughts of ill. Believe this, O believe this ! dear heart." " There is but one promise in all the Scripture that I dare look to," said his dear friend Durham, as he lay near his death, " ' Come unto

---

* " When he first entered on his Sabbath's work, he ordinarily prayed ane hour, for he took in all the publick things in that prayer. . . . His band in the Sabbath would have been all wet, as if it had been douked with tears before he was done with his first prayer. . . . He used to have that expression and petition in many of his excellent prayers, ' O that we may never outlive our integrity nor die undesired.' " Wodrow's ' Analecta,' vol. iii. p. 48.

† Letter from Session of Scots' Church in Rotterdam to John Carstares. Ferrie, p. 36.—" Mr. John Carstares was eminent in many things but he excelled in prayer. Mr. James Wood used to say of him that for lecturing and preaching they could some way keep up with Mr. Carstares ; but in prayer there was none able to hold up with him." ' Analecta,' Maitland Club, vol. ii. p. 148. " He served the first Table " (at Holy Communion) " in a strange rapture, and he called some ministers there to the next, but he was in such a frame that none of them would come and take the work off his hand. He continued at the work with the greatest enlargement and melting upon himself and all present that could be ; and served fourteen or sixteen Tables." Ibid.

me all ye that are weary.' May I venture my Salvation upon
it?" "Yes," said Carstares, "if you had a thousand souls you
might venture them on it.*

Durham, who died at the early age of thirty-six in 1658,
seems to have left his MSS. to John Carstares; and several of
them, on their publication, were prefaced by him. Among
these were the sermons on Isaiah, the lectures on Revelation,
and the 'Unsearchable Riches of Christ,' the last of which was
especially admired and valued in Scotland. Carstares also
wrote the 'Epistle' or preface to Calderwood's 'History of
the Church.' A carefully revised copy of the history having
been sent by him to Macward, in Holland, was printed at
Rotterdam in 1678.† In his preface he contends earnestly
"that there is a particular form of Church government of
Divine Right;" and that in no church has this form been
maintained in greater simplicity and more primitive purity
than in the Church of Scotland.

The ten years of the Commonwealth were years of comparative peace for the Church; during which, had internal
dissensions and political contendings been forborne, Scottish
Presbytery might have established itself on a broad national
basis, which no subsequent revolutions could have under-
mined. Charles Stuart—whether covenanted or uncovenanted,
as bad a king as could have been found for any Christian
state—was fairly out of the way. A government, tolerant,
just, and strong, was in power. The material interests of the
country prospered under the benign influences of peace and
free trade with England. The General Assembly, no doubt, was
disbanded and in abeyance, like the Rump Parliament in the
South; but in spite of its silence and inaction, religion was
alleged to flourish. "The Scotch clergy, persisting in their
own most hidebound formula of a Covenanted Charles Stuart,
bear clear testimony that at no time did Christ's gospel so
flourish in Scotland, as now, under Cromwell the Usurper."‡

* 'Analecta,' vol. i. p. 215.
† Calderwood's History, Wodrow Society, vol. viii. Appendix, p. 4-10.
‡ Carlyle, vol. ii. p. 151.

But throughout all this period the Church was split into two opposing factions, and the hostile clergy strove, with fanatical violence, over the remonstrances, resolutions, and protests, which embodied their political crotchets and their ecclesiastical bigotries.

At Carisbrook Castle, in 1647, Charles I., driven by sore necessity, had entered into a certain engagement with the envoys of the Scots' Estates, promising to sanction the Covenant and to make other concessions to the Presbyterians.

This compact was denounced by the General Assembly; under whose pressure an "Act of Classes," as it was called, was passed, by which every one, who had taken any part in support of the engagement, was debarred from all public employment in the Church, the magistracy, or the legislature. This Act—justly stigmatised as "one of the most bigoted and illiberal pieces of legislation which ever disgraced the statute book of any country"*—was not rescinded till May 1651, after having been in force about three years. This rescission gained a qualified approval from the General Assembly; but a protest against the Assembly's action was given in by twenty-two ministers. The majority, adhering to the resolutions in which the Assembly ratified the policy of the Estates in repealing the Act of Classes, became known by the name of the "Resolutioners;" the protesting minority by that of the "Protesters." The Church was divided between these two parties. The party of the Resolutioners was the larger, and was composed of the peaceable, liberal, and constitutional supporters of orderly Presbyterial discipline, worship, and government, those who in more recent times would be distinguished as the "Moderates,"—the wise men of the "Via Media." The Protesters, early infected with the leaven of the Puritanism, which the sectaries brought to the North with them, were looser in their views of Church government, less reverent and heedful of those forms and usages of public worship which had hitherto been observed in Scotland, and more hot and vehement in speech and ges-

* Cunningham's 'Church History,' vol. ii. p. 168.

ture, whether in prayer or preaching. Their stiff-necked extravagance, and perverse intolerance, blinding their eyes to the plainest rules of policy and laws of human nature, were sufficiently illustrated in their treatment of Charles II., whom they drove even to the degradation of confessing and bewailing his father's sins, and his mother's " idolatry." Their overbearing fervour, noisy zeal, and restless craving for the extinction of opinions differing from their own, gave them that hold over the multitude which zealots and fanatics readily obtain ; but men of calm and charitable temper, of gentle culture, and of sound political experience and judgment, were alarmed and repelled by their extremes.* The most notable name among the constitutional Resolutioners was that of the good and sagacious Baillie ; among the perfervid Protesters that of the pious Rutherford, " the last of that race of Scottish clergy, who were vehement Presbyterians and great scholars."†

It was perhaps natural that John Carstares should take the same side as his old master in theology. At first he seems to have made some effort at peace, or mediation between the factions ; for we find a friendly conference of representatives from each, held in his " chamber," with no satisfactory result. But, like most men who join themselves to any body of pious enthusiasts, he soon became himself enthusiastic in the cause ; whose miserable watchwords, " Treaty with the King "—" Act of Classes "—" Commission's answer to the query," &c. &c., seem now almost beyond the grasp of human interest. Baillie, in one of his long letters, written in 1654, bewailing the predominance of the " heady men " who " waste the Church," and " frame our people to the sectarian model," attributes their undue " prevalence " in Glasgow chiefly to " Mr. John Carstares' zeal."‡

Other attempts, however, to effect a reconciliation are mentioned by Baillie, to which John Carstares was favour-

* See Baillie in many passages, especially vol. iii. pp. 244, 245.

† Burton's 'History of Scotland from Agricola's Invasion,' vol. vii. p. 431.

‡ Baillie, vol. iii. pp. 199, 200, 248, 249.

able, but to no purpose.   At one time, says the former, "We began to hope for a concord;"* but the hope came to no fruition.   When he refers to Carstares again, it is in connection with the prophetic enthusiasms—the jealous strifes—the irrational attempts to "purge out" all opponents, which were the natural fruits of successful fanaticism; and which ran their course, impairing the influence of the Church and dissolving many of the best elements of its corporate strength, until the fatal era of the Restoration.

It is necessary that we should keep in view the character of the times in which the boyhood of William Carstares was passed, and of the influences which surrounded him in his earliest years.   His father's house in Glasgow, where the accomplished Durham and the quaintly witty Zachary Boyd were familiar guests, must have been often the scene of learned and mirthful converse, no less than of piety and prayer; but it must oftenest of all, no doubt, have re-echoed with the Protesting brethren's groans over the defections of the times—their quaint applications of Old Testament names and stories—their mutual exhortations to "testifying" and "purging"—their long and marvellously uttered supplications†— all solemn and wonderful, if somewhat wearisome and perplexing, to the boy.   The first intimation of his existence is in a letter from John Carstares to "his loving sister Katharine" (wife of the Rev. James Wood), dated "Glasgow, 16th February, 1649."—"Your sister is growing strong," he says, "and a fine nurse to her son, yet alive."‡ [He was born on the 11th of February.]   "Let the Lord own him for his."

In Ferrie's collection there is an undated letter to "My dearest nephew," in which an uncle, resident in St. Andrews,

---

* Baillie, vol. iii. p. 297.

† "The man's vehemency in his prayer—a strange kind of sighing, the like whereof I had never heard, as a pythonising out of the belly of a second person, made me amazed." Baillie, vol. iii. p. 245.

‡ (Here, as elsewhere, in quoting these ancient letters and MSS. I modernize the spelling, unless there appears to be some adequate reason for preserving the old peculiarities.)

urges that William should be sent to college there. "He may have a great deal better occasion to follow his studies nor in Edinburgh, where there are so many occasions to divertisements, and will do me and my best half a singular pleasure, and shall be used as our own son." The best half adds a postscript:—"These are earnestly to entreat you to obey your uncle's desire in sending your son to us. . . . I saw your son at Edinburgh. He promised to get leave from his mother to be with us this vacance." This request was not acceded to. He never attended either school or college at St. Andrews. He was sent, "when very young," says McCormick, "to board with the Rev. Mr. Sinclair, a Presbyterian minister, who kept boarders at his manse of Ormiston in East Lothian." "Many young gentlemen of the chief families in Scotland" were educated at Mr. Sinclair's, and so strict was he in their classical training that he allowed no language but Latin to be spoken in his family.* Mr. Sinclair had been, some years before, one of the Regents of St. Leonard's College, St. Andrews, where one of his colleagues was James Sharp, afterwards Archbishop. It is related that in an after-dinner discussion, at the college table, the two regents waxed so hot over the comparative merits of Presbytery and Episcopacy, that Sinclair gave Sharp the lie direct, and Sharp gave Sinclair a box on the ear; and this on "the Sabbath day." † No doubt the minister of Ormiston was more discreet than the regent of St. Andrews.

It appears from the register of graduations that William Carstares entered the University of Edinburgh in 1663, and took his degree in 1667. He studied in the University "under the particular inspection of Mr. Paterson, then one of the regents of the college, afterwards Sir William Paterson, and clerk to the Privy Council of Scotland." ‡ His proficiency is said to have been very marked, not only in the "several branches of the school philosophy," but in theology, the

* McCormick, p. 4.
† See an article on Sharp in 'North British Review,' No. 92.
‡ McCormick, p. 4.

science to which his own and his father's wish specially inclined him. His father, harassed as he was with many troubles, spared no pains to secure to his son the advantages of a thorough education and took a careful personal interest in its progress. In a letter written on the 27th of October, 1662, before William entered college, he says, "I have a line dated Sept. 20, from William, within these two days, wherein he gives me an account of his studies. . . . I find he is not idle. The Lord command the blessing."* From another letter written in June 1664, in which he bids his wife pay her son's quarter, and desire his tutor to "write a particular account to me of Will's carriage and profiting," and refers to his still living with Mr. Sinclair, it is obvious that the long vacation must have been spent at Ormiston; and that William was assisted in his studies by a tutor, under the superintendence of Mr. Sinclair, for at least the first summer after he went to college. Indeed this plan was probably followed as long as he remained in Scotland; for in a letter from Mrs. Carstares written, it should appear, on the 30th of August, 1666—or within a year of the time of William's graduation —she tells her husband, "Your son's education, with his *boarding* and other necessaries, comes to 400 marks, which I have paid."†

After he had taken his degree at Edinburgh he went to Holland, in order to complete his education there. Ere this evil days of darkness and danger had fallen on Scotland, and his father had been called to suffer with his brethren.

The restoration of Charles II. was the beginning of sorrows to the Scottish Church. During Cromwell's Protectorate the party of the Protesters, which, though not the most numerous, was accounted the most zealous, had the favour of the Government.‡ They had consequently increased in numbers

---

* Ferrie, p. 95.

† Ferrie, p. 161. The Scots' mark was in actual value equal to 1s. 1½d. of English money; but its relative value in so poor a country as Scotland was much higher.

‡ Principal Lee's 'History of the Church of Scotland,' vol. ii. p. 376.

and activity; and now, along with the fanatical remnant of
the Ker and Strachan "Remonstrants" that still lurked in
the west, would have urged on Charles, who was, according to
their fond imagination, their "Covenanted King," the old
obligations to extirpate "Popery, Prelacy, superstition, heresy,
schism, profaneness, and whatsoever shall be found contrary
to sound doctrine and the power of godliness." "The Resolutioners," with more moderate and statesmanlike policy, while
desirous that the Covenant should be recognised by way of basis
of the King's restoration, were prepared to accept as sufficient
for their demands, a confirmation of the proper rights and
ancient polity of the Presbyterian Church, as the Established
Church of the country. The grand idea of the Solemn
League and Covenant of one Presbyterian Church established
throughout the three kingdoms had not died out of the
minds of Douglas, Baillie, and other leading "Resolutioners;" but they did not cling to it with the intolerant
tenacity of the opposite party. The Church reaped the har-
vest of the prolonged strife between her two rival factions,
in finding herself in the time of her emergency, when
united counsels might have insured her prolonged peace and
prosperity, divided and perplexed, and speaking with two
voices in the presence of those who were full of jealous suspicion, if not of positive hostility. The representation of the
cause of the moderate party was entrusted to James Sharp—
"a traitor who abandoned all "—who went to London "as an
ambassador in the cause of a Presbyterian polity, and returned as the selected Archbishop of St. Andrews."* It

* Burton, vol. vii. p. 398.

Baillie writes to Spang: "Had we but petitioned for Presbytery at
Breda, it had been, as was thought, granted; but fearing what the least
delay of the King's coming over might have produced, and trusting fully
to the King's goodness, we hastened him over, without any provision for
our safety. At that time it was that Dr. Sheldon, now Bishop of London,
and Dr. Morley, did poison Mr. Sharp our agent, whom we trusted, who,
piece and piece, in so cunning a way has trepanned us, as we have never
win so much as to petition either King, Parliament, or Council." Dated
May 12, 1662. Baillie's ' Letters,' vol. iii. p. 484.

would have needed more than treachery on Sharp's part, however, to have betrayed the cause successfully, had the Church not been both divided against itself, and weakened by the heady policy of the Protesters. They had carried Puritanical pietism and coercion to an excess. Their spirit had not been charitable; their discipline had been irrationally severe; their desire to meddle and rule in civil affairs restlessly obtrusive. Among the elements of revolution which were seething in the country, at this time, there was an irritation, and impatience of moral restraint and ecclesiastical control among the upper classes, which the Protesters' predominance had fostered. The Church was not disliked for its own sake; Presbytery had not lost its hold; but society was provoked and wearied with this intolerant section of the clergy; and few intelligent men had any sympathy with that pertinacity of principle which clung to reasons of division, as eagerly as if they had been bonds of union. The results were the "Act Rescissory," by which all legislation subsequent to 1640, and in the interests of Presbytery, was swept out of the statute book; the "Act for the restoration and re-establishment of the ancient government of the Church by bishops and archbishops;" the execution of the Marquis of Argyll,* and of James Guthrie,† the most zealous of the Protesters; and the burning of the Covenant by the common hangman.

On the 14th of August, 1661, the Episcopacy against which Scotland had struggled ever since James's first intrigues in its favour, was restored by Royal proclamation; and four prelates brought down from London the inestimable gift of the Apostolical Succession, for the benefit and salva-

---

* "Mr. [John] Carstares was called to be with the Marquis, to preach to him in the prison, the last Sabbath of his life." 'Analecta,' vol. iii. p 52. Mr. Graham Dunlop possesses a ring given on this occasion by the Marquis to the divine.

† "Guthrie being minister of Stirling while the King was there, had let fly at him in his sermons in a most indecent manner. . . . This personal affront had irritated the King more against him than against any other of the party." Burnet, vol. i. p. 206.

tion of the Scottish Church and people.* All this was but
in harmony with the policy which in England produced
the Act of Uniformity, and drove 2000 Presbyterian ministers from their churches. But in Scotland the policy was
less exposed to the influence of a healthy and independent public opinion than in England; and it was executed
by more unscrupulous and violent agents. Sheldon and
Clarendon were men of a different stamp from Sharp and
Middleton. In the following year the disastrous effects
of this treacherous and unprincipled policy began to appear. An Act was passed by the pliant Parliament—in
which the bishops had now taken their seats — requiring
from every man in a public office, or place of trust, an
abjuration of the Covenant and declaration of its unlaw-
fulness. Another enacted that all ministers who had, since
1639, been appointed to parishes " without presentations
from the lawful patrons,"† must now either quit their charges,
or accept presentation from the patron, and collation from the
bishop. All who refused to do this were to leave their
manses before the 1st of November, 1662; and were forbidden
thereafter to reside within twenty miles of their old parishes,
six miles of Edinburgh or any cathedral town, or three miles
of any royal burgh. The grinding oppression, which prompted
and applied these and similar Acts of a servile legislature,

* These were Sharp, Fairfoul, Hamilton, and Leighton. "Sharp, the
chief contriver and author of the scheme, solicited for himself the Archbishopric of St. Andrews, because he pretended to be afraid that if a violent
man obtained the primacy the country might be utterly ruined. . . .
Fairfoul, Archbishop of Glasgow, was a man of scandalous life, and totally
destitute of abilities. He had scarcely ever been distinguished at all except
for his jollity and buffoonery. . . . Hamilton, Bishop of Galloway, was
another contemptible driveller. He (as well as Sharp and Fairfoul) had
pretended great zeal for the Covenant, insomuch that before dispensing the
Sacrament he had been in the habit of using a form of excommunication
borrowed from the example of Nehemiah. Shaking the lap of his gown,
he said, ' So may God shake out every man from his house that dealeth
falsely in this Covenant.' " Lee, vol. ii. p. 320; Burnet, vol. i. p. 241.

† Since 1638 patronage had been practically in abeyance. In 1649 it
had been abolished by law.

soon evoked the indignant spirit of Scottish Presbytery. No less than 350 ministers suffered themselves to be driven from their churches, rather than comply with "the Black Acts." In the West the resistance was most determined. There the clergy were, for the chief part, men of good family and high character, and "it can hardly be imagined to what a degree they were loved and reverenced by their people."* Among these was John Carstares. "He was taken to task" by the Parliament itself, in the hope that he and some other "leading ministers in the West" might be brought "to a compliance with the new government,"† and led to influence others to the same purpose. The attempt to pervert his principles failed, and he was sent to prison. His close confinement seems not to have lasted many weeks, and he was then allowed to go to reside at Dalkeith, in terms of the six-mile Act; whence he writes to his wife, still in Glasgow, asking her to send him sundry books from his library, and giving a cheerful account of his health and contentment with his position.‡ "Charge Will from me," he adds, "to make earnest of seeking God, and to be diligent at his books." His troubles were not over, however, with the relaxation of his confinement to prison. In March, 1664, he travelled to St. Andrews to see his brother-in-law, Principal Wood, who was on his death-bed. Sharp, "that bold and impudent calumniator," as he calls the Archbishop, with a vehemence unusual in his language, had stated that Wood was now indifferent about Presbyterianism. The dying man must needs dictate a refuting "testimony," to vindicate himself from such a charge. Carstares subscribed this testimony as witness. He was immediately summoned by Sharp before the dreaded Court of High Commission, which, along with the other appanages of prelacy, had been restored after 1662.§

* Burnet, vol. i. p. 281.
† Memoirs of Veitch and Brysson, p. 7.
‡ Ferrie, p. 90.
§ Here are two samples of the kind of justice administered by the Privy Council and the High Commission :—
In June, 1664, an Episcopal curate having been settled in the parish of

Carstares, however, did not appear, but after writing to the
Lord Chancellor, Glencairn,* that he could not obey the cita-
tion of the court, he fled to a place of concealment. Sometimes from Isle Magee, in the north of Ireland, sometimes
from Cantyre, sometimes from refuges which it is impossible
to identify, he writes to his wife, pouring out his religious
meditations,—telling her of his welfare or his trials, giving
now and then homely and practical injunctions, which touch
chords of lively human sympathies with the much-enduring
man. He writes to her as his " worthie and dear sister," and
calls himself "John Jamesone," and resorts to many other
little artifices of concealment to mask his meaning and
identity, should·the letters fall into unfriendly hands. Thus,
writing very soon after Wood's death, he announces his
arrival at some hiding-place, " that little commodity " (himself) " came hither safe yesterday morning. . . . It is in
tolerable good case. Let me know whether the waiters
will make search for such commodities, and if they know it's

Dreghorn, the heritors and whole·inhabitants withdrew from the Church·
The Privy Council forthwith ordained that a party of soldiers should be
quartered on the parish, with power " to uplift the penalty of 20 shillings
Scots, *toties quoties*," from every parishioner who does not attend the
curate's ministrations.

At Ancrum, the parish minister was ejected, and a curate who had been
excommunicated twenty years before, and who held two other benefices,
was put in. On the day of his induction, amid some crowding and noise,
a poor woman plucked him by the gown, wishing to speak to him ; whereupon he struck her violently with his staff. Seeing this, some boys threw
a few stones at him, but did not hit him. This was represented as a
treasonable tumult ; and there was some local fining and imprisoning ; but
the woman, her two brothers, and four of the boys, were taken before the
High Commission. The woman was sentenced to be scourged through the
streets of Jedburgh. Her brothers, who were fathers of families, were
banished to Virginia. The boys were scourged through the streets of
Edinburgh, branded on the face with a hot iron, and then sent to Bar-
badoes to be sold as slaves. Nine "right reverend fathers in God" were
members of this lenient tribunal. See Wodrow's History (Burns's edition),
vol. i. pp. 393, 400.

---

* Veitch and Bryson, p. 491.

gone by them, what price they will rate it at." Again:
"Send me the Hebrew Grammar I some time looked on
when with you at Glasgow; it's a little grey-skinned book.
Send me also my mickle black satin cap; help it if it need."
"Let me know as near as you may when ye think probably
you will be brought to bed. The good Lord be with you to
refresh and comfort you with his own presence." From
another long letter dated the 12th of August, 1664, it would
appear that at that time William was beside him in his re-
treat, as he says, " Will will direct my letter to you." " My
dear," the wife writes in her turn, "I had reason always to
bless the Lord that ever I knew you; and this day I desire
to bless him more than ever . . . that I have a husband
wandering and suffering for the truth." Again she writes,
with a quiet sadness that is very touching : "It hath pleased
the Lord to remove my little gent. Robert " (the child born
during his father's wanderings). "They sent for me, but he
died before I came. There is many things sadder in our lot
than the death of a child, yet I had my own heaviness for
him."

Colonel Wallace, in his narrative of the Rising at Pent-
land,* states that John Carstares was in hiding up till the
time of the rising; but we cannot either confirm or disprove
this from his letters. We know that on the 28th of November, 1666, Mure, of Caldwell, along with some other gentlemen of the West, among whom was Carstares, met in the
parish of Beith, and organised a squadron of cavalry, chiefly
tenants of Caldwell, with which they set out—Mure taking
the command—to join the insurgents,† who were marching
from the south to Edinburgh.

The skirmish at Rullion Green dispersed Wallace's force
before Mure could unite with him, and the Caldwell contin-
gent, of from forty to fifty horse, was disbanded. Carstares,
who probably had uneasy recollections of Dunbar, with its terrible slaughter and rout, had joined this expedition with little

* Veitch and Brysson, p. 421.
† Caldwell Papers, Maitland Club, vol. i. p. 19.

goodwill; * but having joined it, he could not expect to evade
the penalty of insurrection, however justifiable resistance to
such a government as that of Charles might be.   He was
forfeited both in person and estate, and was expressly excluded from the indemnity, which was granted in October
of the following year.†   We know little of his condition from
this time till 1672, when he was again at liberty.   Wodrow
says that he was in Holland, and returned in 1672;‡ and
Mr. Ferrie, who disputes this statement, on the authority of
the late Rev. Dr. Steven, sometime minister of the Scots'
Church in Rotterdam, produces no evidence to the contrary.
Among John Carstares's letters in the Graham Dunlop collection is one addressed to Mrs. Carstares, and dated the 5th
of February, 1669, written from some place of hiding (in Cantyre, I should say) "with my life,' he says, "in my hand."
In this letter he tells his wife that he thinks of going to
England with some friends; "and whether thence to Holland, or first to Holland, if a fit occasion offer, I cannot so
determinately say. . . . . . One or two days of your company
these twenty days past, that I might have advised and consulted with you, would have been accounted by me a great
favour, but He hath thought good to dispose otherwise, and
I desire to submit, though the exercise of submission in such
a case hath its own great difficulty. . . . Now, my dear, be
not anxious about me. I am in good health. . . . Send me a
good quantity of the filings and nibblings off, with the glasses
of your [*word illegible*] lignum vitæ.   I find it agrees better
with me than tobacco.   I have no other herbs here to purge
my head with ; or rather, send me a little piece of the timber

* Veitch and Brysson, p. 421.

† Ferrie, p. 34.

‡ Wodrow (i. 196) says, "July 18th (1672), Mr. John Scot, son to
Andrew Scot in Tushielaw, being incarcerate for writing to the Reverend
Mr. John Carstares in Holland, is brought before the Council."   And,
"Sept. 3rd : Mr. Wm. Livingstone being imprisoned for correspondence
with Holland, and Mr. John Carstares lately come from Holland, appears
before the Council, and finding caution to appear when called under the
penalty of 2000 marks, is liberate."

that is fit for no other use, that I may get it fresh when
I need." This letter so far corroborates Wodrow, inasmuch
as it proves that in February 1669 he intended to go to
Holland, and upon the whole, we may fairly conclude that
Wodrow is correct.

"Him, who trod in his father's steps, doing mischief as far
as he was able, you have received like fire into your bosom,
of which God, I trust, will in time make you sensible."*
So wrote Cromwell to the Governor of Edinburgh Castle
when, after the battle of Dunbar, Scotland still believed
in her "Covenanted King." The time had now come—a
bitter time of judgment on divided counsels, short-sighted
policy, fanatical intolerance, and that unwise mingling of
things sacred with things secular, which had more than
once imperilled Church and State in Scotland. Such was
the time when William Carstares, having taken his degree
at Edinburgh, began, like Moses, to look on his brethren's
burdens and meditate on their oppression. The prospect
was one that well might stir the wrath—even to "saeva
indignatio"—of a young man of an " active, bold, and enter-
prising spirit,"† loving liberty and hating tyranny, and conscious of formidable powers, which he longed to carry into
the arena, where one after another of his friends and kindred
was falling wounded or slain. Possibly, in distant London,
the " Defender of the Faith," amidst his mistresses and boon
companions, did not fairly realise how his Scottish servants
were dealing with the votaries of that religion, which (unfit
as it was in his august opinion "for a gentleman," and grim
as no doubt were his recollections of its long prayers, longer
sermons, fasts, purgations and covenants) was still the
faith of many who had been ready in other days to die for
him. But, whether Charles knew of all the scandals of his
Scotch government or not, he was constitutionally responsible
for them all; and Presbyterian loyalty under such a government was impossible—impossible, at least, to a man young,
generous, and ardent, like Carstares. He saw his country

* Carlyle, vol. ii. p. 62.   † McCormick, p. 4.

writhing under the merciless *dragonnades* and exactions of
fierce soldiers, such as Turner and Dalzell. He saw the
prisons full of hapless victims, only released from the dungeon
to be crushed in the boots, or marched to the gallows, or
shipped to the Plantations to be sold as slaves. He saw the
ministers of the national church driven from their homes and
churches, celebrating the rites of their religion, in secrecy
and fear, among the broken and scattered remnants of their
flocks. He saw the places of the ancient pastors filled by
those, whom even one of their own order could but describe
as worthless men of little learning, less piety, and no discretion.* He saw his own father skulking from covert to covert,
like a felon, under a feigned name, unable, unless at peril of
his life, to look on the face of wife or child, even in their days
of sickness, sorrow, and death. The spectacle of these wrongs
wrought on his spirit so powerfully that he was ready to rush
into the dangerous melley when yet too young for its strife,
and when he could only have ruined himself, and done the
just cause no good. His father, to whom he—as it appears—
had an access denied to the rest of his family, marking his
disposition, thought it safest that he should not try to study
divinity at such a distracted time, in Scotland. The natural
and congenial refuge of the persecuted Scots was among the
sturdy Dutch, who, in defence of their freedom and their
Reformed Church, had passed through fires as keen as those
which were burning in Scotland. And so John Carstares
sent his son over to acquire his theology, and finish his
education, at the University of Utrecht.

* Burnet, vol. i. p. 279.

CHAPTER II.

Intercourse with Holland—Utrecht—Introduction to the Prince of Orange—Political Intrigues—"Grievances of Scotland"—Imprisonment in Edinburgh Castle.

Holland, which had been the asylum of the Royalists during the Commonwealth, now afforded impartial shelter to the numerous Scottish Presbyterians and English Nonconformists who sought, on the Continent, the freedom which they could not find in Britain. Many Scots had chosen a refuge in Rotterdam, Amsterdam, Leyden, and Utrecht. In all of these cities they found personal liberty under a constitutional government, and the pure worship of the Reformed Church; and in the latter two, a genial and learned society of clergy and men of letters, to which all scholars were frankly admitted. The Latin tongue was still the medium of communication among Scottish, as among Continental, scholars; and Scots and Dutch were able to meet, and to converse familiarly in the language common to the brotherhood of letters. There was, and had been for many years, frequent literary intercourse between Holland and Scotland. Dr. Strang's (Principal of Glasgow College) work, 'De Voluntate et Actionibus Dei circa Peccatum,' came out at Amsterdam in the year 1657; and his other book, 'De Interpretatione et Perfectione Scripturæ,' was given to the world at Rotterdam in 1663. James Koelman, a learned Dutch divine, translated into his own language Rutherford's 'Letters' and Guthrie's 'Great Concern;' and Borstius, a minister of the Dutch Church in Rotterdam, performed the same office for 'Naphtali' in the year 1668.* Baillie's folio on Scriptural and Clas-

* Steven's 'History of the Scottish Church, Rotterdam,' p. 73.

sical Chronology ('Operis Historici et Chronologici libri duo') had been published at Amsterdam. Calderwood's History was printed by Waesberg in Rotterdam. John Brown of Wamphray's 'History of the Indulgence' was also issued from the Dutch press, and the author was minister of the Scots' church at Amsterdam. Rutherford was offered the chair of Divinity at Utrecht, on the death of Dematius, in 1651, and several years afterwards his 'Examen Arminian-ismi' was re-edited there. MacWard, a scholar and author, ministered to the Scotch congregation at Rotterdam. William Spang, a ripe scholar, whose 'Rerum nuper in Regno Scotiæ gestarum Historia' had been published in 1641 at Dantzic, was minister at Campvere. Nevay, one of the revisers of Rous's version of the Psalms, and author of a Latin metrical translation of the Song of Solomon ; Livingstone, who amused his exile with a Latin translation of the Bible, and who was acquainted with nine languages besides his own ; and Fleming, the ingenious author of the still popular 'Fulfilling of the Scripture' (the sixth edition of which was printed in Glasgow in 1801, the first in Rotterdam in 1674), were among the banished ministers who, driven from their parishes and churches at home, were welcomed by the friendly Dutch.*

There was a large British colony at Utrecht, with the usual appanages of an English coffee-house, serving the purposes of a club, and an English church, in which an exiled minister, English or Scottish, officiated. The town, with its varied society, its noble cathedral, its shady mall, and open walks beyond the gates,† must have been, in those days, as it is now, a cheerful and pleasant residence.

Among the professors of the University whose prelections William Carstares, as a student of theology, attended, were Leusden, the great Hebraist, under whose care the two Amsterdam editions of the Hebrew Bible were brought out in 1661 and 1667 ; and Witsius, well known for his strict piety

---

* Scots' 'Worthies ;' Burton's 'Scot Abroad ;' Wodrow, &c. &c.

† Calamy's 'Historical Account of my own Life,' 2nd edition, vol. i. p. 142, *et seq.*

and orthodoxy, and whose works are still in high repute with
Calvinists. Witsius understood English well, was a great
admirer of English divinity and literature, and " was always
very civil to the English." *

We have no record of Carstares's student life at Utrecht.
In the 'Album Studiosorum' (tom. i. p. 127) it stands that
in the year 1669, " Rectore Cypriano Regneri ab Oesterga,"
"Gulielmus Carstaers, Scoto-Britannus," was enrolled as a
student. In the 'Promotie,' or graduation album, of the
corresponding period his name does not appear,† which is, no
doubt, to be explained by his having already taken his M.A.
at Edinburgh. The time which elapsed between his graduation at Edinburgh, in July 1667, and his entrance at Utrecht,
is a blank to us, and so is the time which he spent at Utrecht.
We detect no mention of him anywhere ; and there is no
letter, of his own or his father's, throwing any light on his
history. The first glimpse we get of him is from the following letter to his sister, Sarah Carstares. He had three
brothers, Alexander, James, who died in 1679, aged sixteen,
and Robert, who died in infancy ; and five sisters, of whom
Sarah was the eldest, and presumably only a year or two
younger than William. John Carstares names in his will
his daughters Sarah, Katherine, and Ursula. Mrs. William
Carstares in her will, dated 1724, names her " sister-in-law
Jean Carstares " wife of Principal Drew of St. Andrews.
Besides these there was another sister, Margaret, who married
a Major Coult, Commandant of Edinburgh Castle. She and
Jean must have been born after the date of their father's
will, 1664.

The letter is superscribed " This for his affectionate sister,
Sarah Carstairs ‡ ":—

" *Utrecht, March* 23, 1672.

" Dear Sister,—I take this opportunity of saluting you, and
assuring you that notwithstanding of my silence in not writing to

---

* Calamy, vol. i. p. 166.

† This information was very kindly procured for me by Dr. John Muir,
from Professor de Jong, of Utrecht.

‡ At this time he spelt his name so.

you, yet my affection to you as a sister is not in the least cooled, neither am I forgetful of you nor of the rest of the children, but often beg of God that you may all of you be blessed with spiritual blessings in Jesus Christ, whom if you have for yours, it is not much matter what be your condition in the world. It is his favour that is better than life: it is the enjoyment of him that makes a sweet and comfortable life. If we knew him, sister, and had a discovery of the beauty and excellency that is in him, other things would be so far from bulking in our eyes that they would evanish and disappear. It was a sight of him that made David, a great prince in his time, choose rather to be a doorkeeper in his house than to dwell in the tents of Kedar, and desire to behold his beauty and inquire into his temple as the one thing worthy to be sought after. O! when shall the desires of our souls be towards him and to the remembrance of his name. It is no less than his own omnipotent power must create these soul-desires in us after himself. O! if he would do it: we will never be free till we be captivated by him, his service being choice and excellent freedom,—but who can speak aright of him? For my own part, I am so conscious of my own unfitness to do it in the least measure suitably that I must be silent; but I hope you have seen that in him which makes you ready to sell all and buy this soul-enriching infinitely precious pearl. Now sister, being in haste I must break off, and recommend you to the guiding of his spirit which leadeth into all truth. Remember me kindly to your sister Katherine and the rest of the children. My best respects to young Ralston * and his lady, and to my cousin Glanderston, his mother and sisters, when you shall have occasion to see them.

"Your own brother
"W. Carstairs."

One can fancy that poor Sarah had some suppressed sense of respectful disappointment as she made her way to the last word of this letter—excellent as it is—without finding a syllable of news, or the slightest hint of any of her brother's doings, or interests, or occupations.

This kind of writing seems to have been one of the religious fashions of the time. The letters of John Carstares

---

* Son of Ralston of that ilk. His father married Ursula Mure, a sister of Mrs. John Carstares. "Cousin Glanderston" was William Mure, Mrs. Carstares' nephew.

and all his correspondents abound with it. It, no doubt, was full of reality to the writers and readers, but to the modern critic the constant repetition of Scripture phrase and orthodox commonplace is apt to look tedious and artificial; and the absolute exclusion of what we call "news" from letters, which are in many instances our only sources of information about the writers of them, is provoking.

The next letter in the Graham Dunlop collection is dated "London, Decr. 10, 1672;" and though it begins "Loving friend" and is signed "your affectionate friend and servant Williams," it is evidently intended for the same person as the last, and is of exactly the same character. It contains no indications whatever of the writer's personal history, which at this period must have been sufficiently interesting, for he had already begun that course of political activity and negotiation, which was yet to lead him to much trouble and to much honour. It is impossible to ascertain whether he had at this time entered on any of the duties of his profession. McCormick, whose account of this portion of his life is singularly confused and entirely destitute of dates, says that on completing his theological studies he "passed his trials according to the forms of the Presbyterian church, and obtained a licence to preach the gospel."*

That he returned to Scotland for this purpose is extremely unlikely; nor was it necessary that he should do so.† There was full ministerial communion between the Reformed Church of Scotland and that of Holland. Scotch candidates for the ministry were readily received, as probationers, by the Dutch Synods; and the local "Classis," or Presbytery,

---

* McCormick p. 8.

† The persecuted Presbyterian clergy of Scotland contrived to meet from time to time to examine candidates for the ministry or to give ordination; but the prelates procured an Act of Parliament in 1672 whereby this was stringently forbidden; and at this time, says Wodrow, "there was a sensible decrease of Presbyterian ministers by death, banishment, and the hardships of the time; and it was attended with no small difficulty to get young men sent abroad to other Protestant churches, to be ordained to the holy ministry." Wodrow, vol. ii. p. 198.

conferred ordination or induction, when required, on the ministers elected by the Scotch congregations within their bounds.*

Even the indefatigable researches of the learned author of the ' Fasti Ecclesiæ Scoticanæ ' have failed to discover any record of William Carstares receiving either licence as a probationer, or ordination as a minister, in Scotland; and it may be inferred, with tolerable certainty, that he received orders from the Dutch presbyters. Mr. Ferrie possesses a certificate, dated June 9, 1681, in these terms: "These are to certify all whom it may concern that Mr. William Carstares is to our knowledge a lawful ordained minister of the gospel." This is signed by eight subscribers, among whom the only notable names are those of Matthew Sylvester and Robert Trail.† It proves nothing beyond the fact that Carstares was known to them as an ordained minister.

He had, however, formed associations, during his stay at Utrecht, which were not favourable to his peacefully following the sober calling of a pastor or preacher. On his first arrival in Holland, he had brought, from London, a letter of introduction to the Prince of Orange's physician, who, in his turn, had introduced him to the pensionary Fagel. That shrewd and clear-sighted statesman discerned in the young Scot qualities well worth enlisting in his master's service, and securing in the interests of his policy. Fagel presented Carstares to William, who was at once impressed by his large and discriminating knowledge of parties and affairs

---

* For an excellent account of the relations between the Scotch and Dutch churches, see Steven's ' History of the Scottish Church in Rotterdam.' In the seventeenth century there were Scotch churches in Rotterdam, Campvere, Leyden, Amsterdam, Delft, Dordrecht, the Hague, and Middleburg, beside mixed congregations elsewhere, served sometimes by Scotch, sometimes by English ministers.

† Robert Trail, formerly minister of Greyfriars Church in Edinburgh, was banished, and retired to Holland. In 1670 Charles requested the States General to remove him from the Dutch territories. He secluded himself for a time, but continued to reside, unmolested, in Holland, for several years afterwards. Steven's ' Scotch Church in Rotterdam,' p. 54.

in Britain, and pleased with his courtier-like manner and address. During his residence at Utrecht Carstares seems to have been frequently with the Prince, and to have gained a large share of his confidence and favour. How far the Prince was cognisant of, or countenanced, the intrigues of the Scotch exiles, who made his territories the base of their operations, does not appear. Engrossed, as he must have been, with the war which both France and England waged against Holland, he probably could spare little thought for the designs of Scotch or other British refugees, except in so far as they might tend to farther his own. That he was aware that their bitter discontent, and sense of wrong, expressed themselves in plots against the government of Scotland, we cannot doubt. That he was too astute to compromise himself by any overt approval of their designs is no less certain. It is not likely that Carstares, who had been admitted to the Prince's confidence, and who must have been extremely loth to risk the loss of his friendship, would have undertaken any negotiation to which his Highness was hostile. It was, therefore, probably with his concurrence that Carstares quitted Holland on his way to Scotland, in 1672—carrying with him the letters, "written in white ink," which were his first credentials as an envoy from the exiles to their friends at home. The ship in which he sailed from Rotterdam was taken; and though he managed to escape, the letters were seized. Their tenor was obscure, as the writers had left to Carstares the detailing of their plans; but enough was made out to show that there were plotters in Holland who had sent him over, and who were prepared to send arms and money, if he should find the Scotch malcontents ready to rise against the government.*

It must have been after this escape that Carstares wrote from London, on the 10th of December, 1672, without, as I have said, the slightest reference to his personal history or doings. From this 10th of December, 1672, no trace of him

---

* Burnet, vol. i. p. 621.

is to be found till the 17th of April, 1674, at which date he writes thus to his sister Sarah :—

"**Dear Sister,**—I hope my forbearing to write, (I will **not** challenge you for being more guilty of the same fault) will not pass under a bad construction with you; if it do, I assure you it is without ground, for I am still and shall always be the same what in some measure I have been to you,—and that is your affectionate tho' insignificant brother. If ever any occasion did offer, I hope you should find that you had no less room in my affection than what such a sister deserveth. I am sorry that I have been forced to be so expensive to my parents by my stay here; but one disappointment upon the back of another hath made me do that which I am averse from, and which I hope I shall not always be under a necessity of doing—that is, of putting them to such charge on my account. I confess, sister, this is the one thing that troubles me. It may be at last in providence I may have some door opened, whereby I may be in a capacity to do some little service in my generation, and not always be insignificant in my station ; but alas, what service can I do, or what will God accept from me, who have lived for so many years in his world, and yet for no end ? Just were he if he should reject so unprofitable a servant. His patience hath been extended beyond what in reason could have been expected. Alas, that his forbearance hath gained so little of its end upon me, a leading of me to repentance, and a turning to him from whom I have departed. It is nothing less than a pull of his own arm that can so draw as to make a sinner run. There are days of his power wherein he turneth backsliders and maketh them willing; it is good to wait upon him because he waiteth to be gracious. I desire, sister, to commit you to him, who, I hope, will care for you, and pray that yourself and my other sisters and brothers (who are much upon my heart) may be blessed of him with blessings suitable for you. Remember me kindly to Katherine, and the rest, whom I need not name; and forget not your tossed brother. I have, sister, sent you a small bible bound very neatly in two halves, by Mr. Gabriel Cunningham. Call for it from him, and take it as a small token of my remembrance of you. Let me hear from you, which will not be a little refreshing to him who is, sister,

"Your most affectionate brother,

"W. C."

The nature of the "disappointments" to which he refers does not appear. It is probable that they were of a political, rather than of a clerical, kind. His activities do not seem to have turned at this period towards a clergyman's professional work. He returned to Holland during this year, and again crossed to London in the autumn. Suspected of being on a treasonable errand, he was arrested and sent to the Tower; and papers, which warranted the suspicion, were found in his possession, and taken from him. He was ultimately carried down to Scotland, and committed to prison there, in February 1675. In order to understand the circumstances which led to all this, we must look back for a little way upon the history of the times.

The state of Scotland had not grown happier since Carstares had left Edinburgh for Utrecht. The government of Lauderdale—himself a renegade Covenanter—whose avowed desire was that Parliamentary government should be abolished, and "the good old form of government by his Majesty's Privy Council"* take its place, though less violent than the earlier tyranny of Middleton, was more systematically cruel and oppressive. It fully justified the judgment of Hallam, that "no part of modern history, for so long a period, can be compared for the wickedness of government to the Scots administration of this reign."† The "indulgences" granted to the Presbyterian clergy in 1669 and 1672, although boons in appearance, were not even acts of justice in reality. The indulgence provided that an ejected minister might, when his old parish fell vacant, return thither and exercise his ministry. He was to have the manse and glebe, but only as much of the stipend as the Privy Council chose to give him. He was never to perform any clerical function out of his own parish. He was not to step beyond it without the bishop's licence. He was not even to "lecture" (or expound Scripture) in his Sunday's service (which the bishops condemned as a Presbyterian abuse), but was to preach a set sermon on a set text, and no more.‡ This hampered and clogged "indulgence"

* Burton, vol. vii. p. 465.
† 'Constitutional History,' vol. iii. p. 435.
‡ Burton, vol. vii. p. 458.   Wodrow, vol. ii. pp. 130, 148.

was followed by most stringent legislation for the benefit of those who did not accept it. All public worship on the part of the Presbyterians was forbidden, unless conducted by the " indulged " minister. Any meeting for worship or instruction, in a house or in the open air, was stigmatised as a " Conventicle " and declared treasonable. Persons frequenting such meetings were to be hunted down by the militia; the lairds on whose lands the conventicles were held were to be heavily fined; the ministers officiating at them were to be punished with *death* and confiscation of their goods.* The seeming grace of the indulgence was more than counterbalanced by the actual severity of the persecution. Lauderdale's purpose was to conciliate the moderate party by the one, and to crush the irreconcilable by the other. " The penalties calculated for our western dissenters," he writes to Sir Robert Murray, his confidential agent in London, " it is hoped will be stronger arguments to move them to outward conformity than any divines could use."† He strangely misunderstood the temper of his countrymen. The extreme Presbyterians, the representatives of the vehement Protesters and Remonstrants of the Restoration, and who were still numerous in the West, scouted the indulgence, and denouncing those who accepted it, thronged to their conventicles with a zeal which danger and penalty only kindled into hotter fervour. The moderate clergy, glad to be again allowed to preach the gospel in peace, and ready to make any legitimate concession for the sake of tranquillity and concord, availed themselves of the indulgence, but regarded it while they did so as in itself ungracious and partial. They felt that it was not by such a measure the government, which had so long oppressed them, could hope to secure their confidence and regain their attachment. The common people were, in general, hostile to the indulgence. The ministers who had accepted it were not of that class which had furnished the fiery preachers " to the times," whose semi-political

* Burnet, vol. i. p. 531. Wodrow, vol. ii. p. 150. Burton, vol. vii. p. 458.
† Burton, vol. vii. p. 464.

harangues had, for many years before the Restoration, excited
their passions and directed their fanaticism. They turned
from these preachers of the gospel in disgust, and labelled
them " dumb dogs," and " king's curates," little better than
the " bishops' curates," whom no devices of the government
had succeeded in forcing them to listen to.* The result of
the indulgence on the general community was, thus, the outward conformity of a certain number of ministers; the estrangement from them of the people at large, who adhered more
and more to the extreme nonconformists ; and the emergence
of a body of strenuous protesters against Prelacy and fanatical champions of Presbytery and the Covenant, who held
themselves indignantly aloof, alike from the bishops and their
clergy, and from the indulged ministers.† This body, ever
growing in steadfastness, and (as oppression and misgovernment increased) becoming more distinctly the ark of refuge
for the shattered liberties of Scotland and the rallying point
for all the disaffected, kept alive through years of persecution a political and religious enthusiasm of the keenest, though
not of the purest, type which won its triumph in 1688.

While Lauderdale tried to compel a uniformity by the combined aid of political stratagem and force of arms, a gentler
and wiser attempt had been made within the Church, by the
one man who redeemed the title of Scottish bishop from discredit. During the autumn and winter of 1670, Leighton,
with the concurrence of the government, was endeavouring
to promote an " accommodation," which should fuse the
Episcopal and Presbyterian clergy into the unity of one
national church. Conferences with leading Presbyterian
divines, under Leighton's presidency,‡ were held, first in

* Burnet, vol. i. p. 516.

† These would seem from Wodrow's lists to have numbered about one
hundred.

‡ Leighton also tried to win over the common people, by sending
through the West a deputation of Episcopal divines, of whom Burnet was
one, " to argue upon the grounds of the accommodation." They found
the peasantry far too well versed in controversy to be open to their arguments. "They were ready with their answers," says Burnet, "to any-

Edinburgh, and afterwards at Paisley, at which he urged on the Presbyterians terms of union, that had received the royal assent, and whereby the differences between Episcopacy and Presbytery were reduced to points so small, that he hoped they would not prove stumbling-blocks. It was proposed that the bishop should act simply as the permanent moderator of the Presbytery or Synod; that the vote of the majority of the clergy should control him; that he should be censurable by the Provincial Synods; that every minister at ordination, or on joining a church-court, should be free to declare that he accepted the bishop as his president for peace' sake, and not as in virtue of a "*jus divinum.*"[*]

These proposals, urged with all the apostolic earnestness and gentle wisdom of Leighton, were, after long debate and repeated consideration, finally rejected. George Hutchinson, the leader of the Presbyterians at the conference, gave their decision in the words, "We are not free in conscience to close with the proposition made by the Bishop of Dunblane, as satisfactory." "Before God and man," said Leighton in reply, "I wash my hands of whatever evils may result from the rupture of this treaty. I have done my utmost to repair the temple of the Lord."[†]

A distracted nation, a broken church, hot-brained zeal instead of temperate wisdom, fanatical enthusiasm in the place of Christian charity; licence and tyranny in high places; suffering and discontent, swelling into bitter wrath, among the mass of the people,—this is the aspect of Scotland in these years of the Indulgence and the Conventicles. We need not wonder that eager eyes scanned the horizon for a gleam of

---

thing that was said to them." He mentions also, on the authority of some of the "indulged" ministers, that the people generally, while full of zeal for Presbytery, and ready to argue about the "intrinsic power of the Church," were very ignorant "of the essentials of religion." Vol. i. p. 517.

[*] 'Life of Leighton,' prefixed to Pearson's edition of his works, vol. i. p. 73.

[†] Ibid. pp. 94–5.

light, and that indignant hearts were ready to risk a struggle for liberty and righteous government. The watchers of the night instinctively turned to the United Provinces. There a great company of exiles lamented their country's wrongs, and waited for the day of her deliverance. There a young and sagacious Prince, the head of a free commonwealth, a Protestant and Presbyterian, was maintaining the rights of his people and the cause of religious liberty against all the might of France, and in spite of the hostility of England. If help was to be found anywhere, it must surely be found in Holland.

Indications of a lurking discontent and disaffection were not wanting in England also; and there, as in the northern kingdom, the Court and the government looked nervously to Holland, apprehensive of any sign of sympathy between the malcontents and the Prince of Orange, who, in the event of the Duke of York's exclusion, would stand very near the throne.*   In the autumn of 1674 a discovery was made which revealed a system of treacherous correspondence with Holland, a portion of which was traced to the very office of the Secretary of State. It was on this occasion that Carstares was sent over to London. The paper of instructions, which he carried, confirmed those suspicions of " ill designs "† which had already been rife. Although these instructions, when an explanation was demanded from the Prince, were declared to refer only to the levying of the regiments which the Dutch had been allowed to raise in Scotland for service abroad, the suspicions were not allayed. The government was not sorry to lay hold, in the person of Carstares, of one whom the disaffection and intrigue both of England and of Scotland seemed to have chosen as its instrument. Although,

---

* Even as early as February 1673 the Duke of York anticipated his own exclusion. Jealous of the Prince of Orange, he hoped to arrange a marriage between his daughter Mary and the Dauphin, and allowed French influence to prevent her betrothal to William in 1674. See Dalrymple's ' Memoirs,' vol. ii. (Appendix) pp. 98 and 109.

† Burnet, vol. ii. p. 56.

however, arrested in London for supposed complicity in this
Dutch plotting, whose existence there was good reason to
surmise, there were further charges on which the Scotch
Privy Council was prepared to prosecute him.

A pamphlet had recently appeared which had exasperated
Lauderdale and his friends. It was dated "Edinburgh,
Jan. 27, 1674," and bore the title of ' An Accompt of
Scotland's Grievances by reason of the D. of Lauderdale's
Ministrie, humbly tendered to his Sacred Majesty." The
indictment which it made out was temperately drawn, but
was pitilessly severe in setting down in full and logical
order, enriched with a bitter sarcasm, every abuse of the
Duke's high office, of which he had been guilty.

He had stifled the voice of Parliament by frequent and
arbitrary adjournments, and by an unconstitutional initiative
accorded to the " Lords of the Articles." He had intercepted
the approach of suppliants to the throne.   He had gathered
into his own keeping the patronage of all the public offices
in the kingdom.   He had made nefarious compacts, whereby
the monopoly of salt, and the duties on brandy and tobacco,
were perverted to his own and his friends' advantage.
He had connived at the debasement of the coinage, his
brother, Lord Hatton, being General of the Mint. He had
appointed "ignorant and insufficient men " to be judges of
the Court of Session. He had been corrupt and unjust in
divers transactions, in which he had employed his official
authority for the benefit of private persons, his clients or
favourites. He had been greedy of the emoluments of office,
and had secured for himself a greater number of appointments than he had any right to hold, being not only Lord
High Commissioner, but also sole secretary, President of the
Council, Commissioner of the Treasury, Captain of Edinburgh Castle, Captain of the Bass, Agent at Court for the
Burghs, and one of the Extraordinary Lords of Session. He
had been lavish and dishonest in his administration of the
revenue, and had appropriated to himself not less than
£26,900 sterling in "donatives," and £16,350 yearly since

he became Commissioner. He had exhibited a personal pride, ambition, and lust of power, which rendered him altogether unfit to act as his Majesty's viceroy and representative in his ancient kingdom. These heavy charges were followed by certain proposals, including an Act of Indemnity, the appointment of a new Commissioner, with instructions for the general redress of grievances, and also " for quieting and removing dissatisfaction in matters ecclesiastic ;" which, says the pamphleteer, " will restore that serene peace, which will make our affection and duty again to flourish in most significant acknowledgments." The 'Accompt,' after some racy illustrations of Lauderdale's coarse and overbearing humour, and " his dull and malicious jestings against his old practices and acquaintances," winds up with an earnest appeal on behalf of the Presbyterians, whose special troubles and wrongs it states calmly and fairly. The indictment, while most crushing to Lauderdale and his party, who, according to Wodrow,* never attempted to dispute its accuracy, is noteworthy in respect of two points ; these are—that it combines in one view, and attacks as one huge mass of misgovernment, the whole " grievances " of Scotland, giving no exclusive prominence to the sufferings of the Church, though assigning these a place in the general charge ; and that it draws an obvious distinction between the great body of the clergy, who either had accepted the indulgence, or were willing to forego their functions peaceably, and the zealous party of remonstrants, that would do neither. It names the " Fanaticks " without sympathy or respect. It is, obviously, the production of a Presbyterian, but of a Presbyterian who was not a bigot, and to whom civil and religious liberty was of higher account than any form or theory of Church government—a Presbyterian, who valued Presbytery because it was the ally of that liberty, of which Prelacy had proved itself the foe, and who had nothing in common with zealots,

---

* Wodrow, vol. ii. p. 293. The pamphlet is now a rare one, and is not embodied, as far as I know, in any later publication. I owe the use of the copy, now before me, to the kindness of Mr. David Laing.

who, for the sake of their Presbyterian formulas, would sacrifice the peace and prosperity of the realm.

The chief share in the authorship of the ' Accompt' was ascribed to James Steuart, son of Sir James Steuart, of Kirkfield and Coltness, sometime Lord Provost of Edinburgh. Sir James had fallen into disrepute with the government after the Restoration, being a staunch Presbyterian no less than a staunch loyalist, and an unjust prosecution was instituted against him by the Lords of the Treasury and Exchequer.* In this action he was defended by his son, with such ability that the charges against him fell to the ground. But the son suffered for the father's acquittal, by attracting the resentment of the government, and found his prospects at the bar so blighted, and his position so insecure, that he retired to Rouen.† He had returned to Scotland before the publication of the ' Accompt,' and being already obnoxious to Lauderdale, was at once fixed upon as the most likely author, and the proper object for the offended Commissioner's revenge. Orders were issued for his apprehension, and for the seizure of his papers. He got timely warning, and escaped; but his papers fell into the hands of the Privy Council, who never divulged what they found in them.

Although Steuart was regarded as the writer chiefly responsible for the ' Accompt,' Carstares was suspected of a part in the authorship.‡

Wodrow§ relates that he was sent from London to Scotland to be tried for his alleged share in James Steuart's misdemeanour; but the Records of the Privy Council and of the Court of Justiciary, bear no trace of any trial of the kind.

Probably he was not tried at all. It was a simpler process to shut him up, than to demonstrate his complicity with Steuart, or prove that because the ' Accompt' told the truth, with a stinging plainness which pierced the joints of

---

* Coltness Collections, Maitland Club, p. 38.
† Ibid. p. 359.
‡ Sprat's ' Account of the Rye-house Plot,' p. 77.
§ Wodrow, vol. ii. p. 291.

Lauderdale's harness, it was therefore treasonable. A royal warrant was issued on the 26th of February, 1675, which transferred him from the Tower to the custody of the Governor of Edinburgh Castle, to be kept "a close prisoner" until further orders.

The following letter throws some light on the earlier period of his capture and imprisonment in London* :—

"Novemb. 17, '74.

"Sir,—I have according to your desire sent you a short account of what is my condition and what hath past betwixt my examinators and me; upon the 19 of Septr. last I came to town and was resolved to have kept myself private for some days, because of some informations I had of an inquiry that had been made about me, at an Englishman who was sent to the tower and was but of a very small acquaintance with me, and though my innocence did make me fear no great harm, yet common prudence did advise a short retirement. An hour after I came I went to my chamber, (which I thought had been let) because of some things I had left there, which was convenient myself only should handle; but finding my chamber was not given up nor my things removed as I had been informed they were, I resolved to lodge there that night, but upon second thoughts I resolved to go elsewhere, and went towards night to my chamber to take away some of my things, but thro' the information of my landlord (who as he himself says was made to believe that what he did against me would be useful service to his Majesty) the Messenger was at hand to seize upon me under the name of Williams or Carstares, (either at my chamber or at the house of one Mr. Thomson a Scotch minister,) by virtue of an order from Secretary Coventry dated August 7; (so that my last absence could not be the cause of it) accordingly that same night I was conveyed towards Whitehall, and a strict guard of two men within the room where I stayed set upon me night and day, till I was removed to the tower; the next day after my taking I was brought to the Secretary to be examined, and my confession taken in write, and afterwards subscribed by myself; after a preamble about the great hurt I had done to his Majesty (but I am innocent) and the circumstances of my condition in my native country, I was desired to be ingenuous for my own good, because

* This letter, in Carstares' own hand, is in the Advocates' Library, Wodrow, MSS. folio 59, No. 31, endorsed by Wodrow, " to MacWard."

they had enough against me already, with other expressions which might have frighted, if I had not known my own loyalty. Then I was asked where I resided, I answered sometimes in the City and sometimes in the Country as in Kent. Then, they asked me what gentlemen I knew there. I ans. none, according to truth; then I was asked where I had been in my last absence from the City, I told, because they knew as well as I, that I was at the Pr. of Orange's army being led thither by a curiosity of seeing it, and detained through danger of travelling much beyond my intention. Then I was asked about my being in Holland which I told was upon design of seeing my friends; I was asked from whom I received letters out of Holland; I told I had had some from Mr. McWard and Mr. Brown about general things, and being asked how I durst correspond wt. them and not bring their letters to the Secretary of State, I told that there was nothing in them of moment and that I could not deal so by my friends; this was the sum of what passed then that was material. My examination being ended and the gentleman that wrote what I said being commanded to go out, and I left alone wt. the Secretary, he, with great civility and kindness, told me my hazard and how much they had agst. me and what severity I would meet with from other hands and in another place, to which I would be sent if I did not prevent it by ingenuity in confession; and therefore desired if I would be continued in his hand and not more severely dealt with, that I would bring in others, and it should never be known from whence the information came, and he would do his utmost with His Majesty, who was clement, to procure me favour. I thanked him humbly, as I was obliged, for his kindness, and told him that I desired not to fall into the hands of any others but his, but that I had nothing else to confess; upon which I was dismissed, and told that that would not do my business. Ten days after, I was brought from the Tower to the secretary's house again, whither his Lordship was also sent to examine me; then I was asked about a letter which I had from Rouen from my cousin Archibald Mure, relating to an 100 and odd pounds stg. which he had left with me, to be paid here, according to his order as I did; which I mention because, I hear that my Landlord then in his informations increased this to great sums of money brought in coaches and upon porters' backs, being so blockish as not to distinguish betwixt books and money; and because he would have something to say when so much pressed by great persons, he hath made my few inconsiderable acquaintance multitudes of persons of quality calling for me daily at my chamber.

But great men are wiser than to take notice (for indeed they mentioned none of these things to me) of the stories of a crackbrained drunkard. Then I was asked concerning a letter from one Walker which was but of a very few lines wherein he speaks of his landing in Holland; who this was I told, my Lo. Lauderdale telling me before that he knew the hand, making shifting needless; but being asked from what land Walker had come I answered nothing at all; then was I asked about some books that a letter from one Richardson mentioned, and being much pressed I told that they were 'Scotland's grievances' which I had printed in Holland. My Lo. Laud. telling me that he valued not that pamphlet a straw, pressed me notwithstanding to tell to whom I had given any of those books, which I desired to be excused in telling that I would wrong no man; and being urged again I still refused, and this was all I assure you that passed in this matter; then I was asked about Mr. Durham's book on the Commands which gave occasion to My Lo. Laud. to tell the Secretary what Mr. Durham was, and how well his Majesty knew him and remembered him, as also to ask whose daughter my mother was. Then were produced some few Instructions from one Moulin to me, two of which had been torn out by me; I was pressed to give an explication of those which at that time I refused to do and answered all their questions with silence, saying only that there was nothing there that prejudged his Majesty's interest; and they finding me obstinate in my silence (which in a young man as I am, may well be judged to proceed from an apprehensive fear of great men which maketh gnats camels) did surcease from proposing any more questions, a long catalogue whereof I saw in the Secretary's hand, and Landerd. told me my shins should pay for all, and I should not be believed any more speak what I would, and that so soon as his Majesty had a yacht ready, I should make a voyage; but time will clear my innocence, and make him my friend. This is the ingenuous sum of what passed then; only this I forgot —when there were any questions proposed which I had no mind to answer, and could not shift, I desired to be submissively silent; but this was called *canting*; and I was commanded in his Majesty's name to say either yes or no expressly; but I had no desire to give my answers in an irritating or contemning way; but this not sufficing I was forced to say either Yes or No, the latter whereof I did chuse, then it was set down that I refused to answer. Some few days after this recollecting myself, and knowing that the general meaning of those Instructions was obvious to the reader, (which indeed amounted to just nothing) I did desire after redeliberation to speak with the Secretary, who sent for me; but being disappointed as to what it seems he expected and what I told him amounted to nothing more than might have been communicated to every fishmonger, (but I can only tell what I know and not all that is imagined) as he said, I was not heard out, but was sent away in a passion, and told that now I was off his hand and that he had no more to do with me : but what passed betwixt us you know no doubt by this time, and believe it is true and all that passed of any moment. I forgot to tell you that I was also examined by one Sr. Thomas Chickley a privy Counsellour and a very civil gentleman, but he only asked me concerning the manner of my acquaintance with my fellow prisoner and my acquaintance in the Prince's army.

"This is a true and ingenuous account of all; by which you may see that I am accused formally of nothing, but thus dealt with on suspicions. I hear that they talk in the City of witnesses come from Holland to accuse me, but I value it not, for I know that there is none that can be brought to speak truth against me that will prejudge me.

"I am also informed that it is reported that I desired two things of his Majesty; one was not to be examined by Lauderdale, and the other not to be sent to Scotland ; but it is not so, as you may see by what is above written ; I hear also that I might have favour if I would but tell names, but tho' I know no ill of my friends, yet I hope through grace never to do that which may have the show of wronging of them, and I bless the Lord my imprisonment hath put the thoughts of giving them satisfaction in this matter of names further from me than ever.

"Now sir, I know that your mentioning what I have wrote will be so carried by you that it may not be known there is any way of hearing from me; for my imprisonment continues most strict according to order of authority. This is designed for Mr. Ker too who hath heard of me no doubt ere now."

CHAPTER III.

Imprisonment—Release in 1679—Journey to Ireland—Letters from London—The Dunlops—Renewed Troubles—Marriage—Return to Holland.

THE years of imprisonment dragged wearily on, while the political and religious condition of the country grew worse and worse. The spectacle of a government exerting all its powers, legislative and executive, for the purpose of making people go to church, would have been supremely ridiculous, had not the powers been exerted in such a savage way. Garçilasso de la Vega relates that when Atabaliba was on the road to execution, those about him advised him to desire baptism, threatening, unless he did so, to burn him alive. "Whereupon being baptized he was bound to a post, and there strangled."[*] The government of Lauderdale would seem to have imbibed the spirit of this measure of "careful criminal justice."[†] The people were ordered to go to church; and if they did not go, they suffered for it in the flesh. The Episcopal curates supplied the authorities with lists of the defaulters, who were fined or imprisoned, or hunted down by the high-spirited Claverhouse, and the loyal Dalzell. Landlords and householders were made answerable for the church-going of their tenants and families, under oppressive penalties. Writs of "intercommuning" were scattered through every county, prohibiting, as a crime, any intercourse with persons who went to conventicles,[‡] and offering a bribe to any informer who should report the

* 'Royal Commentaries of Peru,' 2nd part, book i. p. 36.

† The term applied by Mr. Mark Napier, the last (let us hope) of the Cavaliers, to the enactment under which the two women were slowly drowned at Wigton.

‡ Wodrow, vol. ii. p. 318.

name of an offender. The chamber of the Privy Council echoed with the howls of the victims of the boot. There, on one day, might be seen Dalzell striking the prisoners under examination over the mouth with his sword-hilt till the blood sprang : * on another, Lauderdale baring his brawny arms above the elbow, and swearing " by Jehovah " he would force the gentlemen of Scotland " to enter into those bonds."† Day after day, the tyrants in office consigned to their jails and dungeons the victims of the brutal injustice which had made nonconformity treason ; which had changed the ordinary intercourse of life among the Presbyterians into felony ; and had, as if by set design, driven peaceable and loyal subjects into readiness for rebellion.‡ Ship after ship sailed from Leith with its cargo of white slaves consigned to the plantations in Virginia or the West Indies, because they had attended a conventicle, or been kind to an " outed " minister. The " Highland Host," let loose on the Lowlands, ravaged whole districts ; while the lawlessness of the marauder combined with the instincts of the thief to make this Celtic inroad terrible, even to a population inured to the outrages of Turner and Dalzell.

During all these troubles John Carstares abode in Edinburgh. He was invited, in 1677, to become minister of the Scots Church at Rotterdam,§ but declined ; and seems to have occupied himself in Edinburgh with religious writing, and doing good by his prayers, exhortations, and letters, as far as the limited opportunities of a man in his circumstances allowed. He was harassed with the gout, and his wife was broken in health.‖ Even she had not escaped a personal share in the sufferings of the time. She and her sister, Mrs. Durham, were for a short time in the Tolbooth, for keeping a conventicle—i.e., holding a meeting for religious edification

* Burton, vol. vii. p. 452.

† Bonds by which they and theirs were bound against " intercommuning," or going to conventicles. Burnet, vol. ii. p. 137.

‡ Burnet, vol. ii. p. 137.

§ Steven, p. 58.

‖ Veitch and Brysson, p. 501.

—in Mrs. Durham's house.* Well might her poor husband cry, as he does in a letter to MacWard, "O! if I knew of a cottage in the wilderness while I live, and were sure thence to go to the Kingdom!" His spirit grew weary of the contentions of his own people, no less than of the oppressions of the Prelatists; and as his age ripened to its autumn, he became less zealous with the old protesting zeal. In March, 1677, Brodie of Brodie, after calling on him in Edinburgh, says, "Mr. John Carstares expressed his dislike of Mr. John Welwood's expression saying 'It was as great a sin to go to hear those that conformed as to go to a bordel house.' He said he durst not condemn and censure them that heard out of conscience."† "Is there," he writes at a later date, to MacWard, "no place to consider whether it were better to supersede our contendings than to have our Church ruined?"‡

I cannot ascertain that he had any direct intercourse with his son during the imprisonment of the latter. "Most of the time," says William, "I was denied converse with any of my nearest relations, even in the presence of a keeper."§ William's tendency to political intrigue was a grievance to his father; and at the time of his son's release, if not earlier, he "solemnly charged him never to meddle with such things again, but to exercise himself in preaching and prayer, and what other exercises did properly belong to a faithful minister of the gospel."‖

I find only two letters written by William during this imprisonment. The one is dated "Feb. 3," but affords no clue to the year in which it was written. Part of it is addressed to Sarah, and part to a friend whom he calls simply "Mrs." "I return Mrs. my kind thanks," he says, "for what you sent me by George" (his young friend in the Castle, presumably): "and am ashamed you should put yourself to such

---

* Wodrow, vol. iii. p. 10.
† Diary of Brodie of Brodie, p. 384. Spalding Club.
‡ Veitch and Brysson, p. 500.
§ Graham Dunlop MSS.
‖ 'Analecta,' vol. iii. p. 51.

trouble. You are George's great favourite. How you have charmed him I know not."

To his sister he communicates the interesting intelligence, " I intend, if the Lord will, to take that purge upon Monday which the Dr. prescribed: you may therefore send up, then, what is requisite for it : and upon Tuesday, if health permit, and the Lord will, I intend to take the air, and shall be glad to see you at a distance. Farewell. Send up my clean linens." The other letter is dated "May 21, '79," and is a short note, explaining that he should have written sooner had he known of "a sure bearer," and containing nothing worth copying. The only other hints we have of any of the circumstances of his incarceration, are in the Life by McCormick. McCormick, however, with an inexplicable ignorance or carelessness, passes over this first imprisonment without any notice ; but mentions facts in connection with Carstares' second imprisonment, which, investigation shows, properly belong to the first.

Carstares distinctly states, in his own letter to Wodrow,[*] that when he was sent down to Scotland in 1683 he was confined, not in the Castle of Edinburgh, but in the Tolbooth, until his trial. During the trial itself, it would appear that he was kept in the Castle; his "examination," as published by the Privy Council, bearing that he was at the time of his undergoing it, in prison there. Immediately after his trial, however, he was sent away from Edinburgh, and after a confinement at Stirling,[†] was set at liberty. In 1684, therefore, he could not have been in Edinburgh Castle for more than two or three weeks; and the incidents which follow necessarily belong to the only period of prolonged confinement which he passed there, that of the imprisonment which began in 1675.

One day, "not long after his commitment," says McCormick,[‡] a boy about twelve years of age, son of the Lieutenant-

Governor of the Castle, rambling through the courts of the
fortress, came to the grate of the cell in which Carstares was
immured. As the boy looked in, the prisoner came forward
and spoke to him, and that in so kind and pleasant a manner
that the youngster was " captivated ;" and resolved to come
back and pay him another visit. He did so, again and again ;
and at last became Carstares' devoted ally and companion ;
would sit by his cell grate for hours, " lamenting his unhappy
situation, and telling him a thousand stories to divert him."
He brought him little presents of food, and the more substantial favours of paper, pen, and ink ; and when Carstares
had used these to write his letters, the boy would come at
night and take his letters to their destination himself. Probably by this little lad's help, he got some books also to
beguile his loneliness. Among them was a copy of De
Thou's 138 books of the ' Historia sui Temporis.' This he
read over no less than three several times, and his mind was,
by this process, so imbued with the historian's classic style and
idiom, that by the time he ended his perusals he found that
he could think and speak in Latin, as readily as in English.

At last the order of release arrived. It is preserved in
the Graham Dunlop collection, and is endorsed in Mrs. Carstares' handwriting. " This is my dear's releasement out of
prison." It runs thus : " Charles R. Right trusty and well
beloved councillor, we greet you well : whereas by an order of
the 26th day of February, 167⅔, we did require the then
Lieutenant Governor of that our Castle to receive the
body of William Carstares into his safe and sure custody,
and to keep him a close prisoner until he should receive
further orders concerning him from us, or our Privy Council
of that our ancient Kingdom ; and whereas now we are
graciously pleased to extend our compassion towards him, notwithstanding of the sure information we did then receive of
his tampering in several matters tending to the disturbance
of the public peace, it is our will and pleasure, and we do
hereby authorize and require you, to set the said William
Carstares at liberty, whereof (we hope) he will make so good

uso for the future, as we shall have no cause to debar him of the privileges of our other free subjects; and of this we require you to give him notice, to the end he may be sensible that if at any time hereafter he shall be found guilty of the like transgressions, he may expect that the abuse of this our Royal clemency will produce the most severe effects of our displeasure against him, that may be consistent with the laws of that our Kingdom. And so we bid you farewell. Given at our Court of Windsor Castle the 29th day of July, 1679, and of our reign the 31st year. By His Majesty's Command. To our trusty and well beloved Councillor, John Drummond of Lundin, Lieutenant-Governor of our Castle of Edinburgh."

The Lieutenant-Governor has endorsed the paper, "This is the true copy of His Majesty's gracious letter to me ordering the enlargement of Mr. William Carstares. In obedience to which I upon the receipt thereof immediately released him, J. Drummond."

By this time the troubles of the country had reached a crisis. The rigid Covenanting party, embittered by their narrow hatred of the "indulged," no less than of the Prelatists, and becoming more and more deeply imbued with political disaffection, had broken out into actual rebellion. They can hardly be condemned for having done so. The prelates and their party were inconceivably mean, selfish, and unprincipled. The indulged ministers could not move hand or foot to seek the reform of the Church or the abatement of oppression, in peaceable and constitutional ways. The Parliament, which should have defended the liberties of the subject, was the time-serving creature of an insolent and unbridled despotism. The only hope of salvation lay in "the sword of the Lord and of Gideon."

For some time past, the people who came to the conventicles had carried arms. In this summer of 1679 they began to use them. Closely following the unhappy murder of Sharp came the skirmish of Drumclog, on the 1st, and the more serious engagement of Bothwell, on the 22nd, of June.

The Covenanters had drawn the sword, and they perished by the sword. The wild and jealous fanaticism, which filled their noisy camp in Clydesdale with the divided counsels and political harangues of their preachers and leaders,* had not enlisted a force sufficiently strong and disciplined to gain any permanent advantage over the King's troops. But the rising had been formidable enough to show the government the danger of driving a people to despair.

There was now a noble opportunity of trying the effects of that policy of conciliation, which is always most effective when a powerful victor shows clemency, at the very time when the vanquished have good reason to expect revenge. The influence of Monmouth, who commanded at Bothwell Bridge, was all on the side of leniency. The general policy of the Privy Council, however, was not reversed; and the indemnity granted was partial and short-lived. The prisoners actually taken at Bothwell were treated with great brutality;† though an Act of Indemnity was extended to all others who had been at the battle, on condition of their promising never again to appear in arms against the King, or to attend a conventicle; and a new indulgence, allowing ministers not hitherto indulged, to officiate in private houses,‡ was announced. Some also of those who had been forfeited, or in prison, were set at liberty;§ and on the 16th of July the King wrote to Leighton, who, having quitted his episcopate, was living quietly at Broadhurst, his sister's house in Sussex, "I am resolved to try what clemency can prevail upon such in Scotland as will not conform to the government of the Church there; for effecting of which design, I desire that you may go down to Scotland with your first conveniency." ‖

* Veitch and Brysson, pp. 455 and 471.

† Most of them were penned up in the Grey Friars' Churchyard, under the open sky, fed on bread and water, and kept there in filth, hunger, and nakedness, till near the end of November, when 300 were shipped as slaves for the American plantations. Fountainhall's 'Historical Notices,' vol. i. p. 246. Bannatyne Club.

‡ Wodrow, vol. iii. p. 118.　　　　§ Fountainhall, vol. i. p. 229.
‖ 'Pearson's Life,' Leighton's Works, vol. i. p. 148.

But Leighton never went. The Duke of Monmouth's influence declined; few accepted the indemnity; the indulgence was cancelled; and the hunt for " rebels " and " conventiclers " was again begun by the fierce soldiers of Dalzell, that persecutor who, according to the belief of the harassed outlaws, was in league with the devil, and cast no shadow as his gaunt figure crossed the light of day.*

During this spasmodic fit of clemency, however, Carstares was liberated. He does not appear to have stayed long in Edinburgh after his liberation; nor was he likely to wish to remain in Scotland. His being there might have added to his father's existing embarrassments. Besides, he could do no good at home. He could not exercise his ministry, as no indulgence was extended to those who had received Presbyterian orders since the restoration of Episcopacy. He could not conform to an establishment which was based on injustice, and in league with a corrupt and unrighteous tyranny, and which his political foresight told him must ere long be overthrown. He could not ally himself with the fanatics— the "True Presbyterian, Anti-prelatic, Anti-Erastian, and Persecuted party," who, with their hair-splitting and intolerance, their solemn excommunications, and handing over to the devil of the King and the other troublers of Israel, and their uncompromising and extravagant "Sanquhar declaration," were running to all the madness of extremes.† The first distinct trace of him, after his liberation, is afforded by two letters written while on a journey to Ireland, during the winter. He had kindred in Ireland, his mother being niece of Viscount Claneboy, of that kingdom; and the uncle with whom he says he travelled thither was probably either James Mure, of Ballybregach, or Hamilton of Halcraig, who were both Lord Claneboy's nephews.‡ In a short note dated " from

* Pamphlets in Advocates' Library, M. 44, xiii.

† Wodrow, vol. iii. p. 212.

‡ Mrs. Carstares' mother was Jean Hamilton, daughter of Hans Hamilton, vicar of Dunlop. Her brother was created Lord Claneboy, and his son Earl of Clanbrassil.

the Port, Dec. 29, 1679," he tells his sister Sarah, who was then at Glanderston, that he and his uncle are waiting for a fair wind to set sail. "When you return to Edinburgh," he says, "pray wait upon the Lady Lundin" (wife of the Governor of the Castle) "and Mrs. Law, as oft as you can."

The next letter is dated "Port Patrick, Feb. 2, 1680;" and it would seem to imply that he had not yet made out his Irish visit. He says, "My dearest sisters,—You see I include you in one letter, being equally dear to me. It is like you did not suspect to have heard from me after so long a time except from Ballybregach,* or some other of Katherine's old Irish habitations; but we are much crossed with contrary winds; and.what design God may have in it I know not, but I hope it shall be found for advantage. I hope you will not forget the obligations I am under to friends in the Castle; but I do expect your visits to them will be frequent, for I know the lady, when once acquaint with you, will be free and obliging in her carriage to you, and will take it kindly that you divert her sometimes with seeing of her. And for worthy Mrs. Law, I cannot recommend a better companion to you. Present my best respects to her, and to Mr. Lindsay, to whom I know you will be no strangers. I forget not kind Mrs. Mure, to whom I intend not to write anything till in Ireland. . . . . You see I use you as sisters, when I trouble you with nothing else but what will give you some pains; but trouble you as I will, I hope you shall always find me a kind brother. The Lord himself be your portion. I am your affectionate brother, Will. Carstares."

In September of this year, we find him in London. "I desire that your concern for me," he writes on 30th Sept. to Sarah, "may be kept within bounds, lest God be provoked to order providences that shall be vexing to us

---

* Ballybregach, in the County Down, was the residence of James Mure, second son of the laird of Glanderston, and brother of Mrs. John Carstares. He had served in earlier life in a regiment of horse under his uncle Lord Claneboy. Caldwell Papers, part i. p. 25.

both." Whether he had got into any new difficulties does not appear; but shortly after this he undertook regular duty in London.

The nonconformists of England were not exposed to the implacable persecution, which raged against their brethren in Scotland. The Declaration of Indulgence issued on the King's own authority, in 1672, which gave them permission to worship without molestation, had been revoked at the instance of Parliament; but the liberty which that declaration promised had, in practice, been extended to them for several years. Carstares formed a connection with a Presbyterian congregation near London, and became their minister. This congregation met at Theobalds, about twelve miles from London, in the parish of Cheshunt in Hertfordshire. Theobalds, once a favourite residence of King James, had been dismantled by the Parliament in 1650, and was no longer a royal palace; but it seems to have been a favourite resort of the nonconformists. Among others, Richard Cromwell had sought retirement in its neighbourhood; and lived there from 1680, till his death, going by the name of Mr. Clarke.*

The letter which follows, is unaddressed, but must have been meant for his cousin and brother-in-law, Dunlop.

"Theobalds, June 14. 81.

" DEAR BROTHER,—I received yours with my dear sister's postscript, and do easily excuse your former silence, provided I may for the future have long epistles from you both, as to all your petty concerns and those of our relations, and a particular account of public affairs at the sitting of our parliament,—to which you shall have what returns I can make. I have some thoughts of settling here while I am in England, Providence much clearing my way, and the kindness that the people seem to have for me encouraging me. You may tell your wife that I believe nothing that she says concerning the deference she pretends to have had to my judgment; but that I suppose she loved you so that had you but delayed a little longer, she would have been a suitor to you,—tho' I know

* ' National Gazetteer of Great Britain and Ireland.'

not upon what account she should have been so much in love with such a sotchell drunken faced little fellow, but she hath taken one of her own size, and she always longed for one of a ———,* and indeed in so far she hath gained her desire, but now you must both make the best bargain you can. I think I see poor Glanderston,† hovering about the doors of Pollock. Pray let me know what is come of him, for I wish him heartily well, but do not much pity him, being persuaded that he is beyond hazard of pining for his mistress. Disappointments may indeed make him gloom and look sour, (you see I am no affecter of English) but it will be hard to break his heart. I hear honest James hath at last come speed,— but enough of this. Our confusions here are a-growing and seem not to be far from a height.

"Sham plots are the great business of some, but God doth strangely detect them, though I am afraid they may some time take effect.

"I salute kindly my dear sister, and know she will look upon this as written to herself.

"Adieu, dear brother,
"Your very affectionate brother W. C."

On July 16th he writes to Sarah, who had been recently married to this cousin, William Dunlop, eldest son of the Rev. Alexander Dunlop, of Paisley, whose wife was Elizabeth Mure, sister of Mrs. John Carstares. Alexander Dunlop was a man of great eminence for piety, zeal, and learning. He had " great grace and a great gift of preaching; great learning and a great gift of disputing and arguing; and a great painfulness in reading and studying, and in all his ministerial work."‡ He was turned out of his charge in 1662,

* As far as I can make out, "gash gab"—words of rather untranslatable Scottish significance: *gash*, sagacious, verging on the owlish type of sagacity; *gab*, the mouth or utterance.

† The cousin of Carstares already mentioned. He was born in 1654, and became proprietor of Glanderston on his father's death in 1658, and of Caldwell, on the death of his cousin in 1710. Pollock was the house of Maxwell of Auldhouse, or Pollock, in Renfrewshire. Glanderston's great-grand-aunt had married George Maxwell of Auldhouse; and there was a close friendship between the families. Caldwell Papers, part i. introd. memoir.

‡ 'Analecta,' vol. iii. p. 17.

and being too weak to travel over sea to Holland, along with
MacWard, Livingstone, and others then expatriated, he was
detained in confinement at Culross. After the disaster of
Rullion Green he never held up his head. His friends,
visiting him, would find him "sitting with his gown among
the ashes, in a most forlorn and dejected-like condition;" and
his landlord-jailer, who lodged above him, heard him sighing and groaning in the night, as if his heart would break.*
He died before he was fifty, at Borrowstowness, in 1667.†
"As for Will," he said before he died, "he fills all my calms;
he answers all my expectations."‡ The father's estimate is
not belied by the character and history of the son, of whom
we shall often hear as we proceed. He had already been involved, though slightly, in the troubles of his time and
country. While acting as Lord Cochran's chaplain, in 1678,
he had been summoned before the Committee of Privy Council, for officiating without an Episcopal licence, and had
thought it safest to absent himself.§ Immediately before
the battle of Bothwell Bridge, he reappears on the scene,
bearing to the insurgent camp a "Declaration of the oppressed
Protestants now in arms in Scotland," which was in part his
own composition, and which expressed the principles and
aims of the moderate party of Presbyterians, of which he was
a zealous member. This paper, which, avoiding all fanatical
denunciations and "testimonies," temperately stated that recourse to arms was taken simply for the purpose of securing
Protestantism and Presbytery in Scotland; disengaging the
King from Popish plots and wicked counsellors; and exclud-

---

* This worthy man indulged, after a fashion not uncommon until very
recent times, in a kind of groan—"a holy groan," his friend Mr. Peebles
called it—at the end of a specially urgent sentence or appeal. Mr. Buckle
(vol. ii. p. 371) refers to this as a proof that there was "hardly any kind
of resource which these men" (the Scotch ministers) "disdained." It was,
no doubt, a mere natural ejaculation, which may be heard in Gaelic
preaching to this day.

 † 'Analecta,' vol. iii. p. 21.

 ‡ Ibid. vol. ii. p. 149.

 § Wodrow, vol. ii. p. 419.

ing the Duke of York from the succession, was violently
rejected by the Covenanters' Council of War.*

Dunlop again vanishes from the stage; and re-enters, at the
date of this letter, as the bridegroom of Sarah Carstares.

> "Theobalds' July 16, 81.
>
> "DEAR SISTER,—I had yours, and was not a little refreshed to
> hear that you were so well pleased with the change of your habita-
> tion; but it seems a good husband will make any place pleasant,
> and make all other friends to be forgot;—but, sister, it is like I may
> be even with you, and get that which shall put you out of your
> room which now you take up so largely in my thoughts, tho' at
> present I know not how, or who, it shall be. The Lord hath dealt
> well with me in bringing me to this place, where I have, as yet, what
> satisfaction I can in reason desire, the people of which I have the
> charge being, most of them, serious Christians so far as I can judge;
> and God is pleased yet to give me their kindness. But nothing can
> make me forget Scotland, or, I hope, shall detain me from it when I
> shall have a fair opportunity for returning,—which I long for.
>
> "I remember kindly my brother, and do expect to hear frequently
> from him. I am hopeful that as I have heard you are a wife, so to
> hear you are a mother. Farewell, dear sister.
>
> "Thine own W. C."

The "fair opportunity" for returning to Scotland, which he
expected with all the home-sickness of a "kindly Scot," did
not arrive. In this year the forbearance, hitherto shown to
the nonconformists in England, was superseded by a severity
which is described by Howe as a "dreadful storm of persecution, that destroyed not a small number of lives in gaols, and
ruined multitudes of families."† Nonconformist pastors were
imprisoned, and congregations broken up. A Tory reaction,
following the violent excitements of the Popish plot and the
debates on the Exclusion Bill, emboldened the government to
enforce "with extreme rigour,"‡ the dormant laws against
dissenters.

Carstares continued, however, to "abide the pelting of the
pitiless storm;" and not only so, but fortified himself against

---

* Wodrow, vol. iii. p. 96.   † Calamy, vol. i. p. 88.
‡ Macaulay, vol. i. chap. 2.

the depressing influences of persecution by getting married, in the very middle of it. His marriage certificate, which is in Mr. Ferrie's possession, bears that on June 6, 1682, " William Carstares of Chesthunt, in the County of Hertford, gent., and Elizabeth, daughter of Peter Kekewich of Trehawk in the County of Cornwall, Esq.: were lawfully married, according to the Church of England in the parish church of Raynham, in the County of Essex," by Samuel Kekewich, Vicar. The Kekewiches are an ancient and honourable family ;* and the match was an equal one as regarded birth and position. Mrs. Carstares was a little older than her husband. The politics of the house appear to have leaned to Whiggery and Liberalism ; and a Miss Kekewich had become the wife of Speaker Lenthall, in the days of the Long Parliament.

Whether the designation of Carstares in the marriage certificate as " Gent.," indicates that he had for a time laid aside his clerical title and duties ; or is, as Mr. Ferrie opines, simply a mark of the officiating vicar's Episcopalian arrogance, it is impossible to decide. Perhaps he had by this time found it hazardous to continue to officiate as a clergyman, and was therefore content to figure in the register of Raynham as a layman. If he thought it well to do so, he was not a man to stickle about a name. He could hardly deem it altogether prudent to remain with his wife in England ; and, no doubt, would have retired to Scotland had he dared ; but persecution raged there with a steady and relentless violence unknown south of the Tweed. A nonconformist fugitive from England would as soon have thought of running for shelter to Scotland, as a Spanish heretic of seeking his City of Refuge in Seville.

The Duke of York was now his Majesty's Commissioner in his ancient kingdom. The Parliament, which assembled at his summons in July, signalised itself by the passing of two

---

* The late representative of it, S. Trehawke Kekewich, Esq., M.P., informed me he possessed a family history extending back for *one thousand five hundred years.*

Acts; that anent the succession to the Crown, and that anent Religion and the Test.

The first asserted the *Jus Divinum*, with a fervour and fulness that rather resembled the exuberant loyalty of a cavalier club than the staid decorum of an Act of Parliament; and declared that "no difference of religion, nor no Act of Parliament, made or to be made, can alter, or divert, the right of succession."[*]

The other imposed on every person in public employment in the kingdom, from the Lord Chancellor to the sub-collector of customs, from the Archbishop to the youngest curate, —from the Commander-in-Chief to the rank and file, a long and complicated Oath or Test, designed to assert with a more rigid exactness than hitherto the royal prerogative, and the abnegation on the subject's part of every claim to civil liberty, or freedom of conscience.[†] The Test, although the bulk of the Episcopal clergy "went into it very glibly,"[‡] was more than the already strained consciences of some of them could bear. "About eighty of the most learned and pious of them," led by Laurence Charteris, after Leighton the wisest and most liberal of the Episcopalians, left their parishes rather than comply with the terms of the new Act. Fletcher of Saltoun, Sir James Dalrymple of Stair the President of the Court of Session, Lord Belhaven, and others of high position and influence, inveighed against the Test, or pointed out its oppressiveness and inconsistencies.[§] Several of the bishops and clergy issued "explanations" of the oath. The Earl of Argyll drew up an "explication" of the sense in which he would take it, "in so far as it was consistent with itself and the Protestant religion;" and finding that this promised to bring him into trouble, he followed it with an "explanation of his explication,"[||] which, however, did not save

* Wodrow, vol. iii. p. 291.
† See the Test in Wodrow, vol. iii. p. 295.
‡ Ibid. p. 310.
§ Burnet, vol. ii. p. 309; Dalrymple's 'Memoirs,' vol. i. p. 6, &c.
|| See in Wodrow, vol. iii. p. 317.

him from a charge of high treason, and a sentence of death, only evaded by a timely escape from prison.

This course of legislation was not alleviated by any relaxation of the long continued severity of the executive. The whips of Lauderdale became scorpions in the more delicate, but more ruthless, hands of the Duke of York. Ever since Bothwell Brig the victims of the Privy Council had received no mercy.*

In all the circumstances, Carstares could hardly venture to take up his abode in Scotland, although, as we shall see, he probably paid it a short visit. An exodus from Scotland had, in fact, begun. Argyll got out of Edinburgh Castle in disguise, and fled for his life. Dalrymple of Stair, driven from the bench, and threatened with prosecution, also made his escape from the land of bondage. He was followed by

---

* The most notable example was Hackston, of Rathillet, who had been present, though not as an active agent, at Sharp's murder, and who was afterwards taken in arms. Although covered with wounds, he was carried to Edinburgh. At the Watergate he was bound on a bare-backed horse, with his face to the tail. The hangman led the horse, and carried on a halbert the head of Hackston's friend Cameron. Behind the horse came a boy carrying another head in a sack, and three fellow-prisoners on foot, bareheaded, and with their hands tied to an iron "goad." Hackston was conducted to the Tolbooth, and after trial, condemned. The programme of his execution was written out the day before his trial ended. It was carried out with every attention to detail. He was drawn on a hurdle to the scaffold. There his right hand was cut off. After a pause, the hangman began to operate upon the left hand, and as he had taken a long time to get the other off, he, at the prisoner's request, struck on the joint of the wrist, and effected the amputation more quickly. He then, having adjusted the rope, drew Hackston up to the top of the gallows by means of a block and pulley, and suddenly slackening the rope, let him fall to the platform with his whole weight. This was done thrice. He then hoisted him again, and when "choked a little," lowered him till within easy reach, cut open his breast, dug out the heart, showed it to the people, saying, " Here is the heart of a traitor," and threw it into a fire which had been kindled on the scaffold. The body was then beheaded, quartered, and distributed to St. Andrews, Leith, Glasgow, and Burntisland—the head being fixed on the Netherbow. These particulars are vouched by Wodrow and other trustworthy writers. The programme of the execution stands in the records of the Council, of which two " right reverend fathers in God " were members.

Fletcher of Saltoun. Holland was still the natural asylum for these fugitives. The Prince of Orange had paid a visit to his uncle the King in the summer of 1681, and probably Carstares would not lose the opportunity of paying his court to his former patron, now more powerful than ever. Whether an interview with William influenced his movements or not, we have no means of knowing; nor can I discover with any certainty, the date of his return to Holland. He did return, however, after his marriage. Early in 1683 he was at his old quarters, Utrecht. Argyll, who escaped from Edinburgh in December 1681, had after a sojourn in London, found a temporary home in the same city. Stair, Lord London, Lord Melville, Sir Patrick Hume, afterwards Earl of Marchmont, and others of the Scottish nobility, were there. Pringle of Torwoodlee, Denham of West Shields, James Steuart, the author of the ' Accompt,' with many besides, spent their exile, and waited for the dawn of better days, at Utrecht.*

We have no correspondence of Carstares to guide us at this period; and McCormick is so vague, and, as usual, so destitute of dates, that he is of little help. From the end of 1681 to the beginning of 1683 the data on which we can found inductions are very scanty. The outline of Carstares' history, however, which has just been given, is, according to my best judgment, correct.

* Coltness Collections, Maitland Club, pp. 77–9.

CHAPTER IV.

" I HAVE been a conspirator all my life," were the words of
the great statesman who regenerated and united modern
Italy. There are times when honest men, who love truth
and freedom, and who prefer realities to superstitions, cannot
but be plotters. Where open warfare with an intolerable
evil is impossible, recourse must be had to secret craft; and
the citadel which cannot be stormed must be approached
through trench and mine. In the latter years of Charles II.
absolute power, oppression, illegality, and treachery in the
monarch, had grown to such a height that resistance became
the duty of the subject. Although the University of Oxford
might solemnly condemn as " repugnant to holy Scripture,"
and " destructive of the public peace, the laws of nature, and
bonds of human society,"* the propositions that if lawful
governors become tyrants they forfeit their right of government; that the King has but a co-ordinate power with the
Lords and Commons; that there lies on the subject no obligation to passive obedience when the ruler breaks the law;—
the principles of Buchanan's 'De Jure Regni apud Scotos,'
and Rutherford's 'Lex Rex' (which Oxford ordered to be
burnt), and of the works of Milton, Baxter, and Hobbes
('De Cive'), had made progress among all enlightened men.
The day for the doctrine of passive obedience was rapidly
drawing to its close. The authority which had demanded

* See Decree of University, of date 21st of July, 1683, in Wodrow,
vol. iii. p. 506.

that obedience was so nefarious that it supplied the strongest
of all arguments against its own dogma. In Scotland its
divine right proved its vitality through a deliberate system of
religious persecution, carried on with a minute and painstaking
attention to every artifice and detail of brutality. In England, where the public life had long been more orderly as
well as more free, and where there existed the elements of a
sturdier general resistance than in Scotland, the same extremes of inhumanity were not attempted. But in England,
hardly less than in the north, the patience of the sound
Protestants and of the liberal party was worn out. A long
course of dishonourable and disastrous government had tried
it to the utmost. The disgraceful and profitless Dutch wars,
the shameless subservience to France, the persecution of the
nonconformists, the invasion of the rights of the city of
London, the confiscation of the charters, the provision for a
Popish succession, the disuse of parliaments, the profligacy
and extravagance of the Court—all combined to alienate
the loyalty of the wisest and best of Charles' English subjects. If the country was to be governed in the future, as it
had been since the Restoration, they could expect nothing but
a growing subversion of liberty, whether religious or civil, a
deepening corruption of manners, and a thorough degenera-
tion of the people. "An entire revolution of government"
was looked to as the only remedy.*

By the time at which we find Carstares again at Utrecht
—early in 1683—the general discontent and desire for a
change of government had begun to move through those
stages of intrigue which precede revolution ; and he had
been intimately associated with the movement.

There was a great Whig plot, which, had it been successfully carried, must ultimately have produced a revolution.
There was a lesser plot, which designed the seizure, or assassination, of the King and the Duke. The one is associated
with the name of Shaftesbury. The other is known as the
Rye-house Plot. The two were essentially distinct; although

* Dalrymple, vol. i. part i. book i.

it has been the trick of such writers as Sprat, the hireling
historian of the Conspiracies, to represent them as closely
and intricately united. Ferguson, " the Plotter," who lived
in an atmosphere heavy with treason and intrigue, tried to
connect the designs of the greater revolutionists—who used
him as their instrument — with the machinations of the
inferior conspirators, who acted under his malign influence ;
but he failed in the attempt. There is no evidence to prove
that the Rye-house Plot was, in any way, countenanced by the
party that acted with Shaftesbury, Russell, or Argyll.

Ever since the illness which had seized the King in the
spring of 1681, Shaftesbury,

> " For close designs and crooked counsels fit,
>   Sagacious, bold, and turbulent of wit,"*

had pressed on Monmouth, William, Lord Russell, and others,
the necessity of an armed resistance to the Duke of York's
succession, in the event of the King's death. He was suspected and disliked by many of the brave and patriotic men,
whom the wrongs of their country and the suppression of
constitutional government had urged towards revolution ;
but Lord Russell, Lord Essex, Lord Gray, and Hampden,
the grandson of the great Commoner, united their councils
to his. Algernon Sidney alone, " who derived his blood
from a long train of English nobles and heroes, and his
sentiments from the patriots and heroes of antiquity," stood
aloof, and refused to ally his own designs with those of the
Earl.† It was resolved to promote an insurrection, without
waiting for the death of the King. Shaftesbury, who averred
that in the City he had " 10,000 brisk boys, ready to start
up at a motion of his finger," ‡ was to raise the standard of
revolt in London. Monmouth and Russell engaged to secure,
through their friends in the country, the support of the provinces. The negotiations and arrangements, preparatory to

---

* Dryden, ' Absalom and Achitophel.'
† Dalrymple, vol. i. part i. p. 20.
‡ Ibid. Hume, vol. viii. p. 176. Edition of 1825.

this rising, went on all through the year 1682. Again and again the fiery Shaftesbury pressed for immediate action, and when met with the cautious excuses of his allies, who did not think the right hour had come, he overwhelmed them with threats and reproaches. At length, in November 1682, stung with rage and chagrin at a fresh delay on the very eve of the outbreak he had planned, he quitted London and fled to Holland, where he soon afterwards died in the arms of Ferguson and Walcot, who only, of all his coadjutors, kept by him to the last.* His flight and death loosened the hold of the conspiracy on the city of London, and it became all the more necessary for its managers to gain new aid elsewhere. Branches of the plot were spread more widely through the English counties, and communications with the Scottish malcontents, which had begun during Shaftesbury's life, now assumed a more definite character. A council of six managed the affairs of the conspiracy. The six were Monmouth, Russell, Essex, Howard, Hampden, and Algernon Sidney. Monmouth, through his marriage with the heiress of Buccleuch, and his own lenient policy while in the North, had acquired great influence and popularity in Scotland, and had been careful to cultivate the friendship of Argyll, when that nobleman was hiding in London on his way to Holland. Argyll seems to have formed a project of insurrection almost as soon as he reached London, and it had been agreed between him and the Earl of Granard that a simultaneous rising should be organised in Ireland and Scotland, Granard to lead the one and Argyll the other, and 5000 trained Irish soldiers to be sent over to the west of Scotland as soon as Argyll should land there. This design, however, came to nought, and Argyll had carried his baffled plans with him to Utrecht,† when the English conspirators bethought themselves of securing his adherence to their scheme of a general insurrection.

It is at this point, in the winter of 1682–3, that Carstares appears on the scene. He had been in Holland during the summer of 1682, and when he returned to Britain had left

* Dalrymple, ut supra.   † Veitch and Brysson, p. 142.

his wife there with some of his sisters beside her. After this he had, it should appear, hazarded a brief visit to Scotland,* where he found his brother-in-law, William Dunlop, and other gentlemen, proposing to escape from the intolerable evils of life at home by an emigration to Carolina. Sir John Cochrane, and Sir George Campbell (son of Campbell of Cessnock) had been negociating with the King for a grant of land, which they expected to obtain on moderate terms.† The existence of this negociation about Carolina, in which many of the English proprietors of lands in the colony were interested, afforded a favourable pretext for establishing confidential relations between the English and Scottish malcontents. While Dunlop and his friends attended to the business of the emigration (and eventually went out and settled in Carolina), Carstares, Baillie of Jerviswood, Fletcher of Saltoun, and other patriots, prosecuted in London their correspondence with the revolutionary party.‡ The communications with Argyll were carried on through James Steuart and Carstares. The Earl heartily concurred in the proposals of an English insurrection, and undertook to head a similar revolt in Scotland, provided the English party would assist him with £30,000 in money and a force of 1000 cavalry. Without these, he thought he could not venture, with any hope of success, to raise the West of Scotland. There was great difficulty in the way of meeting these demands, and, unfortunately for the character and the fate of the conspiracy,

---

* I infer this from McCormick, and also from what Sir Andrew Forrester writes to Lord Aberdeen on the 14th of August, 1683. "Carstares," he says, "stiflly denies knowledge of the plot, and positively says that when set at liberty from Edinburgh Castle, it was on no condition of banishment from Scotland." Aberdeen Letters, Spalding Club, p. 152.

† "Towards the end of the year, the King signified to the Council that Sir John Cochrane of Ochiltree, and Sir George Campbell had come up from several of his subjects in Scotland, as commissioners to deal with him about a settlement in Carolina, and recommends to the Council to encourage them therein." Wodrow, vol. iii. p. 368.

‡ Wodrow, vol. iii. p. 368. Dalrymple, vol. i. part i. book i. McCormick, p. 9. Burnet, vol. ii. p. 351.

the help of Ferguson—who, as Shaftesbury's former agent, had ready access to the wealthy City malcontents—was invoked. He became again associated with the plot; but even with his assistance no promise could be given to Argyll for a larger sum than £10,000.

Carstares, in his dealings with Ferguson, soon discerned that the latter secretly harboured schemes of a very different order from those of the chief plotters. Ferguson threw out hints of the advantage of saving the lives of thousands by the sacrifice of two, and tried to discover how far Carstares and the other Scots would be likely to go along with an assassination plot. The disgraceful suggestions were indignantly repudiated. Carstares told "the plotter," once for all, that when he engaged in these transactions, he thought he had to do with men of honour and of public spirit; that he and his friends confined their views to the obtaining of a free Parliament, redress of notorious public grievances, and the exclusion of the Duke of York; that they felt they were justified in an armed demand for those constitutional remedies for the ills of the State, which had been denied to their peaceable remonstrances; but that, as men and Christians, they refused to listen to any proposal of an attempt upon the life of the King or his brother, and that if Ferguson wished to find accomplices in such a plot, he might go to the fanatics in the wilds of Scotland, but must not come to them. The idea of assassination was never again mooted, and Carstares, believing it to be the offspring solely of the plotter's own restless and unscrupulous brain, did not altogether withdraw from such intercourse with him as he deemed to be necessary in the interests of Argyll.* These interests, however, seemed to languish. There was no readiness to guarantee the money wanted, and there appeared to be a disposition to concentrate the insurrection in England, and to include in the programme the overthrow of the monarchy and the establishment of a commonwealth—schemes with which Argyll

* McCormick, pp. 10-12. Very confused, as usual, as to sequence of events and dates.

and the Scots would never concur.* In the course of a few weeks Carstares learned from Shephard, a wine merchant in the City, in whose house the plotters often met, that Sidney was wholly averse to any union with Argyll. Sidney was at bottom a republican, and he suspected that the Earl was too much attached to the existing constitution in Church and State to be a hearty rebel.

In face of all these difficulties, judging that his presence in London was of no use, Carstares crossed over to Holland and joined Argyll, Stair, Lord Loudon, and James Steuart, at Utrecht. Many and long were the consultations they held. Argyll was eager to cross to Scotland, if only he could get his cavalry and his £30,000. Stair was very doubtful of the wisdom and the probable issue of the attempt. Steuart also was understood to be opposed to it, although he guided the conspiracy, as far as he could, with sage and moderate counsel.† At length a basis of feasible co-operation with the English faction was agreed on, and Carstares, fully accredited by the refugees, and in possession of an intricate cipher devised by Steuart for their correspondence, moved from Utrecht to London.

On the day after his arrival he had an interview with Sir John Cochrane, and shortly afterwards another with Lord Russell, from whom he found that, although Sidney no longer objected to alliance with Argyll, the subsidies required were as unattainable as ever. Russell could promise no more than £10,000 in money, and could hold out no certain prospect of being able to muster the 1000 horse. On this rock the whole plot seemed likely to go to pieces. In the hope of finding some available aid in Scotland, and also in order to prevent any premature movement there, it was resolved to send a messenger to the North to gain infor-

* Sprat, p. 65. Sprat was employed by the King to write the history of the Plots; and his book must be quoted with caution, as he admits that the statements he makes were altered to suit the royal wishes; *cooked*, in fact. See Howell's 'State Trials,' vol. ix. p. 358.

† McCormick. Coltness Collections, p. 365.

mation, and, if necessary, allay excitement. Robert Martin, late clerk to the Justice Court, and one of the confederates, was deputed on this errand by a meeting of the Scotch confederates held in Jerviswood's lodgings, which Lord Melville, Jerviswood, Veitch (who had assisted in Argyll's escape), and Carstares attended.* The Scots met often thus as they had opportunity; but nothing in their own conferences, in their communications through Martin and others from Scotland, or in their correspondence with the English party, occurred to remove the standing difficulty as to the 1000 horse and the £30,000. Carstares, on Argyll's behalf, was ready to accept £10,000, although the Earl had named the larger sum as the very least which he thought sufficient; but even £10,000 seemed beyond the resources of the disaffected in the City.†

The Scots began to lose patience as excuse after excuse was offered for the deficiency of the money, and as their emissaries brought them tidings of the unabated oppression in the North. "The people of England do nothing but talk," said Jerviswood. "They should go more effectually about this business. The only way to secure the Protestant religion is for the King to suffer the Parliament to sit, and pass the Bill of Exclusion, which he might be led to do if the Parliament took brisk measures with him." The English were taunted with being only fit for "fireside plotting," and the more eager of the Scots threatened that, for their part, they would rise, if there were more delays, "though they had nothing but their claws to fight with."‡ Some weeks passed in fruitless debate, proposals and counter proposals; Carstares in the meantime becoming more and more suspicious of the tendency of the whole negociation, and of the probable result of the conspiracy. He, at last, resolved to try to put a stop to these ineffectual preliminaries, and to withdraw, along with his countrymen, if they would be ruled by him, from

* ' State Trials,' vol. x. p. 673.
† Sprat.
‡ ' True and Plain Account of the Discoveries, &c.' Edinburgh, 1685.

an engagement which was sure to expose them to much danger, and yet do Scotland no good. Accordingly, a meeting of the Scotch conspirators was summoned, and attended by Melville, Baillie, Cochrane, and Sir Hugh and Sir George Campbell of Cessnock—father and son.* Carstares addressed them, and pointed out the unsatisfactory nature of their present relations to the English cabal. Among the members of it, he said, were men, so divided in principle and aim, that combined action for a definite end was hopeless. Sidney the philosophical republican, Russell the constitutional Whig, Monmouth the vague aspirant to his uncle's crown—each with a different ideal, were not likely to concur in the same practical measures. They lost their time in chimerical projects and idle debate, while every day the risk of detection grew, and they were losing sight of the only course that could really serve the country, which was instantly to resort to arms and to demand a free Parliament. Since the English were thus languid and irresolute, he advised that the Scottish confederates should consult their own safety, and instead of hurrying on a rebellion in Scotland (where recent tidings assured them many of the people were willing to revolt, but lacked the means of levying a successful war against the government), they should immediately arrest all preparations there, until the English were thoroughly equipped for action, and should limit their further negociations with the English to the announcement that the Scots would no longer act in concert with them, unless a definite plan of immediate action were adopted. This counsel was stoutly opposed by Baillie. That the English were slow to move and irresolute in their purposes seemed to him no reason why the Scots should not strike for liberty. If it was more difficult, it was also more glorious, to risk the enterprize alone. If they should succeed, as he believed they should, it would not be the first time, since the Stuarts came to the English throne,

---

* The Campbells of Cessnock had an hereditary call to be zealous for the Protestant faith and liberty of conscience. George Campbell of Cessnock, in 1491, was one of the "Lollards of Kyle." Scots' 'Worthies,' p. 11

that Englishmen would owe their deliverance from oppression to the Scots. The advice of Carstares, however, prevailed;
and an intimation, such as he suggested, was sent to the
Council of Six. At the same time a letter was despatched
to Scotland, to entreat the discontinuance of all warlike preparations.*

Before the council had time to frame a reply, the English
plot was discovered. The discovery is traceable to Ferguson's
wild and violent machinations.

During the whole progress of the great conspiracy, both
while he was acting as Shaftesbury's aide-de-camp in the
City, and since his patron's death, this unprincipled schemer
had been the centre and moving spirit of an inferior cabal,
whose object, as far as contrived by him, was the assassination of the King and the Duke of York. He had, as we have
seen, tried to engraft this rascally offshoot on the larger stem,
and had been deterred by the indignant rebuke of Carstares;
but he had not abandoned his murderous design. He had
even managed, by veiling the cowardly nature of the scheme,
to enlist the aid of some men of high character and principle,
who went in with his proposals to the extent of agreeing to
an attack on the King's escort and seizure of his person, when
an opportunity should appear. By what casuistry men, who
would have recoiled from assassination, could justify their
taking part in an attack on the royal cortege, which must
necessarily endanger the King's life and render his murder,
if such should be attempted, comparatively easy, it would be
hard to determine. But nothing is stranger, in the annals of
those disordered times, than the evident integrity of heart
with which good and brave men resorted to questionable
means, in their search after the civil and religious liberty, of
which the government had robbed them. The spectacle of a
government thoroughly immoral seems to have corrupted
their own natural sense of right and wrong. Walcot and
Rumbald were Ferguson's associates; and yet they were men
of religious character and self-sacrificing patriotism—very

* McCormick. 'True and Plain Account.'

unlike the "profligate knave" "remarkable for saving himself in all plots," on whom Dryden pours his blistering
satire :—

> " Judas, that keeps the rebels' pension-purse ;
> Judas, that pays the treason writers' fee ;
> Judas, that well deserves his namesake's tree."*

Walcot was a gallant and high-principled Irish officer. He
had served with Cromwell, and had stood on guard at the
scaffold of Charles I. Rumbald, whose one eye and bold
spirit gained him the name of Hannibal among his comrades,†
had also held a commission in the republican army. He was
now a maltster. Sprat calls him a "desperate and bloody
Ravaillac ;" but except that he offered his house for the use
of Ferguson's conspirators, and that the saying is ascribed to
him that " God did not make the greater part of mankind
with saddles on their backs and bridles in their mouths, and
some few booted and spurred to ride on the rest," there
appears no reason for an epithet so harsh.

In the cant phrase, which passed among Ferguson's confederates, the two royal brothers were called " Slavery " and
" Popery." These two were to be " lopped," and this, in
Ferguson's mouth, meant assassinated.‡ There were many
debates as to where and when the "lopping" should take
place. Some of Ferguson's crew proposed to shoot the
brothers from Bow steeple ; others to attack them in Saint
James's Park, or at the bull feast in Red Lion Fields, or in
their barge on the river. The road between Hampton Court
and Windsor, and that between London and Winchester, frequently travelled by the pair, were also suggested. At last
Rumbald proposed that the conspirators should meet at his
house, the Rye, about eighteen miles from London, in Hertfordshire. Close to it ran the byroad from Bishop's Stortford
to Hoddesden, which the King constantly used in going to

---

* Burnet, vol. ii. p. 358. 'Absalom and Achitophel.' Dalrymple,
vol. i. Book i. p. 20.

† Dalrymple. Sprat.

‡ Sprat, pp. 31, 40.

and from Newmarket. The road was but a narrow lane, and could be stopped by overturning a cart in it. It was over-looked on one side by a thick hedge, and on the other by a long outhouse with several windows. The Ryehouse itself stood hard by, surrounded with a moat and capable of effec-tive defence.* The offer of this advantageous spot was accepted by Ferguson. The offer was made in ignorance of his design to murder; and neither Walcot nor Rumbald engaged to do more than help in overpowering the escort of guards. †

The King was at Newmarket in March; and the attempt was to have been made on his journey back to London. A fire, which broke out in the house he occupied at Newmarket, cut short his stay there; and he drove past the Ryehouse on his way to Whitehall, with a slender retinue, several days earlier than was expected. The golden opportunity was lost; and great was the angry disappointment of the conspirators, who immediately began to cast about for some other way of ful-filling their projects, and to furnish themselves with additional arms and ammunition. They were busy with this when, on the 12th of June, Josiah Keeling, one of their own num-ber, a salter in the City, and an Anabaptist, resolved, as Sprat has it, " after much conflict in his mind, to discharge his conscience of the hellish secret;" and laid an information before Sir Leoline Jenkins, the Secretary of State. A general discovery and dispersion of the Ryehouse plot-ters followed. Ferguson of course disappeared; but he left Rumsey, one of Cromwell's colonels, behind him, the only other conspirator who had, like himself, been admitted to the confidence of the chiefs of the great plot.‡ Russell indeed had always disliked Rumsey, and trusted him but little; but

* Sprat.

† See Burnet and Dalrymple; and Macaulay, vol. ii. p. 145. Rumbald to the very last, when about to be executed after Argyll's rebellion, denied all knowledge of Ferguson's intention to assassinate. He was cruelly treated at his trial and execution; and his head was pickled and sent up in a box to London, to be disposed of as James might wish.

‡ Hume, vol. viii. p. 178: Burnet, vol. ii. p. 357.

Rumsey knew enough of the designs of the Council of Six to make it worth his while to purchase his own safety by their betrayal. In his depositions he mentioned the meetings at Shephard the wine merchant's. Shephard was seized and examined on the 27th of June. He confirmed the statement of Rumsey, and named, as known partners in the plot, Monmouth, Essex, Russell, Gray, Sir Thomas Armstrong, Baillie, and others. When the Privy Council heard the names of Monmouth and Russell they became alarmed, and took measures for the arrest of the chief conspirators. Monmouth absconded. Gray, though arrested, contrived to escape. Russell was found sitting in his study, and was carried to the Tower. Lord Howard was caught hidden up his chimney, and was drawn out blubbering and begrimed with soot. Profligate and cowardly, the only man of the higher order of plotters who knew the secrets of the lower, he turned traitor to his friends; and on his evidence Sidney, Essex, Hampden, Baillie, and many more were apprehended. Baillie was offered his life, if he too would turn king's evidence. He smiled and answered, " They, who can make such a proposal to me, know neither me nor my country."

The first that was brought to trial was Walcot, on the 12th of July. Lord Russell followed on the 13th. Few passages in British history are better known, or nobler and more touching, than those which tell how he underwent that trial, with " the daughter of the virtuous Southampton " by his side ; how he parted for ever with his children and his wife, his eyes following hers as she left his cell, and then turned to Burnet and said, " The bitterness of death is past ;" how bravely and calmly he passed through the crowded streets to the scaffold, and said his last prayer, and died.* It would be foreign to my purpose to trace the destiny of all the accomplices in this conspiracy, but a tribute, ever so brief, is due to one of the noblest of those martyrs of liberty who suffered under the Stuarts.

* Dalrymple, vol. i. Book i. p. 28. Burnet, vol. ii. p. 361, et seq. Hume, vol. viii. p. 179, et seq

Lord Russell was beheaded on the 21st of July.* A few days later, on a Monday, Carstares was taken at Tenterden in Kent, where he was in hiding, under his mother's name of Mure. A short time before Keeling betrayed his confederates, a letter in cipher had come from Argyll to Monmouth, who had sent to Carstares for the key to the cipher. He returned it, when he had used it, to Major Holms, one of Argyll's chief confidants; and on the Major's arrest, it was found in his possession. Lord Melfort no sooner saw the cipher, than he identified part of it as the handwriting of Carstares; and a warrant was issued for his apprehension.

In the King's Declaration for Thanksgiving, dated 7th August, "Carstares, the noncomformist preacher," is named as one of those who have fled from justice; yet at that time he must have been in custody in Kent, as he distinctly states, in a letter to Wodrow, that he was taken "the Monday immediately after the execution of that great and honourable patriot of his country, my Lord Russell."†

The narrative which follows is Carstares's own. It is embodied in a MS. corrected, though not written, by his hand, and which has evidently been intended as a reply to

---

* In spite of this petition : " To the King's Most Excellent Majesty, the humble petition of William, Earl of Bedford, humbly sheweth, that could your petitioner have been admitted into your presence he would have laid himself at your royal feet, in behalf of his unfortunate son, himself and his distressed and disconsolate family, to implore your royal mercy, which he never had the presumption to think could be obtained by any indirect means." [A bribe of £100,000 for royal self or for the Duchess of Portsmouth, possibly ?] " But shall think himself, wife and children much happier to be left but with bread and water, than to lose his dear son for so foul a crime as treason against the best of princes, for whose life he ever did, and ever shall, pray more than for his own. May God incline your Majesty's heart to the prayers of an afflicted old father, and not bring gray hairs with sorrow to my grave.—Bedford." The King, urged by the Duke, refused the petition. Five years later, as the Dutch were approaching London, King James appealed to the Earl of Bedford. " My Lord, you are a good man. You have much interest with the peers. You can do me service with them to-day." " I once had a son," was Bedford's only answer, " who could have served your Majesty upon this occasion."—Dalrymple.

† Wodrow, vol. iv. p. 96.

" Sprat's Account," which it pronounces to be a " rhapsody of false, inconsistent, and contradictory, narratives."*

" The apprehending of several of my countrymen," he says, " and the strict search that was made after others gave me the alarm, having found by former sad experience that legal innocency did prove but a slender fence against the stream of violent opposition; but it pleased the only wise and righteous God to order things so as that I was taken at Tenterden in Kent upon suspicion, and desired to take the oaths; and upon my inquiring if upon taking the oaths of allegiance and supremacy I might expect liberty, being told that I must also take the corporation oath and abjure the Covenant, (though the Act of Parliament obliging to the last had been for some time expired) I was upon a very severe and false mittimus, upon refusing these oaths in their complex bulk, sent to a nasty gaol, full of dirt and stones, where thro' the windows neither having glass nor shutters, I was exposed to the view of every boy and girl in the street; and though I offered to the keeper to maintain what guard he should think necessary for securing his prisoner, yet I was denied that favour, which hath been granted often to such as were prisoners only for refusing the oaths. The great instrument of which severity was one Lieut.-Col. Ausden (as I take his name to be), who by an inhuman carriage to a poor stranger did think to reconcile himself to his Majesty, to whose resentments his carriage in parliament did expose him. After a fortnight's imprisonment there, I was sent for to London, and carried before a Committee of the Council consisting of four members of the honourable board—the Duke of Ormond, the then Lord Keeper, Marquis of Halifax and Sir Lionel Jenkins—who were the only persons by whom I was examined,—his Majesty (as I was informed) being out of town. I was twice before these Lords, and asked whether I was concerned in any plot against King and government; to which, according to truth, I answered negatively. Several other

* This MS. is in part much the same as the letter given by Wodrow, vol. iv. p. 96.

questions being put, I gave one and the same answer to the
most important of them, viz.—that they relating to criminal
matters, I could answer them no other way but by disowning
all concern in such affairs,—which carriage moved Sir Lionel
Jenkins to draw a mittimus for my commitment to the Gatehouse, where I was ordered to be kept close prisoner as a
person guilty of high treason, *in conspiring the death of the
King and levying war ;** the strain of which mittimus was the
more surprising to me in that Sir Andrew Forrester (who had
been sent to me twice while I was in the hands of a messenger, to offer me from the Lords of Council then in town,
by His Majesty's order and in his name, life and favour if I
would confess what I knew of the Cessnocks and others,
showing me that this was a kindness beyond what I could
have expected, considering that I came not in voluntarily but
was apprehended.   But after all the arguments made use of
by him, with the greatest civility, had been ineffectual, I
still answering that I had nothing to accuse any man of, he
left me regretting much my condition, and showing me that
my Lord Argyll's letter and Mr. Holms—with other witnesses
whom I did not suspect—would make my concern in the plot
evident,) did declare that the King did not suspect I was
guilty of any design against his life, but did believe I would
abhor any such thing, tho' he did seem to insinuate that I
might have heard of some such base attempt.   But I am apt
to think that one great reason why I was so severely dealt
with was because, not only offers of favour made by Sir

* "Sir Leolin Jenkins, Knight, of his Majesty most honourable Privy
Council, and Principal Secretary of State : These are in his Majesty's name
to will and require you to receive into your custody the person of William
Carstayres herewith sent you, being committed for high treason in com-
passing the death and destruction of our sovereign lord the King (whom
God preserve) and conspiring to levy war against his Majesty, and him
the said William Carstayres to keep in safe custody, until he shall be discharged by due course of law,—for which this shall be your warrant. Given
under my hand and seal at Whitehall the 17th day of August 1683, in
the 35th year of His Majesty's reign.—L. Jenkins. To Anthony Church,
Gent., Keeper of His Majesty's prison, the Gatehouse, Westminster."—
Graham Dunlop MSS.

Andrew Forrester, under secretary for Scotland, were rejected by me, but that the insinuation of having his Majesty's pardon made to me by my Lord Keeper, who desired me to give the noble persons, before whom I then was, some ground to go upon in pleading with his Majesty for favour to me, was not regarded. While I was in the Gatehouse, his Majesty's advocate for the kingdom of Scotland came to examine me, who, not meeting with that satisfactory answer to his interrogators which he desired, told me that the Boot in Scotland should drive out of me what he alleged I refused to confess. Having for some weeks continued close prisoner, my wife having a copy of my mittimus did first petition his Majesty in Council, and having had no answer, did conclude that she might take the ordinary course in law allowed in such cases, which she did by addressing the Court of King's Bench, and petitioning that either I might be brought to a trial, or have the benefit of law, in being admitted to bail,—which petition was recorded by that Court. But when I expected the privilege of a subject of England, I was, in the most open contrariety to plain law, as well as my own expectation, ordered by a warrant under my Lord Sunderland's hand, and superscribed by his Majesty,* to be sent to Scotland, where I had committed no crime ;—nor was it to be rationally supposed I could be guilty of any, having been a prisoner at the time of Bothwell Bridge, and for near five years before ; and leaving my country a few months after I had obtained my liberty, as I had been a stranger to it a long time before my imprison-

* "Charles R. Whereas Robert Bayly of Jervaswood in our Kingdom of Scotland, John Hepburne, and William Carstares stand accused of, or are upon very good grounds suspected to be, guilty of high treason in our said Kingdom, and are now in your custody; our will and pleasure is that you forthwith deliver the said Robert Bayly, John Hepburne, and William Carstares into the hands of Anthony Birns, one of our messengers in ordinary, to be by him carried on board our yacht, the *Kitchin*, in order to their transportation into Scotland, to be proceeded against there according to law; for which this shall be your warrant. Given at our Court at Whitehall, the 30th day of October 1683, in the five and thirtieth year of our reign. By his Majesty's command—Sunderland. To the keeper of the Gatehouse."—Graham Dunlop MSS.

ment: yet upon this warrant I was, upon a few hours' warning, conveyed aboard his Majesty's *Kitchin* yacht, in which, with several gentlemen of my own country, I was transported to Scotland. It may indeed seem strange that this second time I should have been so illegally dealt with, after an express Act of Parliament forbidding, under very severe penalties, that any residing in England should, for any crime committed in it, be carried out of the kingdom in order to trial and continuance of restraint; but this is such a breach of law as cannot be palliated, and for which my Lord Sunderland and others concerned owe that satisfaction to the justice of the nation, and to me, which the statute requires; seeing in all my examinations in Scotland, I was not so much as accused of a crime committed in that kingdom. There needs no great inquiry into the reason of my being so used, seeing it is plain that I and others were sent home, because it was judged that violent tortures which the laws of England— at least the custom—does not admit of—would force to anything."

The yacht sailed from London on the 1st of November, but had a tedious and very stormy passage, and did not reach Leith till the 14th. On board, besides Carstares, Baillie, and Hepburn (a suspected clergyman), were the two Cessnocks; Muir of Rowallan, with his eldest son, and Fairlie of Bruntsfield, his son-in-law; Cranfurd of Crawfurdland; Commissary Monro; Murray, of Tippermuir, and Spence, one of Argyll's servants.

Late at night on the 14th, the prisoners were carried up to Edinburgh, under a strong guard, and lodged in the Tolbooth.*

* Fountainhall, vol. ii. p. 458; McCormick, p. 17.

CHAPTER V.

Second Imprisonment — Examination and Torture — The Thumbkins —
Sir George Mackenzie — The Deposition.

WHEN Front-de-Bœuf was about to wring his thousand pounds
of silver from Isaac of York, by the simple process of roasting
him over a fire of charcoal until he should agree to pay the
money, he had the Israelite carried to the lowest dungeon of
Torquilstone, whence no remonstrant outcries could reach
the upper air. On the same plan, King Charles had his
Scottish prisoners transported to their native country, in
order that there, remote from the freer air of England, they
might, if necessary, be tortured into making the revelations
which he hoped to extort from them.

He dared not have applied the boot or the thumbkins,
even in the darkest cell of the Tower of London; but these
instruments might be freely used in Edinburgh, under the
eyes of Scottish peers, prelates, and privy councillors. The
King, his brother, and his Council, had been thoroughly
alarmed by the discovery of the two plots; and he was determined to force from the victims in his power full disclosures
of the names and designs of all, who had been privy to their
schemes. The prisoners had not been in the Tolbooth a
week, when a letter came from his Majesty to the Privy
Council, ordering Gordon of Earlston and Spence "to be
tortured in the boots, to extort a discovery of the late designs."[*] Gordon had been taken at Newcastle in June,
and had been condemned to death, but once or twice re-
prieved; and this was the second time the King,[†] against the
remonstrance even of his Scotch advisers, had ordered him
to be tortured, while under sentence of death.

[*] Fountainhall, p. 163.   [†] Fountainhall, p. 452.

The Privy Council began with Gordon, and he was brought up for torture on the 23rd of November. The boot, however, was not applied. Gordon either went mad, or pretended to do so. He "roared out like a bull, and cried and struck about him so that the hangman and his man durst scarce lay hands on him;" he said General Dalzell was to head the plot; and, in short, so comported himself that the Privy Council was glad to send him up to the Castle and finally to despatch him to the Bass.* Processes against the Campbells of Cessnock, Craufurd, the Cochrans, and others, seem to have occupied the government during the winter, for Spence is not mentioned until the 22nd of April, on which day the Council allow him to be " taken out of the irons," in which, presumably, he had lain since November; but order him to be kept close prisoner.†

It was on the 26th of July that he began to undergo the torture. He was, first of all, required to swear that he should answer whatever questions might be put to him, although the law expressly forbade the exaction of such an oath.‡ He refused, and his leg was placed in the boot. This instrument was an iron cylinder, into which the leg was inserted up to the knee; and wedges were then driven in between the case and the limb:

> " On the ankle the sharp wedge descends,
>   The bone reluctant with the iron bends,
>   Crushed is its frame—blood spurts from every pore,
>   And the white marrow swims in purple gore."§

Spence stood firm, and would not reply to the interrogatories. He was thereupon sent back to prison, and entrusted to General Dalzell, who directed him to be clothed in a hair shirt, and to be watched, night and day, by soldiers who, by pricking him, kept him for seven or eight days and nights from a moment's sleep.‖

* Fountainhall, p. 465.
† Wodrow, vol. iv. p. 95.
‡ Burnet, vol. ii. p. 429; Wodrow, vol. iv. p. 95.
§ Lines by Thomas Gibbons, prefixed to Crookshank's ' History.'
‖ Graham Dunlop MSS.

Although worn out with this treatment, he revealed nothing; and on the 7th of August he was carried to the Council Chamber again, to be tortured with the thumbkins.*

This little engine had been known in Muscovy, and brought home, as a useful contribution to the resources of the executive, by General Dalzell.† It is not unlike a miniature pair of stocks, in steel, with a strong central screw. The thumbs are inserted in two apertures, and the upper bar is screwed down until the bones are crushed.‡ The thumbkins were applied, but still Spence kept silence. The boot was then brought out again, and his leg was about to be encased, when he asked for time to consider what he should do, which was granted. Believing that nothing he could tell would reveal more than the government already had found out, he, on the 19th of August, made a declaration to the effect that he knew a plot for the defence of the Protestant religion, and the liberties of the kingdom, had been going on for two years. He also agreed to decipher certain letters of Argyll's which had been found in Holmes's keeping, and the key to which the Countess, on being cited by the Council, alleged she had burned. The cipher, which was that devised by James Steuart, is given by McCormick and Sprat, and is embodied in the 'True and Plain Account.' It is extraordinarily intricate, and, even when deciphered, is found to be full of private marks and names, and to require to be read in a

* Fountainhall, pp. 454, 548.

† Ibid. p. 548.

‡ Dr. Hill Burton ('History,' vol. vii. p. 454) describes the thumb-screws differently. I speak on the authority of the pair with which Carstares was tortured, and which are now in Mr. Graham Dunlop's possession, along with the ring given by the Marquis of Argyll to John Carstares, a ring inclosing King William's hair given to William Carstares by the King, and other Carstares relics.

On the 23rd of July, 1684, the Privy Council resolve that "whereas the boots were the ordinary way to explicate matters relating to the government, and there is now a new invention and engine called the 'Thumbkins,' which will be very effectual to the purpose aforesaid, the Lords ordain that when any person shall by their order be put to the torture, the said boots and thumbkins both be applied to them, as it shall be found fit and convenient."

certain order, the key to which is given, in cipher also, at the beginning or end of each communication in which the cipher is used. The letter whose contents proved to be of most importance was dated the 21st of June, and addressed to Major Holmes. It was written in Argyll's own hand, and when unravelled by Spence ran as follows:—" I know not the grounds our friends have gone upon, which hath occasioned them to offer so little money as I hear; neither know I what assistance they intend to give. And, till I know both, I will neither refuse my service, nor do so much as object against anything is resolved, till I first hear what Mr. Red,* or any other you send shall say. Only, in the mean time, I resolve to let you know as much of the grounds I go on, as is possible at this distance, and in this way. I did truly, in my proposition, mention the very least sum I thought could do our business effectually, not half of what I would have thought requisite in another juncture of affairs; and what I proposed I thought altogether so far within the power of those concerned, that, if a little less could possibly do the business, it would not be stood upon. I reckoned the assistance of the horse absolutely necessary for the first brush; and I do so still : I shall not be peremptor to urge the precise number named; but I do think there needs very near that number effectually; and I think 1000 as easy had as 8 or 600. And, it were hard that it stuck at the odds. I leave it to you to consider, if all should be hazarded upon so small a differ. As to the money, I confess, what was proposed is more by half than is absolutely necessary at the first week's work; but, soon after, all the sum was proposed, and more, will be necessar, if it please God to give success; and then arms cannot be sent like money by bills. There are now above 1200 horse and dragoons, and 2000 foot at least, of. standing forces in Brand,† very well appointed, and tolerably well commanded. It is right hard to expect that country-people on foot, without horse, should beat them, the triple their number; and if multitudes can be got together, yet

* Carstares.   † Scotland.

they will need more arms, more provision, and have more trouble with them. But the case is, if something considerable be not suddenly done at the very first appearing, and that there be only a multitude gathered without action, though that may frighten a little, it will do no good. The standing forces will take up some station, probably at Stirling, and will, to their aid, not only have the militia of 20,000 foot and 2000 horse, but all the heritors, &c., to the number, it may be, of 50,000. And, though many will be unwilling to fight for the standing forces, yet the most part will once join, and many will be as concerned for them as any can be against them. And, though we had at first the greatest success imaginable ; yet it is impossible but some will keep together, and get some concurrence and assistance, not only in Brand,* but from Birch† and Ireland. It will not then be time to call for more arms, far less for money to buy them. No money nor credit could supply it. We should prove like the foolish virgins. Consider, in the next place, how Browne‡ can employ so much money, and so many horse, better for their own interest, though the Protestant interest were not concerned. Is it not a small sum, and a small force, to raise so many men with, and, by God's blessing, to repress the whole power of Brand, that some hope are engaged against us ; besides, the horse to be sent need possibly stay but a little time to do a job, if future events do not bring the seat of the war to Brand, which is yet more to the advantage of Birch. As to the total of the money that was proposed, by the best husbanding, it cannot purchase arms, and absolute necessaries for one time, for a militia of the number they are to deal with ; and there is nothing out of the whole designed to be bestowed upon many things usual and necessary for such an undertaking, as tents, waggons, cloaths, shoes, horse, horse-shoes ; all which are not only necessary to be once had, but daily to be re-cruited. Far less, out of the whole sum projected, was any thing proposed for provisions of meat or drink, intelligence, or incident charges. Some very honest, well-meaning, and

* Scotland   † England   ‡ Dissenting Lords.

very good men, may undertake on little, because they can do little, and know little what is to be done. All I shall add is, I made the reckoning as low as if I had been to pay it out of my own purse; and, whether I meddle or meddle not, I resolve never to touch the money, but to order the payment of necessaries as they shall be received; and I shall freely submit myself to any knowing soldier for the lists, and any knowing merchant for the prices I have calculated. When there is an occasion to confer about it, it will be a great encouragement to persons that have estates to venture, and that consider what they do, that they know that there is a project, and prospect of the whole affair, and all necessaries provided for such an attempt. If, after I have spoke with Mr. Red,* I see I can do you service, I will be very willing; if I be not able, I pray God some other may. But, before it be given over, I wish I had such a conference as I writ of to you a week ago; for I expect not all from Browne.† Some considerable part of the horse may, I hope, be made up by the help of your particular friends. I have yet something to add, to enforce all I have said, which I cannot at this distance; and some things are to be done to prevent the designs of enemies, that I dare not now mention, lest it should put them on their guard. I have a considerable direction in my head; but all is in God's hands."

The references to Carstares here were not to be overlooked, and afforded the Privy Council sufficient pretext to proceed actively against him. The suspicions of which he was the object, and the strong desire to hold him implicated in the worst portions of the Ryehouse conspiracy, may easily be understood from the tone in which Sprat mentions him in his 'Account.' He speaks of him as "a Scotch conventicle preacher to a numerous meeting at Theobalds, where *Rumbald* was his frequent hearer;" and again, as "a zealous and fierce preacher to the sectaries of both kingdoms," formerly prisoner in Edinburgh Castle, "being accused for publishing a treasonable pamphlet called the 'Grievances of Scotland,'" and now "much em-

---

* Carstares.   † Dissenting Lords.

ployed in many messages relating to this conspiracy," "dispersing Argyll's libellous books, and carrying to and fro his letters." *

A Scot, against whom the English could lay such charges, and whom they evidently regarded as one of the chief agents of the plot, could not be let easily off. There would appear, however, to have been a kindly feeling towards him, from whatever cause, in the mind of the Lord Advocate ; and had he but agreed to betray his friends, his own share in the conspiracy would have been condoned ; but this, of course, he would not do. He was not brought before the Council till September. The long confinement in the Tolbooth was sometimes very strict, sometimes relaxed, so as to admit of his seeing his wife, who had followed him from London, and was with his father and mother in or near Edinburgh.

His father, though not more than sixty years of age, was now very feeble, not able for many months past " to walk alone without much trouble, if at all, betwixt the Cross and the Tron." His last public appearance had been in November 1680, when he was summoned before the Council, on suspicion of being concerned in some of the extravagances of Cargill's followers, and when he " came off with a great deal of respect and applause," although he had taken the opportunity of protesting against Paterson, bishop of Edinburgh, sitting in a civil court, and of refusing him his title of bishop.†

Few, if any, of the uncompromising national clergy, were held in such esteem as John Carstares. When Rothes, the Chancellor, lay dying, he sent for him that he might hear him pray. The prayers were so beautiful and touching, that almost all who were present were moved to tears. A lady— so violently Episcopal that she would not stay in the room with the Presbyterian minister—overhearing him, was forced to own she never knew the difference between a Prelatic and a Presbyterian minister till then. " This is a strange thing," said the Duke of Hamilton, who was with the Chancellor, " we are aye hunting and pursuing these men in our time of

* Sprat, pp. 27, 77.   † Wodrow, vol. iii. p. 241

life and health, but we are, many of us, made to call for them at our death."*

The good man was sorely displeased at his son's fresh political embarrassments. He and his kindred had already, and even recently, suffered so much, that he seems to have resented, with a sense of personal injury, William's bringing new troubles on the family. Since his own wife's experience of prison, Caldwell's widow, with one of her daughters, had been seized on the false evidence of a single witness, and, without a trial, incarcerated, first in Glasgow jail, and then in Blackness Castle, whence she was not allowed to go out, even with a guard, to visit another daughter who was sick, and who died without her mother's farewell. Young Glanderston had been thrown into jail because, when in the extremity of a fever, he had been bled by a nonconformist apothecary. Porterfield of Duchal, Maxwell of Pollock, Hamilton of Halleraig, all kinsmen or dear friends, had each been in prison;† and now William must arrive to vex his father's soul as a suspected plotter of seditious plots, instead of comforting him amidst all these distresses. If the solemn advice he had given his son when he was released in 1679 had been laid to heart, this would not have happened. He was sore displeased. "I have a son called Mr. William," he said to one of his visitors, "and a good-son [i.e. son-in-law], Mr. William Dunlop; they will be aye plotting and plodding till they plod the heads off themselves. And this is very grievous to me, for as they are ministers of the gospel, they are not called to meddle with that work which noblemen and gentlemen may very lawfully be called to." ‡

William's wife, let us hope, was dutiful to the worn and saddened old man, and helped to soothe his troubled spirit. There are several letters of her husband's, which appear to have been written during this imprisonment, and which are mostly addressed to her. Nine of them—eight to her and

* 'Analecta,' vol. iii. p. 48.
† Wodrow, vol. iii. pp. 439, 466, 474.
‡ 'Analecta,' vol. iii. p. 51.

one to a sister—are published from the Graham Dunlop MSS., to which Dr. Burns had access, in the appendix to his edition of Wodrow. From these and from the rest of the collection I make a few extracts, to illustrate the character of the letters, which are in general short, and written, without date or signature, on small bits of paper :—

"Your news of an indictment were surprising to us, because none of us can see upon what ground they can found one, while we have been such strangers to Scotland, and have been guilty of no crime in it ; but we doubt not but our innocency shall appear, and that we shall have no reason to complain of our native country. My dearest, my greatest outward concern is for thee. Thou liest near to me, and deservedly, for thou hast been a most kind and conscientious wife to me,—the Lord bless thee, and be thy comforter and portion, and, if it be His will, restore us to one another again."

He adds, on the same sheet, to his sister, Mrs. Dunlop :—

"Dear Sister,—It was not a little refreshing to me to hear of your being in town. I much longed for you, and am sorry I cannot see you, for there are so many eyes upon us that Mr. Benham cannot do us the kindness he would ; but you may see his wife and try if you can be in Mr. Hogg's room to-morrow night, when the maid comes for her things, and it may be Mr. Benham may admit you.* Leave some money at the cheeque-lock if you come, and give Mr. Benham some if he admit you. I am sorry you brought not your son with you. If he could be brought without hurt I should be glad to see him."

"My Dearest.—(Monday night.)—I had my dear father's letter. It seems things run high. A number of groundless reports are spread of me as to crimes for which there is no ground ; but hard things seem to be abiding me, if God do not interpose. He can disappoint fears, and support under any troubles that come ; he is my hope and strength, and in His infinite love and mercy in Christ I trust. It may be He will make light to arise upon me as to my

* Thomas Hogg, of Kiltearn, had been often in and out of prison. He was finally banished, early in 1684. "A coach came for him to the door of *the Tolbooth*" (another proof that Carstares' place of confinement was the Tolbooth, and not, as McCormick would have it, the Castle), and he drove off and reached Berwick on the 3rd of April. Wodrow, vol. iv. p. 512.

spiritual and outward condition, but if I have his favour I cannot be miserable . . . . I shall be glad to see thee once a day, either about eleven in the forenoon or four in the afternoon; and if reports be refreshing then hold up both hands; if otherwise hold up but one."

"My dearest Sister . . . . Consider your husband's true affection, which I do not doubt but he hath for you, and how much it must afflict him, in his voyage, to leave you as sorrowful as I perceive he is like to do; and besides, I think you ought to consider the poor child you have already, and your present condition, so as to guard against excessive sorrow upon the account of what Providence thinks fit to put into your lot . . . . Pray weigh with yourself how you would carry if your husband were in my place and circumstances. I am apt to think you would reckon it a mercy to have him a free man, though upon the condition of going the voyage,* the thoughts whereof do now so much perplex you. The serious consideration of what we deserve from God,—of what we might have met with that He hath not measured out unto us,—of what we have been sometimes, it may be, afraid of, that yet we have been disappointed in,—and of what we see others meet with that is not in our lot — would, thro' God's blessing, contribute much to a cheerful acquiescing in the will of God as to lesser afflictions."

"My Dearest,—My Lord Advocate was with me this day, showing me that Mr. Sp—, after long enduring of torture, did at last decipher some letters of Arg—, by which it did appear that I was deeply concerned in this affair, so long talked of, as to raising of money for a rebellion, and therefore had begged leave of the Council that he might first speak to me, having a kindness for me, and therefore obtested me to be ingenuous, as I loved myself, for that torture had made Mr. Sp— do, at last, what he had so long refused to do, and would make me do it too. He expressed a great kindness for my father and you. I told I knew nothing, and I did not know what I might say in torture. He desired me to swear. I told him I could not swear in anything criminal in itself, whatever it might be made to me; and did, as I had reason, and as it became an honest man, clear myself of all plots whatsoever. My dearest, thou liest near my heart. God bless thee. Be encouraged. He will be thy God and portion whatever He do with me. He is just and righteous, and I desire to love Him. O! for such a fear

* To Carolina.

of Him as might fortify me against all unsuitable fear of any else.
Himself be my strength, for I have none of my own. My duty to
my dearest parents, and love to sisters. Farewell, my poor afflicted
wife. Thine in true affection."

This last letter brings us to the eve of his appearance
before the Privy Council.

Some of the Lords of the Council had held an interview
with him as early as January, with the object, apparently, of
entrapping him into admissions which might be useful to the
government; but had failed in their attempt. After Spence's
torture, other members of the Council besides the Lord
Advocate, and specially the Earl of Melfort, "several times
very earnestly" urged him to confess what he knew of any
designs against the King and the government, but in vain.

"I giving no satisfaction," he proceeds in the MS. I have already
quoted, "though I had favourable conditions offered me, one of
which was that I should not be brought as a witness against any,
my Lord Chancellor was so enraged that he had these expressions
to me, which, in so far as I remember, were that the kindness I had
met with from his brother * in the pains he had been at with me,
should be laid to my charge; and ' before God,' said he, ' there
shall not be a joint of you left whole.'—I did resolve, through
divine assistance, to adventure upon the torture, rejecting at that
time the conditions which Melfort had difficultly obtained for me
from the Privy Council. My reasons were because I imagined, if
I could once endure so severe torture, either the Lords of the
Council would have some regard to my character, and not put me
further to torture, or what I suffered might throw me into a fever,
and so I might be carried off the world; for I can declare that
death, either by a sentence or any other violence, wherein my own
hand was not concerned, would have been welcome to me."

On the 5th of September, a little before noon, he was
taken out of the irons, in which he had lain since the

---

* The Earl of Perth was now Lord Chancellor. In his youth a zealous
Presbyterian, he had become an Episcopalian. On James's accession he
declared himself a Roman Catholic. His brother was the Earl of Melfort,
Lord Treasurer Depute, and one of the chief favourites of the Court. Both
the brothers, after the Revolution, followed James to France.

19th of August, and brought down to that long, low-browed chamber in the Parliament House, where the Privy Council held its sittings and tortured its victims. The great, brutal, domineering Lauderdale was no longer there; he and the rough Rothes had gone to render their bloodstained account. Perth filled the Chancellor's seat, and his brother Melfort, who had been Lieutenant-Governor of Edinburgh Castle during Carstares' first imprisonment, sat beside him as Lord Treasurer Depute. Two other brothers were members— John Paterson, Bishop of Edinburgh, and Sir William, Clerk of the Council, who had been Carstares' "regent" when he studied as a lad at Edinburgh College. Claverhouse had been sworn in as a Privy Councillor in May 1683; and when he could spare time from hunting and shooting the Presbyterian peasantry of Galloway and Ayrshire, came to join his counsels to those of his commander-in-chief, Dalzell, whose place at the board was marked by the savage manner which he had learned in Russian camps, and by the long white beard which he had never cut since the 30th of January, 1649. The most remarkable man among them all was the Lord Advocate, Sir George Mackenzie. A man of wide culture and great learning—"that noble wit of Scotland," as Dryden calls him *—an author who clothed his subtle thought in an admirable style, as clear as Swift's, as piquant as Montaigne's; an accomplished jurist and an enlightened politician, he yet lent all the weight of his character and his abilities to the cause of misgovernment and oppression. In early life the defender of the Marquis of Argyll, he was now the relentless persecutor of the Covenanters, who knew and hated him as the "bloody Mackenzie." The philosopher who could write, "It fares with heretics as with tops, which, how long they are scourged, keep foot and run pleasantly, but fall how soon they are neglected and left to themselves," † was the willing instrument of the most prying and painstaking persecution of insignificant and

* 'Discourse on the Origin and Progress of Satire.'
† 'The Stoic's Address to the Fanatics.'

fanatical offenders that Christendom has ever seen. In his study he could pen the sentence, "Opinion kept within its proper bounds is a pure act of the mind, and so it would appear that to punish the body for that which is the guilt of the soul is as unjust as to punish one relation for another,"* and could step out thence to apply the boot and the thumbkins to sufferers for conscience' sake. It was this high official who was now to direct the measures to be taken against Carstares.

The design of the Council was, partly, to satisfy the English government by proceeding against one of the most suspected of the Scotch accomplices in the recent conspiracy, but chiefly to extort from Carstares the secrets, which it was believed he possessed, relative to the plans of Argyll and the other malcontents abroad; for though all the Whig plotters who had not escaped from England had borne their penalties—though Sidney's noble head had fallen on the scaffold, and though Monmouth was powerless and in disgrace and exile—the dread of Argyll and his associates in Holland remained to trouble the government with a vague surmise of evil to come.

It must have been with no ordinary anxiety that he took his place at the bar, for though prepared to disclaim all share in any plot against the King's life or the established monarchy, and to palliate his concurrence in the designs of Russell and Argyll, on the plea that they only aimed at the redress of existing grievances, he did not know whether or not any discovery had been made of his own private correspondence with the most trusted agents of the Prince of Orange. He had kept up this correspondence with Fagel and with Bentinck until the very time of his arrest in England.† What the secrets of it were he would never, even after the Revolution, reveal; but Fagel spoke of them to Burnet as affairs of the greatest importance, the betrayal of which would have secured his free pardon, and laid the King and government under lasting obligation to Carstares.‡ Of

* 'The Stoic's Address to the Fanatics.'   † McCormick, p. 24.
‡ Burnet, vol. ii. p. 431.

these secrets, however, the Scotch inquisitors were ignorant; and the question to which they addressed themselves was Carstares' engagement in, and knowledge of, the recent plot.

When brought before the Privy Council in London the declarations of Shephard and Holmes had been read to him; but neither Shephard nor Holmes was confronted with him, to be cross-examined on what they had deposed. Their declarations both specified Carstares as engaged in the plot.[*] These were now again read over to him; and, upon his declining to own their truth, and objecting to depositions made in his absence, by deponents whom he had had no opportunity of cross-examining, being taken as evidence against him, he was asked, would he then answer, on oath, whatever questions should be put to him. He positively refused, although assured that the questions should be few, that they should concern others only, and not be allowed to tell against himself, and that if he did not reply to them he should be treated as Spence had been treated. The practice of requiring such answers, Carstares firmly said, was so bad a precedent in criminal cases, that he was determined they should not begin it with him.[†] Upon this the Council paused, and the prisoner was removed and carried back to prison. On his leaving the Council several questions were written out and sent after him, with a message that he must answer these on oath that evening, or be tortured.

In the evening accordingly he was brought down again; and still declining to answer the queries, he was asked if he had any reason to urge against his being put to the torture. "I answered," he says, "I did humbly judge that I could not be any ways tried *there;* for the order by which I was sent down to Scotland was express, that I should be tried for crimes committed against the government in that kingdom; and I desired to know if my Lord Advocate had anything

---

[*] Sprat. Copies of Deposition. 'True and Plain Account.'
[†] McCormick. Graham Dunlop MSS.

to charge me with of that nature. He declared he had not, but that I was now in Scotland, and if I had been guilty of contriving against his Majesty's government at Constantinople, I might be tried for it. I told him I thought it was true, but that the crimes I was accused of were said to be committed in England, where his Majesty's laws were equally in force for the security of his government as they were in Scotland, which at Constantinople they were not. But this was overruled, and yet this was a notorious and unjust breach of the law of the *Habeas Corpus* Act, which was made expressly for the security of the liberty of Scots and Irish men. They then asked me if I had anything further to offer against being tortured. I told them that I did not pretend to any skill in law, but that I was informed that *semiplena probatio* was necessary in order to torture, which was not in my case; for neither the depositions of those at London, nor what was said in my Lord Argyle's letters, did amount to any such thing. They told me presumptions were enough to warrant torture. Then they asked me *again* if I had anything further to say why I should not be brought to torture. I told them I had only an humble petition to them that I might meet with no greater severity in my own country, than the laws of that in which the crimes I am accused of are said to be committed do allow of."

Without further parley the torture began. One of the bailies of Edinburgh and the executioner had been ordered to be present to conduct the operation; and the King's smith was also in attendance with a new pair of thumbkins, of an improved construction, by which much greater force could be applied to the screw. Carstares' thumbs were put in, and screwed down till the sweat of his agony poured over his brow and down his cheeks. The Duke of Hamilton, who was entirely opposed to the torturing system, rose and left the Council room, followed by the Duke of Queensberry, who exclaimed to the Chancellor, "I see he will rather die than confess." All the reply Perth made was to order the executioner to give another turn, which was given with such

violence that Carstares broke silence and cried out, " The
bones are squeezed to pieces!" " If you continue obstinate,"
roared the Chancellor, " I hope to see every bone of your
body squeezed to pieces!" Again and again he was asked,
would he answer the queries of the Council; and assured
that if he did not, he should be tortured day by day while
he had life. General Dalzell at last in a rage left his seat
at the table, and coming close to the prisoner, vowed that he
would take him and roast him alive the next day, if he would
not comply. Carstares did not waver for a moment from
his resolute refusal. A sterner test must be applied, and
the order was given for the boot. While his thumbs were
still held fast in the thumbkins the boot was brought forward, and an attempt made to fit it on. The hangman, however, had only been in office since the 15th of August, (when
his predecessor had been consigned to the " Thieves' Hole "
for nearly beating a beggar to death), and was so inexpert
that he could not adjust the boot and the wedge. He had
to take it off after a good deal of bungling, and applying
himself anew to the thumbkins, the screw was turned again
and again, until Carstares appeared to be on the verge of a
swoon. The torture had lasted " an hour," according to the
Minute of Council, " near an hour and a half," according to
the victim's own report, when " the Lords thought fit to ease
him of the torture for that time." The executioner was ordered to remove the thumbkins; but when he attempted to
loosen them he found it beyond his strength to undo what
he had done; and the King's smith had to be called to fetch
his tools to revert the screw, before the broken and mangled
thumbs could be released.* Carstares was then sent back
to the Tolbooth, with due notice that if he remained " obsti-

---

* After the Revolution the thumbkins were presented by the Privy
Council to Carstares. King William expressed a wish to see them and to
try them on. They were accordingly fastened on the royal thumbs, and
Carstares gave the screw a courtier-like turn. " Harder," said the King,
and another was given. " Again," and Carstares turned the screw pretty
sharply. " Stop, Doctor, stop," cried William. " Another turn would
make me confess anything."

nate," he would be tortured with the boot by a skilled ope-
rator next morning at nine o'clock.*

All night he lay in a fever, through the greatness of his
pain; and in the morning the surgeon who attended him
went to the Chancellor, to beg that the further torture
might be delayed for two or three days. This was peremp-
torily refused, and he was carried down to the Council hall
to be again practised upon, "which," he says, "I was resolved
to endeavour to undergo." Lord Melfort, however, met him
in an ante-chamber, and renewed his friendly persuasions
(which he did, it appears, by direction of the "Secret Committee") that he should come to terms with the Privy Council,
by making some reply to their interrogatories. "He was
willing to grant," says Carstares, "that I should not be
brought as a witness myself against any; but I absolutely
refused to say anything, till I obtained that my depositions
should not be made use of at the bar of any judicature against
any person whatsoever, which the Lord Melfort, after going
twice or thrice from me to know the mind of the Council,
did at last yield to; when I objected the case of Mr. James
Mitchell, as what did give me ground to fear that conditions
would not be kept with me, he answered in these words: that
that was a d——d perjury, and the stain of the government,
for which the present Earl of Lauderdale was forced to get
a pardon.† Upon which reply I thought myself secure."
On Melfort's reporting Carstares' capitulation to the Council,
their Lordships drew up a paper embodying the terms, in
which, however, their engagement not to use his evidence
against any accused party is not so distinctly expressed, as his

* Graham Dunlop MSS. Wodrow, vol. iv. p. 98, et seq. McCormick.
Burnet, vol. ii. p. 430. Fountainhall, pp. 554, 556.

† Mitchell, apprehended at Sharp's instigation, confessed to the Privy
Council, on the assurance that his life should be spared, that he had once
fired at the Archbishop. After this, the Privy Council forwarded his confession to the Court of Justiciary; and Mitchell was, by that court,
tortured, condemned, and executed. Lauderdale, Rothes, Sharp, and
Hatton (who succeeded to the earldom of Lauderdale) all swore (falsely)
that no promise of his life had been given him. Burton, vol. vii. pp. 482–
490.

own report of his agreement with Melfort would have led us to expect. The paper is as follows :—

" Edinburgh, the 6th day of September, 1684.—The Lord-Chancellor having acquainted the Lords of His Majesty's Privy Council that the Lord Thesaurer Depute, being by the Secret Committee appointed to treat and deal with Mr. William Carstares, for bringing him to an ingenuous confession upon the interrogatory yesterday put to him in the torture, that the said Lord Thesaurer Depute had brought him that length as that he would depone and be ingenuous, conform to, and in the terms mentioned, in the paper underwritten, exhibited by the Lord Thesaurer Depute, of which paper the tenor follows.—*Primo :* that the said Mr. William Carstares, upon his part, answer all interrogatories that shall be put to him betwixt and the 1st day of October, upon his great oath.—*Secundo :* the which he doing, in that case, the said Mr. Carstares shall have his Majesty's pardon for his life limb fortune and estate.—*Tertio :* that he shall never be brought as witness against any person whatsomever, for things contained in his answers above named.—*Quarto :* and further the said Mr. Carstares shall never be interrogate, in torture, or out of torture, upon anything preceding the date of this paper, after the day above mentioned, except he himself be delated as accessory, and that accession to be after the date of these presents, or his remission.—*Quinto :* that the Council shall allow one of their number to promise, in their name, the performance of their part, who shall promise, upon his word of honour, to see the premisses punctually observed on their part.—*Sexto :* that all being transacted on Mr. Carstares' part, as above said, the said Mr. Carstares shall continue free prisoner only, and have a moderate allowance for his subsistence from the King, and shall be kept only till His Majesty think fit to grant his liberty.—Which paper being read and considered, by the Council, they do unanimously approve of the same, and haill articles thereof; and do hereby authorize and impower the said Lord Thesaurer Depute to give his word of honour to the said Mr. William Carstares for performing the Council's part of the above-said articles contained in the said paper, in so far as relates to them, he the said Mr. William Carstares performing his part accordingly.

" Extr. by me, GEORGE RAE, Cl. Deputatus Str. Clii."

We shall soon see that the Council understood the bargain made in a sense different from that in which Carstares understood it, and that the terms for which he had specially stipulated with Melfort, and which Melfort told him the Council had granted, were deliberately violated. The paper given above is evidently the official document, as approved by the Privy Council. In the Graham Dunlop MSS. there is another paper (embodied in a continuation of the narrative from which I have already made several quotations), in which the terms are significantly different; and these are, says Carstares, " the conditions granted me, in the *very words* of my Lord Treasurer Depute." In this paper it is expressly provided that Mr. William Carstares shall "never be brought as a witness, directly nor indirectly, against any person whatsoever." The omission of the words " directly nor indirectly," in the Council's copy of the conditions, left a loophole for the treachery of which they were afterwards guilty; and the probability is that the one paper was adopted by the Council, and the other, including the words " directly nor indirectly," was accepted by Carstares, in the natural belief that the copy brought to him tallied exactly with that kept by the Council.* It is not likely that a man as shrewd as he, even though unnerved with pain, would accept, in writing conditions less satisfactory on the most vital point, than those which he had verbally discussed with the Lord Treasurer, and which the latter had not agreed to until after repeated consultations with his colleagues.

At the same sitting, the Council ordered Carstares to be removed from the Tolbooth to the Castle. Spence, when expected to confess, had been sent thither as to " a place where he would be freest from any bad advice or impression;" and now Carstares also is transferred, no doubt with the same intention. It was specially ordered that " none are to be permitted to speak or converse with him, and particularly Mr. William Spence is not to be suffered to see him, and a

* Carstares' copy is given, as it stands in the MS. by Wodrow, vol. iv. p. 102; who also gives the interrogatories prescribed before the torture. As it does not appear that these were afterwards adhered to, I do not think it necessary to reproduce them here. They will be found in Wodrow, vol. iv. p. 100.

surgeon is allowed him for his cure." After a day's repose he was called before the Lords of the Secret Committee, who met in the Castle to examine him. They put a number of queries to him, which, according to his promise, he answered. They then framed his answers into a " deposition,"* in which the questions that elicited them are suppressed, and the answers are reported, not exactly as he gave them, but in a condensed form, which did not appear to Carstares to do full justice to his statements. Worn out with pain and anxiety as he was, he signed it, however, and it was carried off to the Privy Council.

* See Appendix.

CHAPTER VI.

Publication of Deposition—At Stirling—Trial of Jerviswood—Use of
Carstares' Deposition—Release—Return to Holland.

CARSTARES' deposition is not preserved in the registers of the
Privy Council, and appears never to have been recorded
therein. Whatever may have been the reason for this suppression, it was not any desire to bury his statements in
oblivion. The digest of them, framed by the Council, was
kept for ten days, after which he was again examined in the
Castle,* and " adhered to his former deposition in all the parts
of it ;" such, at least, was the allegation of the Privy Council.
Within a few hours afterwards, men were hawking through
the streets of Edinburgh a paper entitled 'Mr. Carstares'
Confession.' Some of the chief members of the Council
had told Carstares that the deposition was to be published.
He had strenuously remonstrated, but to no purpose. He
said he had indeed put his name to the paper as his deposition, but it was a very unfair version of what he had
actually stated. It neither contained the interrogatories put to
him, nor " the just extenuations," both as to the plot itself
and the persons he had named, with which he had guarded
his statements. Had he not been, at the first examination,
in such " disorder " from pain and other causes as to be incapable of calm reflection, he should not have been thus
taken advantage of; and on the second examination he had
not been allowed to make any alterations in the prepared

* Wodrow states that he was removed to Dunbarten Castle on the 13th ;
but he was at Edinburgh on the 18th of September.

reports of the first.* What stung Carstares most in the injustice of this publication of a deposition, which he had considered was to be the private property of the Privy Council, was the suspicion of unfaithfulness to his friends to which he imagined it would expose him. The public—knowing nothing, possibly, of the torture he had undergone, and believing that (as Sprat alleged) no undue means had been used to obtain a single confession about the plot—would read the garbled version of his disclosures, and would haste to the conclusion that he had bought an ignominious safety, by the betrayal of his companions. On a superficial view of the deposition, and with no knowledge of its secret history, such a conclusion might seem natural enough. But a careful examination of the document, garbled as it was, would show that Carstares really unfolded nothing that he did not believe either to be already known, or to concern persons whom his statements could not injure; and these statements, it must be remembered, he had, by strict treaty with the Council, provided should never be employed in any court of justice whatsoever. He had therefore made his declaration with a clear conscience, and he felt all the more keenly the moral cruelty of his persecutors, in exposing him to undeserved suspicion of treachery towards his friends. "I doubt not," he writes, "my friend, but you will have the charity for me to believe that death would have been more welcome than life attended with the prejudice of my friends; and I can, in great sincerity, say that death was digged for by me as for hid treasures."

On the 27th of September a warrant was signed by the Earl of Murray, Secretary of State, authorizing "a letter of remission to be passed (*per saltum*) under the great seal of Scotland, indemnifying and remitting unto Mr. William Carstares all crimes preceding the date hereof."† He was not, however, set at liberty, but was removed to Stirling Castle, where he was still kept a prisoner, though allowed to

* Graham Dunlop MSS. 'Acts of the Parliament of Scotland,' vol. ix. p. 102.
† Graham Dunlop MSS.

be at large within the walls of the fortress.   He writes thence to his wife, on the 4th of December :—

"My Dearest,—I had yours on Saturday last, and am glad to hear of your being in very tolerable health, though sorry that you are in the least indisposed.   I long indeed to have you with me, and shall have no small satisfaction in your return, though it should be attended with disappointments of what you and I both would have desired.   God does all things well, and as he is a jealous, so is he a compassionate, God. . . . . I would fain think he will never forget what he did for my soul in Tenterden, and the Gatehouse : he allured me then into the wilderness ; and how great terror soever I was under, yet he spake comfortably to me ; and it was, I hope, a time of love, the fruits whereof will remain. . . . . . Have a care of yourself.   It is like that business, which you wait for, when you have got it, will neither please you nor me, but we must be silent and patient.   If you have money, I would have you acknowledge my Lord Register's gentleman, for he was civil to me, and I suppose to you too ; it is he that came to the Castle for me. . . . . . My duty to my very dear parents.   I am much concerned for my mother's indisposition.   Pray let me hear how she is.   I would not have you leave her till she be pretty well ; and so soon as that is, haste you, so soon as your affairs will allow, to, my dearest, thine own most affectionate husband,

"W. C."

Meantime the Lords of the Council were maturing one of the most nefarious of their many unjust procedures.   Robert Baillie, of Jerviswood, had long been hated and suspected by the government of the Restoration.   A chivalrous, gifted, and devout champion of freedom could not fail to be obnoxious to a government, which dreaded every development of civil, intellectual, and religious liberty.   His attachment to Presbytery incurred for him the enmity of the prelates. His attachment to the political rights of his country incurred for him the enmity of the government.   He had been associated with Dunlop, and the other promoters of the scheme of emigration to South Carolina.   He had, at the same time, as we have seen, taken a leading share in those negotiations, by which the patriots of England and Scotland hoped to secure such a change of policy, and of measures, from the government of Charles, as should reconcile the liberties of the subject with the prerogatives of the crown. He was no republican or revolutionist. He was, like Argyll, Stair, Fletcher, Carstares, and other leading Scotchmen of the time, content with monarchical government, if only the monarch would not override the law and the constitution; and though a keener Presbyterian than any of these, he was not irreconcilably hostile to an episcopal establishment, should that establishment but admit the doctrines and practice of toleration. A man of chivalrous honour, of loyal sentiments, and of high religious principle, the vulgar intrigues and projects of bloodshed and assassination, in which Ferguson delighted to dabble, were abhorrent to his nature. He loved his country, and religion and freedom, with a pure and high-hearted affection, which, for their sake, would not shrink from danger, obloquy, and ruin, but would not stoop to arts like " the plotter's." It was, however, an alleged complicity with the originators of the Ryehouse Plot that the Privy Council resolved to bring home to him. No legal evidence had been found to inculpate him in that or any other plot; but, after several months' imprisonment, he had been ordered to answer on oath certain ensnaring questions of the Council, and on his refusal was fined £6000 sterling, although he had already suffered a long and severe incarceration.* Such a fine was virtually equivalent to a forfeiture; and he remained in prison, utterly unable to pay it. He was now an old man and feeble, and his health, impaired through the rigour of his confinement, rapidly declined. But the Council were determined he should not escape. No new evidence had reached them on which they could proceed; but as he was likely to die, and thus " escape and prevent fining or any other punishment whatever,"† the old evidence must be made to suffice. On the 22nd of December his indictment was served upon him, charging him with traitorous conspiracy against his Majesty's person and government; and on the next day he was carried, " in his nightgown," to the bar,

* Fountainhall, vol. ii. p. 555. † Ibid.

where, so worn and weak as to need the support of frequent cordials, he underwent his trial.* The evidence was vague and insufficient, but the Lord Advocate was prepared to buttress it with a disgraceful prop. This was the deposition of Carstares.

Carstares had been fetched from Stirling, and "earnestly desired, and pressed with many arguments," to appear in court, and make ever so brief a declaration as to Jerviswood's connection with the London negotiations. This he had indignantly and absolutely refused to do. He was told that if he would do this, it would be so arranged that he should not be confronted with the prisoner. "If it were possible," replied Carstares, "I had rather die a thousand deaths than be a witness against any that have trusted me."† Would he then, he was asked, appear before the Lords of the Council, and own, judicially, that he had emitted the depositions which had been published in his name. This too he positively declined. The paper containing his original signature was then produced, and he was asked if that was his signature. He owned that it was, but took the opportunity of reminding his interlocutors (who were the Earl of Perth, the Duke of Queensberry, and one or two other Privy Councillors) of the express conditions, on which he had appended that signature to their digest of his deposition. This interview was not held at a regular meeting of the Council. Next day, however, Carstares' deposition was produced in court, and sworn to by two clerks of the Council as having been originally signed by him, and as having been adhered to, and "*renewed upon oath before the Lords of his Majesty's Privy Council,*" on *the* 22nd *of December.* The deposition was then taken up by the Lord Advocate, and used as an "adminicle of prolation" in the trial.‡

* Wodrow, vol. iv. p. 105.

† Graham Dunlop MSS.

‡ 'The Tryal and Process of High Treason, &c., against Mr. Robert Baillie, &c. By his Majesties special command, as a further Proof of the late Fanatical Conspiracy.' Edinburgh, 1685.

Sir George Mackenzie, in the course of a speech in which he took pains to identify the Ryehouse Plot with the larger design of Russell and Argyll, charged Baillie with a leading part in the worst schemes of Ferguson.* He was in close correspondence, he averred, "with Ferguson the contriver, Shephard the thesaurer, and Carstares the chaplain of the conspiracy." Carstares, he continued, was a "chief conspirator," and after suffering "violent torture" rather than disclose the plot, deponed to all those facts which tended to incriminate Jerviswood, and twice reiterated his deposition on oath "*after much premeditation.*" With a refinement of treachery, Sir George proceeded to connect Carstares' reluctance to depone at all with the knowledge that his deposition was to be used against his friend, and to found an argument upon that honourable "scrupulosity" which the Privy Council had cheated and overreached. "Mr. Carstares knew," he said, "when he was to depone, that his deposition was to be used against Jerviswood; and he stood more in awe of his love to his friend than of the fear of the torture, and hazarded rather to die for Jerviswood than that Jerviswood should die by him. How can it then be imagined that if this man had seen Jerviswood in his trial it would have altered his deposition; or that this kindness, which we all admired in him, would have suffered him to forget anything in his deposition, which might have been advantageous in the least to his friend? And they understand ill this height of friendship, who think that it would not have been more nice and careful than any advocate could have been; and if Carstares had forgot at one time, would he not have supplied it at another; but especially at this last time, when he knew his friend was already brought upon his trial, and that this renewed testimony was yet a further confirmation of what was said against him? And albeit the King's servants were forced to engage that Carstares himself should not be made use of as a witness against Jerviswood, yet I think this kind of scrupulosity in Carstares for Jerviswood

* 'Tryal,' p. 30.

should convince you more than twenty suspect, nay, than even indifferent, witnesses."*

Jerviswood, who had listened, with evident amazement, to the Lord Advocate's speech, said a few words when he had finished, emphatically denying all participation in any design against the King or the Duke of York. Then, looking his accuser full in the face, he said, " My Lord, I think it strange you should charge me with such abominable things. When you came to me in the prison you told me such things were laid to my charge, but that you did not believe them. Are you convinced, in your conscience, I am now more guilty than before? You remember what passed betwixt us in the prison?" "Jerviswood," replied Mackenzie, "I own what you say. My thoughts were then as a private man, but what I say here is by special direction of the Privy Council. He" (pointing to Sir William Paterson) "knows my orders." "Well," said Jerviswood, "if your Lordship has one conscience for yourself, and another for the Council, I pray God forgive you. I do. My Lords, I trouble your Lordships no further."

The trial lasted till past midnight. Next morning the jury found him guilty. He was a dying man, and, says Fountainhall, "the holy days of Yule were approaching," so the government, at once bloodthirsty and pious, could not delay the sacrifice. The Court of Justiciary, ever the obedient assistant of the Privy Council, sentenced him to be hanged, drawn, and quartered the same afternoon, between two and four o'clock. Within two days of the serving of his indictment, and within five hours of the pronouncing of his sentence, he was to die. "My Lords," he said, as he left the bar, "the time is short, the sentence is sharp; but I thank my God who hath made me as fit to die as ye are to live."† He was executed in the afternoon. He had to be helped up the ladder. When he got up he began to speak. "My faint

* 'Tryal,' p. 35. 'State Trials,' vol. x. p. 686 et seq. Fountainhall, vol. ii. pp. 587-95.
† Wodrow, vol. iv. pp. 106-12.

zeal for the Protestant religion," he said, "has brought me
to this end." At this the drums were ordered to beat; he
was silent, and the sentence was carried out.*

Whatever may be thought of the justice or injustice of the
prosecution and condemnation of Jerviswood, the employment
of Carstares' deposition at his trial was indefensible, and
plainly violated the conditions made between the deponent
and the Council. This was admitted by the Lords of the
Council themselves. When Carstares heard what had been
done, he went to the Lord Clerk Registrar, Sir George Mackenzie, of Tarbat, afterwards Viscount Tarbat, and complained of the gross injury that had been inflicted on him.
" He told me," writes Carstares, "that he was as angry at it
as I could be; but that the deposition was not offered by the
advocate as a legal proof, or sustained as such." He went,
next, to the Lord Advocate; but the only satisfaction he got
from him was the flimsy excuse, that at the time of Carstares'
agreement with the Council he had been ill, and did not know
what had been agreed upon. Carstares then sought an interview with the Chancellor, the Duke of Queensberry, the Lord
Clerk Registrar, and the President of the Court of Session,
and anew represented the wrong done him through the treacherous use of his deposition. The Chancellor called for the
record of the agreement, and having read it, said there had
undoubtedly been a breach of the conditions, but all he could
say was that it should not be repeated. For the stain which
the whole transaction tended to cast on his honour; for the
positive breach of the Council's solemn engagement; for the
deliberate falsehoods by which the Lord Advocate had attributed to him a knowledge of the Council's design to use his
deposition, and a renewal of it, on oath, with this knowledge,
and at the very time of his friend's trial, Carstares could
receive no redress.

* "The Lady Graden, a daughter of Warriston's, and his sister-in-law,
with a more than masculine courage, stayed on the scaffold till all his body
was cut in coupons, and went with the hangman to see them oiled and
tarred." Fountainhall, vol. ii. p. 594.

It was not until the better days had dawned that such reparation as was possible was obtained. In July 1690 Carstares petitioned the Parliament, that " in testimony of their abhorrence of so foul a breach of public faith, the sacredness whereof is the security of a government," they should order his misused depositions to be " razed, and for ever delete out of the records of these courts where, contrary to the public faith, they were made use of." This petition, which was accompanied by a brief narrative of the transactions which we have examined, was found, on investigation, to be " sufficiently instructed, and verified by a declaration under my Lord Tarbat's hand of the date of these presents, and other testimonies." The Parliament declared that Carstares was " highly injured contrary to the public faith," and ordained his petition and accompanying letter to be " recorded in the books of Parliament, and books of adjournal, or any other Court books wherein his testimony was made use of."*

Carstares was informed by the Lord Chancellor, at the interview which he had with him and the other lords, after Jerviswood's trial, that he might now consider himself a free man. By the way of indemnifying him for what he had undergone, an offer was made to defray the expenses he had incurred during his imprisonment. This he declined ; nor would he even memorialise the King, as he was advised (by Melfort, apparently), " to consider his trouble and losses." His reply to these amiable suggestions was, that from the government of the King he would not accept a farthing ; and that he would never return to his native soil until he saw things there go " in another channel."† He resolved to leave Scotland at once ; but it was the 20th of February, before he could get his passport. Then he set out for England. It

* ' Acts of the Parliament of Scotland,' vol. ix. p. 192 ; and Appendix of same vol. p. 161. Carstares states, in one of the Graham Dunlop MSS., and also in the letter above referred to, that notwithstanding Perth's promise that no further use should be made of his deposition, he had been informed that it was read in the Parliament of 1685, " in the cases of some that were then forfeited." See, in proof of this, Fountainhall, vol. ii. p. 644.

† ' Acts of Parliament,' ubi supra.

must have been a sad enough journey. He was again to be
an exile. He was leaving—in all probability for the last
time—his parents and kindred. Keen and angry feelings had
embittered their few days together. For some time after his
release from prison his father, irritated at his political em-
broilments, had refused to see him.[*]

His wife accompanied him, suffering from illness. " It is
your great mercy and my great satisfaction, that your
husband is so far away," he writes to his sister Sarah, " and
I hope God will order things so that he shall not see Scotland till he may with safety, which now he cannot."[†] He
went by sea to London, where Lord Melfort was at the
time. He applied for a passport for the Continent, which
his Lordship promised he should have; but appeared to
think he should wait upon the King, before leaving the
country. The king was now that grim bigot, whose exclusion from the throne had been one of the principles of
the Whig association, for his connection with which Carstares
had suffered so painfully.[‡] The severities of the earlier
years of Charles's reign had not been prompted by any
special excess of intolerance, or love of arbitrary-power, on his
own part. They had been rather the result of a violent reaction in public feeling, and in the political forces of England,
which told malignantly upon the class in Scotland that
sought to grasp the reins of power, under the King. But the
liberals and Presbyterians had not been wrong, in thinking
that they discerned in the policy of Charles's later years the
influence of a spirit far more relentless and inhuman, more
bitter and rigid, than his own or that of his earlier advisers,
and in ascribing that spirit to the Duke of York. Carstares
had no desire for any passages of courtesy with one, whom he
regarded as the chief oppressor of his country, the harshest
foe of Presbytery and political freedom, and beyond the
limits of whose gloomy jurisdiction he was about to fly, in
despair of finding liberty or peace within them. He told

* 'Analecta,' vol. iii. p. 51.   † Graham Dunlop MSS.
‡ Charles had died on the 6th of February.

Melfort that if he were to wait upon King James, he should feel constrained to say several things to him which would reflect but little honour on his Majesty's servants and administration in Scotland, and that the interview could be agreeable to neither. Melfort, on reflection, " thought it more advisable to dispense with that ceremony."* The less the King heard or saw of Carstares, he said, the better. He advised him to go abroad, and live there quietly; and without further delay gave him his passport for Holland.† After an absence of two years, almost the whole of which he had spent in a variety of prisons, the Gatehouse, the Tolbooth, and the Castles of Edinburgh and Stirling, he once more found friendly shelter and repose among the Dutch, and beside those other British exiles, to whom the Commonwealth afforded a temporary home.

* Wodrow, vol. iv. p. 100. † McCormick, p. 24.

CHAPTER VII.

Peace—Tour, and Journal.

CARSTARES left his wife behind him in England, until he should settle where he was to pitch his tent abroad. It is probably to this we owe the careful journal, which records his journeyings during part of the summer of 1685, while he was wandering about Holland, and through the regions of the Rhine and the Meuse. This journal is printed among the 'Caldwell Papers ;' and I give it just as it stands in Part I. of that valuable collection ; only excluding a few sentences about the foreign nunneries, in which the writer might be thought to step across the boundaries of modern propriety. The original MS. was given by Carstares to his cousin William Mure, and is now at Caldwell. It is written in Carstares' own hand, in a small parchment-bound memorandum book.

It is noteworthy that in this journal Carstares, although writing at the very crisis of their disastrous expeditions, never refers to Monmouth, and only once, in a merely incidental way, to Argyll. He must have followed their fortunes with the keenest interest that a partizan and former associate could feel ; and yet, even in his private diary, he does not allow one compromising allusion to slip from his pen. Nothing could tell more forcibly than this designed omission, with what sharpness the iron of persecution had entered into his soul. Argyll sailed from Holland on the 1st of May ; published, at Campbelton, the declaration, drawn up by James Steuart, which set forth the wrongs of Scotland that he hoped to redress (among which a prominent place was given to the torture of Carstares * and misuse of his deposition), strove, in vain, to rouse a dispirited country, and to animate his own few and discordant forces ; was foiled, deserted, captured, taken to Edinburgh, and beheaded, before the 1st of July.†   Monmouth landed at Lyme on the 11th of June, fought his hapless fight of Sedgmoor on the 5th of July, and was beheaded on Tower Hill on the 15th.   Carstares' Journal begins with May the 10th, and ends with July 6th.

JOURNAL.

" We landed at Newport, May 10th, having struck several times on the ground in our entering the channell leading to it.

" May 11.   We came to Bruges, which is seven hours from Newport.   In companie we had a secular priest, who discoursing with me in Latin about the affairs of England, told me that he did believe there would be a change of religion there, and that his Majestie, for removing of scruples, would in the ensuing Parliament take some course for taking away all fears of the restitution of Abbey lands to the Church of Rome.   There was in our company a gentlewoman who lamented the abounding superstition and ignorance of the times, giveing an instance of one whom she knew, who being sick of an ague did, according to some advice given to her, read frequentlie some sentences in order to a cure ; and being askt by this gentlewoman how she durst adventure to doe so, seeing it would be difficult for her to obtain an absolution for such a practice, she answered that tho' one father had refused to doe it yet another did, which she and others in our company did disprove of.   I heard likeways in this company of one Monsr. Mons, one of the learned preachers of Bruges, who had been lately silenced by the Bishop, because he did by his subtle notions suggest so many scruples to the people

---

* See Declaration in Wodrow, vol. iv. p. 286.

† For original narrative, see ' Case of Earl Argyll,' &c., in Advocates' Library Pamphlets, vol. cclii.

that they did not know what to do. What were his doctrines I could not distinctly learn ; only I heard that one was, that after the wife had conceived the husband ought not to bed with her.

"At night in my quarters at Bruges I came to supp with some gentlemen, one of whom falling into discourse about England, told me that some extraordinary thing was set on foot by the French, or Dutch and others, for disquieting the King of England, which would suddenly make a great noise in the world, and would come as a clapp as it were 'of thunder, or some unsuspected thing. I found also this day in discourse a great expectation of some disagreement betwixte the Kings of England and France.

"May 12. I took boat from Bruges to Sluyse, which is three hours. Nothing occurred remarkable this day.

"May 13. I took boat from Middleburgh to Port; nothing occurred worthie noticeing.

"May 14. At night I came to Port, where, upon the 16th I discoursed with a Dutch gentleman, who, as he told me, had been severall times in company and familiar converse with Cardinal Norfolk at Rome three years agoe or more ; who speaking of England told him, that whatever noise there was at present of popish conspiracies, yet in a little time things should be so that England should be popish.

"On the 20th in the afternoon I went from Port, and came to the Bosch earlie next morning, when I had occasion at supper to discourse with a Burgomaster of Amsterdam, and another gentleman that had latelie come from the East Indies, having been in some considerable office at Battavia. Among other things we came to speak about the business of Bantam and the ruin of the English factory there, of which the last gentleman gave us an account, shewing that the old King of Bantam had willingly resigned the government to his son, but would have afterwards reassumed it ; which the son not being willing to part with, a warr did thereupon ensue, the father haveing been assisted by the English and French, the son by the Dutch ; who being conqueror, would have destroyed the English, but that the Dutch interposed for the preserving both their persons and goods, tho' their factorie was from that time ruined in that place. This gentleman told us that he came in company with a Dutch Ambassador from Batavia to Bantam, where they were very civilie received by the King, who was he said a man of understanding, but lived like a beast with his wifes and mistresses, and entertained him almost with no discourse but of them, and that the most immodest, even in the presence of one of the chief of them, who was sitting by decked richlie with jewells. He ledd them also to his father who was his prisoner; and tho' he detained him as such, yet when he came into his presence, he did him all the honour and obeisance that became a son to doe to a father. But falling into discourse with him upon the late businesse that had been betwixte them, the old man only replyed : 'Son, fortune hath given you the victorie, and there is no place for discoursing those things with the Conquerour ;' and so would undertake no discourse further upon the subject. The Burgomaster upon this occasion told me what I much wondered at, that the East India Companie of Holland had very little advantage by the India trade, they haveing not above four in the hundereth, which he had reason to know, because he himselfe had a stock in it. He also told me that two or three days before the time of my discourse with him, there had been a friendship made betwixt the King of England and the Prince of Orange.

"On the 22d, I went before four o'clock in the morning in the post waggon, which is very commodious, and haveing only two wheels goes with an easinesse beyond what could well be thought before tryall. In those waggons we goe to Maestricht from the Bosch in one day, which is near seventy English myles. We change horses six times by the way, which is most part heathie, but not without, in some places, pleasant groves of trees and corn fields ; we dine at a place called Hammond, which is about halfe way, and before we come to it we come to a prettie large town called Endoven, which is well watered; the fields about Maestricht are very pleasant, and the river of the Maes adds much to the beautie of the place. From thence there is occasion every morning at nine of the clock to goe by water to Liege, where you arrive about six or seven at night. It is but eighteen myles from Maestricht, but it is against the stream.

"On the 23 I came to Aiken * by waggon, betwixt which and Maestricht the country is hillie, but pleasant, and abounds with much wood, as also it doeth about Aiken which hath hills round about, itselfe being prettie large but not very populous; it stands upon the descent of a hill, part of it on the hill,—part on the plain. Thither they come from all parts for the Baiths, and the water, which is drunk by many and thought good against many distempers. The fountain of this hot water is in a publick place of the town, and there are two distinct places for men and women to retire themselves to after drinking of their water. The Baiths are within houses, and in one house you shall have severall rooms, where there are some greater, some lesser, baths, that will goe to the midle of an ordinarie man and somewhat deeper. The waters are lett in by conduits into these rooms, in which there is as it were a great cistern, into which you goe down by steps and there bathe.

"There is a place without the Citie a bowshot, called Putsen, where there are also good baths.

"This little town is under the jurisdiction of an Abbey of the same name which I did see; the ladies are very civill and readie to shew anything that is to be seen; they are all persons of good qualitie, for none but such as are noble for eight generations upon both the father and mother's side are admitted into it, as I was informed. The Abbesse hath great revenues. There are in Aiken severall of the reformed religion, and some of them rich, but cannot meet within the citie, but they have their severall Churches about three myles without the citie, within the territories of the States Generall. There is a French Church, and a Calvanist Dutch Church,

* Aachen, or Aix-la-Chapelle.

and a Lutheran Church. I went to hear the Dutch minister, who is an orthodox man and concerned for the Protestant interests. He is a German; upon acquaintance with him I found him very civill and desirous to know how it went with the Dissenters in Brittain. I saw in this Dutch congregation a gentleman of good qualitie in Switzerland, and a Lieut. Coll. under the King of France, and much respected by him ; I was very much taken with his seriousness and attention in hearing ; the minister did very much commend him to me ; his name is Mons. de Salis. In Aiken is a very pretty garden of the Capucins, in which they allow strangers to walk at pleasure. The Papists of this place boast much of the reliques that are here, some of which are shewn but once in seven years, which causeth a great concourse of people. I had acquaintance here with two brothers, merchants, of the name of Romer, whom I found very obligeing ; and one Mons. Holts, that lodgeth strangers.

" On the 27th I went to convoy a friend and his wife to Maestricht, at which time I had an opportunitie of viewing the place better than I had before. Amongst other things I went to a hill halfe a myle or a myle from the citie, which is all hollow underneath, there being many windings and turnings all cutt out of stone, and the height ordinarlie of the vault will be 20 foot. I had a guide and a torch, and did walk near two English myles under that hill, and came out again at another passage, near a cloister which stands very pleasantlie upon the descent of the hill, at the foot whereof runns the river of the Maes, and from which there is a very pleasant prospect. This cloister hath pleasant gardens. I fell into discourse with one of the chiefe fathers of it ; his name as I remember was Corcelius; who seemed to be a man of some learning, and I am sure of great vanity and confidence ; for he told me he would make it out that nothing was maintained now by Papists but what was received in the four first centuries, and nothing maintained by Protestants as such but what was then condemned ; and that he or some of his brethren had written against one of the ministers of Maestricht but had gott yet no answer, tho' he

much longed for it. He also told me, without my asking,
but upon discourse about English affairs, that at Brussels he
had spoke with the present King of Brittain six hours in
end, and that he did communicat thrice in their convent, not
being desirous to goe to the publick Churches; he told me
also that he had a letter from a father that was present
at the action, telling him that the late King died Catholick,
receiving the Sacrament and holy unction. And yet this
did not seem to reconcile him to him, for he said he had professed himselfe Papist at Bruges, but had disowned that
religion when he came to his kingdoms, and thereupon made
use of the words of our blessed Lord : ' he that denyeth me
before men I will deny him &c.' He told me likewise that
his present Majestie of Britain had some of their order at
Brussells, which he brought out of England with him ; one
of which was his confessor ; but that they all went in other
clothes than that of their order, which was the Minorites.
He likewise told me of some private contrivances that there
were on foot betwixt some Protestant Princes and the Pope
about a reconciliation, and amongst other things that were
sought by those princes, this was one: that the married
Clergie might retain their wifes; but this he told me would
be a businesse that would come to light shortly. What
truth is in these things I cannot determine.

" At Maestricht, ever since it came under the States government, the Papists and Protestants both have the publick
exercise of their religion ; but the former have more
churches than the latter, and I am apt to think more of the
inhabitants of the town for their followers ; this they obtained
by articles betwixt the Spaniard and the States, upon the
first surrendering of the town to the later. These articles
were also confirmed, upon the King of France his leaving
that town a few years agoe, and with this addition, that the
Jesuits, who for some contrivances against the States had
been by them banished the town, should be readmitted, as
they are and have now there a great Church. On the 30th,
I returned to Aiken, where I was told of these two customs ;

one that at each corner of the town, upon a turret, stands a man and gives notice upon the approach of any man upon horseback to the town, by so many windings of his horn as there are horsemen comeing. Another which I saw was that when there is a very good and fatt oxe to be slain by a butcher, he is lead through the town, decked with flowers and a pipe playing before him, that the people may see him and be induced to buy pieces of him. Another custom they have, that they have a fair in one parish of the Citie, and not in another at the same time; but have in the severall parts of the town fairs at different seasons.

" While I was at Aikin I had occasion to be in company with one of the Popish ministers of that town. The man seemed to be of a good humour, and entertained me and some others at his house very kindly and invited me again to his house; but I went not. He seemed to be bigott in his religion, and not without learning. I had been but a few minutes in his company, when perceiving, I know not how, that I was of the reformed religion, he would needs have me to debate with him about our principles. I told him that he was gray-haired in his religion, and no doubt well read in controversies about, which made me afraid to encounter with him; notwithstanding we fell into some discourse about the marriage of the clergie. He told me that was the great thing that galled us; and so began to jest upon our ministers for their wifes. I only answered him that whatever he said of the wifes of our ministers, yet I should not entertain him with discourse of the wenches of their clergie; which stirred him a little, and made him solemnlie protest that he not only never knew a woman, but never lusted after any; I suppose he meant since a Clergieman. Yet this man would drink drunk, and I myself saw him in such a condition upon a Lord's day at night that he was ashamed to come into my companie, and my Landlady putt to apologise for him as being easilie overtaken, and having been at some extraordinarie encounter. But I remember one thing in our discourse about the Apostles some of them having wifes, which I

could not chuse but smile at, and it was this: that having
granted to me that some of them had wifes, which they did
carrie about with them for serving and being otherwayes use-
full to them, but that, after their being Apostles, they did
never know their wifes, and that it was my part to prove
that they did. At which I, heartilie laughing, told him he
putt a very hard task upon me, which I could not undertake; for I supposed he did not doubt but there were many
married people in Aiken concerning whom I did believe he
could scarce prove what he would have had me do as to the
other.

" This man told me also in discourse about the decay of the
Latin tongue and increase of the French; that he had a case
of conscience which he proposed to some great Doctors at
Liege in Latin; but that to his astonishment they did not
understand him, but desired him to do it in French. This
man told me that in Aikin there were four parishes, and that
he himselfe had in his parish two thousand of age to communicat; so that I judge there may be nine thousand commu-
nicants in the citie; for some parishes he told me were larger
than his. Being in company with him and some regular
Canonicks, he told them they had an easie life in respect of
what he had, for they had nothing but their prayers to mind,
but he both preaching, prayer, visiting the sick &c.

" They have in this town a sword, which is said to have
been worn by Charles the great, and some other royalties,
that must be made use of at the instalment of every emperour. The people here are civill; a stranger of any fashion
passing through the streets is almost troubled with salutes.—
June 9. I went from Aikin to Maestricht, and next day
from thence to Luych * by water, in a large boat drawn by
five horses. We were seven hours longe upon our way, but
it is exceeding pleasant through the hills on both sides,
covered either with wood or corn. One may have meat and
drink aboard. I went out at a place a myle on this side
Liege called Harstall; from whence you can goe on foot

* So written. Liege.

much sooner than by the boat to Liege. It belongs to the
Prince of Orange; but the inhabitants are papists. Liege
is a great and very well peopled citie. It lyes part upon a
plain along the river Maes which divides it, over which
there is a very fair bridge of stone, and part on pleasant hills,
on one of which the English Jesuits have a very fine house,
and a curious garden lying upon the side of a high hill
towards the south, and that above the house, though even
before you come to the house you must goe up near fourscore
steps from the ground. The garden hath pleasant Parterras
and walks one above the other to a considerable height.
Upon a very high hill overtopping the citie the prince is
building a Cittadell to keep it in subjection. There was,
indeed, one there before, but in the year 72 it was taken
and demolished by the French in part, but wholly by the
citizens, who were glad to have that restraint upon their
liberties taken away; but through their late divisions among
themselves grounded upon their liberties, the Prince hath
gott his will of them, and hath built a kind of a fort in
fashion of a gate upon the middle of the bridge, in which he
hath some pieces of cannon and some few souldiers. This he
did to keep the two parts of the town from meeting together.
He hath laid a sore taxe upon the cittie for defraying the
expenses of his fortifications and other things. But it is
thought that this cittie will not remain long in peace. They
told me that it, together with its district which is but a small
bounds, can send forth upon a necessarie occasion above an
hundereth thousand fighting men. Here I saw the iron
mills, and how they make the potts, which they send in
great quantities to all places. Here they also make allum,
and have abundance of coal and wool.

" Here I saw also a solemn procession, which I blesse God
did convince me afresh of the folly of poprie. There are
scarce any protestants in this citie; yet I was told by one
that hath traded with this place near fourtie years, that
there are many that out of fear own poprie, who if occasion
did offer would professe the reformed religion; and that

there was one worth 15000 lib st., that did openlic own himselfe Protestant, and keep fast to his principles; but that he
hath been so troubled by his enemies, that with much adoe
he obtained a year's time to dispose of his goods and be
gone.   I was told that his father also was Protestant, but out
of fear went to Church; which yet did not keep him from
being persecuted, as not being cordiall.

"I was told that about five or six myles from Liege there
is a large village the most of the inhabitants of which are
Protestants.

"On June 12 I went from Liege to Spaa, which is about
six or seven hours. The way for some myles beyond
Liege is very hillie, but afterwards it is prittie pleasant,
through grounds part heathie, part cornclad, but within view,
and at no great distance, of hills cloathed with wood. When
you come near to the Spaa, you have for a long way a
descent from the tops of high hills, which goe in a range
almost round the town, but pleasant because of the woods
that cover them.   It is true there are in many places but
short bushes of oak, yet often they are intermixed with
trees, which make the place very convenient for retiring.
There are four wells; the one is in the middle of the town,
of which all almost drink. Another is about a myle and a
halfe out of the town hard by a wood. The other two are
about the same distance from the town on the other side, in
the midst of a wood, a little way one from the other.

"There is a pleasant garden of the Capuciners, where
drinkers of the waters generallic walk, and from thence,
about ten o'clock, such as please goe to prayers in the Capuciners church hard by; and from thence to dinner which is
ordinarlie ready about eleven o'clock. In the afternoon they
generallic walk till six, at which time they supp; and after
supper walk an hour or two, and so to bed; rising about four
o'clock. There is a meadow at the end of the town, where
generallic the most of the companie meet and converse; and
such as please dance or otherwise divert themselves. The
ordinarie custom is to take chambers by the night or week,

which you may have for six, nine, twelve, eighteen, styvers or more a night, according to the goodnesse of them. The people of the house furnish you fire and other things for dressing your meat. But many gentlemen go to an ordinarie at twelve to dinner. The best in the town is at the sign of the Spinet, where I staid, and paid for my chambers and dyet twice a day a rix dollar a day. I mett here with a very civill gentleman, who was pentionarie of Tournay ; who, though under the French, yet was no lover of them. There was here a fashionable gentlemân, who could discourse well almost of everything; who was supposed to be a spye for the French king, observing the sentiments of the various companies that came to that place. The best chambers are in a great house at the sign of the Pomelet, where persons of greater and lower quality are lodged, and with great convenience. It is but a small dorp Spaa, and lyes at the very foot of high hills.

"On the 16 June I came from thence to Aiken, in the companie of four young merchants of Amsterdam. It is about seven hours betwixt the two places. We baited at Limburgh, where, as also in many other places, you have the sad instances of French crueltie ; for in this town there are very few houses left standing ; the fortifications are demolished, and a castle that hath been a very strong and fair one quite ruined. This town stands upon a very high hill, and a river runs below it in the valley. The way is pleasant from Spaa to Aiken, though in some places uneasie for waggons.

"When I was at Aiken I fell to be in the house with a gentleman and his lady who were both Catholicks, but great enemies to the Clergie, especiallie the regulars ; which made me take occasion to ask the Lady how it came then that she confessed all that she knew to such persons. She told me plainly that she did not confesse all ; and speaking of their lasciviousnesse she told me, that before she was married, when she came to confesse, they would have askt her questions about things that she never knew before nor thought of; they were about lust. The gentleman told me, and she too, that the mischiefs of their unmarried life were so great, that it were a thousand times better they did marrie, and that he did hope in a little time to see a reformation in that matter. We came to discourse of nunns, many of whom are young gentlewomen of good qualitie. He told me that many of them were forced by their parents to take that course of life, because they were not able to give them a portion suited to their qualitie; and that therefore the consequences could not but be sad, and the lewdnesse of Abbacies great; of which he told me two stories from his own knowledge.

"One was of a gentleman, an officer in the souldierie under the Spanish king, who was in suit of a young Lady who had a kindnesse for him: but not having the consent of her parents could not marrie him, but was forced by them to enter a nunnerie, which made the gentleman think upon marricing another, which accordingly he did. But his wife dying, and he coming afterwards into that place where his former mistrisse was, old love began to revive, and it was aggried that he should come privatlie to her chamber, where he was hidd and entertained by her a fourthnight. But being at last discovered he was taken, and to his own and others' surprise he was sentenced to die; the execution of which sentence the gentleman told me that he himselfe delayed for a small time (his office it seems putting him in a capacitie to doe it), hopeing that the Marquisse de Grana, then governour of the Spanish Netherlands, would have sent a remission. But he was inexorable in that matter, and so the gentleman was executed, but nothing done to the gentlewoman. He told me also that the young Ladies in their Abbacies have conveniences in their chambers, where they can keep a person undiscovered, and that they keep often good confections in their rooms for entertaining one another, or others where they can have them, and are so inclined. But these are religious persons not of the strictest order, but who have a libertie to converse in the world, and some of ym once in the year the freedom to goe out of their Abbacies for six weeks together amongst their friends.

 * * * * *

"On June 19 I went from Aiken to Juliers, which is about five hours. This for the most part is indeed a pleasant journey, for Tulicher land as it is called by the inhabitants, is for the most a plain countrey, mightie fruitfull of grain. The citie of Juliers is not very great, but well fortified. The D. of Newburgh, to whom this country belongs, hath here a house for his residence, which we could not see. There are about six hundereth men in the town in garrison. I could not but smile to see in the evening near two hundereth cows comeing into the town, and every one of them of themselves parting to the severall streets and houses to which they did belong. Here is very poor accommodation for strangers.

"On June 20 I went for Cullen,* and past through a pleasant wood near nine miles long.

"Cullen lyes in a pleasant plain on the Rhyn, in way of a halfe moon. It is a large Citie, hath a good magazin and some of the antient Roman bows and pikes. Here I saw severall poor Hungarians who come to this place everie seven years to doe their devotions in the behalfe of their Countrey, which otherwise they superstitiouslie believe would be plagued with famine. They are maintained at the charge of the citie during their stay which is not long, and are once or twice served by the Burgomasters who attend them at table. Here is a church of the reformed, about two myles out of town. The congregation is prettie numerous.

"There is no other but a floating-bridge upon the Rhyne here, which runns with a great stream.

"On the 22 of June I saw Dusseldorp, and therin the Prince of Newburgh and his Princesse, the Emperor's sister. They had been some myles out of town at a procession, and were attended with four or five coaches with six horses and a small guard of horse. This town is pleasantlie situated

* Cologne.

upon the Rhyn, and the prince hath here a large palace; the place is fortified. I went this day an hour further than Dusseldorp on the other side of the Rhyne, to a countrey place where we were but soberlie accomodated; we had travailed about nine hours this day.

"On the 23 I went towards Wesel, crossing the Rhyne to see it. It is a fine town and pleasantlie situated and fortified, and is under the Duke of Brandenburgh. Before we came to it we passed through Rhynberg, stronglie fortified and garrisoned by the Bishop of Colen.

"From Wesell we went the same night to Marianborne, a countrey place, where there are two or three harboroughs; in one of which we were very well entertained. Before we came to it we passed through a town called, as I remember, Sant; prettie pleasant, and well built in some parts of it. This day we travailed about eleven hours.

"On 24 June I went towards Cleve, which is most pleasantlie situated, part upon a hill and part in the valley. The Duke of Brandenburgh hath a fair palace on the outer side of it, upon a hill from which there is one of the pleasantest prospects of a fine country, with many steeples for several myles, that ever I saw. There seems to be here not a few people of good fashion. I here met with a gentleman at dinner in our ordinarie, the Hoff Van Hollant, who told me that he had severall times dined with the Earl Argyle and another gentleman and his son, in a private house in that town. He said that they lived very devoutlie, haveing a minister with them that performed worship punctuallie twice a day; and that they checked Lord Gray for his extravagancies.

"Before I came to Cleve, about a myle beyond it, there is a pleasant place called Bergendale, where the late Maurice of Nassaw lived sometimes, and where he died. The house is but ordinarie but there is a prettie park stored with deir. Here also I saw severall of the Roman urns of various shapes, with some other antiquities; as the images of Jupiter, Juno, Minerva, &c. in stone, with Latin inscriptions; most of the urns were found by the above-mentioned Sant. On this side of Cleve there is a place called the Deer garden, where you have four pleasant fountains; and upon the top of the hill all cloathed with wood you have a pleasant prospect of severall fine walks through the wood. From Cleve I came to Nimevegen, which is five hours. This is a good town, and stands upon a riseing hill, declining towards a branch of the Rhyne called the Waal, which makes it very pleasant. This day I travailed eight hours.

"On the 25 June I took boat from Nimevegen to Rotterdam, but came no farther by the ship than Gorcum because of the wind. In my way I saw Tiell, Bommell, and Lyvenstein, the last whereof stands upon a point of land betwixt the Maes and the Waal where they meet, and is a small fortification.

"I had in the boat, besides others, a Lieut. Coll. in the Dutch service, who gave me an account how the late D. of Bavaria came to be so much on the French side, which was thus. His Dutchesse was a french lady, and had been mistresse to the King of France before he was married; for whom he had such love that he intended to marrie her, but was diverted from it by some of his courtiers, who procured a marriage for her with the said Duke; by whom haveing besides other children had a daughter, when she came to be marriageable, she resolved that what herselfe had been disappointed of her daughter should be honoured with, to witt being Queen of France. In order to which, when the King of France was engadged in his late warrs with the Emperour, she caused propose a match betwixt her daughter and the Dauphin, promiseing to engadge the Duke in the French interests if this match were aggried to, which accordinglie was done.

"On the 26 June I came to Rotterdam, where I staid privatlie without seing anybody but those of my cusin's familie.

"I forgott, when writeing what was remarkable at Spaa,

to sett down the inscription that is upon that fountain that
is in the town; which is this:—

> 'Obstructum reserat durum terit humǐda siccat,
> Debile fortificat, si tamen arte bibis.'

" It is not permitted to women to enter into the Cloisters
of the Capucins or their gardens; only here in Spaa it is
permitted for the convenience of strangers, that all persons
may walk in their garden.

"On July 3 I went from Rotterdam to the Hague, and
came back again at night, haveing only walkt about the
town without seing any acquaintance.

"On July 6 I went to the Hague again, where I staid
one night without goeing to visit any of my acquaintance.
1 had this day one of the oddest encounters with one that
was in the habit of a very fashionable gentlewoman, that
ever I had in my life. It so fell out that I satt by her
in the boat, without speaking anything but one or two sentences. When we came to pay I had no small money,
and the skipper not being able to change presently the
piece I gave him, she tooke the opportunitie of telling me
with very much seeming civilitie, that she could serve me
with small money; which accordinglie she did, paying the
skipper my fraught. I kindly thanked her, and putt her
to the trouble of changeing my money, which she did, only
I wanted some styvers, which made me tell them that she
should pay my fraught from Delpht to the Hague, and so
we should be quitts. When we came to the end of Delpht
the Hague's scuyt was gone, so that being to stay halfe an
hour, and she pretending to be faint, and that some quarm
came over her stomach, we went to one of those houses
where it is ordinarie for people to stay and drink a glasse of
beer or wine, or eat any litle thing that is readie, which
ordinarilie is only eels, till the scuyt be readie to goe. I
haveing from somewhat of her discourse been suspicious of
her being a slight person, would goe into no room with her,
but staid in the outer entrie where any person came that

pleased. At last, finding more clearlie what she was, and being resolved to be ridd of her, I pretended I had some businesse in town. She told me very brisklie she would goe with me, and went to the door before me, which made me stay in the house; but she, finding that I did not follow, came back againe. Then I told her that I must be gone. She still persisted in offering me her company; but I haveing answered that I was not for such company, I was glad to get away with all the hast I could, she still crying she would goe with me. But I was not a little pleased that she was left behind, tho' I had not the rest of my change from her.

"I this day dined at an ordinary with some gentlemen, some of whom carried themselves very indiscreetlie, endeavouring to bring me to speake of publick affairs in England; but they came short of their design, I not concerning myself in their discourse."

With this the journal ends. It is accompanied with a careful list of the writer's receipts and expenses, from which I make a few extracts that illustrate the rates of charges for travelling, living, &c., in those days.*

On the 6th of April he bought a "perriwig," in London, which cost him £1 10s., and on the 9th of April a silver picktooth case for 3s. Next day he gave a dinner "to some friends upon an extraordinary occasion" for the modest reckoning of 7s. 2d. He travelled from London by Gravesend, Rochester, and Canterbury; and the fare to Gravesend for himself and a friend, coach to Rochester, dinner there, and coach to Canterbury, came altogether to 10s. 2d. Posthorses from Canterbury to Dover cost 8s., and the fare from Dover to Newport, with fees to porters and sailors and " money to the searchers," 10s. " For supper and dinner next day and lodging that night I landed, having also paid for a poor Englishwoman that came from England with us, and given drink money to the maid, 3 gilders 6 stivers."

† For a catalogue of Carstares' library, of the same date, see Appendix.

He lodged for three nights at Dort, and paid, for lodging, diet, and "extraordinaries," 9 gilders 3 stivers, the charge for dinner at the ordinary having been 30 stivers, and for supper 24 stivers. Things appear to have been cheaper at Maestricht, where for the same time he paid 5 gilders 7 stivers. He took fourteen baths at Aachen at a charge, for the set, of 4 gilders 4 stivers. "For beer at the several times of my bathing, 12 stivers." For a "car" from Aachen to Cologne, "being fourteen hours, 2 gilders 8 stivers." A pair of stockings at Liege cost 4 gilders 10 stivers. A night's lodging and "diet" at Rotterdam were had for 1 gilder 8 stivers. On another occasion a night's lodging there, with supper and breakfast, came to 2 gilders 8 stivers. "I reckon not," he says, "what was given on several occasions to the poor." "A pistole," he adds, "gives but 9 gilders in Flanders, and 17s. upon the road in England, though I paid to the goldsmith for it 17s. 6d." His receipts are noted thus :—

"Received April 11 by bill at Aiken from my
　　cousin James Dunlop . . . . . . £61　0　0
Received at Dort before I went to Aiken . 100　0　0
Received at Rotterdam . . . . . . 35　7　0
I brought from London with me . . . . 10　15　6
Received August 24/85 of Mr. Parsons, by bill 335　8　0"

CHAPTER VIII.

Cleve—Death of Father and Mother—Leyden—Chaplain to William of
Orange.

THE next three years of Carstares' life were outwardly uneventful, his residence in Holland being disturbed by no
persecution, and marked by no visible engagement in political or ecclesiastical adventure or intrigue. He took a house
at Cleve, to which he brought his wife before the end of
August, 1685, and remained there for more than a year.

He appears to have had enough of money to provide comfortably for himself and his household, but the source of his
income is not indicated in any of his extant letters and
papers.

Mrs. Dunlop's circumstances seem to have been somewhat
straitened during her husband's prolonged absence in Carolina; and again and again her brother urges her to consider
his purse her own. "Take, dear sister, for your own use,"
he writes, "what you shall need, and the more freedom you
use with me I take it the more kindly. I need say no more
as to this, only you will do me a very great injury if you shall
not take as freely of mine as you would do of your own."

He never had any children.

Sad news from home reached him immediately after he
had finished his tour in Holland. He writes to his sisters,
under cover to Mrs. Dunlop, on the 28th of July :—

"MY DEAREST SISTERS,—I know not what to write to you, and
yet I cannot be silent, though I am not much in a capacity to say
anything suited to your condition—only I bear a large share with
you in your affliction, and indeed such a share as bows me down—
there being many things in this heavy stroke of the removal of my

dearest dearest mother, that make it peculiarly afflicting to me. The Lord sanctify it to us, and help to carry aright under it. My heart bleeds for my dear father. His God be his support. I must confess it was surprising to me to hear of this providence, having suspected no such news, for there came none of all the letters my wife hath wrote to me since parting safe to hand, till the 7th of this month, and then her tenderness of me made her loath to write such heavy tidings, of which I had no account till yesterday—which I must confess are such as are exceeding heavy. It would be some satisfaction to me to hear that I had any place in her remembrance, and if she left any commands for me, in obeying of which I might in some measure make up those defects of duty to so very kind a mother, when alive, which I have been guilty of; but one thing she hath often desired of me, that I should be kind to you all, if God did take her away; which if I know how to perform I shall not be defective in. If it were any way convenient I would come over and pay my duty to my afflicted father; but providence seems to stop that door; but if his body could bear it to be transported hither, there is a place up the country,* in the dominion of the Duke of Brandenburg, to which we can go by water till we come within fifteen miles of it, and then we can have a coach. I intend to go there with my wife, and I cannot tell you what a satisfaction it would be to us to have his and your company. Pray speak to him of it, for I am in no capacity to give him at present the trouble of a line, being in some perplexity and confusion; but pray give my duty to him, and rest all of you assured that I shall never be forgetful of my very dear mother's desire to me about you, and that you shall find me, I hope, while I breathe, according to my capacity, my dear sisters, your faithful and very affectionate, though at present very much afflicted brother, W. C.

"I know I need not desire you to be very careful of your worthy father. The Lord be with you. This is wrote in much confusion, and I do not know whether it will come to hand or not. I have been here some weeks, but have not made one visit."

This was written from Rotterdam, where he awaited his wife's arrival, and where he had the society of his brother Alexander and his cousin James Dunlop (brother of Sarah's husband), who were now successful merchants in that city. We have no record of his life at Cleve. He intended to make

---

* Cleve.

his residence there a time of quiet mental improvement, if we may judge from the following Rule, which he drew up, and which is dated "Cleve, Jan. 5, 1686:"*

"A digested method of spending of time contributing much to the redeeming and right improving of it, I desire (tho' without taking any vow upon me in reference to what is afterwards set down about my course of study, but leaving to myself a warranted liberty to act as in discretion shall be fit) for three months to endeavour to take the following course in study.

"I would not willingly be diverted in the morning by company, but would reserve that time for myself. Besides time spent in reading of Scripture and duties of God's worship, I would spend, at least, an hour in acquiring the French language, being, because of its universality, so very necessary for converse. I would read a particular portion, every day, of my compends of Philosophy and Theology. I would spend two hours a day upon what I design for a just vindication of myself, principles, and friends, from the aspersions cast upon them in the narrative of the plot printed in England. I would be careful of giving offence in the use of recreations. I would endeavour to moderate my passions upon all occasions. I would guard against evil speaking, being so very unbecoming a Christian. I would endeavour to commit myself unto God in well doing without giving way to sinful anxiety upon the one hand, or indiscreet managing of my affairs on the other. I would endeavour to acknowledge God in providences of one kind and another. I would endeavour to be meek and lowly, and yet labour in a prudent way to keep up the respect and authority of my ministerial station, and so much the more that it is under such contempt both with good and bad."

Carstares' kind design of bringing his father away from the saddened home in Edinburgh, and the oppressed life of Scotland, to the peace and freedom that he had found on the banks of the Rhine, was not to be accomplished. While his

* Caldwell Papers, vol. i. p. 108.

son was lying in prison in November 1684, and when the
Privy Council were dealing with the Presbyterians in a spirit
of more than usual harshness, John Carstares had made up
his mind to quit Scotland, and had applied to the Secretary
of State for a passport. "Seeing," he wrote, "as it would
seem, it is resolved that all Presbyterian nonconform ministers shall be either perpetually imprisoned or exiled his
Majesty's dominions, I beseech your Lordship to grant me
your Lordship's pass to go out of my native country (where
I thought I would have been permitted to die, being an aged
man . . .) unclogged with any gravaminous condition, as
of not exercising my ministry, &c." * But now heavier sorrow
and infirmity had bowed him down, and he was in no condition to leave home and join William in the pleasant Rhine-
land, where Cleve looked, from its gentle slopes, across the
ancient river. The day of his own departure was drawing
near, and he was never to see his son's face again. Not the
least among the griefs, which saddened his last days, was the
thought of the exiled son, and of the daughter whom he
feared he was about to lose—for Sarah had resolved to go
out to her husband in Carolina, much to the distress of her
family. William writes to her in November, while she was
entertaining this project: "Thou art very, very dear to me,
and thy afflicted condition goes very near to me. I cannot
without heaviness think upon thee and thine. God himself
be your comforter, and clear your way before you—helping
you to quiet submission to his holy will. The Lord that
hath fed you all your life long until now,—the angel which
hath kept you from many evils that you might have been
trysted with, even the God before whom our dear father doth,
and our now glorified mother (upon whom I cannot think, or
speak, with dry eyes) did walk—bless yourself, husband, and
the lads. . . . It was judged convenient for preventing of
after trouble that upon my coming here I should apply
myself to some of the government, shewing that I came
out of Britain without being concerned in late businesses

* Wodrow, vol. iv. p. 39.

there, which I did. And in answer to the underwritten paper,* which you may shew your father, I have had a return from the Duke of Brandenburg,† under his hand and seal, giving all protection and encouragement within his lands, not only to me, but to all others coming for conscience' sake out of Britain, excepting only those who have been concerned in the late insurrections some months ago, whom he says he cannot but upon the King of England's desire, cause to remove out of his territories."

On the morning of the 5th of February, 1686, John Carstares died, in his lodging in Edinburgh. His daughters were beside him, and he gave them all his blessing, adding, as he did so, " Yea, and they shall be blessed." He called Sarah specially to him, and gave her a solemn charge, which he enjoined her to convey both to her husband and her eldest brother, that they should never again meddle with any work but what properly belonged to them, as ministers of the gospel. Some one asked him what he thought now of the times and the state of the nation. " If I be not far mistaken of the words and ways of God," he answered, " the heart of God is not toward these men. Notwithstanding all their successes and prevailings of a long time against the people and work of God, I am persuaded *tandem bona causa triumphabit.*" "I leave," he said, " my children and family to God, who gave them, and who

* " A copy of the paper given in by me to the government here : Cum Gulielmus Carstares huc ex Britannia, sedem hic per aliquod tempus figendi, ergo venerit, sui esse duxit officii illustre hujus ducatus Regimen certius facere, se ob nulla crimina inde discessisse ; sed tantum ut libera, in exteris regionibus, frueretur conscientia, cum sese omnibus quoad ecclesiastica in Britannia institutis conformare non possit ; humillime igitur petit ut serenissimi Electoris protectione fruatur, et hisce in regionibus, bona cum Regiminis venia, secure degat, Deoque suo libere inserviat."

† The Duchy of Cleve fell to the Duke of Brandenburg in 1666 : " a naturally opulent country, of fertile meadows, shipping capabilities, metalliferous hills ; and at this time, in consequence of the Dutch-Spanish War, and the multitude of Protestant refugees, it was getting filled with ingenious industries." Carlyle's 'Friedrich,' vol. i. pp. 363, 347. The present Duke was Friedrich Wilhelm, " the great Elector," the Prince of Orange's uncle by marriage, " a pious God-fearing man rather, staunch to his Protestantism and his Bible." Ibid. p. 352.

will be their portion.* If it were possible that Christ and his interests could ruin, I had much rather ruin and fall with him, than stand with any, or all, the powers in the world; but as I am persuaded those cannot perish, so am I confident in the Lord they shall revive in all the churches of Christ." Among his last words were, "I am dying, and dying in the Lord, and now I have nothing to do but to die."†

On the 24th of February, Carstares writes to his sisters: "I have had the heavy tidings of the removal of my dearest and very worthy father, whose death hath many aggravating considerations as to me, beyond what it hath to any of you. O for the blessing of so sad a stroke! It hath a loud language, God himself help to know and to conform to it. Our loss is such as can be made up in none but God. O let us seek to have this great want supplied there! Let us be on our guard against distrusting despondence upon the one hand, and unconcernedness on the other. The holy God be submitted to and not quarrelled with, and yet his rods suitably regarded. The taking away of our very dear and tender-hearted and concerned parents carries on it very visible marks of great love on God's part to them, whom in tender care he would not have to see the evils that seem to be at hand, but would house them before the storm should blow; but O! the dispensation looks dark as to us:—Lord grant that we may walk humbly with him. Now, dear sisters, let me once again desire you to rest assured that you shall find me a faithful affectionate and concerned brother. The want of your parents, and of such parents, cannot be made up by me, but what shall be in my power for your comfort and help shall not be wanting. I would have you ordering your affairs so as we may be together as soon as is possible. My poor wife is equally concerned with me in you all and most affectionately remembers you." In a paragraph specially addressed to Sarah he says: "Pray leave behind thee (tho' thy going is heavy to me, but alas! thy great ties are loosed) one of

---

* For John Carstares' Will, see Appendix.
† Ferrie, p. 46.　'Analecta,' vol. iii. pp. 52-3.

thy babies, and Johnie if thou please, that I may shew to
him the kindness I owe to thee, and the savoury memory of
him whose name he bears."

In a subsequent letter (April 10), he says: "I thank you
heartily for Johnie. He shall be as my own. I take it very
kindly also you sent me those things, which I shall prize much
as remembrances of my dear and tender-hearted parents.
I would have my sisters with me so soon as they can
come. We shall very well agree how to live together; and
I would have all my dear father's books brought to Edinburgh, for it is like I may send for them shortly. I am not
yet fully determined where to take up my settled abode for
the rest of the summer and the following winter, if the Lord
shall spare so long, but shall quickly, I hope, come to a
resolution. My wife will go to England, I think, in a little
time, but make as short stay as may be."

Johnie, after all, was not sent to his uncle, and Mrs. Dunlop, instead of emigrating to Carolina, joined with her sisters
in taking a house (in Edinburgh, I conclude), where they
lived together until the Revolution.

Before the beginning of the winter of 1686–7 Carstares
left Cleve, and took up his abode at Leyden. There were
many advantages in this change. At Leyden he was near
his former friends, and the large Scotch colony, in Utrecht.
His old tutor, Mr. Sinclair, who had been for several years
an exile, was close at hand in the Scots' church at Delft.*
Rotterdam—the home of his brother and his cousin, and a
port in constant communication with Britain—was only seven-
teen miles distant. But no doubt the chief attraction of
Leyden was its immediate vicinity to the Hague and the
Court of the Prince of Orange. Carstares' discreet and
courageous silence under his torture, when a few words
would have secured his own release, and made revelations
disastrous to the Prince, had greatly enhanced the esteem
and confidence which William had long entertained for him.
He was now admitted to his most confidential counsels, and

* Steven, p. 295.

he became also the intimate friend of Bentinck. On Carstares' judgment of characters and circumstances William felt he could rely, no less than on his well-tried silence and discretion. In consulting him, he ran none of the risks which he incurred from Burnet's talkative officiousness and self-sufficiency; and when Burnet, at the peremptory desire of King James,[*] was forbidden to see the Prince and Princess, Carstares was drawn into still closer relations with William —relations which gained an official sanction from his appointment as one of the Prince's chaplains. Of all this, however, we learn nothing, or next to nothing, from his letters to his sisters, which are the only ones extant of this period. They are occupied with family affairs, or such personal details as lie apart from any political connection. He does not even announce the appointment which he received early in 1688 to be second minister of the Scots' church in Leyden,—a charge founded by the Prince solely on his chaplain's[†] account, and endowed as a kind of provision for him. The letters are full of his brotherly interest in his family at home, and especially in Sarah, who evidently was his favourite sister. "You are dear to me," he writes to her, " and shall find that you are so, if Providence shall capacitate me to testify it. My wife hath sent each of your babies a ducaton to buy them gloves, and each of you two, as a small token of her great respect. You must not take this ill, for it is much the fashion in England to send their friends, upon occasions, some such little small things as remembrances of them."

"If there shall be an Act of Indemnity," he writes in September 1687, " I intend, if the Lord will, to be with you for some months; but I have little inclination to be in the reverence of some men, tho' I have a strong inclination to see you all."

He had vowed never to return to Scotland until he should see " things there go in another channel." Had the turn of the tide begun then? Had a Stuart learned wisdom

* Burnet, vol. iii. p. 173.   † Steven, p. 312.

and charity, and forsworn bigotry and despotism? How came Acts of Indemnity to be expected from the master of Claverhouse, and the patron of Jeffreys? A glance at the history of the unquiet years, which had passed since Carstares got out of prison, will throw some light on these points, and will prepare us for the great crisis, now fast approaching, which was to bestow on the Dutch Stadtholder the sceptre wrenched from the mean and incapable hand of James, to restore the exiles of liberty and religion to their native soil, and to regenerate the political life of Britain.

CHAPTER IX.

Infatuated policy of James in England—Party of the Prince of Orange —Affairs of Scotland—James Steuart, Carstares, and Fagel—The Invasion.

"NEVER king mounted the throne of England," says the judicial Hume,[*] "with greater advantages than James, nay possessed greater facility, if that were any advantage, of rendering himself and his posterity absolute; but all these fortunate circumstances tended only, by his own misconduct, to bring more sudden ruin upon him. The nation seemed disposed of themselves to resign their liberties, had he not, at the same time, made an attempt upon their religion; and he might even have succeeded in surmounting at once their liberties and their religion, had he conducted his schemes with common prudence and discretion." He possessed a large revenue independent of parliamentary control, and a standing army, strong and disciplined, of which he was the absolute master. The old malcontents and champions of liberty, in the days of his father and brother, were no more, and no others seemed prepared to follow in their steps. The efforts made, early in his reign, by Argyll and Monmouth, to overturn his government in Scotland and England, came to an ignominious end in both kingdoms. When the King opened his English Parliament in November 1685, he stood before his peers and commoners, prosperous, powerful, and confident. But the blind lust of arbitrary power, and the bitter zeal of superstitious fanaticism which infected his hard heart and narrow intelligence, early betrayed themselves, and dissipated whatever hopes his subjects had formed of a free and peaceful reign.

* Hume (chap. lxx.), vol. viii. p. 230.

His leading idea was soon perceived, and it was to rule his kingdoms, independent of the law and of Parliament, and in the interests of the Church of Rome. The sturdy spirit of English Protestantism was not long of being roused, and expressed its alarm through the warning voice of the houses of Lords and Commons. Even the slavish Parliament of Scotland, which, after the King's accession, had solemnly expressed its " abhorrence of all principles which are contrary or derogatory to the King's sacred, supreme, absolute power and authority,"* shrank from the proposal to grant full toleration to the King's co-religionists. Both Parliaments were speedily prorogued, and James essayed to govern alone and absolute. The infatuated and suicidal course of his policy in England is too well known to need recapitulation. The standing army, the assertion of the " dispensing power," the official employment of Roman Catholics, the High Commission, the " regulating " of the charters, the embassy to Rome, the illegal remission of tests and penal laws, the dismissal of Rochester and Clarendon, the appointment of Tyrconnel in Ireland, were all grievances, lesser or greater, which not only alarmed and irritated the nation, but seemed to mark a reckless and unresting progress away from Protestantism and liberty, towards Popery and tyranny, the end whereof none liked to forecast. At length things began to ripen and draw together to the consummation. The King had practically abolished Parliament; he had overstepped the sacred precincts of the law, and he thought he might with impunity venture to interfere with the rights of the Church and the Universities. Here, however, he reached the limits of forbearance. The attempt to extort from the University of Cambridge a degree for a Benedictine monk forced that great, learned, and conservative corporation, whose loyalty was unquestioned, to a simple choice between the orders of the King and the laws of the land.† The attempt to

* Dalrymple, vol. i. p. 75.
† " I could not tell what to do—decline his Majesty's letter or his laws." Letter from Dr. Peachell (Vice-Chancellor) to S. Pepys. Pepys' Correspondence.

foist a Roman Catholic president upon Magdalen College, Oxford, drove that university, whose attachment to the throne was proverbial, to the same fatal dilemma. In either case, constitutional principle triumphed over courtly tradition and feudal sentiment; and the triumph was the beginning of the end for the blind and bigoted monarch.

The loyalty of the Church was shaken to its foundations by the assault on the universities; and the trial of the seven bishops only completed the alienation of the clergy from the King, which that assault had first engendered.

When Lord Dartmouth came to James to give his report of Monmouth's execution, he said, "You have got rid of one enemy, but a more dangerous one remains behind."* When Argyll was carried prisoner into Renfrew, at the close of his disastrous expedition, he said to Thomas Crawford of Crawfordsburn, "Thomas, it hath pleased Providence to frown on my attempt, but remember, I tell you, ere long One shall take up this quarrel, whose shoes I am not worthy to carry, who will not miscarry in his undertaking."† In neither case was the reference obscure. Had James possessed even slight political sagacity, he would have understood that the thoughts of every British subject, who dreaded his arbitrary power and his popish superstitions and intrigues, must naturally turn to William of Orange.

That wise and ambitious prince was, through his marriage to the heiress of the throne, bound to take a watchful concern in the affairs of England; he was the sworn foe of that great potentate, the enemy of civil freedom and of the reformed faith, to whom Charles and James had meanly truckled; he was the recognised head of the Protestant interest in Europe. Long ere James had ascended the throne the Scottish exiles, and sufferers for conscience' sake, had hoped in his son-in-law, as the future champion of their rights; and now the mind of England, also, turned to him as the only possible deliverer from evils that were becoming in-

----

* Dalrymple, part i. book ii. p. 69.
† Wodrow, vol. iv. p. 299.

supportable. No doubt William had foreseen that it would
thus turn to him. He had done nothing, openly, to form a
party in England, or to promote opposition to the King; but
indications are not wanting that his influence had been at
work, in more than one of the disaffected movements of the
time. The expedition of Monmouth was organised with his
connivance. Carstares, acting for the Prince, paid Wishart,
the master of the vessel in which Argyll sailed from Holland
("of whose honesty and willingness to serve his Highness," he
was fully assured.*) In either case we note the influence;
we perhaps cannot decide as to the motive; though in the one,
a rival was certain to be put out of the way; and in the
other, it was not improbable that the allegiance of a whole
nation might be shaken by a successful insurrection.

Now, however, in 1687, William began to lend himself
more frankly, though still with caution, to English political
intrigue. He had been anxious to maintain a dutiful friendship with his father-in-law as long as he could hope, through
this friendship, to secure the alliance of England in his
designs against France. When he saw that the King no
longer represented the nation, or commanded the sympathies
of his people, and that the support of England against the
aggression of France could be gained without her King more
easily than with him, he did not scruple to become the head
of the secret and rapidly-spreading combination of parties
hostile to James.

The missions of William's envoys, Dykvelt and Zulestein,
compacted the alliance between their master and the English
opposition; and by the time Zulestein returned to Holland,
while the forms of decent friendship were still preserved between King James and his son-in-law, the reigning monarch
and the foreign prince were practically rivals for the same
sovereignty. Although James seems to have had a dull
perception of the truth, and might easily have divined the
causes of his own unpopularity, he never swerved in his anti-
Protestant crusade. Office after office was taken from

* McCormick, p. 35. Afterwards an admiral of the English fleet.

Churchmen to be bestowed, in virtue of the dispensing power, on Roman Catholics. Step by step the Romish ecclesiastics were advanced to greater liberty and honour. The King would listen to no counsel; though there is no doubt his Roman Catholic advisers, and even the Pope himself, suggested to him the necessity of mingling discretion with his zeal.*

It was hard for any intelligent observer of James's character and policy to believe that he was, at heart, a lover of the rights of conscience and civil and religious liberty; and accordingly, his measures of toleration in England were regarded with general suspicion. The common conviction was that, under the flimsy cloak of an indulgence to the long harassed dissenters, he intended to introduce Popery with all the authority and dignity which it had arrogated before the Reformation. Even the dissenters looked askance upon a freedom, conferred by a prince who had been the most rigorous oppressor of the Covenanters of Scotland, and who had congratulated Louis XIV. on his revocation of the Edict of Nantes.† The Church regarded his indulgences with a mixture of professional jealousy and Protestant alarm. Statesmen, however they might approve, in theory, of equal religious freedom for every communion, could not but dread the practical results of the concession of the boon in the case of Roman Catholics, and disapprove of the royal prerogative being employed to force upon the nation measures, not only repugnant to public feeling and opinion, but absolutely contrary to law. The republication of the 'English Indulgence' in April, 1688, and the remonstrance of the seven bishops, their trial and acquittal, and the sympathy which attended that acquittal, hastened on the crisis, and marked the last severances in the rupture between the nation and the King. The ill-omened birth of the Prince of Wales only quickened the universal sentiment of national distrust and dread. Within three weeks of that event, and on the very day of the

* Dalrymple, part. i. book iv.
† Dalrymple. Appendix, part i. p. 177.

acquittal of the bishops, a formal invitation, signed by the seven chief conspirators against King James, was despatched to the Prince of Orange.

Meanwhile, how had things gone in Scotland? They were at a dark enough pass at the time of James's accession. The extreme party of the Presbyterians, who now went by the name of the Society men or the Hill men, had drawn off farther than ever from all commerce with the indulged, or even with those moderate men, who were disposed to await in patience the issue of events.

In October and November, 1684, they had published the 'Apologetical Declaration,' drawn up by their leader Renwick. It was a stern and threatening manifesto,* which, practically, declared a war of retaliation against all the minions and emissaries of the government, all abettors of the persecution, all informers, especially "viperous and malicious bishops and curates." "The 'Apologetic Declaration' carried terror into many breasts. Several curates, afraid of their lives, abandoned their parishes. Magistrates and informers could not go out in the dark, scarcely in the day, for fear of being shot down by some unseen hand. The very soldiery required to be more on their guard. A keen marksman, from behind a dyke, might empty a saddle and be off in a twinkling. But government had now a stronger pretext than ever to hunt these men down, as professed murderers, and they did not fail to take advantage of it. An oath solemnly abjuring the declaration was formed. Different officers were commissioned to proceed to different parts of the country, with a sufficient military force. The inhabitants were to be brought before them, and if any one hesitated to take the abjuration oath, he was to be shot upon the spot. To make matters still more sure, no one was to be allowed to pass from one part of the country to another without carrying with him a certificate of his loyalty, and this he could obtain only by taking the abjuration

* See Wodrow, vol. iv. p. 168.

oath."[*] Claverhouse scoured the country, quartering troops
on recusant parishes, assisting those favourites, on whom
government had bestowed forfeited estates, to secure possession; ferreting out, early in the week, and punishing,
those parishioners marked "absent" at the previous Sunday's
service; shooting such as would not take the oath.[†] The
offer, on James's accession, of an indemnity to all persons
below the rank of heritors, life-renters, or burgesses, who
should take the oath of allegiance, was so clogged with conditions as to be, in effect, illusory;[‡] and the merciless action
of the Parliament more than counterbalanced the limited
concessions of the King. A series of Acts was passed, directed
against the Presbyterians, and exceeding in severity all previous legislation. These acts made it treason to acknowledge
the Covenant; treason to refuse evidence against attenders
at conventicles; treason, and a capital crime, to preach
either in a house or in the fields, or to attend a conventicle
out of doors. The insurrection of Argyll afforded only too
fair an excuse for redoubled rigour in the application of these
enactments, and for a harsher licence to the military oppressors of the western regions, in which Argyll had hoped
to find his chief support; but where he discovered, to his
ruin, that the heart and energy of the people were too
thoroughly crushed to respond to his appeal.

No effort has been spared, by the apologists of the government of James, to impart a constitutional and clement
aspect to his Scotch administration, and to throw a dubious
haze around the alleged sufferings of the Presbyterians.
Probably, as in all cases where popular passion has been
deeply stirred, the sufferings have been in some points ex-
aggerated, and the story occasionally has been touched with
imaginative or picturesque details. But, on the whole, there
is no possibility of denying a vast mass of arbitrary cruelty
and illegal oppression.

* Cunningham, vol. ii. p. 236. † Burton, vol. vii. 545.

‡ Fountainhall, p. 621.

The banishments to the Plantations, the enormous fines, the horrors of Dunnotter,* are proved historical facts. Without undue credulity, we may say the same of the great majority of Wodrow's cases of murder, torture, fining, and imprisonment. It has been a fashion among Jacobite and Episcopal writers to decry the historian of the "Sufferings;" but his narrative is in too many instances authenticated by external testimony to be thrown aside as legendary. Hume, who wrote his own account of the reigns of Charles and James within seventy years of the period, considered Wodrow a much better authority than Burnet.† The credulity and prejudice which Mr. Hill Burton lays to his charge,‡ although he testifies that "few works are more truthful than his History," were qualities inseparable from every Scotsman who, attempting to decipher and relate the history of his church and country between the years 1662 and 1688, should sit down to the task within thirty years of the Revolution.§

The battle of Wodrow's trustworthiness has been lately fought at two crucial points—the story of the "Christian Carrier," and that of the "Wigton Martyrs;" and at each he has gained a decided triumph. The late Mr. W. E. Aytoun‖ lent all the enthusiasm of the poet of the cavaliers, and all the skill of an accomplished lawyer, to the enterprise of proving the Christian carrier to be little else than a mythical

---

* Where 167 men and women were crammed together into a vault, ankle deep in mire, and with but one window. Afterwards some of them were removed to another vault; where they could get a little fresh air only by lying down, in turns, beside a chink in the wall. Some trying to escape were caught, laid on their backs on a bench; and matches tied between the fingers of both hands, were kept burning for three hours until the bones were calcined. Wodrow, vol. iv. p. 324.

† Hume, vol. viii. p. 164.

‡ Burton, vol. vii. p. 570, note.

§ My own experience of Wodrow, as far as it goes, is in favour of his accuracy. In every important detail where I have been able to compare his statements with other, and original, authorities, I have found him right. Mr. Fox, I may remark, bears a similar testimony in his 'History of the Reign of James II.'

‖ Appendix to later editions of 'Lays of the Scottish Cavaliers.'

personage; but he fails to shake the narrative of Wodrow, or to explain away the damning facts of the case, as admitted by Claverhouse himself.* In the delirious pages of Mr. Mark Napier† every conceivable pretext for disbelieving the execution of the Wigton martyrs is paraded at length; but the dispassionate and exhaustive investigation of the Rev. Dr. Stewart, of Glasserton,‡ has left no doubt, in any impartial mind, that the story as told by Wodrow is in all important particulars substantially correct.

The persecution gradually concentrated itself upon the outlawed Society people. The great body of the Presbyterians was by this time effectually crushed. Very few of the ministers survived, in Scotland. The nonconforming gentry were either banished, forfeited, or forced into inactive submission by ruinous fines. The yeomen and peasantry were much reduced in numbers by slaughter, exile, and imprisonment; and those who remained were quite unable to contend longer against a ruthless military coercion. Thus, from very want of fuel, the fire dwindled, although there was no reason to believe the principles of persecution had been renounced by the King or government. It was, therefore, with a mixture of wonder and doubt, that the nation heard it alleged that the King proposed to grant an indulgence, and that he was in favour of the removal of the tests and penal laws. James was not adroit enough to do anything to disarm the shrewd suspicion of his designs. He openly announced his wish to relieve his Roman Catholic subjects from tests and penalties; and finding that his Parliament would not help him in this, he did it by virtue of his royal prerogative, but tried to render the act less generally offensive by extending his toleration to the Presbyterians also.

* Napier's 'Life and Times of Claverhouse,' vol. i. p. 141.

† 'Case for the Crown.' Any student, anxious to catch a last glimpse of all the ugliest features of Scotch Jacobitism and Episcopacy, should nerve himself to read Mr. Mark Napier, although the bluntness of moral discernment, the unconscious brutality of sentiment, and the elaborate friskiness of style, are very trying to one's patience.

‡ 'History Vindicated, &c.'

By the first Indulgence, of the 12th of February, 1687, though all persons countenancing field conventicles were to be prosecuted according to the utmost severity of law, the "moderate Presbyterians" were allowed to meet, in private, to hear indulged ministers; while all laws, customs, and constitutions against Roman Catholics were abolished, and they were made free to exercise their religion and eligible for all public offices.* The inequality between the boon to the Presbyterians and that to the Roman Catholics was so glaring, and created so much distrust, that the King, by a proclamation of the 5th of July, though still proscribing field meetings, greatly relaxed the former limitations, and left the Presbyterians virtually at liberty to worship God freely and openly, according to their conscience.†

Even among the Privy Councillors and bishops, some were found who refused to follow their master here and to concur in this policy, or sanction by their approval his unconstitutional exercise of the royal prerogative. But the King could pack a Privy Council as easily as revoke a penal law. The recusant Dukes of Hamilton and Queensberry were displaced. The Archbishop of Glasgow and the Bishop of Dunkeld were turned out of their sees. Sir George Mackenzie was superseded. A ministry was formed, partly of Roman Catholics, partly of Presbyterians. Among the former was the pervert Perth, with his brother Melfort; among the latter was Sir John Dalrymple, son of the exiled Lord Stair. James, when Duke of York, had been the means of driving Stair from his high office of Lord President; Sir John had himself lain for many months in prison, but now he accepted a place from his former oppressor, and was appointed Lord Advocate in the room of Sir George Mackenzie. Sir John's elevation was counselled by Sunderland, who hoped thereby to promote a political union between the Presbyterian and Popish parties. His own purpose was a different one, and embraced revenge for the past injuries inflicted on himself and his family, and the overthrow of the despotism under which his country was

* Wodrow, vol. iv. pp. 117–18.   † Ibid. vol. iv. p. 427.

ground down. Associated with him, and with Melfort, was James Steuart, the accuser of Lauderdale and the adviser of Argyll.*

The very fact of attempting such a union is the clearest proof of the political imbecility of James. The fusion of two irreconcilable forces was impossible. A hatred of popery, and of the ecclesiastical domination which popery symbolised, was one of the most powerful and pervading constituents in Scottish national character. Prelacy—especially popish prelacy—was held in general and sincere abhorrence. Even those who accepted Episcopacy did so with no mediæval faith in the order of bishops. To men like Sir George Mackenzie, the establishment of Episcopacy seemed the simplest way of putting an end to wearisome religious quarrels and disputes, and to the coarse sway of a body of clergy whose religion was full of puritanism, and whose politics were dangerously democratic.† A moderate Episcopacy, favoured by the Court, and backed by the august example and traditions of the Church of England, appeared more likely, than a somewhat divided and turbulent Pres-

* Dalrymple, part i. book iv. Burnet, vol. iii. Fountainhall. Wodrow.

† Among many corroborations of what I state, one may be specially quoted. Evelyn, in his diary (9th of March, 1690) says, "I dined at the Bishop of St. Asaph's . . . with the famous lawyer Sir George McKenzie . . . . He related to us many particulars of Scotland, the present sad condition of it, the inveterate hatred which the Presbyterians show to the family of the Stewarts, and the exceeding tyranny of those bigots, who acknowledge no superior on earth, in civil or divine matters, maintaining that the people only have the right of government; their implacable hatred to the Episcopal order, and Church of England." He then proceeds to a statement, which Mr. Disraeli must have recollected when he penned his account (in 'Lothair') of the origin of the United Presbyterian Church. "He observed that the first Presbyter dissents from our discipline were introduced by the Jesuits' order, about the 20 of Queen Elizabeth; a famous Jesuit among them faining himself a Protestant, and who was the first who began to pray extempory, and brought in that which they since called and are still so fond of, praying by the Spirit. This Jesuit remained many years before he was discovered, afterwards died in Scotland, where he was buried at ——— having yet on his monument 'Rosa inter spinas.' " Evelyn's 'Memoirs,' edition of 1827, vol. iii. p. 293.

bytery, to foster a national religion, under whose auspices thoughtful and peaceful men could live, and cultivate trade, or letters, or politics, in quiet. Scottish Episcopacy became persecuting through its unprincipled use of the engines, which the State provided for the purpose of establishing it on a firm basis; but in itself it was the nerveless creature of the State, and not one of its bishops dared to lift his voice, with the old independence and authority of a Douglas or a Guthrie. When, therefore, James showed his intention of forcing upon Scotland (where Episcopacy, by dint of twenty-six years of persecution, had almost succeeded in making a solitude which it might call peace) a new agent of religious strife, a new element pregnant with all the worst characters of the discord, schism, and spiritual tyranny, with which moderate and enlightened men must always be at war, there was a revolt. No wise man desired that the old battle should be fought over again, and with deadlier weapons.

The majority of the bishops, Privy Councillors, and nobility, who were the minions of the Court, gave way to the royal will; but a few, who, amidst all the excesses of the persecution, had not lost the instincts of statesmen, either openly remonstrated or stood silently aloof. Others, like Dalrymple and Steuart, who had hitherto been among the persecuted, now saw the turning of the tide, and came forward to take advantage of it; understanding well that when the issue came to lie between Popery and Presbytery in Scotland the decision would be sharp and quick, and probably not caring much how it should fare in the meantime with the Episcopal establishment, which stood perplexed and disarmed between the two.

The King's indulgence was, of course, indignantly scouted by the extreme Covenanters, who disdained to acknowledge an earthly monarch's right either to sanction, or to prohibit, their worship of their God. The great body of the Presbyterians, however, availed themselves of the indulgence. Several of the exiled ministers returned from Holland. Those who were scattered through Scotland met in Edinburgh, and sent up a letter of thanks to the King, to which

he graciously replied in the unwonted terms: " We love you
well . . . We resolve to protect you in your liberty, religion, and properties, all your life." *   Congregations began
to be formed, and to " call " the ministers of their choice in
the old fashion, Carstares, for one, receiving a call to Glasgow.†
Large and spacious places of worship were erected in many
of the towns, and even in some country parishes. The old
meetings of Presbyteries and Synods, under their own moderators, were partially revived. The strong Presbyterian
leaven revealed its presence and power all through the South
and West, as soon as the iron repression of the " killing time "
was lightened.

This, then, was the position of affairs when Carstares,
expecting that an Act of Indemnity would accompany the
indulgence, spoke of coming over to spend some months
with his kindred in Scotland. He had been led to look
for an indemnity by James Steuart, with whom he was in
constant correspondence, and whose letters played no unimportant part among the preparatives of the Revolution. ‡
In the end of the year 1686 William Penn went to Holland
on a mission from King James. His instructions were to
represent to the Prince of Orange the wisdom and charity of
the King's policy of toleration, and to influence, if possible,
the British refugees in its favour. The plausible Quaker
did his best, and believed that he made a convert in James
Steuart. On his return to London he told the King no man
could do him better service among the fanatical Scots.
Steuart's pardon was made out; Albeville, James's envoy in

* Wodrow, vol. iv. p. 428.   ' Hind let Loose,' p. 209.

† Graham Dunlop MSS.

‡ Lord Macaulay (chapter vii.) gives a very imperfect outline of Steuart's
actings before the Revolution. He speaks of " a letter " addressed by him
to Fagel, which drew forth Fagel's celebrated reply. There was no such
letter. Steuart corresponded with Carstares, and Carstares conveyed his
views to Fagel and the Prince. There are twenty-two of his letters to
Carstares among the Graham Dunlop MSS., copies of which, in Wodrow's
hand, are to be seen in 8vo. No. 30, of the Wodrow MSS., in the Advocates'
Library.

Holland, assured him he should find himself not only in safety, but in favour, in Britain, and he accordingly left Utrecht for London, having first assured William of his steadfast fidelity to his interests.* His conduct at this point, and subsequently, is one of the many moral enigmas of that unhappy time. That a man so astute, so experienced—whose great legal skill and learning all his contemporaries admired —whose loyalty to Presbytery and to liberty had been proved by years of forfeiture and exile—should have been won over, by William Penn, to believe in James's honesty of purpose in the matter of the indulgences and penal laws, is almost incredible. That a man apparently so honest and religious, so intelligent in his moral discernments, should have stained himself with the treachery of acting as he did, if he had no confidence in James's good faith, is as hard to believe. The problem evidently perplexed those who knew him better than we do. His own kinsman, the author of the 'Denham Memoir' in the Coltness Collections, confesses that he finds it hard to judge of his motives. Burnet† cannot decide whether he really believed in the King's sincerity or not. Dalrymple‡ is uncertain whether he was actuated by " the affectation of loyalty natural to a new convert, or by a refinement of revenge." Probably the real explanation of his conduct is, that wearied of exile, and hopeless of upsetting the established order of Church and State in Scotland by further plotting, he deemed it his wisest course to fall in with the King's policy, and adapt it, as best he could, to the end (which as a patriot he held in view) of securing some measure of civil and religious liberty for his native country. Like all moderate men, or trimmers, however, he attracted the suspicion and dislike of the vehement among both parties. The more rigid Presbyterians thought he betrayed the principles of the Covenant. The ardent royalists accused him of undermining the throne of the sovereign whom he

---

* Coltness Collections, pp. 88-9.
† Burnet, vol. iii. p. 214.
‡ Dalrymple, part i. book iv.

professed to serve.* That he helped to pave the way for the Revolution is, at all events, certain.

In a long series of letters addressed to Carstares, extending through the whole of 1687, he urges on the Prince of Orange a compliance with the policy of James. The tone of the earlier letters is not so confident as that of those written under the immediate inspiration of the King's presence, which evidently had a certain influence, not the less distinguishable by the reader because of the writer's disclaimers. On the 18th of July he writes, from Windsor, that it is a mistake to imagine that "the liberty" was originated by priests or Jesuits, and not by His Majesty's "own good sense and reason." The King, who must have either been at his elbow as he wrote, or have sketched what he was to say, is full of regret at the Prince's and Princess's disapproval of his measures. They ought to yield to his wishes, and in so doing gratify not only him, but the "far greater and better part of the nation;" and then they might depend on the King giving the Prince full satisfaction as to the succession to the throne.†

Again, on the 29th of July, he thinks he has answered all the objections urged in a letter he has received from Carstares, ‡ and has given such a confirmation of all that he had previously written, "from His Majesty himself, that I must still think it a fatality if your people remain obstinate . . . You wish for a union among all Protestants—and who would not ?—but believe me, the Church of England's irritation is such, and is now so visible in daily prints, that, if the Protestant dissenters shall not at this time obtain a legal establishment, they shall be crushed more than ever, when once this precarious liberty expires."

* Burnet, vol. iii. p. 215. Balcarres' 'Account, &c.,' p. 11, 1st edition of 1714.

† It was alleged that the King aimed at disposing of the crown, by way of testament, to whom he should think a proper successor; and it was hinted that his choice might fall on his natural son, the Duke of Berwick. McCormick, pp. 27–8. Fountainhall, p. 812.

‡ Carstares' part of this correspondence is not to be found.

He urges that the only security for the nonconformists is to have the liberty, which the King had granted by royal prerogative, fixed by law, and that in opposing this the Prince is opposing the interests of the Protestants—not, as he may think, obstructing the elevation of the Papists. " I intreat," he continues, " let me, at least, prevail with you to come over *incognito*, and appoint me a meeting, were it but for an hour. If you have a secret permission from the Hague it would promise more. But, however, let us endeavour good all we can; and I assure you I have my warrant, though I was sorry to find it given so despondently, with a ' Well, well, but you will find him inflexible.' You say the want of an indemnity makes the Scots' liberty suspect; but I assure you His Majesty is most free to it, and it is only hindered at home by you may guess whom, but such as never were for this liberty, and like well of the fining; without that the very liberty is more than Scots Presbyterians can bear, and that an indemnity with it would make them insupportable. But I'll tell you plainly, let the Prince consent and concur, and the Scots will get an indemnity, and his Highness all the satisfaction in other things he can demand."

This letter was written, he says, subsequently, " not only with permission, but, according to His Majesty's mind, sufficiently expressed," and he is hurt at Carstares' long delay and great " coldness " in replying to it. He is ready, and has the King's commands, to cross to Holland, if a personal interview would be more effective than letters. The Prince and the Protestant dissenters, especially the Presbyterians, by opposing the liberty, are, in his opinion, only playing " the bishops' game," and " keeping up a scourge for their own backs," the intolerance of the Church of England being sure to increase. And they are doing this under a false impression, for ever since he came to England he has seen that "security to a few Roman Catholics, and ease and safety to all his people, is that which His Majesty only desires." To all these pleas Carstares replied so cautiously and " coldly " as to show that they were urged to no purpose; and Steuart

at last writes, in October, from Edinburgh, that he sees he
need add no more to what he has said in vain already.

Finally, from London, on the 6th of November, he says:
"To tell you the truth, Presbyterians are so feared and
hated by you know whom in Scotland, and so strangely represented here, that it is much to keep up the liberty granted
them, especially when they are so foolish as to give their
[blank] all the advantages they can desire . . . . . . I am
resolved to meddle no more in these matters. I hope men
will not still say that I have been seeking self when they see
I truly get nothing.* His Majesty truly doth rather increase
his favour, and that is all I crave. Nay, I offered to him
that, if he thought good, all Presbyterians should be excluded
from public trust, provided they might have liberty only;
but he said he would have no such exclusions, though he
knew I made the offer to remove the jealousies of some
opposers."

This long correspondence was carefully considered by the
Prince, in consultation with Fagel, Carstares, and Burnet;
and it was decided that a reply, upon the whole subject,
should be prepared, which might serve as a useful declaration of William's opinions and intentions. Fagel accordingly
drew up a letter, that was rendered into English by Burnet,†
in which, while it was declared that the Prince and Princess
would gladly concur in- abolishing any laws which attached
penal consequences to certain religious opinions, they could
not approve of the removal of the tests, or the admission of
Roman Catholics to office. Steuart received this letter, and
communicated it to Sunderland, to Melfort, who was "satisfied" with it, and to the King, who was not. The King, he
found, was "quite over that matter, being no way satisfied
with the distinction made of the tests from the penal laws;

* In January, 1688, he got a pension of £300, said to be for "defraying
his expenses to London." Fountainhall, p. 847.

† Burnet, vol. iii. p. 215. Fagel's letter and Steuart's reply to it, and also
several extracts from Steuart's letters to Carstares, were printed at the time,
1687–8. They will be found in the Advocates' Library, in a volume of
'Tracts,' numbered 567; No. 47, and one of pamphlets, numbered $\frac{2}{3}$.

and no less positive that his Highness is neither to be prevailed upon, nor so much as to be further treated with in this matter." This being the King's attitude, the report of the publication and dissemination of Fagel's letter alarmed and irritated Steuart, who probably dreaded both becoming the scapegoat of the royal anger at the utter failure of an undignified negotiation, and exposure to public dislike and distrust, on the discovery of the part he had played in the correspondence, to which Fagel's manifesto purported to be a reply. He writes to Carstares, on the 9th of December, begging that his letters be " suppressed and destroyed;" but they had already served their turn. Fagel's manifesto was dispersed through England in thousands, and the late and rather lame response which Steuart published, in May, did nothing to erase the strong impression which the Dutch declaration had made upon the public mind.

During the whole course of these negotiations Carstares was near the Prince, and in confidential intercourse with him. William, in particular, consulted his judgment in regard to the antecedents and characters of the many British refugees and malcontents, who resorted in ever larger numbers, to his Court, and he used to assert that he never in a single instance found Carstares attempting to mislead him.*

Burnet's complete silence about Carstares is rather odd. It is probably the result of jealousy. In his answers to the criminal letters issued, in Scotland, against him in April 1687, he says he is " wholly a stranger to Mr. Carstares, who is named as a witness against him," and does not know his face ;† but that this ignorance of his great patron's intimate counsellor and private chaplain should have continued until after the Revolution is exceedingly unaccountable, unless the one Scotch clergyman designedly avoided the other. Even in his narrative of his interview with the Prince after the landing at Torbay, at which Carstares was present, Burnet does not refer to him, nor does he mention the religious service which followed the disembarkation, and which Carstares

* McCormick, p. 25. † Wodrow, vol. iv. p. 409.

conducted, at the head of the troops. Either the vain and
forward Episcopalian thought the grave and discreet Presbyterian chaplain beneath his notice; or he discerned in him
a rival influence with the Prince, strong enough to stir his
jealousy and dislike.

The malcontents mustered more thickly. The emissaries
passed more and more busily between London and the
Hague. Letter after letter reached the Prince assuring him
of support. The very army and navy of his hapless father-
in-law wavered in their allegiance. Scotland, managed by
Sir John Dalrymple and well-chosen agents of his father's,
was ready for revolt. At last the cool and wary champion,
the centre of two nation's hopes, saw that the time had come
to answer to the call, and raise his standard in defence of the
"Protestant religion and the liberties of England." The
final preparations, the voyage to Torbay, the successful
landing, and the triumphant march to London, are among
the most familiar pictures in history.

Along with his Court-chaplaincy, Carstares held, as I have
already said, the office of second minister of the English
Church at Leyden, to which he had been appointed early in
1688.* On being required by the Prince to accompany the
expedition to England, he obtained leave of absence from the
burgomasters of Leyden, but, with characteristic caution, he
offered no resignation of his charge, while the issue of the
enterprise was still uncertain. He sailed for England in the
same ship with the Prince, and landed with him. Burnet—
who also was one of the royal chaplains, and who was in
another vessel, with the Prince's household—got ashore as
quickly as he could, and bustling up to the place where the
Prince stood, began to ask inopportune questions about the
proposed time and line of march. William, who had heard
some heedless remark of the talkative divine, to the effect
that it seemed predestined his Highness should not set foot
on English soil, took him good-humouredly by the hand;
but made no further answer to his queries, than by asking

* Steven, p. 312.

him what he thought of predestination now, and bidding
him—if he would be busy—go consult the Canons.*   Carstares, who was standing beside the Prince during this
colloquy, interposed with the suggestion that as soon as the
troops should be safe on shore, it would be right, and would
produce a salutary effect not only on the army, but on the
people of the country, that a solemn service of thanksgiving
should be held.   The Prince cordially assented.   When the
men were all on shore, they were drawn up on parade, and
Carstares performed divine service ; after which the troops, as
they stood along the beach, joined in singing the 118th
Psalm before they encamped.   This religious rite produced
a profound impression on the army.†

Carstares remained in constant attendance on William in
his advance, and on his arrival in London.

---

* McCormick, p. 34.   Burnet; and note, vol. iii. 328.

† McCormick, p. 34. Dalrymple, part i. book vi. p. 160. Dalrymple says
this suggestion was the foundation of " the future favour of Carstares." The
regard in which William held Carstares was, however, of earlier date and
deeper foundation. I find in the dedication to Carstares of Robert Fleming's
" Pindarick Poem," in memory of " William the Great," " to have been
eight and twenty years in his service, and to have had free and constant
access to him all that time, and all this without a frown, is a thing, all
circumstances being considered, that can hardly be paralleled in history."
Twenty-eight years from 1702 carry us back to 1674—the time at which
as we have seen, Carstares' first imprisonment began.

CHAPTER X.

Farewell to Leyden—Scottish Revolution—Carstares' position—Presbyterians and Episcopalians—Dundee—Ecclesiastical condition of Scotland.

CARSTARES never went back to his congregation in the "Begyn Chapel," at Leyden. William could not dispense with his services at Court; and soon after the successful revolution had established the Prince at Whitehall, Carstares gently took leave of Leyden in the following letter:—

> "*A Leurs Seigneuries, Messeigneurs Les Bourgue-Maistres de la*
> "*Ville de Leyden.*

"Ayant des obligations si grandes, et en si grande nombre, a vos Seigneuries, qui eurent la bonté de me considerer d'une maniere si particuliere lors que j'estois en votre ville, comme estranger, et reduit à quitter le pais de ma naissance, a fin de pouvoir ailleurs jouir du repos de ma conscience, que je ne pouvois avoir en ma patrie, je creu qu'il estoit de mon devoir, de me conduir d'une maniere, qui ne donnoit a vos Seigneuries aucun sujet de croir qu'elles avoient repandu leur faveurs sur une personne qui ne sceut pas les faire valoir comme il faut, et en avoir toute la reconnoissance possible. C'est pourquoy, Messeigneurs, comme je ne voulois pas, sans le consentment de vos Seigneuries, entreprendre de disposer de ma personne en accompagnant sa Majesté du present, en sa derniere expedition, laquelle fut entreprise avec autant de hazard qu'elle a esté suivie et couronné d'un succés glorieux; qui, comme il a eté, sera encore a ce que j'espere a l'avenir, pour la sureté de l'interest des protestans, et a la confusion des desseins de leurs adversaires. Ainsi, je ne scaurois estre content, si je ne fais scavoir a vos Seigneuries, que je continue a etre ici, en vertu des mêmes commandemens par les quelles vos Seigneuries m'ordonnerent d'y venir, et que je ne aurois pas plutot obtenu de sa Majesté la permission de quitter l'Angleterre; que ma premiere et

principale tasche sera de vous rendre mes devoirs, comme a mes
genereux bienfaiteurs : Et je travaillerai, avec l'aide de Dieu, ou a
m'aquitter du devoir de mon ministere envers l'eglise Angloise, qui
est sous la protection de vos Seigneuries, ou du moins a vous rendre
des raisons pourquoy je ne puis pas le faire, lesquelles seront
telles que j'espere qu'elles ne satisferont pas seulement vos
Seigneuries a mon egard ; mais aussi qu'elles les engageront a
continuer envers l'eglise Angloise la meme faveur que vous avez
eu la bonté de commencer en ma personne. Et je ne doute point,
que cela ne tournera a l'avantage de cette grande ville, et de cette
fameuse université, ausquelles vos Seigneuries ont un si grand
interest. Cependant je tascheray de tout mon pouvoir de faire en
sorte que cela reussisse au bien de l'une et de l'autre.

> " Messeigneuries
>> " de vos seigneuries, le tres humble
>> " et tres fidelle sujet et serviteur,
>>> " WILLIAM CARSTARES."

The settlement of the affairs of Scotland was an enterprise
which made a sagacious Scottish counsellor specially useful
to the Prince of Orange. Scotland was remote. Its factions
were embittered with a bitterness hardly known in England.
Its political life was demoralised to an extent a stranger
could scarcely understand. Its religion was deformed on
one side by an irrational fanaticism, on another by a hard
and insolent intolerance. Its public men were needy,
selfish, and unprincipled. It possessed a national independence, in virtue of which it might legally refuse to grant the
Scottish crown to the sovereign of England. The revenues
and the troops, which it could contribute to his resources in
the event of foreign war or domestic turmoils, were of little
account, compared with those of England ; although, if disaffected or hostile, its means of annoyance to its powerful
southern neighbour were almost unlimited. Its Highlands
were inhabited by a half-savage people, alien in race, language, manners, and religion from the Lowlanders ; and the
two races were full of mutual hatred and distrust. Every
political difficulty, which arose in a country disorganised
through misgovernment, and seething with the elements of

revolution, was intensified by the infusion of religious discord and sectarian enmities. At a time when continental statesmen, accepting the principles of Richelieu, were trying to remove religion from the political arena, the Scots were stubbornly insisting on mixing the secular and sacred, and were constantly intruding the *odium theologicum* on the conflicts of the senate and the field.* The keenness of Scotch faction, the fervour of Scotch jealousies and feuds, the pettiness of many of the interests involved, the difficulty of knowing what to believe and whom to trust, the pertinacity of the place-hunters, the contradictory claims and assertions of the religious parties, were all baffling and tedious to a foreigner used to politics of a larger scope, sufficiently preoccupied with the affairs of England, and personally a stranger to almost all the men with whom he had to deal. That familiar knowledge of the intricate questions at issue, and of the persons on whom their settlement must chiefly depend, which he did not possess, and could not acquire, he obtained in Carstares; and amongst a multitude who sought their own advantage, and were ready to serve him or betray him for the highest bribe, William knew he could always find in this one man a calm, experienced, and impartial judgment, a proved and unselfish fidelity, and counsel which was neither warped by personal desire of gain, nor inflamed by political or ecclesiastical ambition. The official position which Carstares already held at Court, as chaplain, was in due time confirmed, and had a proper stipend added to it; but from the beginning of those transactions which ended in the offer of the crown of Scotland to William and Mary, and in the re-establishment of Presbytery, he was virtually William's confidential adviser and secretary for Scotch affairs, and, as such, wielded a greater power than that of any of the ostensible ministers and officers of state.

* "The English were for a civil league : we for a religious Covenant," writes Baillie ('Letters,' vol. ii. p. 90) in the days of the Westminster Assembly ; and the words indicate at once the weakness and the strength of all Scotch political action from the Reformation to the Union.

William had, before leaving Holland, addressed to the people of Scotland a declaration, in which their wrongs were rehearsed, and concurrence in his enterprise was invited.* It made its way to Scotland, and, in spite of the prohibition of the Privy Council, was freely circulated, and received with general rejoicing. The bishops, however, hastened to protest against the common sentiment, by an offusive expression of their own unalterable loyalty. Many years had passed since Gladstanes, the "tulchan" Archbishop of St. Andrews, had said to James VI., "No estate are your Majesty's creatures as we are;" but the "creatures" of James VII. were not ashamed to repeat the confession. The King asked the English bishops to declare their "abhorrence" of the Dutch invasion.† They declined. Their existence did not depend on the caprice of a despot. It was "broad-based upon a people's will." Their office was secured by English law, and reverenced by the English nation. When James sent seven of them to the Tower, he raised a storm of wrath from Cumberland to Cornwall. Had he laid up all the Scotch prelates in Edinburgh Castle, and fed them there with the " bread of adversity and the water of affliction," the one half of the Scottish nation would have looked on with a kind of humorous surprise, the other would have believed he had been divinely led to do justice on those who had worn out the Saints of the Most High. The English bishops regarded James's throne with an attachment which was rooted in a constitutional principle, and not in a personal affection: the Scotch with an attachment, akin to that of the hound to the master who has fed him when he wanted food, and lashed him when he needed discipline. They gave utterance to this attachment now; addressing the deceitful, dull-witted, hard-hearted, loose-living convert to Popery and votary of absolutism, to whom they owed their places, as the "darling of Heaven;" praying that his hapless baby might inherit "the illustrious and heroic virtues" of his father; promising to foster in their flocks a steadfast

* Wodrow, vol iv. p. 470. Burnet, vol. iii. p. 302.
† Burnet, vol. iii. p. 315.

allegiance to King James "as an essential part of their religion;" and not permitting themselves to doubt that Heaven
would bestow on him two gifts (which were never to be his),
"the hearts of his subjects, and the necks of his enemies."*

The bishops' address did neither James nor themselves
any good. The Prince of Orange's declaration had free
course, and was publicly read at the crosses of the chief
burghs; and in Glasgow the two archbishops, along with
the pope, were burned in effigy by the students of the
university, without any interference on the part of the
authorities. A savage riot followed in Edinburgh, ending in
the wreck of the beautiful chapel of Holyrood. The King's
troops having been drawn up to England, on the rumour of
invasion, all control of popular passion was lost;† and the law
had been too long the associate of tyranny and injustice to
be respected for its own sake. The spirit of insubordination
spread. Before the end of the year, all the western and
south-western districts, where lay the strongholds of Presbytery, were in disorder. The fanatical "Hillmen" descended
from their coverts, and, inflaming the passions of the more
peaceable peasants and burghers, roused them to wage a petty
war against the obnoxious Episcopal ministers. No life was
taken, and no gross outrage committed; but many of the
"curates," as they were called, were driven from their manses,
and forbidden, with insults and threats, to return. Many, conscious of their unpopularity, and dreading the hatred of their
parishioners, deserted their charges of their own accord.‡
Meanwhile, men of "all sorts, degrees, and persuasions"
were flocking to London, in the hope of winning some of the
prizes of the hour, or of exercising some control upon the
course of events.§ The Presbyterians mustered numerously

---

* Wodrow, vol. iv. p. 468.

† Wodrow, vol. iv. p. 473. Balcarres' 'Account' (original edition of
1714), p. 37, et seq.

‡ Grub's 'Ecclesiastical History,' vol. iii. p. 294. 'A Memorial of the
Affairs of the Church of Scotland since the Revolution,' among the Graham
Dunlop MSS. (not in Carstares's handwriting).

§ Balcarres, p. 48.

and confidently. William's Scotch friends and advisers in
Holland had all been Presbyterian, as he was himself. The
expectations of their correspondents in Scotland had been
flattered by reports of the Prince's sympathy with their
sufferings, and desire to recognise their claims.* Besides
Carstares, he had brought with him from Holland, or been
followed by, Fletcher of Saltoun, Sir Patrick Hume, Lord
Melville, Lord Stair, and the Earl of Argyll, son of the
martyred earl, and grandson of the martyred marquis. The
official representative of the Episcopal clergy was Rose,
bishop of Edinburgh, who had been commissioned by his
brethren, in the month of November, to repair to London, in
order to assure King James of their devotion, and to consult
with the English prelates on the alarming malady of the
affairs of Church and State. By the time Rose reached
London King James was a fugitive; and the bishop had to
wait to see what favour he might find with his successor.†
Had he been a man of more policy, or of less obstinacy
(perhaps even in a Scotch bishop clinging to the tattered skirts
of James VII., it deserves to be called fidelity), he might
have found much favour, and might, possibly, have saved
the Scottish hierarchy from downfall. To William at
Whitehall, Scotch Presbyterianism did not appear to be so
potent an element in the national life, as to William at the
Hague. During the twenty-eight years of its enforced suppression, Presbytery had undeniably dwindled in numbers
and in influence. William, who was a Broad Churchman, or
" Latitudinarian " (as the phrase ran in his own day), looked

---

* Wodrow, vol. iv. p. 436.

† Evelyn in his diary (15th of January, 1689) says he dined, on that
day, with the Archbishop of Canterbury, where were Sir George Mackenzie
and a Scotch archbishop. "I found," he says, "by the Lord Advocate"
[Sir George had been restored to the office in February 1688] "that the
bishops of Scotland (who indeed were little worthy of that character, and
had done much mischief in that church) were now coming about to the
true interest, in this conjuncture which threatened to abolish the whole
hierarchy in that kingdom," &c. The "Scotch archbishop" must have
been Bishop Rose, as neither of the archbishops went to London.

upon forms of Church government with indifference; and while prepared to tolerate all, was inclined to give the sanction of national establishment to those only, which were upheld by supporters of his own authority. A thorough Erastian, he would yield no recognition to dogmatic or hierarchic pretensions, which were advanced by the avowed opponents of his government and policy. While tolerating all sections of the Church, he would help to establish that one, and that only, which he understood would be most in harmony with his own government, and with the wishes of the people. He would not maintain a church hostile to himself. He would not impose one hateful to the people. With these principles, the ecclesiastical settlement of Scotland perplexed him. He saw that Presbytery had lost ground; and he saw also that Episcopacy was Jacobite and intolerant. He did not wish to put it down; but if it would not abjure Jacobitism and intolerance, it must be put down. He had the promise of hearty Presbyterian support. Rose might have given him a promise equally gratifying, on behalf of the Episcopalians. Those whom Rose represented were not the men to quarrel with his policy, if its result should be to keep them in safe possession of their sees. William, through Compton, bishop of London, intimated to him that if the Scotch bishops and clergy would give him their support, he would give them his, and "throw off the Presbyterians." * Rose would not take the hint. At length he was admitted to an interview. "Are you going for Scotland?" asked William. "Yes, sir," answered Rose, "if you have any commands for me." "I hope," replied the Prince, "you will be kind to me, and follow the example of England." The bishop's answer was, "Sir, I will serve you as far as law, reason, or conscience, shall allow me." William turned on his heel without a word; and the fate of the Scotch Episcopal establishment was virtually sealed.† He had desired to

---

* See Cunningham, vol. ii. p. 264. Grub, vol. iii. p. 297, and the authorities there quoted.

† Ibid.

save it because he believed it was acceptable to many, if not most, of the powerful, though unprincipled, nobility of the kingdom ; because its continuance would secure a uniformity in the established religions of the three kingdoms ; and because he wished to disturb, as little as possible, the existing machinery of Church and State : but to preserve a disaffected Episcopate and a nonjuring clergy was impossible.

His finessing with the Episcopalians must have been disapproved by Carstares ; and the result, confirming the truth of Carstares's opinion of them, would no doubt lead William to lean more trustfully than ever on his chaplain's judgment. Carstares had warned him to beware of the Episcopal party. He had induced the Presbyterian ministers to send up commissioners to London with a dutiful and grateful address ; and he had introduced the deputation to the Prince, and used his utmost influence in their favour.* He assured the King that those whom they represented had been, and must necessarily be, his truest supporters in Scotland. The Episcopalians, on the other hand, had been, and were likely to remain, his enemies. In a paper entitled ' Hints to the King,' which McCormick possessed, written in Carstares's hand, we find the substance of the arguments which he used in behalf of the Presbyterians.† " The Episcopal party," he writes, " were generally disaffected to the Revolution, and enemies to the principles upon which it was conducted : whereas the Presbyterians had almost to a man declared for it, and were, moreover, the great body of the nation ; none, therefore, could think it strange that the friends of a government should enjoy all the encouragement it can afford,

---

* The address presented by the commissioners of the clergy, as well as that from the city of Edinburgh, was drawn up in Carstares's handwriting, and no doubt they were his composition. McCormick says he had the original copies, but they are not now to be found. McCormick, p. 37.

† Dalrymple says (part ii. book vi.) : " The person who persuaded King William to settle Presbytery in Scotland was Carstares. . . . . . The Rev. Mr. McCormick, in whose hands Carstares's papers are, gave me the heads of his discourse to King William, the freedom of which does equal honour to him who spoke and to him who listened to it."

whilst it withheld its countenance from open and avowed enemies. The Episcopal clergy in Scotland, particularly the prelates, had been so accustomed to warp their religious tenets with the political doctrines of regal supremacy, passive obedience, and non-resistance, that it would be inconsistent with the very end of his coming, to continue Episcopacy, upon its present footing in Scotland. As it was impossible for his Majesty to show that favour to the nonconformists in England, who were a numerous body, and at the same time zealously attached to revolution principles, which he was naturally disposed to do, because such a conduct would naturally awaken the jealousy of the Church of England, here was an opportunity of effectually demonstrating to them that the discouragements, they might labour under during his administration, were not owing to any prejudice he entertained against them, but to the necessity of the times, and the delicate situation in which he was placed."

Whatever pleas might be urged, however, on either side, for Presbytery or Episcopacy, the ultimate decision must mainly rest, as William knew, with the Scots themselves. The clergy, Episcopal and Presbyterian, were eager; but the laity, especially the Episcopal laity, were comparatively apathetic. Of the large number of them that had gathered in London, few seemed inclined to pronounce decidedly either for the bishops or the presbyters. They were, in fact, feeling their way among many pitfalls, and were more concerned for the security of their properties, and a share of the spoils of office, than for the liberties and religion of their country. Many of them who had hitherto been Episcopalians, had been so simply because Episcopacy was the official religion. Some of them, who sided in politics with the Presbyterian party, were not attached to Presbyterianism from religious conviction.

The thirty peers and eighty gentlemen, who took counsel together in London at William's invitation, and who, after three days' deliberation, begged him to assume the administration until a convention, summoned for the 16th of March, should meet, exhibited not a few of the unpleasant

characteristics which degraded the political life of their time
and country. Under the outward unanimity of their proposal to the Prince, there lurked dissimulation, mutual distrust, greedy self-seeking, predetermined treachery. The
course of their debates, as far as we can follow it, illustrated
the wary cunning with which the chiefs of the great houses,
and owners of large estates, tried to forestal the chances of
ill fortune on either hand. The Duke of Hamilton declared
for the convention ; his son, the Earl of Arran, for the recall
of King James, and the summoning of a free parliament.*
This division of interests between father and son was a
favourite device to save the lands and honours of the house,
whichever party should prevail. As Hamilton and Arran took
opposite sides ; so did Queensberry and Drumlanrig. The
Marquis of Atholl and his eldest son followed their example.
Stair was with the Prince, while Sir John Dalrymple had
been Lord Advocate to King James. James Steuart had
been the trusted agent of the late King, while his brother
was noted for his enthusiastic Presbyterianism. When
Montgomery took to plotting, at a later day, it was his
own brother who betrayed him.

It is not out of such materials that heroic history is made;
and the history of the Scotch Convention, in which men like
these were the leaders, is not heroic. The Convention itself
was, strictly speaking, an illegality. Its members were
chosen by electors who had set at naught the restrictions of
the still existing Test. But it could not, otherwise, have
been a fair representation of the opinion of the country.
Had the test been observed, the Convention would have been
full of Tories ; as it was, it was well filled with Whigs, sent
up from the counties and burghs. There were fifty members
for burghs ; forty-nine members for counties ; forty-two
peers, and nine bishops. Hamilton was proposed as president
by the revolutionary party. He was but a trimmer at the
best, with little tact, no firmness, and no sincerity of principle ;
but his election was carried against that of Atholl, the

* Balcarres. Dalrymple, vol. i. book vii.

Tory nominee, by a large majority. This victory determined the fate of the revolution. The waiters upon Providence went over to the winning side.

When the next vote was taken upon the resolutions declaring that James had forfeited the throne, and that William and Mary should be declared King and Queen of Scotland, only five members voted "Nay." The Convention wasted no time. Amidst much agitation and wavering within, and the conflicting terrors of Dundee and the westland rabble without, the revolutionary business was pushed on. The "Claim of Right" was rapidly adjusted; the "list of grievances" drawn up. In the former it was declared that "Prelacy and the superiority of any office in the Church above presbyters is, and hath been, a great and insupportable grievance and trouble to this nation, and contrary to the inclination of the generality of the people ever since the Reformation, and, therefore, ought to be abolished."

The Earl of Argyll, Sir James Montgomery, and Sir John Dalrymple were despatched to London, to convey to the elected sovereigns the offer of the crown, and to tender to them the coronation oath. On the 11th of May these commissioners executed their trust in the Banqueting House at Whitehall. Argyll, whose grandsire had crowned Charles II. at Scone, rehearsed the words of the oath, which William and Mary, with uplifted right hand, according to the Scottish mode of affirmation, repeated after him. At the last clause, which contained a promise to root out all heretics and enemies of the true worship of God, William paused. "I will not," he said, "lay myself under any obligation to be a persecutor." Neither the words of the oath, nor the laws of Scotland, replied the complaisant commissioners, laid any such obligation on him. "In that sense then, I swear," said William; and the ceremony was completed.* The liberal and Protestant hero was the

---

* This significant incident might, one should suppose, have been regarded as introducing and sanctioning, with a high authority, an era of lax interpretation and subscription of formulas. But, for all that, the framers of tests and exactors of subscription have scarcely, even yet, been discouraged.

sovereign of Scotland. In northern as in southern Britain the Revolution was an accomplished fact.*

The only real and energetic devotion to the lost cause was concentrated in the person of Claverhouse, now Dundee. His star burned brighter towards its setting, and his romantic title of "Bonnie Dundee" gains a certain chivalrous lustre from his unselfish faithfulness to a ruined master; and nobler associations gather round it than round his earlier name. Among the many false, time-serving, and mediocre politicians of the Convention, his character shines out in a fine light of military genius, personal daring, quick insight, and single-hearted loyalty, which almost persuade us to overlook for the time his cruelty as the persecutor of the Covenanters, and the harsh instrument of the tyranny of the Privy Council. His last walk along the Mall with King James and Lord Balcarres, when, on the eve of his own flight, the King confided to him the charge of the military affairs of Scotland; his brief attendance at the convention; his interview with the Duke of Gordon at the postern of the Castle which the Duke still held, half-heartedly, for King James; his retirement, with his squadron of veterans, beyond the Forth; his raising of the Highland clans, and the artfully prolonged campaign in which he evaded and perplexed his slow antagonist, Mackay; and, finally, his eagle swoop upon his enemy from the heights of Killiecrankie, on the summer eve, when "the evening star was shining on Schiehallion's distant head," are familiar to all Scotsmen—scenes of our country's stormy history too intensely coloured with native hues of passion and perfervid force, to be regarded without a throb of sympathy. Not so well known are the keen political ability, the fiery power of influencing and controlling men, the humorous discrimination of character and motive, that mark the last period of Dundee's career—emerging into their fair proportions when, relieved from the drudgery of a base

* Among the older authorities for the narrative given, I would refer the reader to Dalrymple; among the more recent, to Grub, Cunningham, and Hill Burton.

military police, he found himself the last stay of an ancient dynasty, and the head of an army which was to be the arbiter of a nation's fate. These characteristics reveal themselves in his conduct, and in his letters, which are the grains of salt that preserve Mr. Mark Napier's third volume of his 'Memoirs.' One letter, of date "27 June, 1689, Moy, in Lochaber," to Melfort, who was with King James in Ireland, is·so characteristic, and illustrates so vividly the broken and distracted condition of persons and affairs in Scotland, that it may be quoted. He is referring to letters which had been sent to him, for transmission to supposed loyalists.* "Most of the persons to whom they are directed are either put under bond, or in prisons, or gone out of the kingdom. The Advocate is gone for England, *a very honest man, firm beyond belief;* and Atholl is gone too *who did not know what to do.* Earl Hume who is very frank is taken prisoner to Edinburgh, but will be let out on security. Earl Breadalbane keeps close in a strong house he has, and *pretends the gout.* Earl Errol stays at home. So does Aberdeen. Earl Marischal is at Edinburgh but does not meddle. Earl Lauderdale *is right* and at home. The Bishops? I know not where they are! They are now *the Kirk invisible.* I will be forced to open the letter and send copies attested

* A great deal too much has been made by Sir Walter Scott and Lord Macaulay about Dundee's bad spelling. It was no worse than that of most of his contemporaries. Here are some samples, in proof, from the Leven and Melville Papers. *Duke of Hamilton:* "I cannot answer yours till the nixt, so shall only add that I ame, &c. I hope your Lop. will accquaint the King with what I have writt." *Earl of Eglinton:* "I cannot sufetiantly apologis for my self, for the only falt I ever was giltie of." *Sir John Dalrymple:* "I see clearly the Lords binch in Parliament is very right, except Ros, Annandaill and Mortoun. The barrons are pretty weill, bot the borrows are all possest. Argyl is not yett arryved. *Lord Melville:* "Between nyn and ten of the cloake last night at Hamptown Court." *Marquis of Atholl:* "I understand that my poor misfortunat sone Mungo oues his inlargement to your favour." *Lord Balcarres:* "The Counsell order me to wreit to the Vicount of Dundie and procure the Leard of Blairs liberty or I must goe to closs prisson agaiu." *Sir William Lockhart:* "Som tyms tuo, thrie or four did it. . . . Pray your Lordship mynd my brother Harie for L. C. Douglas companie."

to them, and keep the original till I can find out our Pri-
mate. The poor ministers are sorely oppressed over all.
They generally stand right . . . . Tarbat is *a great villain.*
Besides what he has done at Edinburgh, he has endeavoured
to seduce Locheil by offers of money, *which is under his
hand.* He is now gone up to secure his faction, (which is
melting) the two Dalrymples and others, against Skelmorly,
Polwart, Cardross, Ross, and others now joined with *that
worthy Prince Duke Hamilton* . . . . Even Casillis is gone
astray *misled by Gibby* [Burnet] . . . . All these will break
out, and many more when the King lands or any from him."[*]
And then he goes on with eager and sagacious plans for the
campaign and the recovery of the government; and all the
answer he could get was a promise of reinforcements that
never came, and a lying declaration from King James, containing an offer of a general indemnity and indulgence,
which his knavish secretary, in an accompanying letter,
explained could be withdrawn whenever His Sacred Majesty
pleased.[†] Just one month later, on the 27th of July, Dundee
fell at Killiecrankie, and the cause of James fell with him—
the cause of mediæval feudalism in government and in religion, as opposed to that of modern liberty,—never to rear its
head again in Scotland, except in spasmodic and wasted effort
to recover the irrecoverable.

Scotland had now an elected king, the chosen of the national
representatives. In the very act of mounting the throne of a
country, in which religious feud had raged with virulence for
more than a century, he had paused to refuse to assume any
function as a defender of a creed, or a rooter out of heretics
and schismatics. And though royal intrigue and Erastian
policy had, for a century, been devoted to the establishment
of Episcopacy, the formal instrument, which accompanied the
offer of the regal power, denounced that mode of church
government as an intolerable grievance. While the King's
refusal sprang from his own loyalty to the great principles of

<hr>

[*] Napier's 'Memoirs,' vol. iii. p. 601.
[†] Balcarres, p. 109. Burnet, vol. iv. p. 47.

religious freedom, and could not be altogether pleasing to a people very ignorant of these principles, and among whom one religious faction had never willingly tolerated another, the denunciation of Episcopacy proceeded from the representatives of the people themselves, and seemed to be the solemn expression of a national conviction. The conviction, however, was little better than a mongrel. There were among those who avowed it politicians, such as the Earl of Crawford, whose love for Presbytery was combined with an anxious hankering after the rents of bishoprics.* There were nobles, whose pride of place and family brooked ill the parade of episcopal titles, and the gravity of ecclesiastical rank, which put the dignitaries of the Church on a level with themselves. There were men, such as Stair (who had served alike under Cromwell and under Charles), or his son Sir John (who, as James's Lord Advocate, had hanged Renwick, the last of the "martyrs," and was now an eager revolutionist), to whom forms of church government were matters of indifference, but who found the Presbyterian form most in accord with their own political ideas and ends. There were those who had a sincere hatred of the wickedness of the system of which, since the Restoration, Episcopacy had been a central part. There were, especially, many truly attached, from education and conviction, to Presbytery, and who, though contemning the wild extremes of the fanatics, and with none of the old Covenanters' hope of seeing their own model and creed established throughout the empire, rejoiced to think that the day of their re-establishment, in Scotland at least, had now come. Even those who were inclined to maintain Episcopacy were little hopeful of being able to do so. It had done wickedly. It had been upheld by brutal force. There was no counting on the compliance with it, which years of persecution had produced, being a sincere compliance. If Episcopacy were to continue, the disaffection and fanaticism of the "Hill-

---

* "The bishoprics that my father had right to were many; but those he was possessed of were only Caithness, Ross, Murray, Dunkeld, and Dunblane." Lord Crawford, Leven and Melville Papers, p. 580.

men " must continue also, and increase. If it were abolished, the whole country might unite in a moderate Presbyterianism. Besides, William had been accepted as the king of England. Unless the union of the crowns was to be revoked, he must be made king of Scotland too; and without the concurrence of the Presbyterians of all parties, he never could be made king. Episcopacy must go, or the country must gird up its loins for a civil war within its own borders, and for a war with England. Considerations such as these appear to have ruled the decision of the majority of the Convention, in voting Episcopacy an intolerable grievance, which it behoved the redresser of the nation's wrongs to abolish.

The decision, though more or less agreeable to the mass of the people, was of course grossly offensive to the Episcopal clergy, and yet fell far short of the desires of the fanatical Presbyterians. Nothing would satisfy these, short of a denunciation of Episcopacy as sinful in itself, and a renewal of the Solemn League and Covenant. The low ground of practical policy, on which the Convention had taken its stand, was in their judgment unworthy of the children of the Covenant, and to promise allegiance to an uncovenanted king little better than apostasy. They held excited meetings and used violent language; but the dragoons no longer dispersed their conventicles, and their stern military spirit was judiciously allowed to expend itself in legitimate warfare. The " Cameronian " regiment, 800 strong, was drafted from their ranks, and under the gallant Cleland played a noble part in retrieving the disaster of Killiecrankie. The main body of the grim religionists, thus reduced in aggressive strength, and no longer stimulated by persecution, watched in sullen acquiescence the progress of events. They had done their work. Their injuries, their martyrdoms, their passionate protests, their inextinguishable vitality, their armed resistance to a "tyrant's and a bigot's bloody laws," had been powerful agents in producing the Revolution. But in the political settlement which followed it the remnant of the Covenanters and the Protesters had no part; nor indeed were they fit to have any.

On accepting the crown, William reconstructed the government of Scotland, which had been practically in abeyance since Perth had fled from Edinburgh, amidst the first riots of the Revolution. The new appointments had a strongly Presbyterian bias. The zealous Crawford was made President of the Parliament; Lord Melville, a staunch Presbyterian, sole Secretary of State; Stair became President of the Court of Session; his son Sir John, Lord Advocate; the Duke of Hamilton, whose church principles were vague, obtained the exalted office of Lord High Commissioner. Among the minor appointments was that of Carstares, as Scottish Chaplain to the King and Queen. To this office were annexed, for his life-time, the whole revenues of the Chapel Royal. The King assigned him apartments in Kensington Palace, and " intimated to him that he required his constant attendance upon his person."*

The condition of the Church in Scotland during the year 1689 was anomalous. The representatives of the nation, first in the Convention, had voted its established form of government an intolerable grievance, and next, when assembled in legal Parliament, had by a formal Act† abolished that prelatic form. But nothing had been substituted for it. Prelacy was overthrown; but Presbytery was not set up. The Church, without any rulers of its own, was entirely at the mercy of the State. The State's first exercise of authority was to order all ministers, officiating either in parish churches or in the meeting-houses of the indulged, to pray for William and Mary; and a commission, which sat from the dissolution of the Convention till the meeting of the Parliament, was empowered to eject those who disobeyed this order. After the meeting of Parliament the same power was assumed by the Privy Council, who, on the report of any parishioner, inquired into the minister's disobedience, and on finding it proved, deposed him, and obliged him to quit his manse and glebe within six months. About 300, chiefly in the southern,

* McCormick, p. 38.   Graham Dunlop MSS.
† 22nd of July, 1689.

western, and midland districts, were thus evicted; but in the northern retreats of Episcopacy and Jacobitism, few could be laid hold of, although Lord Crawford laboured zealously to purge out the adherents of the late king. The bishops did not venture to claim their former seats in the Parliament House. The "Kirk invisible" did not emerge from its hiding to raise a voice in its own behalf; and an appeal to Parliament, from some of the clergy of Aberdeen, pleading for the convocation of a national synod, was earnestly opposed by the Presbyterians, and rejected, although supported by the Duke of Hamilton. An attempt was made to procure the re-establishment of Presbytery on the ruins of the overturned Episcopate, but it was defeated; and the Parliament of 1689 separated without having sanctioned any church establishment. The work of demolition had gone far enough; but that of reconstruction was not even begun.*

The ecclesiastical elements capable of re-arrangement and re-distribution were those within, and those without, the late establishment. The clergy of the Church at the Restoration numbered rather more than 900. Of these about 350 were ejected for non-conformity on the establishment of Episcopacy. Their places were filled with the men whom Burnet describes as so unworthy of the clerical office. About eighty of the established clergy, along with Laurence Charteris, were turned out for refusing the rigid test of 1681. Their places again were filled up; in all likelihood with inferior men. At the Revolution about 300 were "rabbled" out of their parishes; and after the Revolution, as many more were removed on refusing to pray for the new King and Queen; leaving less than 500 actually in their parishes. Outside the former establishment, were ranged such of the clergy deprived in 1681 as remained in Scotland, and about sixty who still survived of those "outed" in 1662. Besides these, there were a few irregular preachers, who had skulked with the Hill-men, or

* Dalrymple, part ii. book iii. Burton (from 1688), vol. i. chap. ii. and chap. v. Grub, p. 299, et seq. Cunningham, &c.

led a precarious life from town to town, during the days of persecution.*

The late establishment, in its ritual and internal order, had little or nothing resembling the features of the Episcopal Church, as now existing in Scotland. It was episcopal in government, but no more. It had no liturgy. Scotland had lost this noble possession. The first liturgy used in the Reformed Church was that of Edward VI. It was superseded by the 'Book of Geneva,' as modified by Knox,† which remained in force till about the date of the Westminster Assembly. It then began to fall into gradual disuse. 'Laud's Liturgy,' which provoked the legendary cutty stool of Jenny Geddes and the civil war, never was accepted in Scotland, and was formally abjured by the General Assembly of 1638. At that time Henderson, Baillie, and the leaders of the Church were equally hostile to the liturgy of Laud, and to the Puritanic and Brownist innovations, which discarded liturgical forms altogether. These innovations, with their malign tendencies, however, gained strength as the civil war went on, and, finding high favour with the Protesters, became predominant influences during the time of the Commonwealth.‡ At the Restoration, that opposition to the churchly usages common to the Scotch Church and all the Reformed churches, which had vexed the soul of Henderson,§ had made such way that read prayers were unknown, and even the Lord's Prayer, the use of the Gloria Patri and of the Creed, and private devotion on entering churches, were discountenanced by the Established clergy.‖

---

* Wodrow, vol. iv. p. 127. Burton (from 1688), vol. i. chap. v. Sage's 'Fundamental Charter of Presbytery,' Preface. Grub, vol. iii. p. 305.

† Knox's 'History,' book i. Caldewood, vol. ii. p. 284.

‡ For a condensed account of the liturgical history of the Church, see Mr. Sprott's 'Introduction to the Book of Common Order.'

§ Baillie, vol. i. p. 249.

‖ "All the Presbyterian ministers in Scotland made use of the Christian forms of the Lord's Prayer, Creed, and Doxology, until Oliver's army invaded Scotland, and the independent chaplains in that army thought their own dispensation was above that of Geneva. Upon this, such of the

Under the bishops, the only liturgical effort that was made
was directed, and with but partial success, to the restoration or
preservation of those few bare usages, which the sound Presbyterians of the prior generation had, in vain, tried to protect
from the self-sufficient disrespect and condemnation of the
disorderly party. "The Covenanters of 1638 had a liturgy,
and the Episcopalians of Charles II.'s reign had none."* In
the subordinate government of the Church, the divergence
from the Episcopal model was as wide as in the matter of
ritual. The "curate" was aided in the discipline and rule
of his parish, as the Presbyterian minister had been, by a
kirk session. Nay, King Charles II., moved by a pious admiration of the kirk session, as an ecclesiastical institution,
issued in 1684 a proclamation empowering the curates to
select "elders" in their respective parishes, and ordering
those so selected to accept the office within fifteen days,
"under the pain of rebellion."† The presbytery too existed
as a legal church court, and exercised some of its ordinary
powers, such as examination of the fitness of presentees to
benefices.‡ The difference, indeed, between the Church with

Presbyterians as would recommend themselves to the usurper, and such
as had his ear, forbore those forms in the public worship, and by degrees
they fell into desuetude." 'Apology for the Clergy of Scotland,' London,
1693, p. 45.

* Hill Burton, vol. vii. p. 478.

† Wodrow, vol. iv. p. 178. See also 'Introduction to the Directory,'
by Rev. T. Leishman, D.D. (Blackwood, 1868).

‡ 'Apology for the Clergy,' p. 16. In Moodie's 'Present State of Scotland' (1682), the writer, a strong Episcopalian, gives many interesting
details upon the government of the Church during the enforced Episcopacy,
which show how slight the internal distinction was between Presbytery
and Episcopacy. He describes the Kirk Session, as it might be described
now, as being "in every parish," and consisting of the "chief and most
grave men of the parish, who are called elders and deacons," whose functions
he defines as the strictest Presbyterian might. The Presbytery comes next,
and his description would suit any presbytery now in Scotland, excepting
his statement that the moderator is chosen by the bishop; and that the
candidates for orders are, after examination, returned to the bishop for
ordination, instead of being ordained by the Presbyters themselves. He

bishops, and the Church without them, was so slight, and was embodied so entirely in the office of the bishops themselves, that it becomes the most striking illustration of the utter offensiveness of their office, and their persons, to the mass of the nation. Except that they held certain dignities, exercised a very slender spiritual authority over certain districts called "dioceses," and had seats in Parliament, the existence of the bishops would hardly have been obvious to their fellow-countrymen; had they not rendered themselves the instruments of an intolerable tyranny, and had not the maintenance of their order been made the excuse of its most inhuman excesses. They reaped as they had sown. Whatever dubiety might exist among the members of the Revolution Parliament as to the re-establishment of Presbytery, there was none expressed as to the abolition of an Episcopacy, which to them meant nothing greater or more reverend than the title and function of a few clergymen raised by the Court to a higher rank than that of others, but who found in that rank no claim to general respect, which might qualify its challenge of popular hatred. The bishops were overthrown. The national instinct felt that this was a relief, and read in it a promise of freedom and peace. Troublers of Israel, no doubt, might succeed them, but whosoever should succeed them could not, in any event, be worse than the right reverend fathers in God had been.

describes the synod as presided over by the bishop—the only apparent difference between synods in 1682 and in 1873. The General Assembly receives a great deal of abuse from him, and the model of the correct Episcopal General Assembly is laid down: a supreme court composed of bishops, deans, and two members from each presbytery (one of them to be the nominee of the bishop), and one member from each university: the calling of the Assembly to rest wholly with the crown; nothing to be proposed in it but by the King or his Commissioner, and nothing done by it to be of force till ratified by the sovereign. Moodie gives a deplorable account of the social position of the "curates." "Men," says he (p. 153), "think it a stain to their blood to place their sons in that function; and women are ashamed to marry with any of them." "They are accounted by many as the dross and refuse of the nation."

CHAPTER XI.

Dunlop—Montgomerie's Plot—Carstares in Ireland—Letters—Church affairs
in Scotland—General Assembly—Re-establishment of the old Church.

THERE is a dearth of Carstares' letters during the progress
of the Revolution and the year 1689. Most of those that
are extant of a later date are addressed to his brother-in-law,
William Dunlop, who had returned to Scotland after the
Revolution. Dunlop had lived an active life in Carolina,
where he had discharged, for a time, the somewhat incongruous functions of Presbyterian clergyman, and major of a
regiment of the provincial militia. On his return to Scotland, he had the choice of becoming minister either of Ochiltree or of his father's old parish of Paisley; but through his
brother-in-law's influence he obtained preferment to the
higher office of Principal of the University of Glasgow, to which
he was appointed by the King in November 1690.* Visitors,
with Lord Crawford at their head, were appointed in that year
to " purge " the universities, by exacting from the professors
oaths of allegiance to the new sovereigns and to the Confession of Faith. Several vacancies were caused by the removal
of those who refused to take the oaths; in some cases their
successors were not men of conspicuous ability, and the
Episcopal pamphleteers made merry with especial glee over
the dog Latin of Gilbert Rule, who took the place of the
learned Dr. Munro, as head of the University of Edinburgh.†

* Graham Dunlop MSS.

† 'The Spirit of Calumny and Slander Examined, &c.,' London, 1693.
'An Apology for the Clergy of Scotland,' London, 1693. Rule is accused
of having spoken of " guiltus idolatriae;" of having said of a lost bunch
of keys, " Nescio quid factum est de iis ; habui mox :" and of other equally
heinous transgressions.

Dunlop's appointment, however, in room of Dr. Fall, was
open to no reproach. His ability and his scholarship were
alike above challenge. It was a great satisfaction to Carstares
to have his sister and her husband pleasantly settled in
Glasgow; and he knew that in Dunlop he had a confidant
with whom he could freely and safely communicate on ecclesiastical affairs, and on whom he could rely as an able coadjutor in directing the general policy of the Church. King
William considered himself under particular obligations to
Dunlop, for the part he took in unravelling the Montgomerie
Plot. This conspiracy originated with a knot of disappointed
politicians, who went by the name of " The Club," and who,
having failed in the scramble for places after the Revolution,
grew seditious, and at last opened a correspondence with the
Jacobites, and intrigued for the restoration of King James.
Sir James Montgomerie, of Skelmorlie, was their leader.
One of his confederates was the Lord Ross. The old schemer
Ferguson, and Neville Payne, who was to suffer bitterly for
his share in it, were in the conspiracy. Ross either found
his courage fail, or his conscience trouble him. He sent
for Dunlop, and unbosomed himself to him,* and Dunlop,
with his approval, conveyed intelligence of the plot to
Lord Melville. From the following letter it may be inferred that before Ross's confession, Dunlop had been able to

---

* Lord Macaulay (ch. xvi.) has given an account of Dunlop's relations
to Ross, and of the conduct of both, which is full of absurd rhetorical
exaggerations. A reference to the only authorities he quotes (Balcarres,
and Leven and Melville Papers, ' Notes of Ross's Confession ') is enough to
show the amount of imaginative dressing he has given to the simple facts.
Here is the narrative of Balcarres, a strong Jacobite partisan, Lord Macaulay's
sole authority for this part of his story. " He sent for one Mr. Dunlop, a
fanatick minister, and revealed all he knew to him, and also told him that
he was under great troubles of conscience, and desired his prayers to enable
him to open his heart to him. After long prayers and many sighs and
tears, he told him all he knew; God was thanked, as being the effect, Mr.
Dunlop's prayers being heard. . . . Mr. D. (according to the custom of
his profession) made no secret of his confession." Here is Lord Macaulay's
amplification. " He pretended to be greatly troubled in mind, sent for a
celebrated Presbyterian minister, named Dunlop, and bemoaned himself

send Carstares some information bearing on this intrigue, as its date is prior to that at which the general disclosure was made.

Carstares to Dunlop.

" I had your surprising letter which His Majesty hath considered, and looks upon it as a business of moment, and is very desirous to know further particulars of it, as what may be of concern to his affairs.   He is willing to give a full indemnity to particular persons, but is not as yet so clear as to a general one.   You have done good service to your country, and a good King, who is very willing and desirous we should be happy.   He is sensible that the Presbyterians of that kingdom are his best friends, and will, I doubt not, treat them as such. . . . I hope to be with you ere long. . . . . Pray excuse me to Mr. Kennedy and Mr. Law, with such other ministers of Edinburgh as you shall think fit, that I did not see them when I was last down, nor did not acquaint them with my journey, first nor last, for both were a surprisal to myself, and I was not master of my time.   I hope that they will consider I am, in a manner, His Majesty's domestic servant, and therefore in different circumstances from what the rest of the brethren of the Presbytery are ; but you may show them that as (to say no more) the interest suffered no loss by my last journey,* so it shall be my endeavour that it sustain no prejudice by this. . . Adieu.   May 14, '90."

On the 4th of June the King set out on his expedition to Ireland.   Carstares accompanied him to Highlake, near Chester, whence he writes a hurried line to Dunlop to let

---

piteously.   ' There is a load on my conscience : there is a secret which I know that I ought to disclose : but I cannot bring myself to do it.'   Dunlop prayed long and fervently.   Ross groaned and wept ; at last it seemed that heaven had been stormed by the violence of supplication ; the truth came out, and many lies with it.   The divine and the penitent then returned thanks together. . . . Dunlop was in the meantime magnifying, wherever he went, the divine goodness which had by so humble an instrument as himself brought a noble person back to the right path."

---

* The " last journey " had probably been early in this year.   " By all means," writes Stair to Lord Melville in January, " bring down Mr. Carstares with you, whose prudence may be of much use."   Lord Melville came to Edinburgh soon after as Lord High Commissioner.   Graham Dunlop MSS.

him know that the King cannot see his friend Lord Ross,
but that he allows him to go to London and make what
terms he can with the Queen, who is acting as Regent in
her husband's absence. Ross accordingly, after some dubiety
and delay, went to London to plead his cause with Mary,*
somewhat, it should appear, to Melville's annoyance, who
wished, if it were possible, to get Montgomerie, rather than
Ross, safe out of the scrape. "I am under no particular
engagement to Ross," he writes to the Queen. "If we have
any, it's from the King himself by Mr. Carstares."† Mary
made a searching inquiry into the conspiracy, in the course
of which Ross was kept for a time in the Tower. The inquiry revealed a mass of treachery and intrigue, involving
more or less directly not a few notable partisans of Presbytery and of Episcopacy, of William and of James. No one,
however, was brought to trial for it. Montgomerie went
abroad; Ross, after a time, gained the confidence of William,
and was permitted to re-enter the public service. The conspiracy would have collapsed, without leaving any reproach
of severity upon the government, had not Neville Payne (an
English squire, who had retired to Scotland to be out of the
way of the law of England) been seized, and brutally tortured
with boot and thumbkin, in order to extract from him what
he knew of the secrets of the plot.‡

From Highlake, Carstares—charged by William and Portland (to whom the King had entrusted the general superintendence of Scotch affairs) with messages for Melville, who
had superseded Hamilton as Lord High Commissioner§—

* It is to Ross probably that Mary refers in a letter to William of the
8th of July, when she says, "This evening there has been a person with
me, from whom you heard at Chester, and whom you there ordered to come
to me, as he says." See Burnet's 'Memorial of Mary,' Appendix, p. xiii.

† Leven and Melville Papers, p. 493.

‡ Payne was the last person ever tortured for political causes in Scotland.
His case was as discreditable to the government of William as that of
Carstares was to the government of Charles. William signed the order for
his torture. Burton, vol. i. p. 85.

§ Leven and Melville Papers, p. 442.

came down to Edinburgh. There he appears to have been for some time busied in the expiscation of the various machinations, which had again exercised the unscrupulous activities of his old acquaintance Ferguson, and had engaged, in a treacherous correspondence with King James, one of the very commissioners who had conveyed the offer of his Scottish crown to King William.* He writes from Edinburgh on the 23rd of June: "We have been, of late, much alarmed here with the discovery of a conspiracy against their Majesties' government, in which persons of different qualities and interests are concerned. The thing is certain, tho' legal proofs cannot yet be got." Again he writes to a friend at Court on the 13th of July: "I was surprised to hear of the confinement of my Lord Ross, because I was informed he had fully satisfied the Queen, which if he have not done, I shall not presume to speak one word for him; but, Sir, if I could acquaint you at this distance how much my reputation is concerned in his safety, if he be not guilty of any new conspiracy, or concealment of any knowledge he may have had of former plots (in neither of which case I will offer to own him), you would not blame me for being concerned for him."†

Early in August he travelled by Chester and Holyhead to join the King in Ireland. William had won the battle of the Boyne, entered Dublin, taken Waterford, and begun the siege of Limerick.

"This place gives no news," writes Carstares to Dunlop on the 22nd of August, from the camp before Limerick, "but of hot work at this siege, which advanceth apace. We did upon Wednesday last take a fort that was near to the walls. The enemy made a brisk sally with foot and horse, but were quickly beat back. We are, this day, firing hard with great guns, and have beat down one of their towers upon the wall, and are in a fair way of making such a breach as shall capacitate our men to make an assault. The King is well and hearty. I thank you, dear brother, for your care of my

* Leven and Melville Papers, p. 478.   † Ibid. p. 469.

concerns. I hope Mr. Bruce will get for me all the money he can; I shall stand in need of a bill shortly. My dear love to my sisters, and Sarah in particular, with Sandie and Johnie. I am, I bless God, very well,—it is pleasant in a tent at this season. I believe you wish yourself with me. I hope you shall, in God's goodness, have comfortable news from us ere long. 23 *August.*—I cannot leave this till I have an opportunity of discoursing at some length with the King, which the heat of the siege doth not yet allow of. . . . We are bombing the town."

The siege of Limerick had to be raised, and the King returned early in September to England. "The King hath been so busied with a siege, which a sudden change of weather hath made unsuccessful," Carstares writes from Waterford on the 2nd of September, "that no affairs could be spoken of, and therefore the business of the Universities is not yet done. . . . We only wait a fair wind." He reached London on the 10th of September, along with the King, who had been entertained on the road from Bristol by the Dukes of Beaufort and Somerset, and who was received in his capital with many demonstrations of rejoicing. Carstares writes, thence, on the 4th of October, to Dunlop, who must have been applying to him on behalf of some delinquent: "I was surprised with your enclosed. Can you think that it is fit to direct such letters to me, or that I will deliver them? I have nothing to do with any against whom my master hath any displeasure. I shall do what is just and loyal and no more. . . . I am not certain if I shall be down against the Assembly, or some time after, and therefore I would have you employing my man as your servant, till you hear from me, and I shall be at the expence. Pray let me hear particularly from you, and endeavour that things be moderately managed at the Assembly." Again, on the 10th : "Dear Brother,—I leave you to my dear friend Mr. Gab. Cunningham* for news and

* One of the pre-Restoration ministers, of the moderate party. He was minister of Dunlop, and accepted the Indulgence. His biographer, in Wodrow's ' Analecta ' (vol. iii. p. 118), says, "He was great with all sort

my thoughts of things; only I must desire that your utmost
endeavours may be used for having a good issue put to this
Assembly. If they enter upon possession, and do some things
absolutely necessary for the settlement, I think it is enough
at this time, and an adjournment for some months may be
expedient.   I think all the pains I have been at, and the
success that in some small measure I have had, might at least
be acknowledged by some of the Ministry, and a letter wrote
to me to continue my endeavours; but this is to yourself, as
a confidant. Adieu, and love to sisters and cousins. Dear
brother, yours sincerely, L." *

These references to the Assembly need the illustration of
a slight sketch of the position of ecclesiastical affairs, in
Scotland, in this autumn of 1690. The Parliament had assembled in April. It was understood that the settlement of
the Church could not be again postponed; and the friends of
peace and order were uneasy, lest the crisis should only open
the way for new ecclesiastical contentions. The Viscount
Tarbat, who, despite the contumelious epithets of Dundee,†
bore himself, in those dubious days, more like a wise and
judicious statesman than almost any other politician of the
time, had written months before to Melville: "Pray consider
the matter of the Church, with such an eye as impartially
to consider not only what will satisfy one party, but the
whole." He had followed this up with a weighty memorial,
in which he sketched a plan of comprehension, that would
have kept in the establishment all ministers well affected to

---

of ministers, ~~indulged~~ and not indulged; all had a great veneration for
him. . . . He thought I was too long in preaching, and he told me what
the great and worthy Mr. John Livingstone said anent long preaching,
'that we that were ministers endeavoured sometime to preach the Spirit of
God into people; and then by our long preaching, ere ever we were aware,
we preached the Spirit of God again out of people.' Mr. Livingstone
hardly exceeded half an hour at a time."

* Why L., I don't know; but it is so in the MS.
† See *ante*, p. 171.

the government, and have reconciled moderate Episcopalians
to Presbytery, and moderate Presbyterians to Episcopacy, by
the adoption of Leighton's device of perpetual moderators.*
Crawford, on the other hand, would hear of nothing but
Presbytery pure and simple, neither "clogged" nor "restricted," and the Church "purged" from all leaven of
Prelacy.† The King's own leaning was in favour of comprehensive, and reconciling measures, as he had, anew and
recently, proved by his energetic promotion of the Toleration
Act, which had passed in England, and of the Comprehension Bill, which, to his chagrin, had been defeated by the
jealous bigotry of the Anglican clergy.‡ But large principles
of charity and tolerance had to yield precedence to the practical exigencies of Scotch politics. Week by week the
Episcopal ministers—even those who had stayed in their
churches on the condition of allegiance to King William—
grew more seditious.§ They "preached King James more
than Christ," and lent all their influence to the cause of
Jacobite stratagem and plot.‖ The possibility of a broadly
conciliatory and comprehensive settlement, which would have
pleased a moderate like Tarbat, decreased as loyalty to the
elected King became more and more the distinctive mark of
the staunch Presbyterians, of whom Crawford was the perfervid type. As in the days of the "tulchan" bishops of
James VI.; of the first enthusiasm of the Solemn League
and Covenant; and of the Restoration, political considerations ruled the destinies of the Church. Her own voice was
not consulted. Had a General Assembly been invited to
decide how the Church was to be governed, the vote of the
majority would undoubtedly have declared for Episcopacy; and
therefore Parliament took care to put that question out of
court before a General Assembly should get leave to sit, and

----

* Leven and Melville Papers, pp. 108 and 125.
† Ibid. pp. 140, 145, 172.
‡ Burnet, vol. iv. pp. 16–21.
§ Leven and Melville Papers, p. 140.
‖ General Mackay's 'Memoirs,' pp. 77, 210.

took care also to summon such an Assembly as should be certain never to recall that question.

The " Revolution Settlement" was, of all conceivable settlements, the most " Erastian." Parliament had broken down Presbytery, and set up Episcopacy in 1662. Parliament broke down Episcopacy, and set up Presbytery in 1689 and 1690. The one Parliament, no doubt, was but a servile junta; the other was a fairly representative body. But in neither case was the Church, whose fate was decreed, a party to the procedure. The State dealt with her as its obedient handmaid. It cannot be disputed that the cause of truth and freedom gained by this absolute conduct on the part of the State, and by its refusal to concede an independent and autonomous jurisdiction to the Church. Had the clergy, who claimed to represent the Church, been allowed to settle her affairs, the social and political life of the nation would have been likely to relapse into serfdom and corruption. It said little for the clergy, who had enjoyed an absolute predominance for twenty-eight years, that the general instinct should have recoiled from entrusting them with new or further power. But so it was. Men felt that it was safer for the common weal, that the reason and conscience of the people should speak through Parliament, than that the clergy should get their own way in a church court.

The first step towards the reconstitution of the Presbyterian establishment was the abolition of the Act of 1669, which had made the King supreme over all persons, and in all causes, civil and ecclesiastical. The next was to restore the surviving ministers, in number about sixty, who had been ejected for not conforming to Episcopacy after the Restoration. Then came the last and decisive measure, which established the Church on the basis of the Confession of Faith, and of the Presbyterian polity as defined and secured by the Act of 1592, which, through all vicissitudes, the Constitutional Presbyterians of Scotland had regarded as the unabrogated and fundamental Magna Charta of the Church. This voluminous measure—which revived the Act of 1592, ratified the Westminster Confession, repealed a long list of laws in favour of Episcopacy, legalised the illegal " rabblings " of the curates, vested the government of the Church in the survivors of the ejected ministers of 1661, and appointed a meeting of the General Assembly—was drafted by the wily pen of James Steuart,* and submitted to the King for his revision.

William had never wavered in his Scotch Church policy. He had always put the principles of toleration above theories of ecclesiastical government, and had maintained an impartial attitude between the rival parties. " Do not," said Carstares, in a paper addressed to the King, " do not afford the smallest suspicion to either party, whether in Church or State, that your Majesty is so far engrossed or monopolized by the other, as to adopt those private animosities or resentments, with which they are inflamed against each other."† The King acted on the advice. " If you find that that interest is strongest which is for restoring the government of the Church in the Presbyterian way, you shall endeavour to have it, with provision that the rules of discipline may be adjusted, and all occasion of complaint for rigour taken away." These were William's " instructions " for the Convention in March 1689.‡ " You are to pass one or more Acts, as the Parliament shall agree to," are his orders to Melville in February 1690, " for settling Church government, conform to the former instruction given thereanent."§ And now that the re-establishment of Presbytery was inevitable, he tried so to liberalise the measure as to render it not unwelcome to all but the bigots on either side who preferred their own dogmas and their own way to the general peace and good of Church and State.

On receiving the draft of the proposed Act, William sent for Carstares, and went over it with him, clause by clause;

* Coltness Collections, p. 94.
† McCormick, p. 40.
‡ Leven and Melville Papers, p. 2.
§ Ibid. p. 414.

after which he dictated to him the result of their consultation in a paper of "Remarks," which here follow: they were sent down to Lord Melville, and the Act was modified in conformity with them :—

"1mo. Whereas in the draught it is said, that the church of Scotland was reformed from popery by presbyters, *without prelacy*, his Majesty thinks, that, though this matter of fact may be true, which he doth not controvert; yet, it being contradicted by some, who speak of a power that superintendants had in the beginning of the reformation, which was like to that which bishops had afterwards, it were better it were otherwise expressed.

"2do. Whereas it is said, their Majesties do ratify the presbyterian church government to be *the only government of Christ's church in this kingdom*, his Majesty desires it may be expressed otherwise, thus, To be the government of the church in this kingdom established by law.

"3tio. Whereas it is said, that the government is to be exercised by sound presbyterians, and such as shall hereafter be owned by presbyterian judicatories *as such*, his Majesty thinks that the rule is too general, depending as to its particular determination upon particular men's opinion; and therefore he desires that what is said to be the meaning of the rule, in the reasons that were sent along with the act, may be expressed in the act itself, viz. That such as subscribe the Confession of Faith and Catechisms, and are willing to submit to the government of the church, being sober in their lives, sound in their doctrine, and qualified with gifts for the ministry, shall be admitted to the government.

"4to. Whereas it is desired to be enacted, that the general meeting of the ministers do appoint visitors for purging the church, &c. his Majesty thinks fit, that, for answering the objections that are proposed against this method in the reasons sent up to him along with the act, that what in these reasons is expressed by *may be*, as to the concern of his privy-council in that matter, and the presenting of these visitors to the commissioner, that he may see they are moderate men, be plainly expressed in the act itself, *that it should be*, &c.

"5to. As to what concerns the meeting of synods and general assemblies, his Majesty is willing that it should be enacted, that they meet at such and such times of the year, and so often as shall be judged necessary, provided always that they apply to him or the privy-council to know if there be any inconvenience as to public affairs in their meetings at such times, and have his approbation accordingly.

"6to. Whereas it is desired to be enacted, that the parishes of those thrust out by the people in the beginning of this revolution, be declared vacant, upon this reason, *because they were put upon congregations without their consent,* his Majesty desires it may be expressed in such a manner, as is perfectly consistent with the rights of patrons, which he hath the more reason to insist upon, that, in the paper sent up along with the act, it seems to be acknowledged that this procedure is extraordinary, and, therefore, ought not to be drawn into consequence.

"I A. B. do sincerely declare and promise, that I will own and submit to, and peaceably live under, the present government of the church, as it is by law established in this kingdom, and that I will heartily concur with and under it for the suppressing of vice and wickedness, the promoting of piety, and the purging the church of all erroneous and scandalous ministers.

"It is his Majesty's pleasure, that such as shall declare, as is above written, and assent and consent to the Confession of Faith now confirmed by act of parliament, as the standard of the protestant religion in that kingdom, shall be reputed sound and orthodox ministers.

"It is his Majesty's pleasure too, that those, who do not own and yield submission to the present church government in Scotland, shall have the like indulgence that the presbyterians have in England.

"His Majesty's desire to have what he grants to the church of Scotland to be lasting, and not temporary, makes him incline to have the above mentioned amendments made upon the act."

"The above remarks" (says McCormick) "were sent down to the Earl of Melville, along with a letter from the King. The original is in the possession of the Right Honourable the Earl of Leven, and is thus entitled :—

"'Remarks upon the Act for settling Church Government, with the King's Letter, May 22, 1690, whereby it will appear, Instructions were exactly observed, in so far as was possible, without hazarding the Ruin of the Kingdom.'

"There is only one particular in which the paper in my Lord Leven's custody differs from that which is in the hands of the publisher, and it is remarkable, viz. after the 6th remark, in the copy sent down to Lord Melville, it runs thus: 'His Majesty's resolution to be candid in what he does, and his desire that what is granted by him to the church may not be uneasy to him afterwards, incline him to have the above mentioned amendments in the act.'

"Then follows the letter.　　　　(*Supra scribitur*)　　W. R.

"'Right trusty, and right entirely beloved cousin and counsellor, We greet you well. We have considered the act anent church-government, and have returned the same, with the alterations we have thought proper should be made upon it; however, we leave you some latitude, which we wish you would use with as much caution as you can, and in the way will be most for our service. Given under our royal hand, at our court at Kensington, the 2d of May 1690, and of our reign the second year.　　　W. R.'"*

This famous Act was not passed without some difficulty and opposition.† When the House was about to consider the article which ratified the Confession of Faith, the Duke of Hamilton moved that the Confession itself "be read all over with a distinct and audible voice." The Laird of Craignish, either in grim joke or preternatural earnest, proposed that this should be done on the Lord's day, if done at all. The Duke's motion was adopted, and the long Confession was read. When the reading was finished, it was proposed that the Catechism and the Directory for Public Worship should come next. But this was too much for the wearied senators; the reading of the Confession was voted to be enough, and the Catechism and Directory were passed over, and so escaped embodiment in the Act.‡ At various points the Duke of Hamilton offered an opposition to the Bill, in the interests of a more indulgent treatment of the Episcopal ministers, which did not fail to rouse the suspicion of being dictated by resent-ment at Melville's preferment to the commissionership, quite as much as by real charity and liberality. At last, before the House divided on the article which, with undeniable injustice,

* McCormick, p. 46. Leven and Melville Papers, p. 436. McCormick prints from the copy in Carstares' hand. The copy in the Leven and Melville Papers has a few verbal differences.

† June 7, 1690.

‡ 'Account of the late Establishment, &c.,' London, 1693, pp. 42–3.

proposed to confirm the ejections by the " rabble," the Duke's temper gave way. "The vote should stand," he cried, "approve or not approve the deed of the rabble;" and when the article had passed, "he was sorry," he said, "that he should ever have sat in a Scottish Parliament where such naked iniquity was established into a law;" and, much in wrath, he marched out of the House, followed by several other members. As soon as he was gone it was proposed to pass the whole Act *in cumulo.* A voice was heard: "Fie! make haste! despatch, lest he return again, and create more trouble." It came from a Presbyterian minister, who had made his way into the House, and in the excitement of the moment called out to the members near him. The hint was taken. The whole Act was approven, and laid on the table to await the royal assent.*

It erred, as the legislation of the Parliament of the Restoration had erred, in an assertion and an exercise of powers which, even though tempered by William's impartial tolerance, were too harsh and absolute. The extreme measures of the Restoration were sure to beget a reaction of like extremes, when the oppressed had gained their opportunity of becoming oppressors; and the knowledge of the near danger of Jacobite plots, which might overthrow the still insecure fabric of the Revolution, disposed William's Scottish supporters to be more jealous and rigid than their master.

In one important respect, however, the settlement now legalised was a bolder step towards religious freedom than the Scots had taken since the days of James VI. While the "Confession" was adopted, without any critical examination, as a feasible doctrinal basis on which Presbyterian and Episcopalian could both plant their teaching, the "Covenant," which had been at its beginning the enthusiastic vow and bond of a unanimous people, and afterwards the watchword of a hot fanaticism and the instrument of a coarse religious tyranny, was dropped altogether out of sight. It was well known that the King would never sanction a legal recognition

* ' Account of the late Establishment, &c.,' London, 1693, p. 58, *et seq.*

of it. No voice was raised in Parliament on its behalf.*
The stern Cameronian remnant might lament it, as the Jews
lamented the broken walls of Zion; but it faded hopelessly
away, impotent and gloomy, like one of Ossian's ghosts.
From that day to this it has had no authority in Scotland,
and no living relation to the Church.

The question of patronage had still to be adjusted ere the
ecclesiastical legislation was complete. The King had been
in great doubt as to this point. At one time he had written
instructions that if the Parliament wished it, patronage was
to be abolished.† Again, in his ' Remarks ' he seemed to be
chary of touching the rights of patrons. " The King, as to
the settlement of Presbytery, seems only to stick at the
patronages," writes Sir William Lockhart, in April 1690.‡
" He says it's the interest of the crown and the taking of
men's property." Melville, however, urged by the more
heady of the ministers, and nervous lest he should forfeit
Presbyterian support, when Montgomerie was plotting and a
French fleet hovering on the coast, resolved to assume the
responsibility of sacrificing patronage. A plan was adopted
which took a middle course between purely popular election
and simple patronage; and the envied power of presenting to
benefices was conferred on the Protestant heritors, and the
elders of the parishes.§ This measure was distasteful to
William. He had no faith in popular election, or any approx-
imation to it. Like a lawyer, he regarded the right of
patronage as property, and he knew that his meddling with
it, even in Scotland, would alarm and irritate the English
clergy and the English patrons. The zealous Presbyterians
blamed Carstares for the King's reluctance to abolish this
patrimonial right, which they deemed an ecclesiastical grievance. But, " on the other hand," says McCormick, " Carstares in turn " blamed them " for asking more of King

* Burton, from 1688 : vol. i. p. 199, et seq.
† Leven and Melville Papers, p. 414.
‡ Ibid. p. 430.
§ See Burton, Grub, Cunningham.

William when he was established upon the throne than a compliance with the articles in the Claim of Right, which, without any mention of patronage, only complains of prelacy, or the superiority of any church officers above presbyters, as a grievance."* He proceeds to say that Carstares "knew that, from the Reformation down to the Revolution, in all the vicissitudes of church government, patronage had been the law of the land. He knew that by the Act of 1592, which has always been considered as the grand charter of Presbyterian government, patronages were incorporated with its very constitution. And he knew King William was too tender of his prerogative to allow any authority to the Act of Estates in 1649, which had been expressly rescinded by an Act of Parliament as a violation of the constitution. Besides, Mr. Carstares was too well acquainted with the circumstances of the country, with the King's temper, and with the indiscreet zeal of some of his brethren the Presbyterians, not to foresee the danger of gratifying them in all their demands; and he found himself obliged, in his applications to the King in their behalf, to make a just distinction betwixt what was essential to that form of church government, and what was absolutely distinct from it. Of this last kind he considered the article of patronage; and, instead of advising the repeal of that law as beneficial to the Church, he was afraid that such a step might have a quite contrary tendency, and prove, in the end, prejudicial, not only to the King's interest, but to the Presbyterians themselves, by throwing more power into their hands than they knew how to use with moderation.

"The clergy of that persuasion, having been deprived for near thirty years of the established livings, were then reduced to a state of absolute dependence upon their hearers for their subsistence—a circumstance extremely unfavourable to the dignity of the ministerial character, by deterring men of spirit from entering into that profession, and by debasing the minds of those who do. Mr. Carstares, from the first establishment of Presbytery, dreaded the consequences which

* McCormick, p. 43.

might ensue from intrusting the whole government of the Church and the disposal of its benefices in the hands of a set of men who were tainted with all the prejudices of the people, and at the same time irritated by a sense of recent injuries. Whilst he advised, therefore, the establishment of Presbytery, he was of opinion that it ought to be of the most moderate kind, and so modelled as to admit of the assumption of such of the Episcopal clergy as took the oaths to government upon the mildest terms. This he foresaw would not be the case unless the rights of patrons were preserved as a check upon the clergy.

"Although my Lord Melville did not differ, in his sentiments upon these subjects, from Mr. Carstares, his situation was widely different. As the head of the Presbyterians in Scotland, he saw that his whole credit and influence in administration depended upon that party's maintaining the superiority which it had acquired, and found himself obliged to yield to some of their demands in church matters which he did not approve.

"The Presbyterians, before the Revolution, as well as the dissenters from every legal establishment, had been in use to choose their own clergy, because they paid them for their labours out of their own pockets. As this was a privilege upon which they put a very high value, it was natural for the body of the people to wish to retain the election of their spiritual teachers, even when freed from the burden of their maintenance. They were encouraged to make this demand by the concessions which had already been made to them by King William, and especially by his placing Lord Melville, their patron, at the head of administration in Scotland. And that nobleman found himself so situated that he must either comply, or break with them for ever. He chose the former, and gave the royal assent to the Act repealing patronage."

It is difficult to determine how far William resented this concession. According to Burnet, he was highly offended with Melville;* and certainly, either in anger, or in order to

* Burnet, vol. iv. p. 110.

throw dust in the eyes of the English churchmen, he appeared to withdraw his favour from his Lord High Commissioner; and by-and-by he removed him from his office. Carstares, however, stood Melville's friend; and the report, or vindication of his policy, which the latter laid before the King, bears notes and alterations in Carstares's handwriting, which show that it had been submitted to his judicious revision.*

The Assembly met on the 16th of October, for the first time since Cromwell's dragoons had interrupted its debates in July 1653. Carstares's friend, Gabriel Cunningham, took the chair until the Assembly should, in the usual way, choose its moderator. The moderator chosen was Hugh Kennedy, a member of the old Protesting party. The Assembly numbered about one hundred and eighty members, clerical and lay. There were no representatives from the north, nor from any of the universities, except Edinburgh.†

Lord Carmichael, as the King's Commissioner, delivered his Majesty's "gracious letter," in which it was not difficult to trace the cautious and kindly inspiration of Carstares. "A calm and peaceable procedure," wrote the King, "will be no less pleasing to us than it becometh you. We never could be of the mind that violence was suited to the advancing of true religion, nor do we intend that our authority shall ever be a tool to the irregular passions of any party. Moderation is what religion enjoins, neighbouring churches expect from you, and we recommend to you."‡

The recommendation was not unneeded. Of the sixty ministers who had been restored, and who sat in the Assembly, almost all were of the old "Protesting" party. The younger men, who sat beside them, were those who had either studied and been licensed among the exiles in Holland, or who had

* Leven and Melville Papers, Preface.

† 'Historical Relation.' Cunningham had not been, as Dr. Cunningham states (vol. ii. p. 288), moderator of the last Assembly, but of the last of the two preliminary "General Meetings" of Presbyterians, held in Edinburgh before this Assembly.

‡ 'Acts of Assembly,' 1690.

skulked in Scotland, exercising an irregular ministry under
the ban of the law. The school of persecution is not one in
which men readily learn generosity and tolerance. Upon
the whole, however, the great principle of moderation was
fairly observed. The high-flying claims and dogmas of the
Covenant were quietly renounced in the Assembly, as they
had been in the Parliament. The few remaining ministers
of the Cameronians were allowed to relinquish their divisive
fanaticism, and to come into the Church. The assertion of a
jus divinum for Presbytery was foregone. All clergymen who
should subscribe the Confession of Faith, and promise submission to the Presbyterian government, were to be recognised
as ministers, and allowed to remain in the Church. There can
be no doubt that some external pressure was needed to insure
this moderation. Carstares, who had come to Edinburgh with
letters of instructions from the King, was in constant attendance at the Assembly, although he was not a member, restrain-
ing the zeal of the fanatical, and strengthening the hands of
the moderate. The anti-Episcopal fervour, which could not
find sufficient vent in the acts of Assembly, discharged itself
in frequent sermons in the churches of the town. " In general,
I assure you," writes a keen Episcopal pamphleteer, " they
were very nauseating to all rational persons ; for, except one
or two preached by Mr. Carstares and Mr. Robert Wyllie,
they were either miserably flat and dull, or else full of bitter
zeal against the Episcopal party."*

Before the Assembly rose, however, after a month's session,
it intrusted its "commission" or committee of the whole
House, with powers which were not likely to be used with
as much discretion as its own. This commission, divided
into two branches, was to visit the northern and the southern
districts, to purge out (where purgation had not been already
effected) " the insufficient, or scandalous, or erroneous, or
supinely negligent," and to admit to ministerial communion
those who, upon due trial, should be found " orthodox in
doctrine, of competent abilities, of a godly, peaceable, and

* ' Historical Relation.'

loyal conversation, and who shall be judged faithful to God and to this government."[*]

The course of this visitation brought the commission of divines and elders into dangerous proximity to the officers of the civil government, whose duty it was to exact the oaths of allegiance; and the inquiry into character, conduct, and principles which it authorized, trenched closely on the domain of inquisition and petty tyranny. The visitors, it is to be feared, acted in many cases with harshness and illiberality. "The reforming of the Church," says Tarbat, " by the Cameronian regiment can do no good ;"[†] and he prophesied that the " hot commission " which, in the north, had occasionally to call in the military to enforce its behests, would do more to sow discord than to foster peace. " Fifty thousand of the nation care not for Episcopacy, who now, by the present courses taken, do hate Presbytery; and if Presbytery and peace be settled in Scotland without [unless] presbyters be hemmed in, the former ministers protected from the angry party's wrath, and churchmen kept to the ministerial function, without extravaging on their fanciful jurisdiction, I am far mistaken."[‡] Tarbat's auguries proved true. The commission went too zealously to work. They made, like earlier zealots, in some districts, " havoc of the Church." The King at last was obliged to interpose on behalf of the more humane and indulgent policy, to which he had personally been always faithful.

But although, in carrying out the details of its formal reconstruction, the Church, as represented by its commissioners, might err in judgment and temper, the blame could not be laid on those, who defined and guaranteed the powers which were occasionally misused. No church could exist without a measure of self-government as large, at least, as that accorded to the new establishment; and the State had

---

* Assembly's letter to the King; Leven and Melville Papers, p. 568 ; and ' Acts of Assembly.'

† Leven and Melville Papers, p. 571.

‡ Ibid. p. 586.

undeniably done what it could, to animate that self-government with a spirit as liberal and conciliatory, as was compatible with the orderly reconstruction of the Church, and the perpetuity of the Revolution settlement. The idea of Carstares (for his was the predominating influence which, in the last resort, moulded the councils of the State) was to re-establish, in a country where people for a hundred years "had gone mad"* over questions of ecclesiastical polity, that form of government which the Reformed Church had at first assumed, and which appeared, on the whole, to be the best for, and the most agreeable to, the larger part of the nation. He did not look at Prelacy, or Presbytery, through the mists of mediæval superstition, but in the light of modern statesmanship and reason, believing that order to be the most divine, which did most to promote peace on earth and goodwill among men. He desired to include in the Church all who could be comprehended in an orthodox and loyal communion; and, with this view, no renunciation of Episcopacy was demanded from those Episcopal ministers, who should wish to abide in the national establishment. The only doctrinal symbol they were asked to accept was that "Confession of Faith" which, so far from being intolerable to Episcopalians, had been embodied in one of the oaths which they had readily taken in the days of Charles II. No rigid order of worship was laid down, against which a scrupulous conscience might have rebelled; in this regard there was the amplest freedom. The basis of the Church was essentially liberal; her door of entrance was wide; the policy designed for her was a policy of comprehensive tolerance. This undeniably was the wise and generous idea, of which the reality in some respects fell short. That it did so was in part, no doubt, owing to the fervour of the Presbyterians, but also, in no small degree, to the political and ecclesiastical position assumed by the Episcopalians. Politically they allied themselves, more and more exclusively, with Jacobitism. Ecclesiastically they became more and

* See letter of Lord Tarbat, Leven and Melville Papers, p. 586.

more imbued with "High Church" principles. In each case they retrograded. The unreasoning and immoral absolutism of the Stuarts was political barbarism, when compared with the constitutional order and freedom of the Revolution. The spirit of the Act of Uniformity, which, passing from Lambeth to St. Andrews, had infected the ecclesiastical mind of the North, was narrow, vain, and worldly, when contrasted with the broad and charitable instincts of the Anglican Church in the days which preceded the accession of the Stuarts. Hitherto, throughout all the conflicts of Presbytery and Prelacy, a hope had always survived that, eventually, the two opposing parties might somehow be amalgamated or reconciled. As the re-establishment of the Church progressed, the most hopeful must have become unwillingly, but surely, convinced that the political and ecclesiastical estrangement of Scotch Presbyterian and Scotch Episcopalian had passed out of the reach of reconcilement. Even those Episcopalians who were received into the Church, or rather who were not driven out, were in the Church, but not of it. And outside the Church a body of prelatic separatists was gradually formed, with all their prelatic characteristics hardened by the resentful sense of ill-treatment, who foiled every attempt at comprehension.

CHAPTER XII.

Carstares's position, work, and influence—With the King in Flanders—
Letters—Glencoe.

It would be foreign to the purpose of this book, which designs to present the history of an individual—and not of a
nation or a church—to enter upon the details of Scotch ecclesiastical affairs during the period when the Church was
slowly and painfully settling down upon its new foundation.
The details, indeed, can now hardly be the objects of very
keen human sympathy. The mutual jealousies of Presbyterian and Episcopalian, the harshness of the one, the shifti-
ness of the other, occupy the foreground so noisily and
obtrusively, and cross each other in such involved movement,
that one is apt to watch them rather with a sense of wearied
confusion, than of hearty interest. The scene is ennobled by
none of the heroic lights and shadows of Knox's conflict with
the ancient church. Its tameness is not stirred by any of
the rough but hardy independence of Andrew Melville's
wrestlings with King James. It lacks alike the wild fire of
the early Covenant, and the rich lustre of the varied learning and sound churchmanship, which gave weight to the
counsels, and dignity to the contests, of Henderson and
Baillie.

Many of the least comely features of modern Scottish Presbyterianism began, at this time, to emerge into a prominence
which they had never before attained; some of them, indeed,
had never before existed. The Puritanic and Brownist leaven,
which had tainted the church principles and practices of the
old Protesters, had lost none of its infection during the years
of persecution. There had been too free a growth of tha.

type of piety, at once fervid in feeling and undisciplined in
temper, of which we see a conspicuous illustration in Rutherford. Those points of external difference, which separated the
persecutors from the persecuted, had been magnified into dis-
torted proportions. The old sense of the solemnity of worship
had lost its force amidst the excitements of the conventicle,
and under the ministrations of the fanatical and unlearned.
That deterioration in the order and propriety of divine service;
which, for several generations since, has exposed the rites of
Scottish worshippers to the reproach of coarse familiarity and
meagre slovenliness, had begun. The infrequent communion,
and the preposterous preparatives and accompaniments of the
sacred celebration, had come into vogue. In fact, the Church
as restored in 1690, ill bore comparison with the Church as
restored in 1638. Those old men who remembered the glory
of the earlier temple, might well have wept, like Ezra's exiles,
as they watched the upbuilding of the later, and marked how
much more many of those who sought to direct it, were led
by political tact and secular wisdom, than by the gentle spirit
of Christian tolerance, and the humanising reverence for
catholic usage and tradition.* In such a period, a man like
Carstares, unimpassioned, sagacious, just, charitable, liberal,
of great experience, and of deep diplomatic skill, was of more
practical avail than a hero or an enthusiast. A prelatic Cyril,

---

* The pamphlets of the period bear ample testimony on these heads.
Making all allowance for the exaggerations of the Episcopal pamphleteers,
no doubt remains that during the twenty-eight years of Charles and James,
Scottish Presbyterianism had lost several of the old characteristics, which
were common to it, with all the other Reformed Churches. An interesting
reference to these will be found in Dr. T. Leishman's ' Introduction to the
Directory.' Sage (' Fundamental Charter,' p. 362) is very amusing about
the Presbyterian alterations and defections from better times. Old people,
he says (to take one instance), educated before the Donatism of the Covenant,
" will still uncover on entering the kirk ; but not the younger generation.
Mas. John himself enters church as mannerly as the coarsest cobbler in the
parish. In he steps, uncovers not till in the pulpit, claps straight on his
breech, and within a little falls to work as the Spirit moves him. All the
congregation must sit close in the time of prayer ; clap on their bonnets in
the time of sermon, &c."

or a Presbyterian Savonarola, would have burst all bonds of
Revolution settlements, and plunged Church and State into
chaotic turmoil.   Whether out of the chaos something might
not have emerged, of a higher type than modern Scottish
Presbytery and Episcopacy, is a question which may be left
open.

What work there was to do for Scotland, however, Carstares
did.   It was not work of the high reforming or constructive
sort; chiefly work of mediating, moderating, adjusting, not
less needful in its place than the other ; perhaps not so easy
as the other, because sustained by no loud encouragements of
excited sympathy, and done often silently and out of sight.
" I think," says Carstares, " all the pains I have been at, and
the success that in some small measure I have had, might,
at least, be acknowledged."   Was this a half-pathetic appeal
for friendly sympathy ; or was it a judicious hint for such an
expression of his brethren's approval, as might strengthen his
hands in guiding the policy of the King ?   Possibly, it combined both.   At times he found it hard enough to guide that
policy, partly from the King's actual indifference to Scotch
affairs, partly from the busy intrigues of opposing politicians.
No one, however, was able to supplant him in William's confidence, or to lessen the " extraordinary share "* which he had
in the government of his native country and in the personal
esteem and friendship of the King.   Wodrow, in his ' Analecta ' (which is not so trustworthy as his ' History'), records
an anecdote, in illustration of this, which we may take at what
it is worth.

He was told, he says, by Mr. Andrew Fullarton (minister
at Paisley), who " had it from good hands, that one morning,
when the King was in his closet, some Scotsmen fell a speaking to the King anent Mr. Carstares, and they told him it was
the mind of his best friends he should be removed from about

* Lord Hardwicke's note to Burnet, vol. iv. p. 535.   " Bishop Burnet
never mentions the extraordinary share, which Mr. Carstares a private
Scotch minister, had in the management there and in King William's
confidence."

him; and the English bishops were taking umbrage that he should have so much of his ear. The King gave them no answer. Within a while the King came forth to the chamber of presence, and the onwaiters, nobility, and others, made a lane for him to go through them. At the entry of the lane, Mr. Carstares stood. The King bowed to all as he came through them; and when he came near to Mr. Carstares, he put out his hand to him, and said, in the hearing of all, ' Honest William Carstares, how is all with thee this morning?' This was answer enough to his accusers."*

The great mass of the ' Carstares State Papers,' preserved by McCormick, proves how completely communication between Scotland and William lay under Carstares's control. " Few Scotsmen," says Macky, " had access to the King but by him, so that he was properly viceroy of that kingdom, and was called at Court Cardinal Carstares."† We gather the same from his own letters and papers among the Graham Dunlop MSS. Every question affecting Scotland seems to have been laid before him, and every measure ruled, more or less, by his advice. There was a proposal, for example, that the King should have a Scottish Council beside him in London. It was submitted to Carstares, who reports upon it thus: " In the time of King James the First, there were several persons of quality of Scotland, as I have heard, that had places about the King, which gave occasion to his having a Scots Council near his person, and made the power of his secretaries not very significant, nor much dreaded by the subjects. I do believe that things were much after the same manner in the time of Charles the First. After the restoration of Charles the Second, there was a Scots council at Court, in which there were some English, of whom the Earl of Clarendon was one, who having, as I have been informed, concerned himself too much in Scots affairs—being the great support of a party in Scotland that was opposed to Earl Lauderdale, then Secretary, and was headed by the late Earl

* ' Analecta,' vol. i. p. 264.
† ' Memoirs, &c.'; Characters of the Nobility of Scotland, p. 210.

of Middleton (who was at that time his majesty's commissioner),—Lauderdale for his own security, the hindering of Clarendon's meddling so much in Scots affairs, and the increasing of his own power, did procure the dissolving of this Council: but I did never hear that what he did, in this, was displeasing to the honest solid party of Scotland, for Lauderdale's management was, for some years after that, very fair and acceptable to the country, till engrossing all power to himself, and hindering, as much as was possible, any access to the King but to such as he knew to be his friends, his management came to be uneasy, and gave rise to strong factions in the kingdom. Now, there being at present heats and parties in Scotland, occasioned by what have been the different interests and contrary managements of secretaries (and these heats kept up by the apprehension that the different parties have of what may be the influence of a secretary for a kingdom that is at a distance from His Majesty), the proposal made to the King about having a Scots Council near his person seems to be rational enough.* But the having of a fixed Scots Council here hath, in my humble opinion, these inconveniencies: 1st, It will be a greater charge to the government than at present it can well bear, the least that can be allowed to each of this council being £600 sterling, yearly. 2dly, Such a fixed council would much lessen the authority of the King's Council in Scotland, because all men would have their eyes upon the Council here, and make their interest with it and applications to it. 3rdly, It would not, I am afraid, answer the end for which it is designed, of laying heats, and preventing parties; for as there would be a difficulty in choosing the men, so if they be of one party, the other will have greater apprehensions of their power and

---

* This paper is undated, but this sentence, and the other which alludes to trade, seem to refer to the time when James Johnston, who had been British envoy at Berlin (son of the Johnston of Warriston beheaded after the Restoration) was dismissed from the Secretaryship of State, which he had held as colleague to Sir John Dalrymple.

influence than of the Secretary's; and if they be mixed of
both parties, it will not be possible to hinder their intriguing
in their different ways, and making affairs at least as perplexed, if not more, than they are at present. 4thly, I am
afraid that if it be a fixed council, the King will be in some
difficulty as to the naming of those English that he would
have to be in it; for if they should be only Whigs, then the
other party would conclude that there must be more at
the bottom of this affair than there really is; and if they be
a mixture of Tories and Whigs, it will give a jealousy to
many of the Scots, and be an occasion of continual intriguing;
besides the present ferment betwixt the two nations as to
trade seems to make this business, at present, difficult. I
am indeed sensible that it is very fit that Scotland have an
opinion that secretaries do not possess entirely the King's
ear, nor have an uncontrolled influence in the management
of affairs; but the method the King hath followed this
winter in allowing a fair hearing to both parties in presence
of one another, and what he is about to do in calling a Scots
Council, may, I hope, be of great use to beget such an
opinion in that kingdom; especially if His Majesty shall think
fit to let his Scots Council, when he calls them, know that he
resolves to take such methods as shall ease his subjects
of fears of being prejudged by any unsuitable influence,
or partial suggestions of any particular persons about him.
I do, my Lord,* with all humility and candour, lay these
things before your Lordship with a sincere design for His
Majesty's service. I shall take the boldness, my Lord, to
say only one thing more, which is, that the more I consider the temper of this nation and their notions of government, together with their way of management with a respect
to His Majesty, the more I dread the thoughts of any of the
English being much concerned in our affairs, or of my countrymen having any encouragement to meddle with them as to

---

* Lord Portland, to whom, in general, Carstares's notes, memoranda, &c.,
were formally addressed.

the management of public business; and I must confess, this is one of my great exceptions against this fixed Scots Council here, as it is proposed."*

In another paper, we find him offering suggestions about an inquiry into " the funds of the poll and excise," which are alleged to be " almost sinking ;" about auditing the Treasury accounts ; leases of tithes ; the advantage of a " separate fund " for the King to give " in charity, or for reasonable gratifications to those of the Scots nation that apply to him, here or in Flanders, that may be fit objects of the King's charity or gratification." In another, he supplements the private and public 'Instructions,' which the King designed for his Commissioner to the Scottish Parliament; thus, for example :—" Private Instructions: . . . . The 6th private instruction may run thus; *If the Parliament cannot be brought to give supplies, but by offering Acts which are either contrary to your instructions, or not contained in them, you are then to adjourn, &c."*—" Public Instructions: . . . . To the end of the 17th instruction these words may be added : *But you are not to be sudden in passing this Act, because upon a further consideration of the matter of it we may more fully instruct you about it. . . . This may be added to the private instructions, if His Majesty think fit: As to our 23rd public instruction, about encouraging trade, you are to take particular care that nothing be done in that matter that may raise jealousies, or disturb our affairs in our kingdom of England.* This private instruction may also, if His Majesty please, be added : *You are to endeavour that supplies for the forces, of as long continuance as can be obtained, be one of the first things granted by the Parliament, and that other business that would delay them be as much kept off as can be, till they be expeded."*

Amidst the charge of public affairs to which these papers bear witness, Carstares was never neglectful of the claims of private friendship, and seems to have marked with observant

* Graham Dunlop MSS. The proposal was not carried out.

concern, and remembered with tenacity, anything that touched the interests of his kindred or friends. The letter which follows is undated and unaddressed, so that the recipient cannot be identified; but its kindly faithfulness is very characteristic of the writer :—

" My Lord,—Nothing but a dutiful respect to your Lordship, and a sincere and entirely affectionate concern for your Lordship's honour and true interest, could have obliged me to give your Lordship the trouble of these lines, and to lay before you my great grief because of reports, not whispered, but loudly talked of, here, as if your Lordship had forsaken that modest way of managing yourself, that even in your younger years, and amidst many tentations you were honoured for, and highly esteemed. I have, indeed, my Lord, had too much reason to be sensible that when one is envied and hath ill-willers, many methods are used, without regard either to truth or justice, to blast his reputation and lessen his credit ; and I would gladly persuade myself that what is said to your Lordship's disadvantage is only an effect of malice ; and I shall be very unwillingly brought to believe that you shall ever be left so far to yourself as to forget your God, your religion, your honour, and your temporal as well as eternal interest, your noble family, and what the faith of a judgment to come and a future state doth call for from your Lordship, and to follow those whose ways are moveable that you cannot know them, and whose feet go down to death and their steps take hold on hell. Nay, my Lord, the gracious and good God forbid it should be thus. I can, for myself, sincerely say, that I never observed anything in your Lordship that gave me the least ground to suspect that your Lordship was the least inclined to [*words illegible*], and may you never be so ; but after what I heard when I was at London, and what is talked of here, I could not satisfy myself without laying the matter before your Lordship, with the most affectionate concern :—and if there be any impertinency in it, I hope your Lordship will impute it to the greatness of my affection to your Lordship's person, and to the memory of those that are gone, for I shall never cease to be,

" With the greatest respect,

" My Lord, &c."

As soon as the Assembly rose, on the 13th of November, 1690, Carstares returned to London, carrying with him, for the King, transcripts of the minutes.*   "I have been exceedingly obliged to him," says Lord Carmichael, the Commissioner.   "His coming here has been of no small use to His Majesty's service and interest."   Lord Cardross, who had been with Dunlop in Carolina, and was now General of the Mint, takes advantage of his journey to send up some specimens of the new Scotch coins of William and Mary. "The Mint is now going," he writes to Melville, "and I have sent up a few of each species to your Lordship by Mr. Carstares: if your Lordship think fit you may show them to the King and Queen.   The tenpences do not look so clear and well as the next will; however, I could not but send of them as they were, being the first.   The fault is only in the blanching, it being done with old materials that was lying in the Mint; but your Lordship may observe it helped in the fortypences.'

On the 2nd of December, Carstares writes to Dunlop, from London, "I have done what I could for Arran" (Hamilton's eldest son), "and I would fain hope he will not render himself useless to his country by a groundless scruple.   I do find there is no particular prejudice against him."   No sentence could disclose more thoroughly that policy of practical compromise, which was the only course open to a ruler like William.   Arran had finessed at the Revolution, had been implicated in Montgomerie's plot,† and now was not only holding back from taking the oaths to government, but

* "If he would have undertaken to make the report alone," writes Lord Carmichael to Melville (Leven and Melville Papers, p. 570), "it might well have been rested on; but he was unwilling to do it, and was desirous that others should have been sent; he has been very active to have matters go right, which has had very good effect."   This disproves the insinuation of the Episcopal pamphleteer, who says, "It's said that Mr. Carstares, whom the King had sent down with letters of instruction to the Assembly, expected that they would have honoured him with that trust; but whether it was out of any jealousy of his conduct, or faithfulness, or if it was to gratify others who might have had particular designs of their own, they passed by Mr. Carstares and gave the employment to Mr. Gilbert Rule and Mr. David Blair."   'Historical Relation,' p. 63.

† Burton, from 1688; vol. i. p. 81.

actually meddling with a new conspiracy. To the heir-apparent, however, of the great house of Hamilton, much should be forgiven, if only he would lend his influence to the established order.

On the 15th of January he again writes to ..is brother-in-law, telling him he is going to Holland with the King. "I wonder," he adds, "I hear not of Magg's marriage ; but your principalship* makes you neglect all things else." According to Mr. Ferrie, his sister Margaret married, first, the Rev. William Mackay, minister of Markinch, and afterwards, Major Coult, of Edinburgh Castle. It is of her that McCormick relates the incident† which Dean Stanley quotes, as illustrating " the freshness and simplicity of Carstares' pastoral character, amongst the absorbing public affairs which occupied him ;" illustrating also, I may add, that strong feeling of family affection and faithfulness to the claims of kindred, which was one of his marked characteristics. "A few days after her husband's death," says McCormick, " Mr. Carstares came down from London to transact some matters of importance with King William's ministers in Scotland. She, hearing of his arrival, came over to Edinburgh to see him. Upon calling at his lodgings in the forenoon, she was told he was not at leisure, as several of the nobility and officers of state were just gone in to him. She then bid his servant only whisper him that she desired to know when it would be most convenient for him to see her. He returned for answer 'immediately'; and leaving the company, ran to her, and embraced her in the most affectionate manner. Upon her attempting to make some apology for her unseasonable interruption to business, ' Make yourself easy,' says he, ' these gentlemen are come hither, not on my account, but their own. They will wait with patience till I return. You know I never pray long.' And after a short, but fervent prayer adapted to her melancholy

---

* Carstares never employed the modern vulgarism of calling this office a " Principality."

† McCormick, p. 89.   Stanley's ' Church of Scotland.' p. 120.

circumstances, he fixed the time when he would see her more at leisure, and returned, all in tears, to his company."

On January the 18th he sailed for Holland, with William, who was about to open the great Congress at the Hague. When thus on foreign or military service with the King, he had, in addition to his ordinary salary, an allowance for travelling and camp expenses, at the rate of £500 a year. As usual, he kept up a correspondence with his brother-in-law.

Carstares to Dunlop.

"Hague, Feb. 10, st. v. '91.

"DEAR BROTHER.—Nothing can be done as to the affairs of the Universities at present, but I shall not be wanting in doing my endeavours as I shall have opportunity. As for what concerns myself, I have no confidence to act in it,* for I would not do anything that might render me incapable any way to serve, in my capacity, the public interest. Pray, make Duke Hamilton your friend: if he come up to Court, I doubt not but he will be one to me, seeing some of the greatest men know my concern for him and that noble family. Dr. Canaries and Mr. Leask are here, doing what they can for their friends. I shall be faithful in my capacity to the true interest of the King and country. We have here the Electors of Bavaria and Brandenburg, the Duke of Wirtemberg, Landgrave of Hesse, Governor of the Spanish Netherlands, and many other great persons. I hope we shall have a good issue of this great meeting. . . . I hope my Lord Arran will be sensible of the King's kindness, and see, at last, that it is his interest and duty to be upon a bottom with him. My dear love to my sister and your family. Adieu."

This Dr. Canaries was one of the disestablished clergy, peculiarly obnoxious to the Presbyterians,† and was now at Court as the representative of the Episcopalians.‡ He carried to William an assurance of their loyalty, and a

---

* It had been proposed to call Carstares to a church in Edinburgh.

† 'Apology for the Clergy,' p. 103.

‡ Canaries had been at first a Roman Catholic: then minister of Selkirk, and finally suspended from his ministry, by his bishop acting under the orders of Perth, the Chancellor, whose hostility Canaries had provoked by preaching, in St. Giles's, Edinburgh, a sermon against the errors of Rome. Grub, vol. iii. p. 285.

complaint of the hardships they were enduring at the hands of the Commission of the Kirk. The result was a letter from the King to the Commission recommending lenity, and begging that no Episcopal minister, who should qualify to the government, and submit to Presbytery, should be disturbed. It was hard, no doubt, in William's private opinion, that in the midst of the Congress which was to rule the policy of half of Europe, and to direct the great coalition against his life-long enemy, France, he should be molested with the squabbles of Scotch ecclesiastics. If there were any more complaints of hardships (Sir John Dalrymple, who was in attendance at the Hague, writes to Melville) the Commission must investigate and settle the cases "impartially, and put the King to no further trouble."* To Crawford and the zealous Presbyterians, the concession accorded to the aggrieved complainers, ignoring, as it did, the Confession of Faith, was a fatal defection from the path of righteous government. Such ill-advised lenity, Crawford assures Melville, is attributed by the Jacobite and Episcopal party to fear, and not to charity, and only serves to inflame their insolence "to a strange pitch." "It has almost, if not altogether," he groans, "unhinged both Church and State."† The King's letter, however, only reiterated the constant principle of moderation and comprehension, in which his own just and liberal instincts had always been confirmed by the counsels of Carstares.

While William was busy with the statesmen and soldiers of the Congress, Carstares found time to see his kindred at Rotterdam; and to revisit Utrecht, where he met, for the first time, Edmund Calamy, whom he ever afterwards numbered among his esteemed friends. Calamy, who was still a student, about twenty years younger than Carstares, says, "One of his principal aims was to pick up some that might be fit and qualified to make masters of in the several colleges of Scotland, which had been before either too much

---

* Leven and Melville Papers, p. 595.
† Ibid. pp. 596, 601.

neglected, or filled with improper persons. Here it was that
I had my first acquaintance with that excellent person, whose
friendship I had afterwards so much reason to value myself
upon. He found me pretty studious and retired, and was
pleased to enter into considerable freedom with me, which
was afterwards improved both in Scotland and England. He
then several times told me that if, when the course of my
studies was finished, I would look towards North Britain, and
could like a professor's life among them, he would readily
give me his utmost interest towards my obtaining as good
encouragement as I reasonably could desire." *

The wants of the Scotch universities, both in regard to
men and to money, were much in Carstares' mind. Himself
an accomplished scholar, he could not but see, with regret
and alarm, the decadence of learning and culture among the
clergy, which had marked the evil years since the Restoration. The persecuted and expelled ministers had little
opportunity of study. The younger men, who furtively entered
the ministry between 1662 and 1688, set greater store by
Presbyterian zeal than by liberal scholarship or theological
science. The "curates," as a body, were more occupied
with enforcing conformity, than cultivating their minds.
The few men among them of intellectual power and solid
learning became professors in the universities; and many
of these had been removed, by Crawford's commission, for
declining the oath of allegiance, so that the Church was
without the means of training up properly educated candidates for the ministry. Carstares bestirred himself to secure
able professors, and to provide the adequate salaries, without
which it would be neither easy nor honourable to solicit, and
to secure, the services of the erudite or the pious. " I have
spoken to the King," he writes in April, after his return to
London, " about allowing to the universities some part of the
bishop's rents, and he seems to be much more inclined to
do so than to give them to particular men. I shall not fail
to push the matter as far as it will go, because it is service

* Calamy's ' Historical Account of my own Life,' vol. i. p. 172.

to the King and country. I could be content too you fell
upon some method to call a foreign professor, such as De
Vries at Utrecht: if you will get a call, I shall promote it."[*]

In the month of May, the King returned to the Continent,
to take the command of the forces of the Coalition in the
campaign against the French. His visit to England had
been busied with the examination of the plotters, who, urged
by political discontent, or personal spleen, had, during the
winter of 1690–1, been trying to undermine his throne;
among whom were not a few of the very men who were
eating his bread, and had sworn to be faithful to his service.[†]
Arran, on whom Carstares' remonstrances had been thrown
away, was involved in this new conspiracy. He was seized,
along with others of the Scots nobility; but the King, with
a generosity which should have disarmed and shamed disaffection and intrigue, gave orders that the culprits should be
set at liberty, if they would give their word of honour not
to disturb the government. Arran refused. "I will not
give my word," he said, with a kind of perverse candour,
" because I am sure I could not keep it."[‡]

Carstares was with the King for a short time at Loo, and
in June went with him to the camp. While Ginkell and
Mackay were successfully finishing the war which had lin-
gered for nearly two years in Ireland, William conducted a
campaign in Flanders, which was but languid and uneventful.

No great action was fought, calling out that calm courage
and contempt of danger and death, which made the impassive

---

* "M. de Vries, the chief philosophy professor, was very civil to the
English and free in conversing with them. He was no great lover of the
Prince of Orange, but a mighty friend to the Louvenstein faction, and yet
was far from falling in with the Remonstrants in matters theological. He
was prejudiced against the dissenters in England, of whom he had wrong
notions." Calamy, vol. i. p. 158.

† "The Prince of Orange is mortally hated by the English. They see
very fairly that he hath no love for them, neither doth he confide in them,
but all in his Dutch. . . . . He is cursed daily by those of his council,
his bedchamber, and others that have very good employment under him."
Macpherson's 'State Papers,' vol. i. p. 390.

‡ Dalrymple, part ii. book vi. p. 169.

Dutchman, who was a wet blanket to his courtiers, a hero to
his troops.* That courage, Carstares used to say, was not
constitutional hardihood merely; it was fortified and sustained
by religious principle. He had the best opportunities of
judging, for he accompanied the King in his chariot to every
field of battle, remaining with him until the engagement began.† William's tranquillity and composure, before the action,
were only equalled by his " absolute contempt of danger in
the field."

Carstares to Dunlop.

" I had yours concerning the Earl of Arran, and am heartily
sorry that he cannot give his Majesty satisfaction, in giving his
word of honour not to act against the government for a few months,
which is all, as the Master of Stair ‡ told me (he speaks of him
favourably enough), was desired of him. You know how much I
employed myself for him, and what an honour I have for the family;
but the King's service must be dear to me beyond that of any else,
as it shall always I hope be. . . . I wrote to you, long ago, about
the business of the University, and told you that I found the King
inclined to give all encouragement, and I think you may have an
allowance for an extraordinary professor of Divinity, and another of
philosophy; but I would have them from Holland, where they are
very good, and I suppose it will please the King best. . . . . .
At the camp four hours on this side Namur. June 15, '91."

Carstares to Dunlop.

" Gembloux, 3 leagues from Namur,
" July 6, st. v.

. . . . . . " There hath been a design to set fire to Bruges and
Brussells in several places at once, that the French, who were to
have forces near, might possess themselves of these towns, when the
inhabitants and garrison were busied in quenching the fire; but the
treachery is discovered, and several committed to prison upon that
account. There is, we hear, great discouragement in the French
army under Luxemburgh, which we impute to the news from
Vienna and Savoy; from the first whereof it is hoped we shall,
ere long, hear of the conclusion of a peace betwixt the Turk
and Emperor. We have been here three weeks, but a little time

---

* Burnet, vol. iv. p. 2.   † McCormick, p. 38.
‡ Sir John Dalrymple.

will show that our stay hath not been without good reason ; for the King is known not to lose time in acting. . . You want not enemies; I hope they shall have no advantage of you, as to any neglect of the duties of your place. I gave you this hint from London. You are obliged to Duke Hamilton's kindness. You may, if you think fit, give my most humble duty to his Grace and the Duchess. I think now is the time for the Earl of Arran to give his word of honour not to disturb the government any way,—nay, to own it by offering to take the oath of allegiance. He is now under no constraint, and I am apt to think he cannot have a fitter season for doing it with honour and conscience too ; and pray tell my good Lord Carmichael that this is my opinion ; and I speak not in this matter at random. . . . . My humble service to the Provost of Edinburgh, who I hope hath received mine. I do not find that either the King or Lord Portland have any unfavourable thoughts of him ; and this I say with reason. Pray give my humble duty to my Lord and my Lady Cardross, to whom I shall always be a true friend and faithful servant. Show him my news, as also to worthy Mr. Rule, whom I kindly salute, and shall do all in the concerns of the church that shall be in my power, if I be not incapacitated by not having particular accounts of what passeth. . . I did acquaint my Lord Portland with what you wrote to me concerning the frankness of Glasgow for the government. Adieu, goodly principal, and my dear love to Sandy and Johnie. I fancy you will think that in my writing I am like the Muirlandmen in their drinking. . . The King is hearty and well, and so is the Master of Stair, who carries very civilly to me."

Carstares to Dunlop.

"At the head-quarters, 2 leagues from Philippeville,
"August 3rd.

. . . . . "I could wish some way were taken to acquaint some sober men of the Church of England with the reasonableness of their procedure,—I mean the Commission—which, I suppose, would be pleasing to the King. I hope their carriage at this time shall be such as that their enemies shall have no advantage of them, and they may be assured of all the service that is in my power. We have here a strong army, and did upon Friday last march towards the enemy, and stood twenty-four hours within little more than an English mile of their camp ; but they lay still, and had they not been very strongly posted, the King had attacked them in their

tents, and I believe had done so, however, had his generals been of
his mind. We had an alarm in our camp upon Saturday night
last, which was thus: In the very centre of our ammunition waggons two bombs were kindled in two distinct waggons, where there
was also powder, and a lighted match was found in a third; but
some soldiers were so stout as to draw those waggons, in which the
bombs were burning, from among the rest and to overthrow them,
by which, in God's good providence, there was no further harm.
. . . As for your coming to London upon our return, I do conceive
the affairs of your University may make it expedient, and I believe
it might not be amiss that Dr. Fall were upon the place too. . .
Let me tell you Lieut. Gen. Douglas and Breadalban are at Brussells, and will be here with the first convoy. I cannot see how his
negociation, according to my account of it, will be for his credit
here."

This letter is indorsed: "21 Aug., 1691. I opened this
according to allowance. I got it within this half hour, and
am so straitened by the post, that I can add no more than
that the King is expected in England next month, and I am
to you and yours your most affectionate J. Steuart."

Carstares to Dunlop.

"At the head-quarters at St. Gerard,
"betwixt Dinant and Namur,
"17 August, '91.

"Breadalban complains much of the carriage of the Synod of
Argyll to one Lindsay, as I remember he called him. They suspended him for contumacy, though he came two hours after the
time he should have appeared; but none of his entreaties could
prevail with them to take off the suspension. This being a matter
of fact I could say nothing to it. . . . . . Breadalban's negociation *

* The Earl of Breadalbane had proposed, with a view to quiet the
Highlands, that a pardon and £12,000 in money should be given to the
Highlanders still in arms, and that the chiefs should be pensioned, on condition of their keeping a certain number of their clansmen available for
military service at home or abroad. Sir John Dalrymple laid this plan
before the King, and Breadalbane was summoned to Flanders, that the terms
of the project might be exactly adjusted. This negotiation proved to be
the first, unsuspected, step towards the tragedy of Glencoe. See Dalrymple,
part ii. book vi. p. 187, and Appendix, p. 217.

is said not to be so bad as was represented; and he himself told me that some things which I had heard about that matter were utterly false. . . I hear the King did last night make his company at table merry with his asking, at my Lord Breadalban, if there were any wolves in the Highlands, and upon his answering in the negative, with telling him that they had enough of two-footed wolves to need any four-footed ones. We are like to have no battle this season. I wrote you, in my last, of the danger our ammunition was in. We now find, upon the torturing of one taken upon suspicion,* that it was a design set on foot by the French, who were, upon its success, to have largely rewarded the actors, and to have fallen upon our army when in the consternation that such an accident would have been attended with; but God delivered us. We have been troubled and shamed with the application of one Mr. Will. Houstoun, who hath, for some days, haunted the King and Court, complaining of a breach of the claim of right in his late imprisonment, and desiring a warrant for being admitted to a church, to which he is called, and kept from it by the suggestions of some ill-willers. He says he is come in the name of several, who offer to raise a regiment for His Majesty, and desire that he would give a commission to a blank person to be Col., and to Capt. Bruce to be Lieut. Col. He also desires for himself and brother compensation of their losses. I was spoke to about him, and said what I thought was proper, but being desirous to have him out of this place, did desire that some little money might be given him, to carry him on his way, and that he might be dispatched, which I suppose he will be this day, for my Lord Portland is as desirous to have him gone as any man can be, for he is confident and clamorous; and I suppose the best way to deal with such men will be not to make them sufferers."

Carstares to Dunlop.

"At the head-quarter at St. Gerard,

"August 20, '91.

. . . . . "I apprehend my letters must be intercepted by some with you; but it is more than dare be avowed. I write nothing myself, nor have any friends that write anything to me, but what they will own. I know I have ill-willers that think it not their interest at present to own themselves such, but wait for an advantage, which I

---

* This, and the case of Neville Payne, are enough to prove that torture was not so wholly unpractised under William, as Whig enthusiasm for his memory would have us believe.

hope they shall never have—it being my endeavour to carry myself
with that integrity as to my gracious prince and country, that I
dread nothing of what they can do. . . . . We can do nothing here
this summer, the French shunning all fighting, and it not being
possible, as this country lies, to force them to it. Breadalbane goes
from hence in a day or two, with conditions for his Highlanders,
which seem not to be so bad as they were represented. Your friend
hath done his duty with freedom and faithfulness upon this occasion. I can assure you that His Majesty hath good and honest intentions, and it will, I doubt not, appear in time that he hath them."

It is plain from the way in which Carstares here refers to
Breadalbane, and his plan for quieting the Highlands, that
he regarded it as a fair and feasible plan, although at the
first he had evidently been prejudiced against it, and that he
believed that the King's intentions concerning the Highlanders were "good and honest." That he should have
written thus, to an intimate correspondent, about a programme which included the foulest treachery and midnight
murder, is beyond belief. Nor is it probable that at the out-
set, Breadalbane himself, who was selfish and cunning rather
than ferociously cruel, designed such an end to his scheme of
pacification, as the Massacre of Glencoe. But the advantages
offered to those, who should fall in with his terms before the
1st of January, 1692, had to be balanced by the terror of
threats that would come straight home to the blood-boltered
imagination of the marauding Celt; and therefore the issue
of "letters of fire and sword," against such as should not
comply, was a natural accompaniment of a policy of conciliation. The burden of the guilt of the massacre rests on the
Master of Stair rather than on Breadalbane. The Master's
expectation that the clans would not generally accept the
offered terms cannot be misunderstood. He depended on the
letters of fire and sword, and not on the King's amnesty, for
the quieting of the half-savage glens and straths; and with an
exhilaration which has justly been called "fiendish" * by a
grave historian, anticipated the opportunity of applying to

* Hill Burton, vol. i. chap. iv. See also Macaulay's account of Glencoe,
'History,' chap. xviii. Nothing can be added to these two narratives.

the Highlands of his native country the policy which the
Spaniards had applied to the Indians of Mexico and Peru,
and which was not without more recent illustrations in the
Irish campaigns of the Great Protector.* To what extent King
William was actually aware of the import of the measures, to
which he assented, can never now be determined. I am inclined to believe that he knew little, and thought less, about
the affairs of the remote and turbulent districts, among
which these measures were to be put in force ; and I find a
strong confirmation of this opinion in the fact that throughout the whole of Carstares' correspondence, I can light on no
reference, howsoever indirect, to the tragedy of Glencoe.
Had he known anything about its true character ; had he

* See his letters in Dalrymple's Appendix.

In the year 1873 we find the following orders issued in the model
Republic :—

"Head-quarters Army of United States,
"Washington, April 12.

"General Gillem, Modoc Camp, *viâ* Yreka, Cal.

"Your dispatch announcing the terrible loss to the country of General
Canby by the perfidy of the Modoc band of Indians has been shown to the
President, who authorises me to instruct you to make the attack so strong
and persistent that their fate may be commensurate with their crime.
You will be fully justified in their utter extermination.

"(Signed)   W. T. Sherman, General.

" Repeat, as copy, for General Schofield, San Francisco, Cal."

Two days later the General in Chief sent the following to General
Schofield :—

"Washington, April 14.

"General J. M. Schofield, commanding Military Division, San Francisco.

"Your dispatch of yesterday is this moment received. Last night,
about midnight, General Townsend came to my house with a dispatch
from General Gillem to the same effect as yours, which dispatch he had
shown to the President, and I answered General Gillem direct with a copy
of the answer to you. The President now sanctions the most severe
punishment of the Modocs, and I hope to hear that they have met the
doom they so richly have earned by their insolence and perfidy. Consult
Mrs. Canby, and have every honour paid the remains of General Canby.
This is Sunday. I will see the President this evening, and to-morrow
will notify you of any change in the existing command, if made, but you
may be sure that any measure of severity to the savages will be sustained.

"(Signed)   W. T. Sherman, General."

believed it was to be a lasting stain on his master's good name; had he supposed it would afford the most damning accusation against Sir John Dalrymple, with whom his relations were not always cordial, it is impossible that his confidential letters, to Dunlop at least, should not have borne some trace of his thoughts upon this shameful outrage. But he is as silent about it as though it had never been. The crime was committed on the 13th of February. On the 18th of March Carstares wrote to Dunlop, from London, on his way to join the King, who had gone to Holland. He speaks of the General Assembly, which had met on the 15th of January, and had sat for a month; but neither then, nor in his subsequent letters does he say a word of Glencoe.

CHAPTER XIII.

AMONG the many difficulties attending the ecclesiastical
settlement, which followed the Revolution, were some inseparable from the union of Church and State. Absolute as
the action of the State had been in establishing the Church,
the Church, when once established, was co-ordinate with the
State; and it had never been inclined, in Scotland, either
before or since the Reformation, to abate a jot of its own
authority. The claim of " spiritual independence," which
Andrew Melville had urged with his usual intemperance,
had not been forgotten during the prelatic days, when the
adherents of the proscribed religion saw, with contemptuous
amazement, those very bishops, who alleged an apostolical
commission, suspended from their office, or bandied about
from one diocese to another, at the pleasure of a worthless
King. And now, the restored Presbyters, rejoicing in a
recovered power, were nowise ready to copy the prelatic
example, in yielding a servile submission to the dictate of
the civil magistrate. " Cæsar "—that mysterious entity that
has figured so largely, and stood such free abuse, in Scottish
ecclesiastical disputes—had done too much for them to be
openly defied. But it was possible to offer to his policy, if it
did not chime with theirs, an inert and stolid opposition of
inaction and non-compliance, which should defeat it as
effectually as overt hostility. Of this kind were the conduct
and the temper of the Assembly of 1692. The King had
become possessed with the idea that the Church was dealing
too harshly with the Episcopal incumbents. The Church

had become possessed with the idea that the King was too
favourably affected towards them.

There was irritation on the one hand; suspicion on the
other. Carstares and the moderate party dreaded the issue
of the Assembly,* which, after some invidious postponement,
was held on the 15th of January, 1692.

It was the misfortune of the Church, at this time, that its
counsels and actions fell to be conducted by men, who were
not equal to the demands of the occasion.

The race of great ecclesiastics— reformers, scholars, and
statesmen, had died out. Their successors were punier men.
"Who tied Dolabella to that sword?" asked Cicero of his
paltry son-in-law. What fate connected the Hugh Kennedies
and Gilbert Rules of the Revolutionary era, with the final
establishment of a church which had a great history, and
was the representative of exalted principles? They appear
to have scarce realised their position, as trustees of the
honour and justice of Church and State, or to have understood that they were suffered to stand where they did, for the
sole purpose of consolidating—on ground which had been
wasted alike by puritanic fanaticism, and by prelatic exclu-
siveness—a comprehensive Church, whose policy should not
be dictated by dogmatism and tradition, but by the reasonableness and charity of Christian wisdom; a church which
should seem to have drawn from its Presbyterian ancestry the
spirit of Knox and Buchanan, rather than that of Melville
and Guthrie; and from its Episcopal alliances the principles
of Hooker and Taylor, rather than those of Bancroft and Laud.
Those causes of ill feeling and distrust, which are apt to
operate most forcibly on minds deficient in culture and experience, were not wanting. The King had listened with
patient courtesy to Episcopalian statements of grievances; he
had promoted to office men who were little better than careless
Gallios, in the eyes of the staunch Whig and Presbyterian
party; he had indicated, with severe brevity and plainness, his idea of the terms on which the Church should

* Graham Dunlop MSS.

accommodate itself to the peculiar circumstance of the Episcopal clergy.

It was now of moment to William that the Episcopal clergy should, if possible, be allowed to remain in their parishes. As soon as a "curate" was put out, his natural tendency was, either to relapse into active sedition at home, or to travel southwards, inveighing, as he journeyed, against Presbyterianism and Whiggery, until, on arriving in England, he lent his angry voice to swell the chorus of High Church and Tory discontent. But the Assembly, which consisted of about 170 members,* clerical and lay, did not consider the interests of the King's policy at large; and though urged by a letter from him, and by the active superintendence of the Commissioner, would not concur in the royal suggestions. Under the authority of the last Assembly, a large number of the Episcopal ministers had been expelled; but few, if any, had been received into communion with the Establishment. The King complained of this. The Assembly, thus refusing to admit or recognise these clergymen, continued, he said, to restrict the representation of the Church to a minority. He desired not only that the Episcopalians, who duly complied with the prescribed terms, should remain unmolested in their charges, but that they should be admitted, as constituent members, to the church courts. He sent down a formula of declaration, which he considered proper as the condition on which they might be thus admitted. The formula was admirably drawn, strict in its demand of loyalty to the constitution and government of the Church, lax in its exaction of concurrence with the letter of the established creed.†

* "A set of men much younger and hotter-spirited than the last." Letter to Portland from Sir P. Hume (Lord Polwarth). Marchmont Papers, vol. iii. p. 400.

† "I A. B. do sincerely declare and promise that I will submit to the Presbyterial government of the Church, as it is now established in this kingdom, under their Majesties King William and Queen Mary, by presbyteries, provincial synods, and general assemblies; and that I will, as becomes a minister of the gospel, heartily concur with the said government,

Most of the Episcopal clergy, who had taken the oath of allegiance professed themselves satisfied with it, and petitioned the Assembly that they might accordingly be received. The Assembly would neither refuse nor assent. The formula and the petitions were both referred to committees ; and day after day the House spent its time over details connected with individual cases, without making progress towards a measure of general applicability. At last, on the 13th of February, the Earl of Lothian, the Commissioner, brusquely told them that they had sat for a month, and not done what they were called together to do; and thereupon dissolved the Assembly, specifying no day for a future meeting. Upon this, the Moderator, after some parley, named a day, and the clergy, having thus asserted their independence, sullenly separated, muttering against Episcopalian craft and royal Erastianism.*

"Use all endeavours," says Carstares to Dunlop, on the 8th of March, " to keep people from extravagancies upon the account of changes that are made. Patience will be our advantage and cannot prejudge us. I always dreaded the issue of the Assembly. You shall hear more from me when in Holland."

William had just crossed to the Hague, whither Carstares followed him.

He writes from Loo, soon after his arrival, warning Dunlop that Lord Portland had been told that he had encouraged his brethren in the Assembly to resist the King's wishes. Dunlop appears to have been somewhat unguarded in his speech. " It is fit that you take notice of your discourse," says his brother-in-law in another letter ; and he promises to make his peace with Lord Portland.

---

for the suppressing of sin and wickedness, the promoting of piety, and the purging of the Church of all erroneous and scandalous ministers. And I do further promise that I will subscribe the Confession of Faith, and the shorter, and larger, catechisms, now confirmed by Act of Parliament, as containing the doctrine of the Protestant religion professed in this kingdom."

* Burnet, vol. iv. pp. 155–7. Burton, from 1688, vol. i. chap. vi. Cunningham, vol. ii. p. 298 et seq. Cruh, vol. iii. p. 328.

It is evident, however, that the recent Assembly was a sore subject at Loo, and had occasioned angry feelings. "I find no alteration as to myself," he says, "nor is there, as you well know, any reason there should be any. As there is opportunity, I shall mind you and your university. . . . Let us be quiet, and show all duty to our gracious Prince, and we may make amends for the last fatal step of the Assembly—concerning which you know my mind. Adieu, dear brother, and remember few are to be trusted as to discourse or actions."

King William found, on his return to the Continent, that a formidable task awaited him, in reanimating and invigorating the policy of his allies, and bringing their troops to the theatre of war. After many disappointments and delays, the allied forces were brought together, and he took the command. He hastened towards Namur, around which lay the great army, that, before the leaders of the Coalition were half equipped, had already followed the splendid Louis to the field. Carstares, as usual, attended William. He writes from "the camp at Bethlehem, near Louvain," on the 23rd of May, to Dunlop.

"DEAR BROTHER,—I have had three of yours, and am glad you have had an opportunity of confuting the calumnies of your enemies, and manifesting your duty to your King, and concern for your country. The good news of our fleet will, I hope, confound the designs of Jacobins, and some men will be taken in their own snare.* God does his work, and it ought indeed to be marvellous in our eyes. The French have besieged Namur, and batter it from several places. Yesterday they took a windmill near the town, and were forced to quit it again with the loss of several hundreds of

---

* The great sea battle of La Hogue had been won. King James, watching the action from the French shore, saw in the English victory the ruin of his last hopes of his forfeited crown. He "slowly and sadly returned," says Dalrymple (part ii. book vii.), "to bury the remembrance of his greatness in the convent of La Trappe. All his attempts, and those of his family, afterwards, to recover the throne of their ancestors, were either disappointed by the insincerity of French friendship, or were the mere efforts of despair."

men. We go on in our march towards them to-morrow; and it is very probable we shall in a very few days have a battle. We have a great army of 90 battalions of foot, all, almost, of them very full; and 200 squadrons of horse: our men are in good heart,—God give the blessing. . . . I should be glad to hear that Hugh Cunningham had got my rents of '91 and rest of '90,* for I and my wife both do need them. Campaigns are expensive; and three horses and two servants, which are absolutely necessary for me, will be expensive. Pray take your own way to speak to him, and to let me know how much I may draw upon him for. . . . We are just now firing with great and small shot for the victory at sea. We have 100 pieces of cannon." " I have access," he adds at a later date, " often in Angus' [the Cameronian] and Leven's regiments to be employed in my proper work ;"— almost the only reference in any of his letters to his clerical capacity.

The fall of Namur, and the battle of Steinkirk—in which Mackay, of Killiecrankie, fell where the dead lay thickest— left but scant glory to William's generalship at the end of the indecisive campaign. He returned in October to pass the winter in England.

Carstares was still much occupied with the state of the Scottish universities, ill equipped with professors, and poverty-stricken, as they were. Again and again, in his correspondence with Dunlop, he assures him that the universities are not forgotten. Dunlop was an active member of the " General correspondence," or joint-committee for the affairs of the universities, and urged their claims, both publicly and through the private influence of Carstares, who, in the interests both of learning and of the Church, was eager to secure the better endowments, which were an essential part of any university reform. There were but few funds available for the purpose, but at last, in 1693, Carstares obtained a gift from

* There is no indication among the Graham Dunlop MSS, or elsewhere, of the sources of Carstares' private income, or of his possession of any landed property.

the crown of £1200 a year, out of the bishops' rents, which was divided equally between the four universities.   He also procured, at the same time, the place of historiographer for Scotland, with a salary of £40 a year, for his brother-in-law, the Principal.*

Carstares to Dunlop.

"London, Nov. 1.

"I had yours, and against Mr. Johnstone's time of officiating— which will be the beginning of the next month, I shall endeavour to have the business of your university settled, so well as I can: and shall have a meeting of the Bishop of Salisbury,† Dr. Fall, Secretary Johnstone, and myself, for that effect, and the historiographer shall not be forgot. And I assure you not only my nephews, but the father and mother too, are more upon my heart than I confess they have reason to think from what is visible. I am sure you will have good thoughts of us now, when you have got Sir James Steuart for Advocate, and Ormistoun for Justice Clerk, with the good liking of his honest predecessor, who is still in the King's favour."

James Steuart had, till now, lain under the King's suspicion and dislike, owing to the part he had played before the Revolution; but his great ability, and the confidence which the Presbyterian party reposed in him, gave him a claim to office which could not be resisted, the more especially as some recent appointments (such as that of Lord Tweeddale, a suspected Jacobite, to the Chancellorship) had given that party grave offence. Cockburn, of Ormiston, the new Lord Justice Clerk, was one of the most zealous Presbyterians of the day,‡ and now succeeded George Campbell, of Cessnock, who had held the same office since 1690.

Office had also been offered to the Duke of Hamilton, who, offended at Melville's Commissionership, was still sulking, like Achilles in his tent, although Melville had now been

---

* Bower's 'History of the University of Edinburgh,' vol. ii. p. 44. Wodrow, vol. iv. p. 522 (Appendix). Graham Dunlop MSS.

† Burnet had been himself a professor at Glasgow.

‡ McCormick, p. 99. Macky's 'Characters,' p. 244: " Hardly in common charity with any man out of the verge of Presbytery."

relegated to the unimportant post of Keeper of the Privy
Seal. The Duke was one of those men of vast territorial and
social influence, and unemphatic opinions, who are specially
useful in offices of state where parties are bitterly divided,
and where heroic policies have no chance of success.

Carstares was very anxious he should take a place in the
government. "Mr. Carstares," Lord Basil Hamilton writes
to his father, "is much for your Grace's not quitting the
government, for all that is done; and he says he is very sure
that things will come to your hand." The Duke at last was
persuaded, and after refusing the place of Lord Admiral
of Scotland, he accepted again the dignity of Lord High
Commissioner.*

To the extreme Presbyterians, Hamilton was by no means
so acceptable a representative of royalty as Melville, and Carstares' interest in his appointment was regarded, by them, as
a sign of his often suspected lukewarmness towards the Church.
He was quite aware that his temperate and cautious policy
was not popular with the fervid party, though he did not
let the knowledge affect his conduct. Referring in one of
his letters to "some men's jealousies," he says, "I value that
not. I have never concerned myself in the public, with an
eye to thanks from those in Scotland, for whose interest I
have been, and will be, sincerely concerned; but if I had
not more of honesty and principle than some have of charity,
it is like some affairs might have gone otherwise." His constant effort was to instil, into the less disciplined minds of
his compatriots and fellow-churchmen, his own "sweet reasonableness." "Pray let Will Dunlop know these news," he
writes in a letter to his cousin Hamilton of Halleraigs,† which
contains some tidings pleasing to the Presbyterians; "but
let not our people be vain, but carry with modesty." Again,

* Dalrymple. Appendix, vol. ii. p. 207, &c.
† Carstares had five aunts of the Glanderston family; of whom Ursula
married Ralston of Ralston; Jean, Hamilton of Halleraigs; Margaret,
Zachary Boyd, and James Durham; Agnes, Porterfield of Quarreltonn;
and Elizabeth, the Rev. Alexander Dunlop, father of William. Caldwell
Papers. Introductory Memoir.

he says, "There can be no great satisfaction in men bringing themselves into inconveniencies by doing anything that is not absolute duty, and the forbearing whereof is not sinful." His letters during this winter of 1692–3, to Dunlop, and Hamilton of Hallcraigs (who was one of the Lords of Session) are not specially interesting; and refer chiefly to the universities, and to sundry benefactions and appointments, which his friends and kindred seem to have very freely sought at his hands, and in regard to all of which he evidently spared no pains to satisfy their expectations. Sometimes he seems a little worried by their pressure. "I wonder," he remonstrates on one occasion, in a letter to Dunlop, "how you should think that I am capable to serve [*name illegible*]? I am sure, if I should meddle in all affairs recommended to me by friends, I should soon incapacitate myself to do any service at all. I will do for him what I can, but I will promise no success." Again, writing to Hallcraigs: "The Laird of Macfarlan must be preferred to my uncle,* for reasons which the Secretary hath told me, if the business be not already done; and I know the Secretary will do for my uncle another way."

When the Scottish Parliament was about to meet, Carstares, who was going again to attend the King in Flanders, writes to Dunlop; on the 28th of March, 1693 :—

"I must desire you would do me the favour to supply my place in attending His Majesty's Commissioner and the Parliament, this ensuing session; and I hope, my Lord Duke, when you acquaint his Grace with it, will approve my choice . . . The King hath granted me Kilmarnock's ward,†—but this to yourself and my other good trusties, for it must be in another's name; and I am apt to think it will have much to do to defray two campaigns; but I have a very good master." The references to the need of money and expensiveness of his mode of living, which occur in his letters, would appear to

---

* Captain James Mure, of Ballybregach, in the county Down.

† Earl of Kilmarnock, a minor, father of the Earl who was beheaded in 1746.

have been the result, not of any love of filthy lucre, but of a freedom in expenditure, and inattention to pecuniary details, occasionally exposing him to the inconveniences of impecuniosity. "He was such a despiser of money," says the editor of his nephew, Professor William Dunlop's, sermons, "and such a lover of hospitality and charity, that, notwithstanding all the opportunities he had of becoming rich if he had inclined to it, he had nothing at his death to leave his lady—a person of singular worth, and with whom he lived in all the sweetest endearments of conjugal affection—but her own patrimony, which he was careful to reserve for such an event." *

He crossed, early in April, to Rotterdam, joined the King at Loo, and accompanied him to the camp near Louvain. He thus describes the great battle of Landen, writing from the camp on the 24th of July :—"Upon Tuesday last about three in the afternoon, the enemy began to appear, and did that night place themselves in several posts before our lines. We did also dispose our army to the best advantage against any attack. Our baggage was sent away that evening—the King himself sleeping for two or three hours in his coach upon the field. The next morning, betwixt four and five, we began to play with our cannon, and betwixt eight and nine we came to small shot, which continued till about two in the afternoon, at which time, or a little after, we were forced to quit the field, being overpowered by the French—who had forty battalions of foot more than we, and so near double our number; and yet we were once in a fair way to carry the day, so bravely did our men behave themselves. Our King, during the whole action, exposed himself to all hazards, in giving necessary orders everywhere; and himself, in the greatest heat of the action, led on some squadrons of horse to encourage them thereby to do their duty. A part of the fringe of his scarf was shot away, but himself is, blessed be God, in safety. My Lord Portland carried very well upon this

* 'Sermons by the learned William Dunlop, late Regius Professor of Divinity, &c., in the University of Edinburgh,' 1722. Preface.

occasion; he is wounded in both his hands. Count Solms hath his foot shot off by a cannon ball. The Duke of Ormond is wounded and prisoner, and the Duke of Berwick is prisoner with us. We have not lost many men, and our army is getting together apace, and in a few days we shall be stronger than before, for we had detached from our army, before the fight, 20,000 men, who will now join us; and then we shall, as is thought, go after the enemy, who certainly hath a much greater loss than we, and is, we believe, put much out of capacity to do great things this year. This, to the best of my knowledge, is a true, tho' short, account of this affair, in which the King hath indeed appeared very great. Adieu. My dear love to sisters. This will tell you I am well, tho' I was upon the field to the last."

This was the great event of the campaign. In October the King returned to England. While at the Hague, waiting for a fair wind, Carstares had the pleasure of attending the marriage of his brother, at Rotterdam. Alexander, he says, is "oppressed with business. The bride seems to be of a good temper, and a discreet manager." He took up his quarters again in London, for the winter. "I could wish you were here," he writes to Dunlop, "could you have your expenses borne; your university affairs would go the better, and you should have nutmeg for your punch." The Principal, however, had a good office to perform at Glasgow in celebrating the marriage of another of the family, Katherine, whose " marriage warrant," dated the 14th of February, 1694, bears that she is to be married, by Principal Dunlop, to the Rev. John Law. Carstares sends her a present of £20 before the wedding, and promises Mrs. Dunlop, who had, presumably, been desirous to wear a headdress of the latest fashion on the occasion, "we shall send down that head suit you mention."

Among the many scurrilous pamphlets which the rival Scotch factions discharged at each other, one was published in 1693, with the title, ' The Spirit of Calumny and Slander examined, chastised, and exposed, in a letter to a malicious

Libeller.' To this was appended 'A Letter from a Gentleman in Scotland to his Friend in London,' which bore the initials "W. P.," and was generally ascribed to Sir William Paterson. In this letter the writer took occasion to refer to the old story of the Rye-house Plot and the trial of Jerviswood. Baillie, the Campbells of Cessnock, Carstares, and the rest, he declared, all professed their innocence of any plotting with such apparent sincerity, and with such "imprecations," that he actually believed them; and yet, he adds, "Carstares upon the first application of the thumbscrew—even the first touch of it—confessed all, as may be seen in his printed confession."* Carstares naturally resented this mendacious attempt to malign him. The records of Parliament already bore that he had been grossly deceived and injured in the misuse made of his 'Confession'; but his conduct in the chamber of torture had been witnessed by only a few, and of the few but one or two remained, who would be likely to help him to prove that his slanderer was lying. The Duke of Queensberry was one of these. He had been King James's Lord Treasurer, and though turned out of office because he would not concur in the King's quasi-tolerant policy, he had remained a Tory, and since the Revolution had made no advances to the existing government. His testimony would be impartial, and above suspicion. Carstares accordingly asked a friend in Edinburgh to wait upon the Duke, and to obtain his opinion of the statement in the 'Letter from a Gentleman in Scotland to his Friend in London.' His correspondent writes in reply, on the 22nd of February :—

"I have been to see the D. of Queensb., whose indisposition (for he is indeed very ill) keeps him in the country. After I had some occasion to name you, I told him what had happened, and what a letter Sir Will. Paterson had written of you, and which had been printed. He presently took the same apprehension I told you formerly that I had of it, but added—with a great oath—'It has been the knave, his brother,† has made him do it, for I see it has

* 'Spirit of Calumny, &c.,' p. 67.

† The Bishop of Edinburgh, promoted in 1688 to the Archbishopric of Glasgow.

been of design to bring a reproach on the poor man, and I consider not Sir William such a fool as that he would be persuaded by any other body, but by his brother, to do such an ill thing.' As to the matter, he bade me tell you that it was so far from being true that you denied with any sort of imprecation, and that upon the first offering of the torture you acknowledged what you had denied :—that first, he never heard you make any imprecations; that it was never so much as said in the Secret Committee that you had made any, but, upon the contrary, that you would say nothing, and that he did not think it possible that any man could endure what you did with so little perturbation, and that notwithstanding of it you said nothing, and would say nothing ;—that the day following the Secret Committee met in the Treasury Chamber, where the resolution taken was to put you so severely to it as that either you should discover, or die under it. Upon which he said, ' I perceive he will rather die under it. Pray,' said he, ' let me send to him and tell him his hazard, and that if he will deny upon oath, he shall be set at liberty, and that it shall never rise in judgment against him, but that any evidence that we conceive we have against him shall be supprest' (for they had something, particularly a key of Earl Argyll's cipher, which they judged written by your hand); and, on the other hand, that if you would make any discovery, it should not be brought as an evidence against any man. Upon which the then Treasurer Depute, Melfort, was sent to you,—that he himself afterward came to see you, with the then Chancellor, after he had persuaded them to let you be sent to the Castle, as a place of better air, and where you should be as securely kept, for he was then governor of it. He bade me present his service to you and to tell you that he looks upon that whole account as a cunningly devised trick to defame you, and that he will own this to anybody that shall, at any time, happen to speak to him of it."

The letter then diverges to an account of the doings of " that madman, Hepburn," a fanatic preacher, who had been received into the Church, but who retained the vagrant and disorderly habits of his Cameronian associates. " Having a great fervency in expression," says Carstares' correspondent, " and unweariable lungs, are mistaken by the poor ignorant for zeal and piety." *

It was in the spring of this year, 1694, that the incident

* Murray Dunlop MSS.

occurred which has had a dramatic prominence, next to the scene of his torture, in the vague popular recollections of Carstares' life. The story is told, simply and effectively, by McCormick, and (with due deference to Mr. Hill Burton's scepticism)[*] there seems little reason to doubt its truth. It is not one that McCormick or any one else was likely to invent; nor is it one for which there could be the formal documentary evidence, which Mr. Grub desires for its verification.[†] The only persons who could give the details were Carstares and King William, and the latter certainly would not think of committing them to writing. But it is natural to suppose that they may have descended to McCormick (who was Carstares' grand-nephew) in memoranda preserved by Carstares or his kindred; or in oral narrative; and that they were recorded by him as he received them from his mother and grandmother. M'Cormick was a clergyman of high character, and published his book within sixty years of his grand-uncle's death; and it is absurd to imagine that he would have deliberately introduced into it, amidst grave matters of political and ecclesiastical history, a fiction or a legend. The incident is that of Carstares' intercepting the royal despatches to the Commissioner of the General Assembly of 1694.

The summary dissolution of the Assembly of 1692 had caused much ill-feeling; encouraging the disaffected Episcopalians; grieving the sober, and exasperating the violent, among the Presbyterians. " During the following part of that year "—to quote the ' Memorial of the Affairs of the Church,' among the Graham Dunlop MSS.—" notwithstanding all these provocations, the judicatories of the Church not only forbore censuring any more of the Episcopal clergy, but took some of them in,"—among others Laurence Charteris—" and upon terms in effect the same with the formula, except that they owned the Confession of Faith *as believing it*,—for here the great objection against the formula[‡] ceaseth. But the Church by doing it in this manner does not subject itself to

---

* Hill Burton, from 1688, vol. i. p. 235.   † Grub, vol. iii. p. 333.
‡ Suggested by the King.

the consequences of taking in all that shall barely apply."
But while the Church's procedure was thus peaceable and
moderate, the Legislature did what it could to provide the
materials of new discords. The Parliament of 1693 devised
in addition to the Oath of Allegiance, an " Oath of Assurance," which it imposed on all the clergy, Presbyterian and
Episcopal, as a condition of their holding office. The Oath
of Assurance bound the swearer to acknowledge William as
king *de jure*, as well as *de facto;* and it was at once odious
to the Presbyterian, as an unwarrantable encroachment on a
region with which " Cæsar " had no right to meddle; and to
the Episcopalian, as implying "a solemn disavowal of hereditary right."*

The risk of uproar and disturbance seemed but to be increased by an Act which bore the soothing name of 'An
Act for settling the quiet and peace of the Church.' The
Church threatened that it would not be quieted on the
Parliament's terms. The Act declared that all Episcopal
ministers who should take the oaths of Allegiance and Assurance, subscribe the Confession, and acknowledge the Presbyterian government, should be entitled to claim admission to
the church courts; while all who should not thus qualify
might be deposed; and all who should were to be protected
in their parishes, until regularly received into the ecclesiastical judicatories.† The Act further demanded the calling
of a General Assembly, the Parliament being, no doubt, apprehensive of a collision between the civil and ecclesiastical
jurisdictions, if the Assembly should take the initiative, and
meet without the royal warrant. The oaths and the Act set
the whole Church in a ferment. That Parliament should
impose civil oaths as conditions of clergymen holding office,
or doing duty, was as black Erastianism as that of Charles or
James. That the Assembly should be summoned in accord-
ance with a Parliamentary vote, and not in virtue of the
Church's inherent right of meeting and deliberating, was an

* Laing's ' History,' vol. iv. p. 256.
† Cunningham, vol. ii. p. 304.　Grub, vol. iii. p. 330, &c.

outrage on its liberty. Who gave the elected King authority to decide that no one should sit in that Assembly, unless he should first swear that the elected was his rightful sovereign? Or what right had he to prescribe terms of deposition, or to promise to interpose his protection to men unrecognised and unsanctioned by the Church? Why should not the Assembly meet on its own day, and ignore the interference both of Parliament and King? But the growl of gathering wrath in Scotland did not echo to Kensington. Sinister influences, it was alleged, were in temporary ascendancy there. The King had been listening to Tarbat, whose personal leanings were towards Episcopacy, and who looked on the heats and squabbles of rival ecclesiastics with the Laodicean indifference of a man of the world, and the impatience of a statesman who knew how much they retarded national prosperity; and to the Master of Stair, to whose cool and selfish judgment churches, sects, parties, principles, were only so many pieces on the great chess-board whereon he played his wary game, to be moved hither and thither, or swept aside, as best should suit his purposes.

The King called an Assembly, and sent down orders that the ministers must subscribe the Assurance before they took their seats, and that, if they refused to do so, the Assembly was to be dissolved.

The King seemed firm. The Presbyterian ministers, inflamed with a sense of injury, and supported by the expressed sympathy of the English nonconformists, were resolved to stand firm too.* Lord Carmichael was the Commissioner, and to him the royal commands were sent. At this juncture, in the month of March, it is said that Carstares had obtained leave of absence, and was not in attendance at Court. We are now ready to take up the narrative of McCormick, who shall tell his story in his own words:—

"Upon Lord Carmichael's arriving in Edinburgh, and communicating his orders to some of the clergy in town, he

* Burton, from 1688, vol. i. p. 232. McCormick, p. 52.

found them obstinate in their resolutions not to comply. They assured him that their sentiments upon the subject were the same with those of all their brethren in the country; and that, if this measure were persisted in, it would spread a flame over the country, which it would not be in the power of such as had given his Majesty these counsels to extinguish.

"The commissioner saw that all his attempts to bring them to better temper would be vain and fruitless. At the same time, he was sensible that the dissolution of the assembly would not only prove fatal to the church of Scotland, to which he was a real friend, but also to his Majesty's interest in that kingdom. From a sincere regard to both, therefore, he undertook to lay the matter, as it stood, fairly before the King; and, for that purpose, sent off a flying packet, which he expected to return from London, with the King's final determination, the night before the assembly was appointed to meet. At the same time, the clergy sent up a memorial to Mr. Carstares, urging him to use his good offices, in this critical conjuncture, for the preservation of that church which he had so active a hand in establishing.

"The flying packet arrived at Kensington in the forenoon of that day upon which Mr. Carstares returned. But, before his arrival, his Majesty, by the advice of Lord Stair and Lord Tarbat, who represented this obstinacy of the clergy as an act of rebellion against his government, had renewed his instructions to the commissioner, and sent them off by the same packet.

"When Mr. Carstares came to Kensington and received his letters, he immediately inquired what was the nature of the despatches his Majesty had sent off for Scotland; and, upon learning their contents, he went directly, and, in his Majesty's name, required the messenger, who was just setting off, to deliver them up to him. It was now late at night; and, as he knew no time was to be lost, (the general assembly being to sit in a few days) he ran to his Majesty's apartment; and, being informed by the Lord in waiting that he was gone to bed, he told him, it was a matter of the last importance which had brought him at that unseasonable hour, and that he must see the King.

"Upon entering the chamber, he found his Majesty fast asleep, upon which, turning aside the curtain, and falling down upon his knees, he gently awaked him. The King, astonished to see him at so late an hour, and in this posture by his bed-side, asked him what was the matter? He answered, he had come to ask his life. And is it possible, said the King, that you have been guilty of a crime that deserves death? He acknowledged he had, and then produced the despatches he had brought back from the messenger. And have you, says the King, with a severe frown, have you indeed presumed to countermand my orders? Mr. Carstares then begged leave only to be heard a few words, and he was ready to submit to any punishment his Majesty should think proper to inflict. He said,

"'That the King had now known him long, and knew his entire fidelity and attachment to his person and government. Some of his servants in Scotland might find it their interest to impose upon his Majesty, to screen themselves from his merited displeasure. Others might, under the mask of zeal for his service, seek only to gratify their own private resentments; and, whilst they pretended to conciliate all parties to his government, might pursue such measures as would only unite them in opposing it.

"'That this was the foundation of all those factions which had hitherto rent that kingdom, and made its crown sit so uneasy upon his head: That, for his own part, he could call God to witness, that, ever since he entered into his Majesty's service, he had no interest, for he could have none, separate from that of his master: That, though he had been educated a presbyterian, and, on that account, had a natural bias to this form of church-government; yet his Majesty knew, that, when he recommended the establishment of presbytery in Scotland, he did it, because he was firmly persuaded the Presbyterians were the only friends his Majesty had in that country : That his regard to their principles had not rendered him blind to their faults : That he had been aware of the indiscreet use they would make of the liberal concessions in their favour in Lord Melville's parliament, and had freely given his sentiments upon that head : That, with the same freedom, he had remonstrated against the precipitate measures adopted in the last session of parliament, under the pretext of correcting the errors of the former : That the effects had justified his opinion of both. The first had alienated all the episcopals, the last, great part of the presbyterians, from his administration. One thing alone was wanting to complete the wishes of his enemies, and that was, to cement the two parties by one common bond of union : That nothing could be better calculated for this purpose than the advice which had been given to his Majesty to push the administration of the oaths to the ministers before the sitting down of the assembly : That, although there was nothing unreasonable in what his Majesty required, yet some who had credit with them had fallen upon methods to represent their compliance as inconsistent with their principles, and had been so far successful, that they were determined not to comply : That, however unjustifiable in other respects their conduct might be, it proceeded from no disaffection to his person and government ; and that, whilst this was the case, it was more for his Majesty's interest to confirm their attachment, by dispensing with the rigour of the law, than to lose their affections by enforcing it. What avail oaths and promises to a Prince, when he has lost the hearts of his subjects ? Now was the time, therefore, to retrieve his affairs in that kingdom : That, by countermanding the instructions he had sent down to his commissioner, he conferred the highest obligations upon the whole body of the presbyterian clergy, gratified all his friends in that kingdom, and effectually thwarted the insidious arts of his and their enemies.'

"The King heard him with great attention, and, when he had done, gave him the despatches to read, and desired him to throw them in the fire; after which, he bid him draw up the instructions to the commissioner in what terms he pleased, and he would sign them. Mr. Carstares immediately wrote to the commissioner, signifying, that it was his Majesty's pleasure to dispense with putting the oaths to the ministers; and, when the King had signed it, he immediately despatched the messenger, who, by being detained so many hours longer than he intended, did not arrive in Edinburgh till the morning of the day fixed for the sitting of the assembly.

"By this time, both the commissioner and the clergy were in the utmost perplexity. He was obliged to dissolve the assembly; they were determined to assert their own authority, independent of the civil magistrate. Both of them were apprehensive of the consequences, and looked upon the event of this day's contest as decisive with respect to the church of Scotland; when, to their inexpressible joy, they were relieved by the return of the packet, countermanding the dissolution of the assembly. Next to the establishment of presbytery in Scotland, no act of King William's administration endeared him so much to the presbyterians as this. They considered it as a certain proof that his own inclinations were altogether favourable to them, and that any difficulties they laboured under ought to be imputed to his ministers, not to himself. It was soon understood what part Mr. Carstares had acted upon this occasion; it gave him entire credit with the whole body of the presbyterians, who had of late begun to suspect that he had deserted their cause; and it was gratefully acknowledged by most of the clergy after he came to reside in Scotland. In one instance, indeed, he was obliged to put them in remembrance of it. When some of his zealous brethren, in the heat of debate in a general assembly, charged him with want of zeal for the interest of the church of Scotland; which provoked him to such a degree, that, in spite of his natural modesty and coolness of temper, he rose up, and begged leave, in justice to his own character, to observe, 'That such a reflection came with a very bad grace from any man who sate in that court, which, under God, owed its existence to his interposition: That if ever, in any one instance, his zeal had carried him beyond the bounds of discretion, it was in favour of the church of Scotland: That he never had received a frown from the greatest and the best of masters but one, and it was on her account.'"

This incident marked a crisis in the history of the Church. Henceforth the Presbyterians believed in William's honesty and goodwill, as they had not believed before. They were now convinced of his firm intention to maintain Presbytery, and of their own secure position. Conscious of a confirmed power, they were able to use it with greater generosity. The Assembly proceeded to receive, and empowered its commission also to receive, the Episcopal clergy who should apply for reception in the terms of the recent Act. Those who thus conformed were amicably admitted.

Many of those who would not conform were allowed, and even entitled, under the protection of an Act of the next Parliament of 1695, to remain, and to officiate in their parishes; though, of course, debarred from a place in the Presbyteries, Synods and Assemblies, in which the Presbyterian government was vested. The waste and empty places were gradually reached, and filled up. In the North, where Episcopacy still was strong, force was no longer employed to expel Episcopal, or to intrude Presbyterian, incumbents. The complete organization of one homogeneous establishment was left to the healing and restoring influences of time. That no harsh pressure was used to hasten the action of these, and that the policy and practice of the Church were vastly more lenient after the Revolution than after the Restoration, is sufficiently attested by the fact that even as late as 1710, there were 113 Episcopal ministers, of whom nine had not even taken the oaths to government, still ministers of parishes;* and that the Sacrament of the Lord's Supper was not celebrated in Aberdeen, according to the Pres-

* Leven and Melville Papers, Preface, p. xxx.

byterian use, until the year 1704.* The Episcopal Church, as
a church, was now, however, entirely broken up. Those of its
clergy who conformed were henceforth politically powerless,
and were merged, more or less completely, in the Establishment.† Those who kept aloof, and who maintained a furtive
relation to the surviving bishops of the deprived Episcopate,
became, in the natural development of the tendency we have
already marked, a body of political dissidents, whose bond
of union was primarily Jacobitism, and only in an inferior
degree, Episcopacy. The exiled King was their *raison d'être*,
and not a theory of church government. It is perhaps unwelcome to the so-called High Churchmen of the present day,
in Scotland, to acknowledge that they owe their ecclesiastical
lineage to a dethroned oppressor, more than to an apostolic
succession; but so it is. The lonely exile at St. Germain's was
the true source, the *fons et origo*, of the Scotch Episcopacy of
the eighteenth century. The Scotch Episcopacy of the nine-
teenth has no longer any sympathy with, in few cases has
it any accurate knowledge of, its own historical ancestry. It
is not now Jacobite in sentiment; and, although among the
aristocracy and landed gentry it is frequently Tory in politics,
it is not always so. It retains no relic or recollection of its
old Scotch simplicity of ritual, and of its Calvinistic creed.
It has adopted the English Articles; and, of late, has
echoed, in a thin voice, the emphatic protest of the modern
Tractarians against the "Evangelicalism" of the first quarter
of this century. It has clothed itself with all the forms of
Anglicanism of which it could lay hold. It owes its vitality

* 'Spalding Club Miscellany,' vol. ii.; Preface, pp. 72–3. This was no
worse than earlier omissions and irregularities. In Glasgow between 1645
and the Restoration, there were only six celebrations of the communion;
and betwixt the Restoration and the Revolution only two. St. Andrews
and Edinburgh were not much better. See Sprott and Leishman's 'Book
of Common Order and Directory,' p. 346.

† In addition to those already included, Burnet states that about seventy
were received in 1695. Burnet's editor quotes the 'London Gazette,' No.
3122, to the effect that the number was about a hundred. Burnet, vol. iv.
p. 282, and note.

mainly to imitation of English fashion, or the modified reproduction of Anglican modes of thought and feeling; and by reason of the bareness of Presbyterian ritual, it has gained a hold on minds whose æsthetic culture that ritual does not attract; but it is still, as it has always been, essentially an alien on Scottish soil. In as far as it is the religion of Toryism, it is still as opposed to Scottish Liberalism as it was in 1688. As the religion of Prelacy and Sacerdotalism, it has no power whatever over the mind of Scotland; and it exerts no appreciable force in any of the great movements of thought, whether theological or political. That midnight interview of Carstares and William decided that, for evil or for good, Scotland in future was to be emphatically Presbyterian.*

* Since writing the above I have found in one of the volumes of the Wodrow MSS. (8vo. lxxxii., Advocate's Library) a narrative of "remarkable occurents" by a certain Mr. J. B., who was born at Glasgow in 1676, and became a minister of the Church. J. B. relates the proceedings which led to the summoning of this Assembly and the exaction of the oath, the blame of which he lays on Dalrymple and Tarbat.

After the malign instructions were sent down to Edinburgh, Portland, Mr. Secretary Johnstone, and Master William Carstares, the King's Chaplain were, he says, "not idle at Court to get a counter instruction; but all their solicitations were to no purpose till at length Johnstone, with much resolution and bravery, addressed the King one evening as he was going in his night-gown to his bedchamber." The King then gave in; a new dispatch was sent off, and reached Edinburgh at 4 A.M. on Thursday, the 29th March, the day on which the Assembly was to meet.

I have not been able, even with the aid of Mr. Laing, to identify J. B., and therefore can offer no opinion as to the value of his statement as compared with that of McCormick; but it is right the reader should have it laid before him. *Valeat quantum.*

CHAPTER XIV.

Correspondence—Darien Scheme—Ministerial Changes—Death of
William.

The 'State Papers' preserved by McCormick contain little beside the letters received by Carstares. His own letters in reply to those addressed to him by the Scotch public men and officers of state, if still extant, seem to be altogether out of sight and reach. Scarce any are accessible except those written to Dunlop and his more private friends. The loss of so large and important a collection of letters, as his general correspondence must have formed, is much to be regretted. Those that we have show us the tenor of his life and personal history plainly enough, his watchful interest in the affairs of the Scotch Church and State, his constant attendance on William. He was again with him in his annual visit to Holland, and campaign in the Low Countries in 1694. From "the camp at Rousselaer" he writes to Mrs. Dunlop, on the 30th of August, 1694. . . . "The distinct accounts he [Dunlop] sent to me of the proceedings of the Committee in the North * hath done us more service than it is fit for me, at this distance, to write of. . . . We have had no battles this campaign as yet, but we have, by the marches of our army, forced the enemy to live upon their own country; and this place where we now are belongs to their jurisdiction. Huy is besieged by a part of our forces. Your husband will know the place. . . . My brother Alexander crows over me, for he hath a John Carstares, who, I know, will be a darling of yours. I bless the Lord I have my health well."

The death of Mary, on the 28th of December, 1694, was

* The Commission empowered by the Assembly of 1694.

a heavy blow to King William, and threw him more than ever into exclusive intercourse with a few faithful and tried friends immediately around him, of whom Carstares was one. His ungracious distaste to English society and his phlegmatic reserve increased. "The Princess of Orange's popular affability," says Caryll, "did in some measure appease, or at least cover, the general disgust conceived against him : but she being dead, nothing can hinder an increase of aversion between him and the people."* The summer abroad was, perhaps, the only period of his lonely and silent life that he found enjoyable. In it he escaped from the unstable friendship and covert dislike of the English; he was among his trusty friends and compatriots; he had before his eye the familiar scenes of his level fatherland ; he was braced by the keen excitements of war and danger.

We have a few of Carstares' letters while he was with the King during the more eventful campaign of 1695.

Carstares to Dunlop.

"At the camp before Namur,
"July 8, 1695.

. . . . "I am very kindly received here, and am as much for calm methods in Parliament as ever. If your Assembly do not sit, the King is not to blame. We have this evening made a vigorous and successful attack upon the outworks of the town, and have gained most, if not all, of them. What our loss of men is I know not."

The Scottish Parliament had met in May. Hamilton was no more. He had died during the winter, and Lord Tweeddale, the Chancellor, succeeded the Duke as Commissioner. The tragedy of Glencoe had by this time been noised abroad. Party spite and national feeling were alike inflamed by it, and the general indignation chiefly concentrated itself on the Master of Stair.

The King had yielded to the inevitable force of public

* Macpherson's 'State Papers,' vol. i. p. 510. See also Burnet, vol. iv. pp. 403, 442.

opinion, so far as to appoint a commission of inquiry; but this measure of incipient justice was popularly thought too limited, and likely to be used in a way too favourable to the now detested Secretary of State.

Carstares to Dunlop.

"Dear brother, I wonder I hear not from you : I wrote to you some posts ago. The town of Namur is surrendered,* the capitulation being signed this day, which makes amends for the infamous surrender of Dixmuyd and Deinse. . . . . I hear you have a story with you that I concerted matters with the Master of Stair at Rotterdam, and tarried there for him. I tell you, in short, it is a notorious forgery; for I know nothing of his being on this side till I was within three leagues of this place, and saw him not till I came hither. Such methods of malicious defaming men will not, I hope, hold out long."

Carstares to Dunlop.

"Sombreffe, Aug. 29, 1695.

"I wonder I have had none from you, but one, all this campaign, —not so much as to give me notice of the death of my dear sister Katherine. . . . We have had, in the singular goodness of God, hitherto a very successful campaign. The siege of Namur, as circumstances were, having been one of the greatest enterprises of this age. We had just reason to detain the darling Mareschall † of Madam Maintenon prisoner,—whatever was the capitulation, while the French have kept no measures of faith or cartel with our King, who, by this action, shews the French King that he neither values nor dreads his resentments. As to the Assembly—I would willingly know, so soon as is possible (what Mr. Blair and yourself can say upon good grounds), that if it meet, the Episcopal clergy will not be at all meddled with at this time. You may easily judge I have reason

* The town of Namur was retaken from the French under Boufflers, by William, on the 6th of August. Villeroy, who had succeeded to Luxembourg's command (Luxembourg having died since the last campaign), had gained Dixmuyd and Deinse, on terms discreditable to the conquered. See Macaulay, vol. vii. chap. 21.

† Boufflers. He surrendered the citadel of Namur on the 26th of August, and was detained a prisoner in reprisal for the French breach of faith, in sending the garrisons of Dixmuyd and Deinse prisoners into France.

to be informed of this, while if it shall meet, the burden of the consequences of it is like to fall upon me ; for it is adjourned to such a time that the King must determine all things concerning it ere he go to England, and I dare not say that he will incline to do it,—and if it should be again adjourned, I know it will be uneasy to many, and, it is like, will add too to the load of reproaches cast upon me :—but I shall honestly use my endeavours to have you satisfied. I cannot think that the adjournment of it to such a time was with any design to put the thorn in my foot; but it was about the 7th of November ere the King arrived in England last year. . . My dear love to sisters and my brother Law. I cannot but upon many accounts lament his loss and our own. I shall only add, dear brother, that I am heartily concerned for the true interest of my country, as to the present constitution of our Church in it, and its civil interest : and I have no reason, with a respect to these, to repent of what were my methods and advices, which have exposed me so much to the resentment of some and obloquy of others, and do, as I hear, so still. Adieu."

There seems to have been, in some minds in Scotland, a still jealous dread of the King's adjourning the Assembly, as he had already done more than once, beyond a twelvemonth from the date of its last meeting, and thus setting at naught the Church's claim to hold its Assembly every year. After his return to London, Carstares writes reassuring Dunlop on this point. " I know nothing to the contrary but the Assembly will sit, but it is said that there will be a great difficulty to find a man you have confidence in to be a commissioner; honest men having such an aversion from it. . . . . . It is not in my power to serve my cousin Capt. Mure, except I stir up a hive of bees about my ears. He is indeed hardly dealt with, and I am sorry I cannot help him."

In another short note dated merely " Monday at one of the clock in the morning," he says, "Mr. Alsop prayed this day very heartily for your Assembly, and begged that all the devices of Tobiahs and Sanballats against it might be disappointed ; and Secretary Johnston desires me to tell you that he wisheth your Assembly may be worth the praying for." The Assembly met in December, and did but little harm or good. The agony of the struggle between the rival churches was over now, and the chances of a rupture between the ecclesiastical and civil establishments had come to a crisis, which, thanks to Carstares' interposition, had passed safely. The result was that the action of the Assembly, and of the other church courts, was felt to be of less importance, and drew less attention, than hitherto. Political and commercial questions, into which the *odium theologicum* did not enter, began to occupy the foreground.

The commission of inquiry into Glencoe had reported; and the Estates had, in a memorial to the King, invited him to give effect to the commission's severe judgment on the conduct of the Master of Stair and Breadalbane.* The Highland Earl was left unpunished; but the Secretary of State had to pay the light penalty of dismissal from his office. It was scandalously disproportioned to the crime; and so conscious was Dalrymple himself of its insufficiency in his countrymen's opinion, that, on his father's death, this year, he did not venture to provoke their enmity by taking his seat, as a peer, in parliament. The popular discontent, at his inadequate punishment, was no wise mitigated by the popular suspicion, that the King's displeasure was not so much due to a just indignation at a disgraceful crime, as to a Dutch jealousy of the golden promises of a new era of prosperity for Scotland. Lord Tweeddale, the Chancellor and Commissioner, and Secretary Johnston, were also turned out of office, though they had had nothing to do with the Highland massacre. The head and front of their offending was their connection, in which Dalrymple also had a share, with the Darien scheme.†

* The report, which is in McCormick's collection, pp. 236–54, acquits the King—"there was nothing in the King's instructions to warrant the foresaid slaughter"—but lays the chief blame on Dalrymple, whose letters were "no ways warranted" by the King's instructions, and appear to have been the "only cause" of the slaughter, "which, in effect, was a barbarous murder."

† On Darien, see Burton, from 1688, vol. i. chap. viii.; Macaulay, vol. viii. chap xxiv.; Dalrymple, part iii. book vi. p. 96.

The Scotch were, like the Jews, a people who combined with a strong religious faculty, a keen aptitude for finance, and love of the profits of commerce. Hitherto their trade had been much fettered by their foreign wars and internal discords. Only during the years of the Commonwealth, had they known the advantages of free participation in the larger commercial enterprises of England. But the benefits of that period had not been forgotten, although they had been lost at the Restoration ; and the memory of them gave a stimulus to the energy and eagerness, with which Paterson's projects for a foreign trade and a settlement at Darien were received by his fellow-countrymen. Gorgeous visions floated before the fervid national imagination. Darien was to be the site of a new and greater Alexandria ; through which should roll, to the ports of Scotland, a trade richer than that which had flowed from the East to Venice and Amsterdam, from South America and the Antilles to Cadiz and Seville, from the transatlantic plantations to London and Bristol.

But barring the way of the Jasons who should adventure on the accomplishment of these golden dreams, lay the solid and sullen commercial privileges and jealousies of England, Holland, and Spain—none of which could William venture to offend, even had he desired to do so, for the sake of his poor and unprofitable northern kingdom.

The English Parliament lost no time in addressing the King, and representing the disasters that would befall the commerce of England, if the Scottish Company, "trading to Africa and the Indies," to which the Scottish Parliament[*] had granted a charter, were allowed to execute its designs. The answer of the King, was to the effect that he had been ill-served in Scotland, but he hoped some remedies might be found to prevent the ill consequences that were apprehended from this Act.

"There are no means," says Mr. Hill Burton, "of further authenticating this remarkable answer, than by its having

[*] 26 June, 1695.

been generally received uncontradicted."[*] It receives a certain authentication from the paper which follows, and which is written in Carstares' hand. The same term is used in it as that reported by Burnet. This paper, however, appears to have been intended for Scotland, and is probably Carstares' suggestion of the despatch which should be addressed to the government there.[†] "The East India Act hath occasioned much noise, and made me some trouble. I am satisfied if my parliament had foreseen it, they would have prevented both; yet I have reason to say that I have been ill served in that matter by some of my ministers, whom I employed,—since the instruction I gave contains only a warrant for an Act to be the ground of a patent in favour of foreign plantations, with such rights and privileges as we grant, in like cases, to the subjects of our other dominions—the one not interfering with the other; but it leaves the granting of the patent to me, to be timed and ordered by me as I should see cause, so that I must say a patent, by way of Act of Parliament, was a surprise to me, having had no notice of it till it was past; nor had I any account of the particulars of it till I returned to England. I have also reason to be dissatisfied with some, whom I intrusted with the management of my affairs, for their either having encouraged—or, at least, not employed themselves in earnest endeavours to hinder, according to my express desire and order,—those things that were the cause of unnecessary heats in the Parliament, to the delaying greatly of the public business, and making the Session of Parliament longer than

---

[*] Burton, from 1688, vol. i. p. 293. Burnet, vol. iv. p. 292, gives the answer as above.

[†] The earliest printed quotation of the King's speech that I have seen is in a Scotch pamphlet printed in 1700, entitled 'A Short Speech prepared to be Spoken by a worthy Member in Parliament,' &c. The author is very bitter against the "evil councellors," who have guided the government; and amongst other charges, adduces this—"They have remitted £20,000 sterling into Scotland" [for bribes] "which they say Mr. Carstares has done by way of Holland, for the more close conveyance, and that by my Lord Portland's means." p. 12.

was either needful, or was consistent with my instructions;— which is a management, that both the manner of my government, and the quiet and security of my people in that kingdom, have obliged me not to let pass without marks of my displeasure. I must also recommend to you the using of suitable means for the preventing of our people being imposed upon, by false suggestions of ill-minded men."

The following paper of Carstares', undated, belongs to the same period; some of its suggestions obviously pointing to the arrangements rendered necessary by the intended dismissal of the ministers, whose commercial policy had incurred his Majesty's disapproval.

" For the commission of the Great Seal :

> Lord Rosse,
> Lord Carmichael,
> Lord Ruthven.

" His Majesty was pleased to condescend upon the persons above mentioned to supply the want of a Chancellor.

" President of the Council.

" The King did not positively fix upon any particular person for this place. The only persons that I conceive can pretend at present to be candidates for it are Earl Melville, Earl Argyll, and Earl Annandale. If the first of these be preferred to it, he will be acceptable to the body of the Presbyterians, and entirely so to the other party, which seems to be of some advantage to His Majesty's affairs in this juncture; nor is there any connexion between this place and that of President to the Parliament. As for the Earl of Argyll, if he keep his word of giving his lady an honourable allowance and living inoffensively and without scandal, his sense, quality, and interest, make him fit for any place.* As for Earl

* Argyll's character was not without reproach, and his domestic relations were unhappy. He was a constant correspondent of Carstares; and in one of his letters, about this time, says, " As to what you say in relation to myself and my own particular behaviour, I take it very kindly of you. . . . I do assure you my carriage shall be such as I shall give no just cause of scandal or offence. . . . There is one thing I know will be clamoured against, that I have sent my two daughters home to Rosneath, designing to

Annandale, the opinion that many of both parties have of his unfixed temper, and his huffing and encroaching humour, makes me judge that His Majesty will not at all find it for his service to make him president of the Council.* If the King shall think fit to put Earl Melville in this place, then either Argyll or Annandale may be Privy Seal, and the other a lord of Treasury.

"Register.

"The King did seem to incline to Earl Selkirk as to this post, and I then told your Lordship that my Lord Tarbett had said that it required a man of sufficiency, but that I had heard from others that the clerks could supply any want of that nature that might be in the person that was Register; and I am glad to hear that my Lord Stair said the same to the King; though now he says that, upon information of the nature of the place, he is of another mind,— but I have nothing to say further upon this head.†

"Secretary.

"His Majesty made choice of Sir James Ogilvie for this post, and I have not much to object against it. I hope he may do well enough in it.‡

---

take the charge of them myself. . . . . I wish and endeavour that they be bred up in all duty and love to me, as their father, which I cannot expect in the circumstances they have been in hitherto, living with a mother in those terms with me, and who never in her life showed them either the example of goodnature or duty to their parents." McCormick, p. 285.

---

* "Often out, and in, the Ministry, during the King's reign. . . . . not much to be trusted." 'Characters of the Statesmen,' in the Hyndford MS. McCormick, p. 97.

† Tarbat had been Lord Clerk Register, but had resigned. He writes to Carstares, in May 1695, "If the King judge it either fit or easy to please a party with allowing my address for a private life, I can as willingly quit a beneficial object to serve him, as they can trouble him until they get it. When their [i.e. the Presbyterians'] heat cannot bear with the Earl Melville's family, and with you, to whom they owe under the King all the power they have, I can little wonder of their fretting at me: but I hope their folly will not frighten the King from so faithful servants, nor you from giving him counsel for their sakes." McCormick, p. 229.

‡ Younger son of Lord Findlater; at the Revolution opposed to declaring the throne vacant, but afterwards brought over to William's side, and made Solicitor-General, through Secretary Johnston's influence. "Upon Mr. Johnston's and Lord Stair's dismissal, he was made Secretary of

"President of Session.

"The King came to no determination in this matter, and it may admit of delay for some weeks.*

"Lord of Session.

"I presumed to name one Scuggell for this office, and by what I hear of him I do not find much reason to alter my opinion : but my Lord Advocate may be consulted in this matter. I did also take the boldness to recommend Sir John Maxwell for the other vacancy in the Treasury, and I have still good reason to presume to do so.

"I am, my Lord, still of the opinion that the sooner these changes be made, it will be the better, for delays have only embarrassed his Majesty's affairs, and will, I am afraid, do still more so. His Majesty, if he shall so think fit, may allow the Duke of Queensberrie† and Earl Breadalban to speak to him to-morrow, before he declare his pleasure as to these things, for I suppose that Lord Tarbett hath already had the honour of waiting upon the King. There is one thing more that I would humbly suggest to your Lordship, which is that his Majesty would be pleased to call a Scots Council here, and honour them with his presence, as a Council .... I am confident, my Lord, that this method would be obliging, when there is a greater number of Scots councillors here than are at present in Scotland, and would shew that his Majesty doth both well know and take notice of the affairs of that kingdom ..... Allow me only humbly to beg of your Lordship, that when Mr. Johnston is put out, your Lordship would be pleased to intercede with his Majesty to give him ground to suspect that he will employ him another way, for I should be sorry to see him reduced to straits."

State, in which post he continued till King William's reign. ..... His implicitly executing what pleased King William, without ever reasoning about it, established him very much in his Majesty's favour, but his joining with an English secretary to destroy the colony of Darien lost him extremely with the people." Macky, p. 182.

---

* Vacant, through the death of old Stair, on 25th November, 1695.

† Drumlanrig had now succeeded to the title. He had taken the safe side at the Revolution.

This last sentence does not confirm the allegation of
Macky, that Carstares had dealt treacherously with Johnston.
Carstares, says the spy, is "the cunningest subtle dissembler
in the world, with an air of sincerity,—a dangerous enemy,
because always hid. An instance of which was Secretary
Johnstown, to whom he pretended friendship till the very
morning he gave him a blow, though he had been worming
him out of the King's favour for many months before." *
Now the last sentence of this paper of Carstares' is dictated
by a friendly feeling for Johnston; although the writer was
evidently convinced that the good of the State required his
dismissal from office. Nor was Carstares' disapproval of
Johnston's conduct a secret. In a letter to William Hamilton, of Killileagh, written in November, 1695, Walter
Steuart refers to it as well known, and generally sympa-
thised with. "The difference," he says, "between Mr.
Johnstown and Mr. Carstares still remains, and the former
hath a great deal of nobility against him." †

This unhappy Darien was from first to last a national
madness. The design was splendid in conception and outline; but it was impracticable in execution and detail.
William could have encouraged it, only at the cost of
detaching Spain for ever from the Continental coalition; of
alienating the merchants of his own Amsterdam and Rotterdam; of provoking the bitterest resentments of the English.
The advantages of the scheme, even if the Scots had gone
about it more judiciously than they did, were too problem-
atical to justify so great a risk. However much we may
deplore a great national disaster, we cannot, at this day,
blame him, or those of his advisers who concurred in the
course he took. Darien is now chiefly memorable as one of
the proximate causes of that union of the two kingdoms,
which William had much at heart.

* Macky, p. 210. The 'Characters' pass under Macky's name, if not
written by himself.

† Caldwell Papers, part i., p. 193. William Hamilton was Under-
Secretary of State for Scotland. Walter Steuart was of the Coltness
family, and was settled as a merchant in London.

The part which Carstares was understood to have taken, in the ministerial changes, was obnoxious to many of his countrymen in Scotland. As his moderate policy in Church affairs often exposed him to the reproach of being a lukewarm Presbyterian—too complaisant to English bishops and to a latitudinarian king—so the calm foresight, in this first stage of a fatal mania, which led him to anticipate the serious dangers lurking in the delusive future, and to see that the longer Paterson's specious project was encouraged by the government, the worse these would grow, incurred the charge of indifference to Scottish rights and interests, and tame acquiescence in the overbearing dictation of the English. Carstares bore the misunderstanding and ill-will with quietness—perhaps with a touch of contempt. "Be not troubled at stories," he writes to Dunlop, in March, 1696. "I begin to undervalue them as to any public actings I have been concerned in; for I have acted a more honest part in them than, it may be, some of the greatest murmurers against me would have done, and I see no reason that honest men have any reason to complain of any changes that are made."

I find only one short letter of his from the Continent, during 1696, dated "Breda, 18 May." "The King," he says, "is expected here from Loo to-morrow. . . . I shall peruse that book of Discipline you sent me, and give you my poor thoughts of it. Tell my sister I forget her not, though I have not answered her letter, which yet I shall do very shortly. Tell her that her nephew, Johnie Carstares, is a pleasant boy, and hath the nose of the family, which, it may be, you will think is none of the best, but I know it will please Sarah. My kind love to her and sister Jean. Adieu."

A visit to the theatre of war was, in those days, one of the recreations of men of leisure and fashion; and in June of this year Carstares' kinsman, William Mure, of Glanderston, made his way, among others, to the camp. He tells us he travelled from Brussels with "near 200 more in company,"

and with a military convoy, and was lodged at the "quarter
at Corbees, where my friend Mr. Carstares and Mr. Pringle,
the then Scots subsecretary, stayed, in an old bones house.
Within a day or two after I kissed the King's hand, being
introduced by the Earl of Selkirk, one of the bed-chamber
men, and once a day, while there, I rode alongst still with
the King, in viewing the lines." *

The Alexander Cunningham to whom the following letter
refers was a Scotsman of distinguished ability. He was
born at Ettrick, where his father was minister, in 1654, and
died in 1737. He lived for many years in Holland, and
part also of his long life was spent at Venice, where he was
British envoy. He was well known in the literary society of
England, Scotland, and Holland. He seems to have been a
man not only of diplomatic capacity, but full of literary
sympathies and activities.† Wodrow tells us of his proposed
edition of the Justinian Code, edition of ' Horace,' ' Remarks
on Bentley,' ' Vindication of Christianity,' &c. Some of these
projects were realized, some were not. The work by which
he is remembered is his ' Latin History of Great Britain,'
from 1688 to 1714, an English translation of which, by Dr.
William Thomson, was published in 1787. He was, when
Carstares became acquainted with him, tutor of John, Lord
Lorne, afterwards Duke of Argyll and Greenwich, that

> " Argyll, the State's whole thunder born to wield,
> And shake alike the senate and the field."

Carstares to Dunlop.

" London, November 3, 1696.

" DEAR BROTHER,—I have had none from you for some time. I
shall be glad to know how you and the family are, and Katherine's
child. . . . . I take this occasion of giving you an account of Mr.
Alexander Cunningham, my Lord Lorne's governor, whom I more
of late esteem than ever, for in a late conversation I had with him
he discoursed to me of a scheme for proving the divine original of
the Christian religion, and that all the arguments ordinarily made

---

* Caldwell Papers, i., p. 175.
† ' Analecta,' vol. iv., p. 152.

use of against it are clear proof of it; and, indeed, his way seems to be clear and convincing, and hath been so even to some great deists that he hath conversed with. He also designs to show how unreasonable it is for the Socinians to plead for Reason being judge in matters divine, and that the divine original of the Christian doctrine being once proved, faith ought absolutely to take place as to its particular mysteries; and that the Scripture is to be the alone rule of judging of them. I must confess he did much please me by his discourses upon these heads, and the more because I was misinformed of him as to his principles. He is of extraordinary parts, deserves to be encouraged and justified against calumnies, and may be an honour to his country. You may, in a letter to him, take notice of your satisfaction with the account that I have given you of him, and desire he would favour you himself with a short hint of his scheme as to this excellent subject, in a time when deism grows so much. I dearly remember sisters, your children, uncle, aunt, and other friends, and so doth my wife, who hugely blames your wife's silence in not letting her so much as know whether she had her hangings. Let her answer this charge. Godolphin is out of the Treasury. Our secretaries are not yet here. Adieu."

There are no letters of interest during the rest of 1696, nor, indeed, for a considerable time afterwards. The King, after his next year's visit to Holland, returned to London in November 1697, on the conclusion of the Congress of Ryswick, which pledged France to recognise William as lawful sovereign of the British Isles, and ended the long and weary wars. Carstares was detained in Holland by sickness, and did not witness the rare cordiality with which his master was welcomed home by the Londoners. Several of his short notes to Dunlop about this time are partly written in cipher, to which we have not the key, and seem to refer chiefly to passing events in Scotland, in Church or State—the former of little permanent importance—the latter all more or less overshadowed with the impending lurid gloom of Darien. The correspondence in McCormick's collection is full of the "African Company," their shares, their addresses to the King, their wrath at Sir Paul Rycaut, at Hamburg, and general indignation at

the jealousies of England. Interspersed among the letters
of this class are others, beseeching Carstares' influence and
help in obtaining appointments, civil or military. This
reply to one of these frequent appeals is a good specimen of
polite evasion of the request.

> " *To Lord* —— ."
>
> "Loo, Aug. 30, 1698.

"MY LORD,—I have the honour of your Lordship's letter, and
would have given a return sooner had I not been for some days at
Rotterdam. As to what your Lordship does me the honour to
write about, I assure your Lordship my capacity to serve you in it
is not such as some may imagine; and I do not doubt but your
Lordship is sensible that others will have the management of that
affair in their hands, with whom I have the honour to be in such
friendship that, if it were fit for me to make proposals as to posts
of that importance, yet it would be in subordination to their inclinations and desires; and if those your Lordship mentions in yours
befriend you in your affair, I have too great an honour for them,
and am too much a faithful well-wisher to your Lordship, as to offer
to stand in the way of your Lordship's satisfaction. But really,
my Lord, as I have said, I have not that weight in matters of such
importance as some think I have; but your Lordship may be
assured that I am, sincerely, my Lord,

> "Your Lordship's most faithful and most humble servant,
>
> "W. CARSTARES."

The following letter is a sample of the applications for
aid and counsel he was constantly receiving, and also serves
to illustrate the embarrassed condition of many of the great
families in those disordered times; on which the fines and
forfeitures of the persecution, and the divided policy of the
Revolution, had left their evil mark, and in which men still
trod at every turn, "*per ignes suppositos cineri doloso.*"

The Earl of Sutherland's son, Lord Strathnaver, had a
command in the army, and was with the King in all his
campaigns.

> "Edinburgh, April 24, 1697.

"RIGHT REVEREND,—I came safely to this place on the 17th
instant, I thank God, and request you to bless him on my behalf
for so great a mercy. My son is not yet come here; therefore I

must request you to persuade him to haste home, since his absence from this is like to ruin his estate ; and I can command nothing of my own to live upon (for you know he is farmer of all that is mine), unless he return here speedily : so that if the king command him not home, where he can do his Majesty better service than in Flanders, his family will be ruined, and I will be redacted to great hardships, having nothing but my wife's jointure (which was farmed by Mr. Watson for six thousand merks by year) to live upon ; and, for that part of it, which Jarviswood should pay me for, I cannot command a farthing of it, though there be two years rent and a half due unto us. Wherefore, I must entreat you to make this known to both the secretaries, that they may deal with his Majesty to let my son home ; and to send an order to the receivers of his Majesty's rents to make what is due to my wife effectual ; and what he pleases to give myself also ; for without that, we have but the name of nothing. My wife is very valetudinary still, yet gives her most affectionate service to your dear consort and yourself. The confidence I have in your friendship, and the difficulties I now lie under, constrain me to give you this trouble, hoping you will forgive my freedom, and esteem me, as I am in all sincerity, sir, your affectionate friend and humble servant,

" SOUTHERLAND." *

The Treaty of Ryswick was followed by a resumption of diplomatic intercourse between England and France. Portland, who was angry with William for the favours heaped on Albemarle, and unwilling to remain at Court, agreed to accept the embassy. His residence in Paris necessarily withdrew him, for the time, from his former charge of the affairs of Scotland, and left these even more than formerly to the guidance of Carstares. In the spring of 1698, Carstares was for a time in Scotland, on political business, the progress of which he reported to Portland. Lord Portland instructs his secretary, in thanking him for his letters, " positively to let you know the satisfaction he has of your safe return, and that you found things so well to your mind and the King's interest in Scotland—desiring you will continue the same information as you have given hitherto. . . . . His Excellency has no time to answer you himself, but

* McCormick, p. 294.

if anything occurs you want his opinion in, acquaint me with
it, and I will endeavour to satisfy you as speedy as possible
can be done." *   An ambassador to the first Court in Europe
could obviously give little time to the subjects of such a
correspondence as a correspondence with Carstares must have
been,—and as no one in London succeeded to the superintendence of Scottish business which Portland had exercised,
the sagacious chaplain became during his absence, for all
practical purposes, the viceroy.

After the ambassador's return from France however, Carstares writes to Dunlop: "Though Earl Portland hath, for
reasons known to himself, laid down his key, yet he stands
firm in the King's affection, and will concern himself still in
our affairs, so that there will be no changes."

During the years of 1698–99 and 1700, Carstares' Scotch
correspondence is particularly active—much of it in cipher—
most of it purely political, but always with a large admixture
of intriguing, finessing, railing accusation, and begging for
place—which, read in the cold light of after ages, looks
sadly selfish and paltry. Sometimes there are lighter
touches, and glimpses of the social life of Edinburgh; as for
example, when Cockburn, the Lord Justice Clerk, writes one
September afternoon, " They daunced at our court, in the
Abbey, till four o'clock this morning;" or when Ogilvie (now
Viscount Seafield and President of the Parliament) closes a
letter with, " I have an untollerable fatigue; I did proceed
this day in the above for seven hours [Parliament], and did
thereafter give a public dinner." One of the most exacting
and impatient of the correspondents was Argyll. He was
constantly demanding or complaining. His predominant
grievance in 1699 was the appointment of Lord Teviot
(formerly Sir Thomas Livingstone) to the command in
Scotland. " The secretary," he writes, in high dudgeon, to
Carstares, on 16th March 1699, " advises me to live well
with Teviot, when he comes down. I had better not live at
all, if the King redress me not, or allow me, with his favour, to

* McCormick, p. 334.

redress myself." Again—"There is that rogue Forbes, fifteen shillings sterling a day not. There is Major Burnet has eight shillings a day; there is one Dunbar, a cowardly rogue, has eight shillings a day; there is the Laird of Glengary has 200*l* sterling a year of pension, a Papist, and in Lord James Murray's name; and meantime my brothers must want, and I not gratified in a trifle since I came from London. All this I have over and over again represented to V. Seafield; but to no purpose. I am at a deal of drudgery in writting long letters to him; but all is lost: and, if you cannot cause him doe me right, I shall give over my correspondence; and I must tell you, who I conceal nothing from, I cannot easily digest it. He fances me the easy fool—but it is not I. Sir, pray excuse this from one is your's. Adieu."[*]

With all his diplomatic *suaviter in modo*, Carstares could be perfectly firm, if he thought it necessary. We have, as I have said, hardly any of his replies to the manifold letters he received; but one or two survive in stray collections, which give us an idea of his more formal official style.

Sir John Maxwell, of Pollok, wished to be made Lord Treasurer Depute, and had been grumbling to Seafield about his being made, instead, Lord Justice Clerk and Lord of Session, in succession to Cockburn, who was promoted to the envied post (equivalent to that of the modern Chancellor of the Exchequer). Seafield sent the letters of remonstrance to Carstares, who, as usual, was the source of the appointment. Carstares then writes to Sir John. "I have made bold to give my humble advice to my Lord Secretary, that the commissions designed for you should be expeded, notwithstanding of what you are pleased to write to my Lord about them. And though it may be this is too great presumption in me, yet I am sure it is intended in all sincerity for the good of my country, the satisfaction of friends, and the contenting of honest men in general.

"London, February 4, 1699."[†]

[*] McCormick, p. 466.
[†] 'Memoirs of the Maxwells of Pollok,' vol. ii. p. 115.

The deference of tone, tenacity of purpose, and declaration of unimpeachable motive, seem all very characteristic.

Carstares to Dunlop.

" London, May 9, 1699.

" . . . . When I am able to give you a farther account of your African Company I shall do it.   I am desired by more than one to let you know that you are like to lose the right of Mr. Snell's gifts in favour of your University, by delaying to do what is your part in proposing some young men to have the benefit of that settlement.* I hear that the Master of Balliol College hath wrote twice to you upon this subject, and hath no return. Pray mind this affair without delay. There is one Hay, whose father was minister of Kinneuchar, that I am desired to recommend to you, which I do, knowing that you will do for him what you shall find convenient."

In July, 1698, the long-projected expedition to Darien sailed from Leith, " amid bright sunshine and the plaudits of a vast assemblage." In the darkening days of October, 1699, it became known in Edinburgh that the settlement had been deserted by the first settlers.† In the midst of the tumult of rage and disappointment which agitated the whole nation, Carstares was sent down to Edinburgh to give the weight of his presence and advice to the Government. He remained in Scotland till March 1700, and writes to Dunlop, on his return,—" I do meet with all the kindness I can desire," from which we may conclude his conduct had been satisfactory to the King—though what special commissions he had borne we do not discover.

Nothing said or done in Scotland could induce William to sanction or protect the ill-fated colonists ; and the grand scheme and expedition came to their tragic end in the spring of 1700, leaving to Scotland a legacy of financial ruin and political distraction and to William a legacy of

* The Snell Exhibition to Balliol.
† Burton from 1688, vol. i. p. 308.   Dalrymple, vol. iii. vi. p. 96.

national hate, as much more bitter than that engendered by Glencoe, as hard-won Lowland money was more precious to the Scot than lawless Celtic lives.

Amidst the crash of the universal disaster a special blow smote Carstares.

His dear friend Dunlop had been much interested in Darien. His experience of Carolina marked him as one of the few men in the country who knew anything of colonial life. He was made a director of the company, and led the professors of the University, of which he was principal, to invest 500*l.* of their slender funds in the company's stock. Although harassed by the excitements and anxieties of the enterprise, he was not thought to be in dangerously ill-health. On one Sunday evening in March he was supping in Edinburgh, with his friends Sir John and Lady Maxwell; before the next, he was no more. Carstares felt keenly the sudden loss of one so much in his confidence, and bound to him by so many close and familiar ties.

He could not return to Scotland to see his sister, but he wrote to her the following letter from London, on March 16:—

"MY DEAREST SISTER,—Could my sincere sympathy with you, or my concerned tender affection for you, signify anything to you under your heavy affliction, you have them both in a high degree; but I must confess your loss is so great, and I share so deeply in it, that I am at a stand what to say. But He that spoke as never man did, can speak to your soul with such power, as to calm all the stirs that are there, because of the great breach that in infinite wisdom is made upon you. He can say to the swellings of your grief, for what is by His hand taken from you, 'Peace, be still!' Then there will be a holy acquiescing in His disposal of your dearest earthly comfort. O that He himself would speak a word in season to you in your present heaviness!

" Dear sister, endeavour to have it for your language what you have in Psalm xxxix. 7,—'And now, Lord, now, when the affectionate, the useful, the edifying, and comfortable companion of my pilgrimage is taken from me, what wait I for! my hope is in Thee.' O lift up your soul to this all-sufficient God, who can rejoice it. Sorrow not as those that have no hope; you are far from having reason to do so. Fix not your thoughts altogether upon the dark side of what the infinitely holy and sovereign God hath measured out to you, but consider what reason you have for thanksgiving, even in your present circumstances. Bless God that ever you had such a relation; that you enjoyed him so long; that he was not taken from you when he was in the remote parts of the world; that he hath had access to be remarkably and singularly useful in his generation beyond many; and that he hath died lamented and desired by the lovers of Sion. All I shall add at present is, that the God of Consolation can comfort, stablish, strengthen you, and that it is my earnest prayer He would be pleased to do so. You have the affectionate sympathy of my dear wife; we give our love to the children and poor sister Mackie. Allow me, dear sister, to assure you that you shall always find me to be with tender concern,

"Dear sister, your most affectionate, sympathising brother,
"W. CARSTARES."

"You had a father," he writes, on 9th April, to Dunlop's eldest son, "whose memory will be savoury to posterity. He did cast you a pattern of a well-managed zeal for the interest of Christ and the public good, and of faithfulness and affection to his friends. I hope it will be your endeavour to imitate it. I doubt not but it will be your endeavour, too, to be a comfort to your destitute and afflicted mother, and that you will be exemplary to your brethren in your deportment. You and they may be assured of all affection and assistance from me that I am capable of. Your father's memory will always be dear to me. I have wrote to Hugh Cunningham to take out the gift of pension which the King hath given to your mother. It is 60*l.* only a year. Pray give her my dear love, and tell her she is, and shall always be, much upon my heart. I kindly remember your aunts, and your brother John, with little Will. Let me hear fully from you. I know you will have a care of any papers of your father's, that related to the public. I do not think it fit that you should let any of them go out of your hands. I heartily commit you all to the gracious care of an all-sufficient God, who can richly bless you and supply all your wants, and make up your great loss. My wife gives her dear love to your mother, and is as affectionately concerned for you all as I am.

‘ " My brother Alexander is desirous to have John with him in Holland, if he have not an inclination to follow his book." *

Carstares had to take a second journey to Scotland, with the King's commands, in May. He writes to his sister from Carlisle, on the 11th of that month. "I came this western road of purpose to have been a day or two with you, before I went to Edinburgh ; but I am forced to stay here for want of horses, and cannot get away till Monday, though I came hither yesternight ; and I have been longer on the road than I expected, both through the badness of the way and weather, and by a severe fall I had, by which my left shoulder was so much bruised that I was feverish for a day or two, and did ride with uneasiness. . . . . . My desire was to make my first visit to you, but the providence of God hath ordered it so that I now judge it will be fit to go first to Edinburgh, and I will endeavour to see you afterwards. I have a very sincere sympathy with you, dearly remembering you before Him who can supply all your wants. Your concerns shall be more minded by me than my own. Pray, dear sister, encourage yourself in the Lord, and firmly believe that He is infinitely wise and all-sufficient."

Mrs. Carstares, a few of whose letters remain, says, in writing to Mrs. Dunlop, on July 20th :—" I was extremely concerned that my dearest did not see you when he was last in Scotland ; and it was no small disappointment to him that he could not go first to Glasgow. He landed in Holland yesterday was a se'nnight—had a good passage from Gravesend to Rotterdam. He sailed in two nights and one day. At his coming to his

---

* John went to Holland, but did not turn out a creditable member of society.

brother's, he found my sister Carstares' mother dead in the house."

Carstares had carried his report of affairs in Scotland to the King, at Hampton Court, and had reluctantly attended him abroad. The earnest desire of his Scottish Ministers was that the King should visit his northern kingdom; and the policy of such a step was urged on him by Carstares. But William would not take his advice on this head, any more than on that of his marrying again;* and went back to his beloved Holland, to the grievous disappointment and embarrassment of his servants in Scotland—who found themselves obliged to carry on the government in an impeded and ineffective fashion, in the face of a general disloyalty and a large Parliamentary opposition. Queensberry, who was now Commissioner, Marchmont the Chancellor,† wily James Steuart the Lord Advocate, all alike complained of the impossibility of conducting the government with proper firmness and authority. "You do well," writes Steuart to Carstares, "to recommend vigour; but I wish also you would send us a good dose of it, for I protest it is not here to be found."‡ William, however, was habitually indifferent to Scotch politics; and affairs in that kingdom had to right themselves after the shock of Darien as best they could, without his personal interposition. Yet he entertained his Scotch subjects with the prospect of his coming during the autumn. "You tell me," writes Queensberry § on 26th September, "His Majesty desires to know what is the

* McCormick, p. 582.

† Formerly Sir Patrick Hume.

‡ McCormick, p. 547.

§ The domestic and personal references in Queensberry's correspondence are sometimes rather amusing. After the death of the young Duke of Gloucester he writes to Carstares expressing his regret, and then proceeds : "I shall say no more on this melancholy subject at present, nor trouble you with any other business, but to beg that you would receive the King's orders for me in relation to the manner of my mourning. If I shall only put myself and my wife in black, it is a matter of no expense; but, if it be thought fit that I put my servants and equipage in mourning, the charge will be considerable to the King; for I have at least fifty servants shortest time in which things absolutely necessary may be provided for his coming. I know not truly what may be reckoned absolutely necessary. You know the condition of the house and the apartments of it." * The royal visit never was paid, and William died without having crossed the Tweed.

We have but one more letter, dated "Hampton Court, 21st December 1700," written by Carstares during his master's lifetime. It is to Mrs. Dunlop, and refers to the appointment of her husband's successor.

"The College of Glasgow," he says, "was under extraordinary obligations" to Dunlop. "You may be assured that it is my particular concern that there be such a principal as may be both fit for the place and friendly to you. There are three spoken of at present—Mr. Flemming, who is here, and upon whom I can entirely rely; Mr. Cumming, whom you and I both have a confidence in; and Mr. John Stirling, of Greenock, of whom I heard not till yesternight, by a letter from Sir John Maxwell, and whom you need take no notice of; but if he should be the man, I cannot think but he will be according to your mind.† But, dear sister, be at ease. I hope that business will be adjusted with my advice. . . . . Let me know upon all occasions wherein I can serve you. . . . . My love to my nephew, with brother, and sister Drew." ‡

He spent the summer of 1701 again in Holland, chiefly at

that I must clothe, besides my coaches, which I must have from London, it being impossible to get them here. I have privately made an estimate of the prices of things, and do find, that, to have all these things as they ought to be, fifteen hundred pounds will be the lowest it can be brought to; wherefore, as soon as possible, let me have his Majesty's pleasure in this matter."—McCormick, p. 594.

* McCormick, p. 662.

† He was the man.

‡ His sister Jean had recently married the Rev. Joseph Drew, afterwards Principal of St. Andrews.

Loo—whither William had resorted for the last time. The King did not return thence till November. Prospects looked brighter, both politically and personally, for William, in England and Scotland, than they had looked for some time. The recognition by Louis of James's eldest son as the rightful King of England after his father's death, in the spring of the year, had at once quickened the sluggish English loyalty to William's throne, and had evoked a spirit in cordial sympathy with his hereditary hatred and distrust of France.

Although Scotland, as yet half paralysed by the shock of the Darien calamity, was still brooding in bitter and menacing wrath over her ruined hopes, out of the very depth of her misfortunes was rising the dawn of a better day of more assured prosperity. The King's clear eye discerned, amidst the gloom and distraction of all parties in that country, the possibility of giving effect to his long-cherished project of a legislative union between it and England. But he was not to live to wage any more wars with his old enemy, or to ratify the Scottish union. All summer, at Loo, his health had been bad, and the harsh winter had not improved it. On the 28th February 1702 he sent a fresh message to his English Commons, calling their attention to the question of union with Scotland. He despatched Albemarle to Holland to make ready for an early campaign against Louis. But before the House could act upon his message,—when Albemarle came back, on the 7th March, with a favourable report,—the King turning coldly from thoughts of politics and from news of camps and armaments, could only murmur *"je tire vers ma fin."* * The end was at hand. On the morning of Saturday, the 8th of March he died, at Kensington, in the fifty-second year of his age, and the fourteenth of his reign.

We have no record of any intercourse that may have passed between him and his chaplain in those closing days.

---

* Amplified by Lord Macaulay into "I am fast drawing to my end."

But it was remembered afterwards that not long before his death he expressed his unabated regard for his faithful friend and servant. " As for Mr. Carstares," he said, " I have known him long, and I know him thoroughly, and I know him to be a truly honest man." *

* Burnet, vol. iv. p. 559.   Dalrymple, iii. x. p. 169.
' Fame's Mausoleum : a Pindarick Poem,' by Robert Fleming. 1702.
Mr. Graham Dunlop possesses a gold ring containing a lock of William's hair, which, when on his death-bed, he gave to Carstares.

CHAPTER XV.

Queen Anne—Carstares goes to Edinburgh as Principal of the University
—One of the Ministers of the Town.

CARSTARES could never speak of the death of King William
without tender emotion.* Cold and gruff as he appeared,
there was in William's Dutch heart a deep and faithful
centre, which attracted and reciprocated the affection of
strong natures like his own. Heinsius, Bentinck, Carstares,
were not only loyal subjects and trusty servants, but devoted
friends. Their political fidelity was confirmed by their personal devotion. It is easy to understand William's claim
to such attachment on the part of such men. His faults of
manner any lackey of the Court could observe; but men,
who, like himself, had been trained in the stern school of
danger and adversity, held the ungracious manners excused
by the noble principles. Carstares had been nearly tortured
to death under the *régime* of the urbane and fascinating
reprobate Charles. In the unpolished William he had found
a master whose mind was filled with great ideas, whose
intelligence was luminous, whose aims were high, whose spirit
was noble and serene, whose instincts were just, whose sympathies were all on the side of liberty and righteousness.
His character was cast in a large and heroic mould, as one
predestined for other than the "common chances common
men could bear;" and those within the circle of his influence
who were lovers of liberty, of truth, of the rights of man,
and who were haters of immoral prerogative and authority
and superstition, not only recognised in him their proper
leader, but clung to him with an affinity of the heart, no

* McCormick, p. 67.

less than of the understanding. William valued their attachment, and was invariably faithful to his friends.

The friendship of William was no passport to the favour of Anne. His heavy sister-in-law had never been on cordial terms with him, and her dull sympathies were with the Tories and not with the Liberals. She, however, knew and esteemed Carstares, and, without solicitation, continued to him the appointment and emoluments of Royal Chaplain, which he had enjoyed during the late reign.* The Queen was a staunch Episcopalian, and his personal attendance was never required by her, as it had been by William; nor were apartments provided for him at Kensington or any of the palaces. While William lived he had received frequent allowances for special services, but this source of income was now cut off, and except the slender revenues of the Chapel Royal he had no official salary.†

Carstares' direct influence in the management of Scotch affairs, of course ceased with William's death. He could

---

* McCormick, p. 69. Graham Dunlop MSS.

† These allowances had not been large enough to admit of his " laying by." The following is a list of them, from the Graham Dunlop MSS. :—

1. Grant of rents of chapel royal. 26 Feb. 1690.

2. New gift of ditto, with deanery and sub-deanery thereof. 28 Feb. 1694.

3. Letter to Treasury determining the rents of the Abbey of Crossraguel, and Priory of Monimusk and Auchlossan, to belong to Carstares by his former gift, and ordering payment of them, with arrears. 28 Feb. 1695.

4. Treasury warrant for £300 for " acceptable services performed." 30 March 1697.

5. Letter to Treasury, ordering payment to Carstares of £1000 of grassum, due by University of Glasgow, for their tack of the Archbishopric. 22 July 1697.

6. Letter for payment of £200 for services and charges in Flanders. 6 Feb. 1699.

7. Ditto, ditto, £400. 11 Jan. 1700.

8. Warrant for £200 (" no consideration ") on 3 July 1700.

9. Letter for payment of £300 for services with the King in Holland. 8 May 1701.

10. Ditto, ditto. 3 Feb. 1702.

11. A new warrant, by the Queen, of the office of one of her Majesty's chaplains, with the rents of the Chapel Royal, Deanery, and sub-Deanery. Dated at St. James's, 12 May 1702.

never again expect to stand so near the throne as he had stood and to wield his former power. It appears that his first inclination was to withdraw wholly from active life. To renounce public and political functions entirely seems to be easier to some men than to accept a diminished share of them. Diocletian retreated to his garden at Spolatum, and Charles V. to his convent at Yuste, when wearied of the sceptre, to forget, in a thorough change of life, their former toils and cares. But the retirement which Emperors can command, commoners with straitened incomes cannot purchase. Carstares could not afford, at the age of fifty-three, to forego the active occupation which might supplement his private resources; nor could he keep himself, even if he wished it, completely out of the stream of politics. He was too well known, and his experience and counsel were too highly valued by the statesmen of the day, to allow of his burying himself in an idle privacy. After remaining for some time in uncertainty as to his future plans, he resolved to settle in Edinburgh, and to accept the office of Principal of the University.

Dr. Rule died early in 1703, and in May of that year Carstares was elected his successor by the Town Council, in which the patronage of the University was vested.*

The period between his quitting the Court and his coming to Edinburgh was spent in London. It was a time of anxiety to the Liberal and Presbyterian party in Scotland.

The Queen's leanings were known to be towards the reactionary party, to which Episcopacy was dear, and in whose eyes the Revolution was a vile thing. The Tories and Jacobites began to swagger with the air and tone of confidence and success. The hotter Presbyterians were ready to assume, on their part, an attitude of jealous and menacing self-assertion and to make the Parliament-house and the Church Courts ring with their technical war-cries. In the Parliament of 1702, when the party headed by the Duke of

* Bower's 'History of the University of Edinburgh,' vol. ii. p. 27. McCormick gives a wrong date, 1704.

T

Hamilton had withdrawn, the Presbyterians were overpower-
ingly strong, and they did not hesitate to use their strength.
When Bruce of Bromhall ventured to hint, in debate, that
"some of the laws establishing Presbytery contained things
inconsistent with the essence of monarchy," he was unanimously expelled from the House.* (But days were coming
when the Presbyterians were to go more softly.)

The dread of the party's rashness is reflected in Carstares'
correspondence,

In some of the provincial synods, the clergy's apprehension
of a renewal of oppressive and prelatic policy in the Government acting under a malign Court influence, had prompted
indiscreet harangues upon the Church's "intrinsic power."
The more the Church suspected and dreaded "Cæsar," the
more was she prone to vaunt her independence of him; and
she tried to escape from the unpleasant consciousness of her
inability to match him if he took to his own weapons, by a
louder assertion of her peculiar spiritual power. Carstares,
who had a statesman's dislike of extreme formulas and parade
of abstract resolutions, writes to Principal Stirling, the successor of Dunlop,† at Glasgow : —

" London, April 21, 1702.

" Rev. and dear Brother,—Your kind letter was not a little
acceptable, not only upon the account of the sensible and plain
narrative it gave of what passed at your synod, but because it was
so expressed as I was in a capacity to improve it to some advantage.
The proposals as to the intrinsic power, which some few urge with
so much warmth, are at this juncture so visibly inexpedient, and, I
had almost said, destructive, to the solid security of our church,
that I am amazed any should have the countenance to urge them,
and particularly such whose zeal for such heights was little
known till there were factions in our state. I cannot forget the
noise that was made about this affair in the last session of
Parliament, and chiefly by some who would laugh at our folly if

---

* 'Marchmont Papers,' vol. iii. p. 241. 'Lockhart Papers,' vol. i. p. 47.
† Thirty-six letters of Carstares are preserved among the MSS. of the
library of the University of Glasgow. They are to be found in three 8vo
volumes, lettered on the back respectively, 'Letters, Scots, 1701-1714;'
'Letters, England, 1702-1713;' 'England, 1714-1717.'

we should believe that they had the least tincture of Presbyterian principles. I bless God that the Church of Scotland hath such a settlement, and such quiet as at present it doth enjoy; and long may it do so — and such will have little peace, upon serious reflection, that would disturb its peace and expose it to danger by rash and imprudent practices, however disguised and varnished. I am persuaded that our strength at present is to be quiet and sit still. Her Majesty hath solemnly declared that she will maintain the Church as by law established; and those of our country that have the chief management of affairs under Her Majesty have been, and continue to be, friendly to our Church, and solemnly declare their firm resolution to be so.

"What shadow of a reason, then, can there be for our taking new measures to gain new and uncertain friends? Is it not rational to think that we secure better what we have, by a discreet management of it than by grasping at more? . . . .

". . . . The Church may sometimes sustain prejudice from the overacting of its friends as well as from the designs of its enemies. The good Lord Himself direct those concerned" * . . . .

Carstares to Principal Stirling.

"London, June 22, 1702.

" . . . . I hope there shall be no ground to fear that the late King's gift to the University shall be infringed, and you may be assured, dear brother, that I shall not be wanting in my care and endeavour to prevent any prejudice to the University; though I am apt to think that some of your regents have not carried so kindly to my sister as might have been expected; but this is only betwixt you and me " † . . . .

Clouds were darkening the northern sky when Carstares transferred his residence from London to Edinburgh. The political atmosphere was charged with the elements of storm; and in returning to his own country, though he quitted the greater and busier arena of public affairs, he stepped into one far more excited and contentious. That passionate and tortuous strife was beginning which was to end in the Union; and Jacobite stratagems, Episcopal pretensions, Presbyterian jealousies, national prejudices, personal dishonesties, and political corruptions weltered together in illimitable babble

* Glasgow University MSS.   † Ibid.

T 2

and confusion. The presence of the calm and judicious Churchman, bringing his wide experience of courts, councils, and camps, to this narrow and fiery centre of Scotch life and action at Edinburgh, must have been a blessing to the few wise and honest patriots who, in taking their share of the conflict, were trying to direct it to a safe issue of public welfare; while to his fellow-Churchmen, in particular, his name was a tower of strength. He found at Edinburgh many of his old friends, as well as others with whom he had long been on terms of more or less confidential correspondence. Sir James Steuart was still Lord Advocate; Cockburn of Ormistoun had been turned out of the Treasury by Queen Anne, and Marchmont had been deprived of the Chancellorship, but they both continued to take a keen part in politics. Seafield, who, as Secretary of State, had been a constant correspondent of Carstares', was now Chancellor, and his firm friend Queensberry was Commissioner. That Earl of Arran, whom he had tried so hard to win over to William's side was now, as Duke of Hamilton, rising to a position of strong influence, though of very questionable integrity. It was not at a time of much political excitement, and in the midst of the society of such men as these, that Carstares could hope to enjoy the felicities of the " beatus ille, qui procul negociis."

He did not, however, allow his interest in public affairs, and his relations to these leading statesmen, to intrude upon his discharge of the proper duties of his office in the University. In that he was as sedulous as if it had been his sole concern.

The local habitation of the University of Edinburgh was then, as now, at that Kirk of Field which had gained an evil name at the murder of Darnley. Where the spacious edifice of the College now admits its 1500 students, the " Manse and house of the Provostry of the Kirk of Field," along with a " great lodging,"* built by the Town Council, gave humbler accommodation to a much smaller concourse of students, and to the Principal and regents. The houses of the Principal

* Bower's History, vol. i., appendix.

and regents were handsome dwellings, with good gardens attached to them. The college itself was built around three courts, and had a high tower over the great gate which opened towards the city.*

The salary of the Principal had been fixed, in 1609, at 500*l.* Scots, or about 41*l.* 13*s.* sterling; but a short time before Carstares' election (and presumably in view of it), the Town Council agreed to increase this wretched pittance to the still inadequate sum of 1600 marks, or about 92*l.* sterling.† The patrons elected Carstares on the 12th of May: two days later he appeared before them to take the oaths of office; and on the 3rd of June the Lord Provost, Sir Hugh Cunningham, duly installed him at the College.‡

Among the Graham Dunlop MSS. is the paper that follows, endorsed, " What I said when Sir Hugh Cunningham did present me to the Masters as Principal : "—

" You may be sure, my Lord, that I would have called for any rules that concern my post from the keeper of the library, but I shall read this paper which your Lordship hath given me; yet, my Lord, I cannot but tell your Lordship and the other worthy magistrates of this city that are here present with you, that I look upon myself as coming into this post upon no other terms than what my predecessor did; and that, as to my part, all affairs relating to this college remain entire.

W. CARSTARES."

The particularity of this statement records the existence, at the date of Carstares' installation, of embarrassments created by the incongruous relation between the University and the civic Corporation, which only ceased when that relation was, in our own days, abolished by Act of Parliament. The functions of University government and patronage, which, in Padua and Pisa, had been entrusted by Venetian and Florentine Senates to small and carefully selected courts of the most eminent of the citizens,—of

---

* Calamy's ' Life and Times,' vol. ii. p. 175.
† Town Council Records, vol. xxxvii. p. 325.
‡ Ibid. p. 482, *et seq.*

which, in Leyden, the enlightened civic aristocracy of one
of the most intellectual of European communities had
declined to assume the responsibility, were confidently discharged by the municipality of Edinburgh. The natural
result was encroachment—now on the rights of the Town
Council, now on those of the University—jealousy and alter-
cation. One of the frequent disputes had reached its height
just before Carstares' installation. The right of the Crown
to present to a chair of its own creation had been contested
by the Council; in reprisal for an assertion of the independence of the Senatus, the salaries of the professors had
been stopped; the academic discipline was alleged to have
fallen into discredit and abeyance; and the patrons had declared their resolution to revise the whole laws of the University. As a preliminary to this revisal, the laws were
publicly read at Carstares' installation, and to this his initial
statement referred.* His firmness and tact were successful
in guiding the action of the University and in conciliating
the irritated and jealous Town Council. A remodelled code,
framed by the Principal, was adopted by the patrons, who expressed their favour for him by appointing him to the charge
of the Church of the Grey Friars, and raising his salary to
2200 marks,—which, however, appears to have included his
stipend as a minister of the " good town."†

The laws, as remodelled by Carstares, contain some quaint
regulations, illustrative of the state of society at that time, as
well as several of permanent value. " The college meetings
begin with October. In the winter season the students are to
meet in their classes before seven in the morning. . . . . On
the Lord's Day the students are to convene in their classes
presently after sermon, to be exercised in their sacred

---

* Bower, vol. ii. 24 et seq.

† Bower, vol. ii. p. 40. Town Council Records, vol. xxxviii. p. 142, of
date 11 Sept. 1704. "The Council, with the Kirk Sessions of the City,
being convened together, did subscribe two calls, one to Mr. William
Carstares, Principal of the College of Edinburgh, and one to Mr. William
Mitchell, one of the ministers of the Canongate, to be two of the ministers
of the good town of Edinburgh."

lessons. . . . . The students are obliged to discourse always in Latin ; as also to speak modestly, chastely, courteously. . . . . Those who transgress—especially such as speak English within the college—are liable, the first time in a penny, the next in twopence. . . . . None may absent from the college or go out of it without his regent's licence. . . . . Every one is to show good examples to others by his piety, goodness, modesty, and diligence in learning, as becomes the disciple of Christ. . . . . Let all shun bad company, as a corrupting plague. None may carry sword, dagger, gun, and such arms, or forfeit threepence. None in the evening may walk the streets. . . . . The principal and masters being informed that the custom of playing at dice (owing its rise to infamous bankrupts) has lately crept into the college, and knowing what hazard and mischief those portend to studies, piety, and good manners, therefore they strictly discharge students to use cards, dice, raffling, or any such games of lottery. . . . . Those who neglect to go to church shall forfeit sixpence each time." . . . .

Along with the duties of principal, Carstares discharged those of *primarius* professor of Divinity, and of a parish minister. His habits of method, his equable temper, and his great capacity for work, enabled him to overtake the calls of each office with regularity and perfect success. Of his prelections as a lecturer on Divinity none remain, unless a long paper on the comparative merits and authority of Episcopacy and Presbytery may be regarded as written for his students. The teaching of systematic theology, however, appears to have been the duty in those days of a second professor; and the Principal's lectures (probably on special questions in theology) were delivered not oftener than once a-week, in the common-hall, and were attended both by students and professors.* He observed the custom

* 'Account of the Government of the Church of Scotland.' London, 1708, p. 20.

This pamphlet gives a minute account of the system of government and teaching in the University of Edinburgh, which evidently devolved much

of opening each session with an oration delivered in the presence of the Senatus and the students:—

"In his first oration," says M'Cormick, "which he pronounced in the common hall of the University, before a very numerous and respectable audience, he displayed such a fund of erudition, such a thorough acquaintance with classical learning, such a masterly talent in composition, and, at the same time, such ease and fluency of expression in the purest Latin, as delighted all his auditors. Even his enemies were obliged to confess, that in him were united the manners of a gentleman with the science of a scholar. The famous Dr. Pitcairn, who was always one of his hearers upon these occasions, used to observe that, when Mr. Carstares began to address his audience, he could not help fancying himself transported to the forum in the days of ancient Rome."*

Carstares, like the other great divines of the Scottish Church in her best days, took no narrow and provincial view of the position and character of the National Establishment. To him the Church of Scotland, while the rightful representative of the religious life and belief of the Scottish people, was but one branch of the great Reformed Communion, and was bound to live in brotherly alliance with all the other ecclesiastical bodies, which maintained reformed doctrine and Presbyterian government. He desired to strengthen the ties which bound the Church of Scotland to the Presbyterians of the Continent, of England, and of Ireland. With a view to this, he had already done what he could to procure the appointment, in the Scotch Universities, of some professors from those of Holland. He was in favour of sending young Scotsmen to finish their educa-

---

more personal superintendence and examination of the students on the Principal than is attempted now. The curriculum then began with Greek, a knowledge of Latin being indispensable before entrance. There were public disputations before the heads of the University; the candidates for degrees had to defend their themes against the Principal and professors and all comers, and to deliver "harangues" in Latin, Greek, or Hebrew. Is the modern M.A. or B.D. of Edinburgh sufficient for these things?

* McCormick, p. 70.

cation abroad, and of thus keeping up the old connexion, which associated the names of Crichton, of Buchanan, of Mair, of Melville, and of many Scottish scholars and divines, with the honourable traditions of the Continental Universities. And now, as head of the University of Edinburgh, he wished to render the seminary, over which he presided, attractive to those Presbyterian and Nonconformist students whom exclusive tests debarred from an academic career in England, and Ireland. His plan was the establishment of what is now called a "college hall," under the wing of the University, in which these students should be accommodated. They were to have a common table, and their studies and conduct were to be under the charge of an English warden. Thus, while enjoying the advantages of the public instructions of the Scotch professors, they would still be, to a certain extent, amenable to English influence, and under familiar control.

The English Nonconformists went into the project with some heartiness, and money was subscribed to carry it out; but its execution was delayed too long, and at last the death of Carstares extinguished it.[*]

The proposal to appoint the Principal of the University one of the ministers of the town was started at a time when there was no vacant charge, and the Lord Provost, though anxious to co-operate with Carstares' friends in securing his services for a city pulpit, appears to have shrunk from the responsibility of creating a new charge. There was some talk and negotiation about it, which coming to Carstares' ear, he wrote to Sir Hugh Cunningham :—

"My Lord,—Two of my friends, to whom your Lordship spoke about an affair in which it seems I am concerned—I mean a call to be one of the ministers of your good town—have informed me that your Lordship is straitened between the kindness you are pleased to have for me and the concern you are obliged to have for the interest of the town.

* McCormick, p. 71. Bower, vol. ii. p. 48 et seq. Graham Dunlop and Murray Dunlop MSS.

"I have thought it my duty, by these lines, to contribute to your ease in that matter, by assuring your Lordship that, as I have had no manner of concern in seeking after such a call, so I do not desire to be the occasion of the least prejudice to the interest of the town of Edinburgh. And I beg that neither your Lordship nor any others of the magistrates of the city may be in any perplexity on my account.

"Your Lordship knows that whatever might have been the inclinations of my friends to have me settled in my own country, it was with reluctance I brought myself to be so much as passive in accepting the honour the good town conferred upon me, by calling me to the station I now fill. I can safely say it was not the prospect of gain that brought me hither. I bless God, who hath been pleased not to leave me so destitute either of friends or interest, as that I might not have obtained a more lucrative settlement elsewhere."

The proposal, however, was effected, and Carstares became minister—first of the church and parish of the Grey Friars, and afterwards (in 1707) of the historic High Church, or Cathedral of St. Giles.

In the Grey Friars Church his colleague was James Hart, a zealous minister and a fervid Scot. It is of him McCormick relates an anecdote which illustrates Hart's keen temper and Carstares' courtly forbearance and kindly charity.

About the time of the Union, according to McCormick, "a national fast had been appointed, which the violent opposers of that scheme amongst the clergy would not observe, as they could not approve of the reasons for which it was appointed. Mr. Carstares had given his advice against the appointment, but as a zealous friend of the Union, he observed the fast. His colleague, who was equally zealous in his opposition to that measure, not only refused to observe it, but next Sunday took occasion, in the forenoon sermon, to throw out some bitter reflections upon the Union in general and upon certain contrivers and promoters of it in particular, who, he alleged, were traitors to their country and to the Church of Scotland, although some of them were ministers of that Church, and had too great influence over their deluded brethren.

"As this violent attack was directly pointed at Mr. Carstares, it fixed the whole eyes of the congregation upon him, whilst, with great composure, he began to turn over the leaves of his Bible. His colleague's discourse being considered by the people as a formal challenge to Mr. Carstares to vindicate his conduct, a great crowd from all corners of the city were assembled to hear him in the afternoon, when he gave out for his subject these words of the Psalmist, "*Let the righteous smite me, it will not break my bones.*" From which he took occasion, with great calmness of temper, to vindicate his colleague from any suspicion of being deficient in point of regard and affection for him. That difference in opinion was the natural effect of the weakness and corruption of the human mind. That, though he differed from him in his sentiments upon some points, yet he was sure both of them had the same end in view. And that, as he knew the uprightness of his colleague's intentions, and the goodness of his heart, he was determined to consider any admonitions or rebukes directed to himself from that place as the strongest expressions of his love.

This discourse had a wonderful effect upon the whole audience." *

Of Carstares' gifts as a preacher we have no means of forming an estimate. The incidental notices of his sermons that occur in 'Wodrow's Correspondence' and elsewhere, are always laudatory; but nothing remains on which we can found an independent judgment. The editor of his nephew William Dunlop's sermons says: "In his ministerial charge he was equally diligent and prudent, and applied himself with the greatest cheerfulness to the lowest and most toilsome offices thereof. He had an admirable gift, both of prayer, and preaching; choosed always to insist on the most weighty and important subjects of religion, and delivered his sermons so gravely and distinctly, with

* McCormick, p. 72.

such an acceptable *pathos* and well placed accent, and all the other advantages of a natural and easy eloquence, as never failed to fix the attention of his hearers, and greatly to promote their edification. His sermons were of that sort as to be understood by the meanest capacities and admired by the best judges." * McCormick bears similar testimony.

" He discharged the duties of his pastoral office with great fidelity and diligence, qualities which attended him in every sphere of life in which he was engaged. Such of his sermons as he has left behind him are written in a short-hand peculiar to himself, so that we cannot ascertain his character as a preacher from his compositions. It is certain he was much esteemed as a preacher in these times. His manner was warm and animated, his style strong and nervous, and at the same time chaste and correct. And although he had been for a considerable time out of the habit of preaching, yet he had such a comprehensive view of the great subjects of religion and so happy a talent of arranging his ideas upon every subject, as rendered this branch of his duty no great burthen to him." †

In one able thus to turn aside from the envied post of a favoured courtier, and confidential adviser of a great monarch, to the quiet position of a ruler of a small university, and the comparatively obscure and commonplace avocations of a parish minister in a poor and struggling church, there surely were some of the best elements of the sound and equal mind, which carries its possessor safely and serenely through prosperity or adversity. In either place, Carstares appears alike at home, strong, wise, and competent; adapting himself to any circumstances and faithful in every duty. The change, however, from all the habits and interests of the last fifteen years of his life, was somewhat modified by the fact that Edinburgh, for some years after his settlement there, was the theatre of political action more momentous than any that had occupied the Scots, since the Reformation.

* Preface, p. 10.   † McCormick, p. 72.

CHAPTER XVI.

The Union.

THE greatest triumph of the Augustan reign of Anne was the happy Union. King William had often said that the island could never be tranquil without a Union, and that if the two nations understood their own welfare they would not rest until it were effected ; * and he had left the design as a political legacy to his successors, unable himself to carry it through. Never, perhaps, in the history of England and Scotland had the public feeling been more mutually hostile than after the death of William. Never did an amicable incorporation of the kingdoms appear less possible, and yet in a few years that incorporation was accomplished. Sentiment, even of the most friendly and favourable type, is the weakest of all bases of political action; and had the British Union rested on this, it would have been insecure, and probably short-lived. It had a firmer foundation on those political, social, and commercial necessities, which, by their constant tendency to embroil the two nations, proved that national prosperity and peace could only be attained by a combination of interests and rights. England had nothing to lose by changing her northern neighbour from a vindictive enemy, hanging on her most exposed frontier, into a humble rival in her foreign and colonial trade. Scotland had everything to gain through having the wider arena of English political and commercial life opened to her energy and ambition.

She was to lose, indeed, her native legislature; but it was, except, perhaps, the Polish Diet, the most turbulent and

* Defoe's 'History of the Union.' Introductory, p. 32.

impotent legislature in the world. Men like Queensberry,
Stair, and John Duke of Argyll, must have felt, with bitterness, the narrow range to which their genius was restricted
within the Parliament House of Edinburgh. Even Fletcher,
the brilliant Cicero of the "country party," could not but
long, while he denounced the Union, for a grander audience
than that afforded by the Scots' Estates. Even Belhaven's
perturbed and prophetic spirit would have been soothed,
could he have foreseen his country's destined share in im-
perial statecraft, war, and glory,—could a Father Anchises
have unrolled for him the vision of the future, and showed
him a Scotsman on the exalted seat of Lord High Chancellor of England—a Scotsman filling the metropolitan chair
of Augustine,—Camperdown leading the British fleet to
victory—Clyde saving the endangered empire of the East
—Elgin and Dalhousie reigning over vast dependencies, in
which a Scot in Belhaven's day was an alien, — Scotsmen
taking the lead in every advance of science, and second to
none in the ranks of British literature.

The trading and mercantile classes had been convinced,
by the fate of Darien, that extensive enterprise and large
profits were inaccessible to them, unless they could enjoy
free trade with England, and have a right to a share in her
foreign and colonial traffic.

The Church itself, much as it disliked and dreaded the
prelacy of England, was aware that it would run less risk of
assault under the protection of the stable legislature of
Great Britain, pledged to maintain a Protestant succession,
than if left to hold its perilous way amidst the turmoils and
factions of Scotch Episcopacy, Jacobitism, and Cameronianism.

Each class of the community had sound reasons for
desiring a Union with England; yet the general sentiment,
which seldom follows the guidance of pure intelligence, was
averse to the measure which the common welfare seemed to
demand. A federal union might have been accepted without
demur; but an incorporating union, which alone would
resolve all the difficulties of the case, was almost universally

unpopular. All the pride of an ancient nationality, all the prejudices of a small and zealous community, were arrayed against it. It was abhorrent to the politico-religious fanaticism which still reverenced the Solemn League and Covenant. It was dreaded by the Episcopal Jacobitism which clung to the hope of a restoration of prelacy and the Stuarts. It alarmed the rigid Presbyterianism of Cranford. It promised to realise none of the ideals of Fletcher's classical republicanism. The incorporating union, however, was that on which the whole question of permanent amalgamation, or separation, turned; and no small credit is due to those statesmen who, keeping it steadily in view, withstood popular obloquy and rose superior to national predilection, and persevered until the vital point was finally won. In the labours of these, Carstares took an influential, though unobtrusive, part. The times were past when his opponents could reproach the Government with entrusting the whole Scottish Administration to his hands;* but the great influence of his personal character and political sagacity remained, and was an acknowledged power amongst English and Scottish statesmen. While in Edinburgh he was in constant correspondence with the politicians of London; while in London he maintained an equally active correspondence with Edinburgh.

Among his English correspondents was Harley, who was no less keen for union than Somers. I find a letter from Harley after the collapse of the first negotiations in 1703, and when the new Scottish Parliament was fiercely debating the proposals which were shaped into the " Act of Security." After expressing that difficulty of understanding the motives and affairs of other communities, which is a common English

* " Those factious people [the Presbyterians] finding themselves encouraged from Court, where all things were then, and have during all the late reign, to the scandal of monarchy, been managed by the uncontrolled councils of an ambitious Presbyterian clergyman."—'The State of Scotland, under the Past and Present Administration,' &c. 1703.

characteristic, he says, in reference to the affairs of Scotland :—

" To say the truth, very few speak at all about them ; and those who do (I do not mean any Ministers of State), speak with too little concern—less than they do of the King of Sweden and the Pole. I think this is not right ; for though Englishmen may not meddle about their affairs, I cannot but have a zeal for a nation so full of good and learned men, who have, in all ages, given such proofs of their learning and courage ; a nation sprung from the same original, inhabiting the same island, and professing the same religion.

" These reasons, sir, make me a well-wisher and a servant to the nation, and fill me with grief to see a cloud gathering in the North, though no bigger than a man's hand. I wish some of you would do their endeavour to dispel that cloud : that some amongst yourselves (for none else you will suffer) would bind up the wound, would fling a garment over the nakedness of your country. Some papers have made a great noise of the independency of that kingdom ; I cannot imagine to what end, because it hath never been thought otherwise, or treated otherwise, since the days of Queen Elizabeth.

" I must still profess myself full of hearty good wishes for the honour and prosperity of that kingdom ; and should be very glad to be able to answer several questions which now and then fall in my way to hear ; as, Whether such long sittings of parliament will not have fatal consequences, besides the altering that constitution, if often practised ? Whether the whole nation will acquiesce in renouncing the house of Hanover, and agree with another person ? Whether foreign subsidies will maintain the expense of a king and a court ? Whether a king of their own will ever procure them any sort of advantage in trade ; and what shall be given to their neighbours to obtain it ? Whether, under a king of their own, the power of the nobles must not be increased, and the liberty of all the rest of the people proportionately diminished ? Whether the present constitution of their ecclesiastical regimen can be of long continuance under such a government ? and, Whether the hand of Joab is not in all this ?

" I am unwilling to add an objection which strikes me dumb : which is this : Here is a treaty set on foot by the public faith of both nations for an union ; so great a progress is made in it, that trade, and other things desired, seemed to be agreed ; and, without any regard to public faith or decency, &c., all is laid aside, and

England is to be bound by a collateral act of another nation. Are men in earnest? Does any single person believe this is the way to procure what they seem to desire? But, sir, I fear I have said too much. Pardon the overflowings of my affection to your country and the desire of its prosperity. My confidence in your well-known candour, probity, and great prudence, encouraged this address." *

This letter expresses fairly enough the general feeling of the English statesmen : a desire for the security which a union would guarantee; a mild impatience of the apparently unreasonable and illogical Scotch opposition to it; a vague dread of Scotch jealousy and touchiness; dubiety as to the real condition of any party or question in the northern kingdom.

Soon after receiving this letter, in August, 1703, Carstares went to London, where he remained till March, 1704. From the few letters in the Glasgow collection we gather that he was detained there partly by private concerns of his own, and partly by public business, among which he specially adverts to the claims of the universities to the Bishops' rents. There had been a design to deny these; and a letter withdrawing the gift of the rents was ready for the Queen's signature when, with the help of the Duke of Queensberry, Carstares obtained a renewal and confirmation of all that had been granted in William's reign. While securing this provision for the universities, he declined to take any share of that portion of it assigned to his own University of Edinburgh.

We miss in those years of the Union the frequent and familiar letters that used to be addressed by him to Dunlop, and we see little, if anything, of his private life. Nor is his presence in the councils and negociations of the time so obvious that we can everywhere mark the very part he took. We rather discover the extent of his power by the constant respect for his opinion, expressed in the correspondence of such men as Harley, Portland, Seafield, Stair, Argyll, Mar, and others, charged with the conduct of the affairs of State;

* McCormick, p. 719.

U

and by the tacit acknowledgment, which the general deference to him implied, that his influence in the Church could either confirm or defeat the Treaty.

The course of this great measure may be traced in full detail in the pages of Defoe, or, in luminous summary, in those of Mr. Hill Burton. We need not follow it here more closely than is necessary in order to understand Carstares's relation to it. His chief concern was to secure the Treaty from the hostility of the Established clergy. The days were over when ecclesiastical war-cries stirred the deepest passions of the nation. Redress for Darien and free trade with England and her colonies were now watchwords of greater potency than Prelacy or Presbytery. The " country party," animated by the genius of Fletcher, thought to force what it considered justice to Scotland from her southern sister, by giving new prominence to all those points at which Scotch independence was, in English eyes, most menacing and capable of mischief. Hence the rejection of the proposals of extended toleration of the Episcopal clergy; the Act securing the Protestant religion and the Presbyterian government in terms stronger than any Act hitherto had used;* and the Act of Security, which deliberately refused the Scottish Crown to the future sovereign of England unless, before Her Majesty's demise, " there be such conditions of government settled and enacted as may secure the honour and sovereignty of this crown and kingdom—the freedom, frequency, and power of parliaments—the religion, liberty, and trade of the nation—from English or any foreign influence." †

While the sentiment of injured and jealous nationality was thus strong, the clergy, accustomed as they were to bring their politics into the pulpit, could do much to stimulate it and give it direction. Had they zealously opposed the Union, their influence was known to be still sufficient to render their

* " As agreeable to the Word of God, and the only government of Christ's Church within this kingdom."—' Account of the Proceedings of Parliament of 1703,' p. 44 et seq.

† Ibid, p. 242 et seq.—Act of Security.

opposition fatal.* But although they could not be brought to petition or move in its favour, their opposition was judiciously moderated, and restricted mainly to points at which they believed the Treaty was likely to infringe the rights of the Church and the jurisdiction of Presbytery; and when the securities which they desired were provided, they (at the risk of forfeiting their popularity with the commonalty) gave their support to the Union party.† That they did so, was chiefly owing to the sagacious policy of Carstares. We can gather this, as I have indicated, not so much from any extant correspondence of his own (at this period very scanty), as from the tenor of the letters addressed to him, and from the respect which we can see the statesmen were aware his educated countrymen in general, and the clergy in particular, paid to his advice. "It may be questioned," says Mr. Hill Burton, "if any one, not in the immediate and responsible councils of the Crown, had so fully the means of anticipating the general character of the Treaty before it became public; and the hints which he received, assumed the flattering form of applications for advice and counsel." ‡

A letter, unsigned, but evidently written after the conclusion of the Treaty by a member of the English Cabinet, bears the highest testimony to the value of Carstares's interpositions. "Give me leave to assure you, sir," says the writer, "that the part you have acted in this great affair is sufficiently understood by all that know anything of the affairs of Scotland. And I daresay it will not be easily forgot, what all our great men are very sensible of, that the Union could never have had the consent of the Scotch Parliament, if you had not acted the worthy part you did." §

The General Assembly was still, as it had always been, the great focus of ecclesiastical power. Its influence had in earlier times been virtually co-ordinate with that of the Parliament;

* McCormick, p. 75.
† Lockhart Papers, vol. i. pp. 159, 173, 225.
‡ Burton, from 1688, vol. i. p. 430.
§ McCormick, p. 76.

and even now the Estates could not afford to disregard the voice of the Church, as uttered in its annual convention. The Church, indeed, had of its own accord, begun to sap one of the foundations of the Assembly's power by imposing restrictions upon the admission of the laity to its councils, but these had, as yet, scarcely had time to operate.* The right of annual meeting had been fully secured; every district of the country was represented; and the ministers and elders who formed the Supreme Court of the Church were, on the whole, just and influential representatives of the national religious belief and ecclesiastical polity.

It was natural that a Churchman of Carstares's position and power should, as soon as possible after fixing his residence in Scotland, become a member of the Assembly. Accordingly, in the Assembly which met at Edinburgh in March 1704, he took his seat as representative of the University of Edinburgh.† His name appears, along with that of his old friend James Steuart, the Lord Advocate, in the list of a select committee appointed to prepare the " Form of Process," or rule of procedure in cases before the judicatories of the Church.‡ In the Assembly of 1705 he sat as one of the ministers of Edinburgh and representing the Presbytery. He, Principal Stirling of Glasgow, and Mr. James Brown, one of the ministers of Glasgow, were proposed for the office of Moderator; and Carstares was elected by a majority.

He made a formal speech on taking his seat, thus introducing a practice which has continued to the present day, and which, along with other usages attaching to the office of Moderator, has tended to make the election to the chair more orderly and deliberate than it might otherwise have

---

* By the Acts of Assembly of 1700 and 1704, which required subscription of the Confession of Faith from all *elders* returned as members of Assembly —Acts, it should be noted, which never were confirmed by Parliament.

† MS. Records of Assembly, vol. for 1702–5, in College Library of Glasgow.

‡ Acts of Assembly, 1704. The " Form of Process " was presented to the Assembly of 1706, and sent down to Presbyteries for approval, and passed into law in 1707.

been. "The method of premeditated and studied speeches is now come in at the opening of our assemblies," writes Wodrow, in 1715, " and was brought in by Mr. W. C., a good many years ago. It is attended with several inconveniences. It seems to prælimit the vote of the Assembly to a person concerted beforehand, otherwise the person chosen is at a stand, not having his speech ready. Besides, unless very cautious and general, it seems to prælimit the Assembly in their business, by promises in name of the Assembly to the commissioner, &c." * Those results, which Wodrow dreaded as evils, were, no doubt, foreseen by Carstares as among the advantages of the system he adopted; and, upon the whole, the plan of having the choice of the Moderator settled beforehand has tended to impart dignity and tranquillity to the proceedings of successive Assemblies.

The foes of the Church had probably calculated upon the Assembly's indicating a readiness to assume an attitude of hostility to the coming project of a union, in a way which might have been embarrassing to the Government, or on its being divided into two factions of unionists and anti-unionists. Difficulty and dissension were likewise anticipated by the enemies of Presbytery in connection with the case of the contumacious and uncontrollable Hepburn,† who had now tried the forbearance of the Church to its utmost limit. An extreme Cameronian, admitted to the pale and ministry of the Establishment, he had for years set all its laws and usages at defiance, and lifted up a ranting "testimony" against its policy and principles. He was now finally condemned, and, notwithstanding his popularity with a considerable body of the people and the sympathy of the "True Blue" section of the Church, was quietly deposed.‡ The sinister expectations of the troublers of Israel were thus disappointed; and, in his address at the close of the Assembly, Carstares said,—"I hope, reverend brethren,

* 'Analecta,' vol. ii. p. 301.   † See ante, p. 231.
‡ Acts of Assembly, 1705.

that I shall not be judged by you to be much out of the way if I allude, with a respect to this Assembly and the enemies of our Church, to that which we have in the xlviii. Psalm. No doubt many who wish not well to our interest have these days past come hither to spy out our liberty, and to catch at something that might be matter for their drollery; but they have seen the beauty of our harmony, the calmness with which our debates have been managed, the order that hath been in our proceedings, and the civil authority of the magistrates and the spiritual power of the Church kindly embracing each other. They saw it: they marvelled. They were troubled, and hasted away." *

" Your being Moderator," writes John Duke of Argyll, to Carstares, " is a satisfaction to all honest men, and particularly to myself."† " Lord Portland," writes Seafield, " asked kindly about you. I told him you governed the Church, the University, and all your old friends here; that you lived with great satisfaction, and was as much his servant as ever. He said it was some satisfaction to him to find that you and I, in whom King William reposed so great trust, were still f such consideration in the present reign." ‡

Carstares opened the next Assembly with a sermon on Ps. xlvii. 8; and in this, as in the following Assembly of 1707, not being in the chair, he was able to take an active part in the debates. " His manner of speaking in Church courts," says McCormick, " was calm, sententious, and decisive—which, along with his influence over the most considerable members of the house, gave great weight to his opinion in every debate. Such was their respect for his character, that one sentence from him would often extinguish in a moment the most violent flame in the house. This authority, which he had acquired, he knew well how to maintain. In matters of lesser moment he seldom spoke at all; in business of consequence he spoke only in the close of the debate, and it was

<hr>

* MS. Records.   † McCormick, p. 735.

‡ Ibid. p. 74.

a rare instance in which any adventured to speak after him." *

Carstares could not always, however, succeed in restricting the action of the clergy to those which he considered wise and profitable courses. Appointing a fast was a favourite device when they felt that affairs of public importance, of which some official cognizance seemed due from the Church, were in progress. Carstares was aware how inappropriate this way of testifying their concern for the general welfare must appear to English statesmen, and much disliked it. He writes to Principal Stirling, in October 1706, after the Synod of Glasgow and Ayr had been fasting, " I return my kind thanks for the account you gave me of your synod, and should have been glad I had known what reasons were given in for your private fasts. . . . . We are blessed with one memorable success after another against the common enemy " (the Episcopal-Jacobite party), " and how a day of fasting will look at such a time you may judge." † Again, to the same correspondent : " As for what concerns the great affair of the Union, that is the common subject of discourse, I can only say that the most grave and judicious ministers here do look upon it to be a matter of such weight and consequence, that the terms of it ought to be well understood ere positive sentiments about it be expressed, and especially by their brethren in pulpits, or by Church judicatures ; and they seem to think that the plain nature of the affair itself, as well as the multitude of those that wait for our halting, do call for great circumspection in our management. . . . . And it is not doubted, reverend brother, but that you will use your endeavours, as you have access, that the carriage of our brethren may be such in this matter as may be liable to no just exception, as a too hasty and peremptory expressing of a judgment about it (till it be fully known) will be. We here are indeed sensible that it is our duty to be earnest in prayer to God that He would so order this important business as the

* McCormick, p. 74.
† Glasgow MSS., Lett. Scot. 1701-14.

issue of it may be to His glory and the solid advantage of both kingdoms as to religious and civil concerns." *

The Church's interests, in prospect of a union with prelatic England, had often engaged the Scottish Parliament; and Belhaven and his friends had been zealous to maintain that the treaty offered no security to the Church adequate to the danger which she would incur.† The Jacobites eagerly tried to fan the flame of discontent and apprehension;‡ but the great majority of the clergy were too wise, and were too wisely counselled by Carstares, to be led away by the zeal of injudicious allies or the false sympathy of covert foes. The commission of the General Assembly, which, in virtue of its ordinary powers, continued to act when the Assembly was not in session, represented the Church duringt he progress of the treaty with calmness and dignity; and in its addresses to Parliament temperately stated those points in the measure which were considered defective. § The Commission complained of the English Sacramental Test as the condition of holding civil and military office, and urged that no oath or test of any kind, inconsistent with Presbyterian principles, should be required from Scottish Churchmen. They recommended that an obligation to uphold the Church of Scotland should be embodied in the Coronation Oath. They represented the necessity of a "Commission for the Plantation of Kirks and Valuation of Teinds;" and they concluded their fullest and most formal representation with an intimation that knowing, as they did, that twenty-six bishops sat in the House of Lords, which, on the conclusion of the treaty would have jurisdiction in Scottish affairs, they desired to state, with all respect, but all firmness, that it was contrary to the Church's "principles and covenants" that "any Churchman should bear civil offices and have power in the Commonwealth."

* Glasgow MSS., Lett. Scot. 1701–14.
† Defoe. Minutes of Parl., &c., p. 55 et seq.
‡ Burnet, vol. v. p. 289.
§ Defoe: Appendix, p. 13 et seq. Lockhart Papers, vol. i. p. 173.

These representations had due effect.* The bench of bishops of course could not be removed. The operation of the Test Act in England could not be meddled with, though its scandal and injustice were undeniable;† but as a kind of equivalent for this grievance, and to guard the Scotch universities and schools against the infection of prelacy, it was enacted that every professor and teacher should, ere his admission, subscribe the Confession of Faith as the confession of his faith, and bind himself, in the Presbytery's presence, to conform to the discipline and worship of the Established Church. It was provided that the unalterable establishment and maintenance of the Presbyterian Church should be stipulated by an Act prior to any other Act that should ratify the treaty, and should then be embodied in the Act of ratification ; and that the first oath the British Sovereign should take, on his accession and before his coronation, should be an oath to maintain "the government, worship, discipline, rights, and privileges of the Church of Scotland."‡ The minor points, as to kirks and teinds, &c., were satisfactorily disposed of, and the Church saw her firmness and moderation crowned with an adequate success.

The country ministers were, in general against the Union ; § and it is probable that the position which Carstares took on

* There were more addresses than one ; but the above is the substance of the most elaborate given by Defoe; against which it may be noted that Rothes, Marchmont, Polwarth, and some other elders entered their protest. Defoe: Appendix, p. 16.

† "Letter from a gentleman in Scotland to his friend in England, against the Sacramental Test." London, 1708.

‡ Hill Burton, from 1688, vol. i. p. 466 et seq. This is still the first oath taken by the Sovereign.

§ "Many of the clergy (the far greater part whereof being young men of little experience and warm zeal, are too easily imposed upon, and being by a melancholy constitution apt to entertain fears and jealousies) did become very cross and uneasy, and as now oppose, being entangled by the craft of those who pretend friendship of late ; and grown jealous of their old friends, were too busy to fright the vulgar (who are much inclined to follow their preachers) with dangers approaching to the Kirk government, which they are beyond expression fond of."—Letter of Earl of Marchmont to Somers, Nov. 9, 1706. 'Marchmont Papers,' vol. iii. 305.

the side of the Court and Government, was more uncompromising than it would have been, had he not felt that he must concede as little as possible, lest he should encourage the opposition. This may explain the fact of his having abstained, in the Commission, from voting for the address which has been quoted (though he did not join in the protest of Marchmont and the other elders), and which he presumably, like these protestors, considered too provocative of English ill-feeling, by its testimony against bishops, and too suggestive of an unbecoming distrust of the wisdom and goodwill of the Parliament of his own country.* The heat of the country ministers was also allayed by one or two judicious "circular letters," composed by Carstares and sent to the Presbyteries, by the authority of the Commission, as occasion seemed to require. Of these circulars, which were pronounced by Harley to have been "eminently serviceable in promoting the Union," † the following is a specimen :—

"A letter from the Commission of the General Assembly to the Presbytery of Hamilton :—

Edinburgh, December 6, 1706.

"Rev. dear Brethren,—The General Assembly of this Church having appointed us to take care that it suffer no prejudice through

----

* McCormick, pp. 754, 758.

The attitude of the Commission was at the most merely negative, and indicated so little active hostility, that the consternation which their address appears to have spread through the ranks of the Unionists is almost incomprehensible. The Duke of Hamilton, writing on 14th November, refers to the Commission as giving plain proof of the Church's aversion to the Union. "Your lordship may easily perceive, whoever they be who undertook to bring the Presbyterians into this measure have totally failed, for in this Commission of the Church, though there were but thirty lay elders of the greatest consideration amongst them, yet there were but her Majesty's two chaplains and one other minister of the whole Commission of a different sentiment, which shows the greatest unanimity that has been known in such an Assembly; and you may depend upon it this will have the utmost influence upon the people, who are the most affectionate to the present Establishment."—'Marchmont Papers,' vol. iii. p. 425.

† Ibid. p. 757.

neglect of due application to the Honourable Estates of Parliament, or any other judicatory concerned in the management of public affairs, we have in this juncture, wherein a treaty of union with the neighbouring kingdom is under deliberation, before the repretatives of our nation endeavoured, and are still endeavouring, to exoner our consciences in doing what we judge incumbent upon us for securing the doctrine, worship, discipline, government, rights, and privileges of this Church, as now by the great goodness of God the same are established among us; and being informed of disorders and tumults in some parts of the country,* which the enemies of our present happy establishment may be ready to improve, though without ground, to the disadvantage and reproach of this Church, we do look upon it as our duty to recommend to all our brethren that, as they have in their stations access, they do discountenance and discourage all irregularities and tumults that tend to disturb the government of our gracious Sovereign the Queen, to whom we are in gratitude, as well as duty, under the highest obligations; seeing, in the kind providence of God, we by her good and wise management enjoy so many advantages, and upon whose preservation our peace and the security of all that's dear to us do, under God, much depend. This in name, and by the order of the Commission of the General Assembly of the National Church, is subscribed by, rev. dear brethren, your affectionate brother and servant in the Lord,

" William Carstares,

"Moderator pro tempore." †

It is evident that the clergy must have entertained a profound respect for the moral power and political influence, which they knew lay behind an address such as this, else the circular letters could never have exercised the control which is ascribed to them ‡

* There had been disturbances in Glasgow and its neighbourhood, and the most strictly Presbyterian districts had been the most agitated.

† Defoe: Appendix, p. 25. The Union was passed between two general Assemblies, and the Presbytery of Hamilton had petitioned that it should be delayed till after the Assembly met.

‡ Their influence is plainly attested by the correspondence in the Carstares State Papers. Laing, who makes much of the clergy's opposition, says "the violence of the Presbyteries was restrained, or their petitions were intercepted, by circular letters from Carstares, artfully

The English and Scotch Commissioners completed the Articles of the Treaty of Union, on the 23rd of July 1706. After much excitement in Parliament, rioting in Edinburgh, threats of rebellion in some parts of the country, trickery and alleged bribery among the members of the House, the Treaty was finally ratified and approved by the Scottish Estates on the 16th of January 1707. On the 25th of March the Estates were finally adjourned.*

The debates upon the Treaty were proceeding simultaneously in the English Parliament. They betrayed no slight apprehensions of the evils that might ensue from the strong position conceded in the Treaty to the Church of Scotland. The apprehensions were partly owing to Episcopal prejudice, partly to the still vivid memory of the time when the Solemn League and Covenant had swept over England like a tornado, and overturned her Established Church. But common sense and statesmanship prevailed; the opposition, though strong, was unsuccessful; †　and to their honour it is recorded that some of the most strenuous advocates of the Union spoke from the bench of bishops. A correspondent writes to Carstares on the 8th of March 1707.

---

calculated to represent the Commission as indifferent, or as not indisposed, towards a Union; but the English Ministers in vain solicited the approbation of the Church, which that subtle politician was unable to procure." 'History of Scotland' (3rd edit.), vol. iv. p. 371. See also Somerville's 'Reign of Anne,' p. 225 (edit. of 1798).

* The Duke of Hamilton's vacillation and trickery (not to call it treachery) seem undeniable. The disbursement of the £20,000, which Godolphin sent to the North, suggests grave suspicions of bribery. It was expended in sums varying between £12,325, given to Queensberry the commissioner, and £11 2s., allotted to Lord Banff; whose parish minister writes to Carstares soliciting his "kind influence for his lordship's encouragement" in the circumstances of his changing his religion from Roman Catholic to Protestant, and desiring to take his seat in Parliament —we may presume to vote for the Union.

† Burnet (who took a leading part in promoting the measure), vol. v. p. 293.

" When the Act for securing the true Protestant religion and
Presbyterian Church Government was debated by the committee in
the House of Lords, several lords and four bishops spoke very
warmly against ratifying, approving, and confirming it, though
they were not against giving the Scots a security that it should be
maintained among them.   But the A. of Canterbury* said he had
no scruple against ratifying, approving, and confirming it within
the bounds of Scotland.   That he thought the narrow notions of
all Churches had been their ruin ; and that he believed the Church
of Scotland to be as true a Protestant Church as the Church of
England, though he could not say it was so perfect.   Several of the
bishops spoke very much in the same strain, and all of them
divided for ratifying, approving, and confirming the Church Act,
except the four that spoke against it, and the Bishop of Durham,
who went away before the vote.   The other High Church bishops
were not at the House that day."

On the 6th of March 1707 the Act of Union received the
Royal assent, and the first British Parliament was summoned
to meet upon the 1st of May. . . . " I do assure you,"
wrote Sir David Nairn, Under-Secretary of State, to Carstares, " the Queen is very sensible of your services, which
she had several times information of from me, by the Duke
of Queensberry and Earl of Mar's commands." †
Early in the summer Carstares went up to London, and
presented himself at Court.   " When I had the honour to
wait upon her Majesty," he writes, to Principal Stirling,
on the 15th of July, from London, " I was received with all
the goodness that I could desire." ‡   The Queen granted him
a private interview, at which she personally thanked him for
his services in promoting the Union, and presented him with
one of the silver Union medals—" a very few of which,"
says McCormick, " she had made to be cast off for her
particular friends."   Carstares found that his old friend
Portland had gone to the Continent, and wrote to him to let

---

* Tenison. McCormick, p. 759.
† Secretary of State ; afterwards leader of the Jacobite rising in 1715.
‡ Glasgow, MSS. ' Lett. England, 1702–1713.'

him know how he had been received at Court. Portland writes in reply, on the 15th of August, from Sorgvliet:—

"Je vous assure, que ce n'est pas avec peu de satisfaction, que je reçu la votre de Londres du 17 passé, et que je n'ay pas peu de chagrin de ce que je suis ici pendant que vous estés en Angleterre; puis que j'ay toujours conservé mes sentiments pour vous; une honeste homme et un vieux ami est ce que j'estime le plus. Ce que vous me mandez de la maniere dont la Reine vous a reçú, me fait une vraye plaisir; elle temoigne connoitre en vous un veritable serviteur. Je vous prie de me continuer toujours votre amitié, et de me croire inalterablement votre tres humble serviteur,

"PORTLAND." *

A General Assembly had been held in the spring of 1707, ere yet the Act of Union had come into operation. There is no reference to the Union in its printed records; and it should appear that its leaders, finding that their brethren would not, bless the Treaty, thought it best to pass it by in silence. Their calmness and self-control were highly appreciated by the Government. "I am very glad," Lord Mar wrote to Carstares, "your Assembly proceeded so calmly; 'tis not the first time the Church of Scotland has been obliged to your good counsel." †

By the time the Assembly of 1708 met, the ancient Parliament, which the ecclesiastical convention had so often controlled, so often withstood, had passed away for ever. With the demise of the Scottish Legislature much of the strength and glory of the Supreme Court of the Church departed. The Assembly could never again expect to influence the British, as it had influenced the Scottish, Parliament.

The leaders of Scotch political life, attracted to St. Stephen's, and exposed there to all the influences of English society and of a powerful and predominant Episcopacy, were no longer likely to take their seats as elders in the Scotch Church Court, and to lend their weight to its deliberations.

It was of importance that the first Assembly that met in

* McCormick, p. 77.   † Ibid. p. 762.

these altered circumstances should choose as its president
one whose Presbyterianism and Churchmanship had stood
keen tests, and who yet enjoyed the confidence of the Government, and had been a promoter of the Union, and who, by
the worth of his character and dignity of his position, would
do honour to the Moderator's chair. The choice naturally
fell upon Carstares. He was elected Moderator, for the
second time. His election, he told the Assembly, was a
" proof of their moderation, and that they could allow a
differing from them in sentiments as to some particular
things, and retain love and charity." *

The Queen's letter to the Assembly made no special
reference to the Union, although referring in commendation
to the " zeal and affection," which the Church had shown
during the recent attempt at a French invasion in the
Jacobite interest.† Neither in the Acts of Assembly, nor in
the address to the Queen, is the great change in the constitution of the nation named. Carstares's opening speech
is occupied with the threatened invasion, rather than with
the abolished Legislature and the new condition of things.
" The Presbyterians of Scotland," he said, " have too great a
concern for the Protestant Churches, and too great a detes-
tation of Popery and tyranny, and see and hear of too many
dismal instances of French government, not to have an
abhorrence both of the designs of Versailles and the pretences of St. Germains."‡

This avoidance of a subject, which could not but be
uppermost in all minds, indicates no indifference to it, nor
any unanimity regarding it; but rather reveals a state of
feeling and opinion, in which it was tacitly admitted that
the subject could not be approached without danger.
National pride had been too recently wounded, ecclesiastical
jealousy too bitterly irritated, the practical effects of the
Union, in Church and State, in society and in trade, too little

* MS. Records, Glasgow, 1708.
† See Hill Burton, from 1688. vol. ii. p. 1.
‡ Acts of Assembly.   MS. Records, Glasgow.

tested, to allow of any body of Scottish Presbyterians giving it a dispassionate and unprejudiced discussion. Carstares's wisdom and moderation were rewarded by, as they were reflected in, the dignified reticence of the first post-Union Assembly. The predominating control of that Moderate party, which he had largely helped to consolidate, and which he now led,—a control that was to last for more than a century,—was already established.

CHAPTER XVII.

Calamy—Squabble between Universities of Edinburgh and Glasgow—
Carstares and Calamy's Visit.

WE are indebted to Edmund Calamy, who made a journey
to Scotland in 1709, for some picturesque glimpses of
Carstares and of his manner of life in Edinburgh. Before
quoting, however, from the pleasant gossip of his diary, we
may notice a squabble (of which he was the proximate cause)
which arose between the Universities of Edinburgh and
Glasgow, and which stirred many academic passions at the
time. Calamy, like many English Dissenters, was probably
ambitious of obtaining that degree of D.D. or LL.D. which
he could not hope to receive from any university in his
native country; and Carstares was no doubt anxious to do
honour to his friend by making him a doctor of divinity
of the University of Edinburgh. When Calamy came to the
North the degree was accordingly conferred.

A few weeks later the University of Aberdeen granted
him the same degree; and on his arrival in Glasgow, the
university there bestowed on him a silver box containing
a third diploma of D.D.* In this instrument, while his Aberdeen degree was referred to, no notice was taken of his
having been admitted to the doctorate of Edinburgh. This
slight was naturally resented by the Senatus of Edinburgh;
Carstares especially was very indignant,† and felt the affront
all the more because his own nephew, Alexander Dunlop,
was one of the professors in the peccant university. He
writes, on the 28th May 1709, to Principal Stirling :—

* Calamy, vol. ii. p. 212.
† Wodrow's Correspondence, vol. i. p. 17.

"I had one from you some days ago, recommending to me for charity one Mr. Fleming, an Episcopal minister, to whom I gave what I could conveniently spare at that time. I had another from you yesterday, recommending one Mr. Dunlop, a student of divinity at your college, to whom I showed all civility, but could, at present, give him no assistance in what he desired. This is all I have been favoured with from you, since you intented a process against our society, and acted in the affair as judge and parties too ; having by your sovereign power passed sentence upon us, though I hear it was not *nemine contradicente*, some not being willing to drive too furiously till they knew their way. I am sorry that your college should do anything that tends so plainly to break all measures betwixt us, seeing it is a thing that cannot be retrieved ; nor do we intend to give you the least trouble that it may be so, for we indeed treat it more with scorn than resentment, as, we are apt to think, many others of sense will do here and elsewhere too. Mr. Cumming * hath been with me, and acquainted me with the boundless liberality of your society, even when not desired and when he was a professor amongst us. This says so much of itself that I need say nothing. I heard this day from the Rev. Mr. Osburn,† who much laments the circumstances of that country ; but I have had no letter from your very rev. and much esteemed friend Dr. Middletoun ; nor do I think will he load you with compliments for your degrees *ad eundem*. I could have wished that my good friend Pardovan had spared his discourses upon a subject he had not been well-informed of, and when what he said could not but savour a little of partiality. But I apprehend we shall have no great prejudice by all this management, even though supported by the weight and lustre of silver boxes,—which will only oblige you to be at the expense of gold ones when any person of quality gets a degree, which is no rare thing in England."

---

* John Cumming, Regius Professor of Church History in the University of Edinburgh, who had received no degree there, was made "doctor utriusque juris," a doctor of laws, by the University of Glasgow, without any consultation with his own principal.

Bower, vol. ii. p. 25. Wodrow's Correspondence, vol. i. p. 17.

† Osburn was one of the clergy and professors of Aberdeen. Dr. Middletoun had been dean of the diocese of Aberdeen under the Episcopacy, and, having conformed, was now Principal. Walter Steuart, of Pardovan, was the author of the 'Collections and Observations concerning the Worship, &c., of the Church of Scotland,' published in 1709.

To this rather testy reclamation Stirling replies,—

"I could answer the charge so as to satisfy the impartial and unconcerned, yet it is in terms so high, and so far from the Rev. Mr. Carstares's usual strain of temper, that I think it advisable for me to make no particular return at this time, lest I should fall into expressions which you might no less challenge; but I shall be willing, when this heat is over, to subject the angry expression of yours to your own review." *

The sting of the offence lay not merely in the disparagement of the rights of the University of Edinburgh (although these had been amply guaranteed by the charter of James VI. in 1582, and by an Act of the Parliament of 1621), but also in the suspected design of drawing to Glasgow those English students, whom it was Carstares's plan to attract to Edinburgh and provide for there. Among the Dissenters in the South there was a party in favour of Glasgow, with Dr. Williams at its head, while Calamy stood by Edinburgh. He writes to Carstares, after his return to England, "There is a rumour spread among us that your Lord Advocate should say that Edinburgh has no more right to give a doctor's degree than St. Paul's School has with us. This makes some triumph, and keeps others silent. . . . . Mr. Smith, that came to town with us from Glasgow, does ill offices. He magnifies Glasgow to the skies and runs down Edinburgh. I believe he may have some instructions." †

The ill-feeling gradually died away, and Glasgow did not attempt a repetition of the offence; but the memory of it rankled for a time—as can be traced in this letter to Alexander Dunlop, the young professor of Greek, who had owed his preferment very much to his uncle's influence:—

"Edinburgh, Nov. 24, 1709.

"Dear Nephew,—I have two from you, one of which was only recommending to me a young man whom I am in little capacity to serve, though I have got his brother settled, who was also recommended by you. . . . . As for reflections upon the professors of

* Glasgow MSS., 'Lett. Scot.'   † Murray Dunlop MSS.

X 2

your society, none of ours are guilty of them, and for my part I never used such unworthy methods as to any society of learning in my country. ⸱ I detest such a way of retaliating the affront that some of yours put upon us, though it was of a nature that, in its circumstances, was as much levelled at debasing of our society as was in the power of those that did us the injury. . . . . I am much grieved for my dear sister, as to my unhappy nephew, your brother.* I greatly sympathise with her, and shall endeavour to get some account of him. My dear love to her. I shall delay writing to her till I have something to say. He hath drawn a bill of 6*l.* sterling upon his Uncle James, which, you may be sure, he will not pay. . . . . I have not had for some time so much leisure as to write so long a letter. Be assured that I fixedly am, dear nephew, yours to love and serve you,

" W. Carstares."†

Calamy timed his visit to Scotland so as to reach Edinburgh during the session of the General Assembly. In the Assembly of 1709, which met on the 14th of April in St. Giles's Church, Carstares sat as representative of his university; and he, as retiring Moderator, prefaced the proceedings by a sermon on the text (Ps. cxx. 9),—" Because of the house of the Lord our God, I will seek thy good."‡ "His doctrine," says Wodrow—who begins his letters from the Assembly to his wife with this year—"was, in the general, that every good person should be of a public spirit, and be concerned about the good of the house of God as well as civil interests. He proved it from Scripture instances of Moses, and the instance of the woman—1 Sam. iv., two last verses—David, and several others. He gave the reasons of it, and the methods we were to evidence our public spirit in no unlawful thing, but in everything suitable to our station, in prayer, in the keeping up communion of saints, in keeping up the unity of the Spirit in the bond of peace, and in walking wisely towards those that are without—where he recommended charity and ingenuity [ingenuousness] in dealing with those of the Episcopal communion, who did not think it fit to join

---

* John, the eldest.

† Graham Dunlop MSS.   ‡ Correspondence, vol. i. p. 1.

with us, and avoiding harshness and bitterness of spirit towards them ; and told us that morosity and disingenuity will no way recommend us in dealing with them. Which expressions some looked upon as what contained a tacit reflection upon ourselves. He had certainly a very neat and well-worded discourse."

Calamy arrived in Edinburgh on Saturday the 16th, and on Monday was conducted by Carstares to the Assembly. "I was placed," he says,* "upon the bench at the foot of the throne, at the right hand of the Moderator, and had liberty to attend from day to day and hear all that passed, making my remarks and observations. To get the better insight into their affairs, I not only went into the 'Committee of Overtures' and the 'Committee of Bills,'† but had a meeting every evening (over a glass of wine), which had in it one out of each of their synods, who by kindly giving me an account of what had passed in their respective synods, with regard to the several matters laid before that General Assembly, gave me a clear and distinct view of their proceedings.

"When I afterwards told Mr. Carstares of this aim and practice, he, with his wonted frankness, cried out, 'Verily, to spy out our nakedness are you come! and had you spent ever so much time in contriving a way to discover all our defects at once, you could not have fixed on one more effectual.' That which I take to have been more remarkable," adds Calamy (and it indicates how deeply the liberal and moderate principles of Carstares had penetrated the leading minds of the Church), "was that not one in all the company was for the *jure divino* of the Presbyterian form of Church government, though they freely submitted to it."

"No man in the Assembly," he continues, "was heard with more respect than Mr. Carstares. He was commonly one of the last in speaking, and for the most part drew the

* Calamy, vol. ii. p. 152. The quotations which follow will all be found in vol. ii. between p. 152 and p. 192.

† Committees charged with the preparation of the business to be laid before the House.

rest into his opinion, when he thought fit to declare himself with openness. Yet I once saw him a little put to it; meeting with what would have tried some other men, though he got easily through. It was upon occasion of somewhat referred to the Assembly by the Synod of East Lothian. In which case it was moved that the members of that synod should withdraw, as was, it seems, the usual way. Mr. Carstares said he thought there was no great occasion for that now. It would take more time than they could well spare, and the matter depending was of no great importance. But a certain old gentleman stood up and said they both must and should withdraw, according to custom, before the matter proceeded.

"Mr. Carstares replied he was much mistaken if the thing depending was not of that nature that it might be foreseen that the brethren would pretty generally concur in their sentiments without dividing; . . . . however, he offered freely to withdraw with his brethren if it was insisted on. Upon which the old gentleman asked Mr. Carstares for what reason his opinion might not be of as much weight as another's? 'I, sir' (said he), 'am as good a man as yourself, bating that you have a sprinkling of Court holy water, which I must own myself a stranger to, and never affected to meddle with. I tell you again, sir, you shall withdraw, or we'll go no farther.' To which Mr. Carstares, with great meekness, made this reply : ' Dear brother, I can more easily forgive this peevish sally of yours than you perhaps will be able to forgive yourself, when you come sedately to reflect upon it;' and so withdrew. The matter was soon determined with a *nemine contradicente;* but the angry old gentleman afterwards could not rest without asking Mr. Carstares's pardon."

Calamy admits us to a last interview with an old acquaintance :—

" Meeting Mr. Carstares in my way, he desired I would be with him at four o'clock that afternoon, and keeping myself free from all other engagements be ready to go where he would conduct me. Querying where, he replied I might safely venture under his conduct. He carried me to old Sir James Steuart's—the wonder of his age for vivacity and spirit, briskness of parts and readiness of memory, considering his years. Bishop Burnet says he was 'a man of great parts, and of as great ambition.' We found him sitting in an elbow-chair, to which he was confined. He embraced me, and intimated how well pleased he was that I would pay a visit to an old man worn-out and just going off the stage. . . . . Salutations being over, he rang a bell and gave orders to his servant for wine and glasses, &c., straightly charging him to appear no more until he heard the bell ring. If any company came his master was engaged, and not to be disturbed on any account whatever. The servant followed orders, and Sir James entered into free discourse about the civil and religious interests of this island, the great necessity and difficulty of the union between England and Scotland, &c. He showed it impossible to have secured their Church settlement, or kept out the Pretender without it, and how it might be best improved. On all which heads he offered a great many very noble thoughts, which showed a wonderful and uncommon knowledge of men and things. . . . . I cannot remember I ever spent a couple of hours in free conversation with more satisfaction in my whole life."[*]

On the second Sunday of his stay in Edinburgh, Calamy occupied Carstares's pulpit, and preached a sermon on the text, "The disciples were called Christians first in Antioch," which was publicly denounced as Latitudinarian. "Mr. Carstares," he says, "with great mildness and prudence afterwards replying in the same pulpit, I heard no more of the matter."

One more extract and we shall have done with the good Calamy :—

"I was one day invited by the masters of the college to go with them to Leith, to take a fish dinner, with which they were to entertain their Principal, Carstares, according to annual custom. I found the way thither exceedingly pleasant, and that a fine and convenient port. . . . . Among other fish there was one I had neither

---

[*] Sir James Steuart, in 1709, retired from the office of Lord Advocate, and was succeeded by Sir David Dalrymple, fifth son of the first Lord Stair, and one of the Commissioners of the Union, whom he again superseded in 1711.

seen nor heard of before—a sea-cat, the head and tail like those of a cat, but the flesh very white and exceedingly firm ; . . . . an admirable fish, rather beyond a turbot. I was extremely pleased with the day's entertainment and conversation. One thing that gave a peculiar relish was the entire freedom and harmony between the principal and the masters of the college, they expressing a veneration for him as a common father, and he a tenderness for them as if they had all been his children." *

These notices of Carstares, slight as they are, throw some little light on his ordinary walk and conversation among his friends and neighbours in Edinburgh, and bring into pleasant relief the same traits of character—kindliness, geniality, sagacity, charitable tolerance — which we find revealing themselves in his letters, and which are ascribed to him by his original biographer. " His religion," says McCormick, " was neither tinctured with the extravagancies of enthusiasm nor the rigours of superstition." †

" As his piety was unfeigned, so his charity was unbounded, more so indeed than his circumstances could well afford ; for, whilst he had one farthing remaining in his pocket, he could not turn aside from any necessitous object that claimed his assistance. This was so well known to the poor that, whenever he went abroad, he was perpetually harassed by them, and was at last obliged to submit to a regulation, proposed to him by one of his friends who knew his foible; which was, to put only so much money in his pocket as he could conveniently spare for the purposes of ordinary charity. ‡

" Amidst that multiplicity of business in which he was perpetually engaged, it is remarkable that he found abundance of leisure for the duties of hospitality. His house was a place of resort to all the youth of the best families and the most promising

* " A cold treat given the Principal and Masters of the College, one evening, was all that I could prevail with them to accept" (in return for all their civilities, and a degree), says Calamy.

† McCormick, p. 88, et seq.

‡ Among other traces of his charity in giving, I find in his papers (Murray Dunlop MSS.) a receipt from the treasurer of the Maiden Hospital, of date 7th Feb. 1706, for a donation of 100*l.* sterling, a large subscription from a man of Carstares's fortune in those days.

hopes, who were generally recommended to his attention during their course at the University; and he failed not to improve the opportunities which his station afforded him, of instilling into their minds, along with an ardour for study, the best regulations for their future conduct. Many of them, who have since acted their part in the most conspicuous stations, have not scrupled to own that it was to him they were indebted for the best maxims both in public and private life. The Duke of Argyll, in particular, was early recommended to him by his father, and continued to advise with him in every matter of importance in which he was concerned, from the time he entered upon public life until Mr. Carstares's death.

"The clergy of all denominations were welcome to his family; particularly such of the Episcopal clergy as were deprived of their livings at the Revolution. He always treated them with peculiar tenderness and humanity.*   He often relieved their families when in distress, and took care to dispense his charities in such a manner as he knew would be least burthensome to them. Some of them, who were his yearly pensioners, never knew from what channel their relief flowed, till they found by his death that the source of it was dried up.

"He was sometimes ingenious in devising methods of imposing upon the modesty and pride of such as would have rejected his good offices with disdain, if he had not disguised his intentions. We shall give one instance out of many that are told of him.

"One Caddel,† an ejected Episcopalian clergyman, sometimes waited upon him when he came to Edinburgh. One day, when Caddel came to call upon him, he observed that his cloaths were thread-bare; and, eying him narrowly, as he went away, he desired him to call again two days after, pretending he had some commission to give him before he went to the country. He was no sooner gone, than Mr. Carstares sent for his taylor, and desired him to make a suit of cloaths that would answer himself as to length, but not so wide by two or three inches, and to have them sent home

* "At the Revolution, Mr. Carstares laid down a plan for the maintenance of such of the Episcopal clergy as were removed from their churches, out of the Bishops' Rents. But the Ministry always found some pretext for applying this fund to other less charitable purposes."

† Cadell, properly, or Calder, "a dull, scandalous fellow," according to Wodrow (Correspond. vol. i. p. 475), was the pamphleteer, too rudely assailed by the Rev. John Anderson, of Dunbarton. in his 'Curate Calder Whipt.'

about the hour at which Caddel had engaged to call upon him. Caddel kept his appointment; but, upon entering the room, found Mr. Carstares in a violent fit of passion at his taylor for mistaking his measure, so that neither coat, waistcoat, nor breeches would fit upon him. At last, turning to Caddel, who agreed with him that it was impossible he could ever wear them; then, says he, they are lost if they don't fit some of my friends; and, by the bye, adds he, I am not sure but they may answer you: be so good as try, for it is a pity they should be thrown away. Caddel complied, after some importunity; and, to his surprise, found they answered as if they had been made for him; upon which Mr. Carstares ordered the cloaths to be packed up, and sent to his lodgings. Next day, upon putting them on, he found a ten-pound note in one of the pockets, which he naturally imagined Mr. Carstares had forgot to take out when he threw off the cloaths. Returning directly to the college, he told Mr. Carstares, he had come to restore him a note, which he had neglected to take out of the pocket of the suit of cloaths he had sent him. By no means, says he, Caddel, it cannot belong to me; for when you got the coat you acquired a right to every thing in it."

Carstares had borne the brunt of persecution in the days of the enforced Episcopacy. He had guided the Church through the unquiet waters of the Revolution settlement, and had ruled her policy during the negotiations of the Union. Another chapter is still needed to record his management during the troublous times which ensued, when concessions to Episcopacy, and restoration of patronage, threatened to realise the worst fears of those Presbyterians who had denounced, and withstood, the incorporation of the kingdoms.

CHAPTER XVIII.

English Liturgy—Greenshields—Apprehensions of the Church Assembly of 1711—Deputation to London—Toleration and Patronage—Oath of Abjuration.

HITHERTO the liturgical element had entered but slightly into the constitution and history of Episcopacy in Scotland. In the days of King James's " Tulchans," the Presbyterians habitually used a liturgical worship; and the bishops, whom he created, had neither the power nor the wish to alter it. Under Charles I. a disastrous effort had been made to introduce a new service-book; but it had never been repeated.

During the persecuting days of Charles II. and James VII., the Episcopal worship was of the same extempore kind as the Presbyterian had by that time come to be; and it was not the ritual, but the prelacy, of the bishops and their clergy, that was the stone of stumbling and rock of offence to those who refused to conform to the enforced Establishment. Now, however, after the turmoil of the Revolution was stilled and the excitements of the Union were allayed, and when the cultivated and refined classes in Scotland were rendered more amenable to English influences than hitherto, by the transference of the centre of their political and social life from Edinburgh to London, the liturgical element began to make its presence felt in the North. The old Presbyterian propriety had given way to usages in divine service which were slovenly and unattractive ; and the more the comeliness and solemnity of the English ritual were known, the more were educated worshippers repelled by the ill-ordered manner of worship in Scotland. There had been a great influx of English servants of the Government after the Union, who lamented bitterly the loss of their familiar prayers and

services; and not a few Scotsmen, during their sojourns in
the South, learned to contrast, unfavourably, the public
worship of their national Church with that of the Church
of England.*

The English liturgy had scarcely, if ever, been heard in
Scotland until after the Revolution, and then but on very
rare occasions, until after the Union.† In the year 1709
the first determined attempt was made to use it regularly
and openly, and to establish the right of Episcopalians to
celebrate public worship according to the Anglican use.
The General Assembly had foreseen the danger, and had,
in 1707,‡ launched an Act " against innovations in public
worship," which was intended to prevent the introduction
of the liturgy in any of the parish churches, and to assert
the Church's right to interfere with the worship of any congregation which worshipped without Presbyterial sanction.
But this Act was ignored, and the whole question with which
it professed to deal was brought to an issue, two years later,
by James Greenshields.

Greenshields, who had been ordained by one of the deprived Scotch bishops, and who had held an Irish curacy
for some years, came to Edinburgh in 1709, took the oaths
to Government, and opened a place of worship, in which he
read the prayers of the English Church. There had been
no such deliberate invasion of the domain of Presbytery
since the Revolution. Even in the case of English regiments
lying in Scotland, the Episcopal chaplain had not ventured
to officiate publicly. Brigadier Whiteman, who commanded
a regiment of Englishmen and Episcopalians, on being quartered in Scotland, consulted Carstares as to whether his
chaplain might celebrate divine service as he had been accustomed to do in England, the congregation being composed

---

* Even " ruling elders " habitually " haunted " the Episcopal Church in
London.   See Correspondence, vol. i. p. 138.

† Grub, vol. iii. p. 357.

‡ Act xv. of Assembly, 1707.

solely of the regiment. Carstares declined to advise him;
but proposed that he and the Brigadier should both refer
the question to the Secretary of State, and await his decision.
Whiteman agreed to this; and the reply which he received
from the Secretary was, that Her Majesty desired that his
chaplain should neither preach nor celebrate the Communion
on Scotch ground.* On this occasion Lord Sunderland wrote
to Carstares from Windsor, 25th October 1709:—

"I have received the favour of yours of the 13th instant, and
acquainted the Queen with the contents of it, who has commanded
me to let you know how sensible she is of your care to keep all
quiet in your parts, and how well she takes this instance of your
zeal for her service, in relation to what was proposed of having the
liturgy used in Brigadier Whiteman's regiment, whose conduct in
this particular Her Majesty does very much commend, and has
ordered me to tell him so. I am also commanded to assure you of
Her Majesty's intentions not to suffer anything to be done that
might give any disquiet to those of the Established religion in
Scotland, which it is Her Majesty's fixed resolution to support and
maintain. Whatever happens from time to time in your parts, of
this kind, or any other which you shall think it for Her Majesty's
service she should be informed of, I desire you will acquaint me
with it, and I will not fail to lay it before Her Majesty, and let
you know her pleasure; and, in whatever regards your particular
interest, you may depend upon the best services of him, who is
with great truth and esteem, sir,

" Your most humble servant,

" SUNDERLAND." †

It will be seen from this incident that the Court and the
Government were not interested in the introduction of the
liturgy in Scotland. Nor was it in itself agreeable to
the general body of the Scotch Episcopalians, who had
never used it, and who disliked it — partly from national
prejudice, partly from their disloyalty to that Crown to
which the liturgy did ample homage.‡ Those clergymen,

---

* 'Analecta,' vol. i. p. 214. Wodrow gives a wrong name—Weir.

† McCormick, p. 776.

‡ Defoe. Preface, p. xxvii. "They would not pray for the Queen."
Calamy, vol. ii. p. 164.

from England or Ireland, who came into the country, did
not bring with them the political sentiments of the Scotch
Episcopalians, and indeed held themselves aloof from connection with the representatives of the expelled hierarchy,
who were in affectionate alliance with the English Nonjurors.*

The movement was thus, however, not the less, but the
more, alarming to the Presbyterians. They saw in it but
a new instance, in the ecclesiastical sphere, of that overbearing English domination, which had, in the departments
of their civil government, done much to intensify the
general hatred of the Union. Even the friendly intentions
of the Court and Cabinet were of little avail, if a Scottish
institution was to be overthrown, or an English tax or
law imposed.† The haughty Southern seemed to delight
in inflaming the irritated temper of the Northern nation;
and things were so ordered, says a shrewd spectator, " as if
the design had been to contrive methods to exasperate the
spirits of the people there."‡ Even those who had no great
love for Presbytery thought they detected, in the attempt
to set up the Anglican Church service, an invasion of national
rights and a violation of the Union. The Established clergy
naturally were alarmed and incensed. Greenshields, who
had placed himself at the head of the movement, was within
the bounds of the Edinburgh Presbytery; and he was summoned to its bar, and prohibited from exercising his clerical
functions. On his disregarding the prohibition, the Presbytery invoked the aid of "Cæsar" in the person of the
magistrates, who committed the contumacious liturgist to
prison. On appeal to the Court of Session the sentence of

* Grub, vol. iii. p. 357.

† The abolition of the Scots Privy Council was carried against the
Government in the House of Commons.—Burton, vol. ii. p. 24.

" The Queen," writes Lord Glasgow to Carstares, " is much afraid that
the House of Commons proceedings against a Council in Scotland may
much alarm our Church. She is heartily against the measure, and will do
her utmost in the matter."—Murray Dunlop MSS.

‡ Burnet, vol. v. p. 333.

the magistrates was twice confirmed; and thus, "so far as
the institutions of Scotland were concerned, it was clear
that Episcopal clergymen were not to be permitted to officiate according to the English form in Scotland."* Greenshields and his advisers, however, had a remedy in view on
which the Church party had not reckoned. For the first
time in the legal annals of Scotland an appeal was carried
to the British House of Lords; and the Presbyterians found,
with dismay, that a cause affecting the interests and jurisdiction of their Church was to be decided in a court of
which the English bishops were members.†

Meanwhile, public feeling in the South was exasperated
by reports of the renewed stringency with which Episcopalians were treated in Scotland. Old Sir James Steuart was
again appointed Lord Advocate;‡ and the Jacobite party
alleged he was restored at the instance of Carstares, because
Sir David Dalrymple was found too lenient in his dealings
with the disaffected Scotch Episcopalians and the innovating
English.§ There is no evidence of Carstares having had anything to do with his old friend's restoration to office; and
the strict measures which were used to enforce conformity
were opposed to his general policy. He knew too well
how impossible it would be—especially amid the High
Church fervour for Sacheverell—to persuade the House of
Lords, or any English court, that the celebration of divine
service in the English form must be pronounced absolutely
illegal in Scotland—to regard with favour the extreme
position taken up by the Presbytery and the courts of law
in Edinburgh. He knew how hotly the general opinion

* Burton, from 1688, vol. ii. p. 36.

† On the question of Scotch appeal to the House of Lords, which
legislation has brought into recent discussion, see Burton, from 1688,
vol. ii. p. 36, &c.

‡ Mr. Hill Burton makes one of his rare minor errors in stating (vol. ii.
p. 40, note) that Sir David Dalrymple remained Lord Advocate in 1711.
Sir James was re-appointed in that year (see Cothness Collections, p. 367),
and retained his post, notwithstanding the Tory ascendency in the
Ministry, till his death, in 1713.

§ Lockhart Papers, p. 551.

of England would resent the prosecution of a clergyman
(no matter what his special circumstances might be) for
reading the prayers of the Church, and how loudly the
squires and parsons would echo the cry which Swift had
raised in his 'Examiner:' "If these be the principles of the
High Kirk, God preserve at least the Southern parts from
their tyranny."*

"Mr. Greenshield's affair," he writes to Principal Stirling,
on the 9th of March 1710, while the case was still pending,
"hath given us a great blow, and doth very much grieve
me. I pray God may direct us how to manage ourselves, in
such a juncture. We stand in need of wisdom and conduct,
that integrity and truth may preserve us." †

In the Assembly of 1710, the address to the Queen was
drafted by Carstares, and being very much in the usual
form, except in a few references to Protestants abroad, and
to the principles of the happy Revolution ("cast in by
Mr. Carstares," says Wodrow, "in opposition to the Tories
in England"), it was objected to by some members, who
appeared to desire the addition of other paragraphs, with
more direct relation to the existing grievances and difficulties of the Church.‡ Carstares's draft was, however,
adopted, and we trace his influence in the Assembly's
avoidance of the vexed question of the English liturgy. It
was, however, with great difficulty, and at the hazard of all
his personal popularity, that he succeeded in maintaining the
ascendency of the moderate policy. "He was at this time,"
says McCormick, "although the most respectable clergyman in the Church, perhaps the most unpopular. This
made him often complain, both in private and in public, that
his situation was peculiarly hard, to be forced, first to draw
upon himself the censure of his brethren, by encountering
their prejudices and putting a stop to their violent proceedings, and then to justify those very measures to

* 'Examiner' (Swift's Works), No. 30.
† Glasgow MSS., 'Lett. Scot.'
‡ Acts of Assembly. Correspondence, vol. i. pp. 137, 152.

administration, which he had disapproven, and in vain attempted to frustrate.

"He felt this in a variety of instances during the course of those prosecutions which were carried on by his more rigid brethren in different corners of Scotland against some of the Episcopal clergy, who, by virtue of the powers entrusted with presbyteries, were, upon the most frivolous pretexts, turned out of their livings. But he felt it most of all in the case of Greenshields at Edinburgh. Having in vain attempted to dissuade his brethren and the civil magistrates from so unpolitic a step as that of stating themselves in downright opposition to the Church of England at the bar of the House of Peers, he ventured to prognosticate that their severity in that instance would only open a door for other encroachments, and give an advantage to their enemies in carrying on their projects for the subversion both of Church and State." [*]

"I am perfectly tired," he writes, on the 12th of May, to his nephew Alexander, "by continual toil, since the Assembly did meet, which ended calmly this evening. . . . . . I have some thoughts of going to St. Andrews next week, but my motions are very uncertain."

Sacheverell's impeachment pushed the lesser affair of Greenshields into the background; but when Sacheverell's case was settled, and when the Whigs, driven from office, had given place to Harley and the Tories, the appeal came before the House of Lords. Harley and St. John both urged its withdrawal, as a decision was certain to give mortal offence either to the Church of Scotland, or to that of England; but Lockhart and the majority of the Scotch members of Parliament, who were Tories, insisted on its being heard.[†] The sentence of the House of Lords was pronounced in March 1711, and it was, that the judgment of the Court of Session should be reversed, and the magistrates of

---

[*] McCormick, p. 79. [†] Lockhart, 347–48.

Edinburgh—who had imprisoned Greenshields—condemned in costs.*

This decision marked the first phase of a crisis in the history of the Church of Scotland. A full toleration of Episcopacy—the recognition of the Church of England in Scotland, and the restoration of patronage, were foreseen as likely to follow this defeat.

When the Assembly met in May, the unpopularity which Carstares had earned was all but forgotten in the desire to have the Church officially represented, at so threatening a juncture, by his long-tried wisdom and statesmanship. He was for the third time elected Moderator by an overwhelming majority.† In his speeches at the opening and at the close of the Assembly, one can detect the apprehension of coming dangers.

There were not a few, he said, in his inaugural address to the Commissioner, who were watching for the Church's halting, and he knew well that methods had been used by those that were openly disaffected to the constitution of the Church to make Churchmen uneasy, and to tempt them to murmur. Surmises had been raised that patronage was to be restored, though it was notorious what an important security to the Church its abolition had been and how highly the law which abolished it was valued. The Queen, he was aware, had many misrepresentations laid before her; but he could assure his grace the Commissioner, that the often-maligned Presbyterians were yet Her Majesty's most trusty subjects. He never wished to see the loyalty of her people brought to the test; but should a trial ever come, the world would see the difference between those that acted from a firm and solid principle founded upon conscience and those who, "upon a turn," professed loyalty to the Crown only to serve their own purposes. He referred to the loud outcry

---

* Burton, from 1688, vol. ii. p. 86 ; Grub, vol. iii. p. 362 ; Cunningham, vol. ii. p. 348.

† "I think there were not ten votes squandered from him." Correspondence, vol. i. p. 213.

that had been raised about the "persecution" of the Episcopalians,—but, said he, "*quis tulerit Gracchos de seditione que-
rentes?*" There was so little ground for the outcry, and he
would be so much tempted to recriminate if he entered on
the subject, that he would forbear. As regarded the restoration of patronage, or any measure touching the rights of the
Church, he would not allow himself to forebode, but he
trusted in "the Queen's wisdom and equity," in the public
faith, and "the justice of a British Parliament."* "He
was near a quarter of an hour," says Wodrow, and adds
admiringly, "I can scarce think that the freedom he used
could either come so handsomely from, or been so well taken
off the hand of any member of the house as him."

It was significant of the Assembly's dread of the policy of
that "memorable Tory Ministry of Queen Anne's latter days,
which would, it was believed, have restored the British Crown
to the Stuart dynasty had they not been zealously watched
from without and divided among themselves,"† that, for the
first time, the reply to the Royal letter expressed the
Church's steadfast hope in the succession of the "illustrious
family at Hanover;" and an Act was passed "recommending," along with the prayers for the Queen, prayers for the
Princess Sophia and the Protestant house.‡ "I was confident," wrote Lord Seafield to Carstares, "that the Assembly,
being under your direction, would not fail in their duty to
the Queen, and, at the same time, would do something that
would be of consequence for our religion, and which has
accordingly happened; for what the Assembly has done in
favour of the Protestant succession in the House of Hanover,
is thought by all that are well affected to the Constitution
to be of the greatest consequence in the present juncture,
and it pleases me that the honour of doing this is given
to yourself."§

At the close of the Assembly, again speaking at length in

* MS. Records (Glasgow). Correspondence, vol. i. p. 214.
† Hill Burton, from 1688, vol. ii. p. 38.
‡ Acts of Assembly, 1711.   § McCormick, p. 792.

a like strain to that employed at the beginning, and
obviously intending his words to be understood as a deliberate
manifesto addressed by the Church to the Government and
the public, he says, as if to give an additional emphasis to
them, "I have here my papers, which I shall freely consult,
as I find it necessary that whatever shall be spoken by me
shall be under your censure, to which I shall cheerfully
submit myself."

It is very remarkable that Carstares should make no
reference to an Act of this Assembly, which has bequeathed
to the present day a serious practical embarrassment. That
Act, the tenth, assuming the Assembly's right to alter a
formula fixed by Parliament, enacted that all probationers
entering the Church, and all ministers before their ordination, should subscribe a formula much more minute and
stringent than that which had received Parliamentary sanction.* It is obvious, on the most cursory review of the
position, that the Assembly passed the Act as a precautionary
measure, and with the intention of interposing a barrier to
the dreaded admission to parishes (under Jacobite patrons)
of Episcopalian, and disaffected, presentees. Carstares was
too much of a Broad Churchman to love the stringency of
the formula for its own sake; but he regarded it as a necessary safeguard against a grave political and ecclesiastical
evil. He might, however, have shrunk from adopting it,
even in view of this necessity, could he have foreseen that,
ages after every political cause for its existence had passed
away, its precarious legality would be still asserted, and the

---

* In the Act "for settling the quiet and peace of the Church"—1st
William and Mary (1693), cap. 22. "That no person be admitted a
minister or preacher within the bounds of this Church unless that he . . . .
subscribes the Confession of Faith, declaring the same to be the confession
of his faith, and that he owns the doctrine therein contained to be the true
doctrine, which he will constantly adhere to; as likewise that he owns and
acknowledges Presbyterian Church government . . . . to be the only government of this Church, and that he will submit thereto and concur there-
with, and never endeavour, directly or indirectly, the prejudice or subversion
thereof."

burden of its subscription laid on the conscience of every
entrant to the ministry, not by the law of the land, but by
the injunction of the Church alone. He was not likely
to anticipate that the protection against the intrusion of
Episcopalians and Jacobites would, in course of time, trans-
form itself into a check upon liberty of thought and of
conscience, and, notwithstanding, still be maintained as an
indispensable part of the constitution of the Church.

The Church had begun to feel the practical inconvenience
and disadvantage of having the seat of the civil government
fixed in a distant city, and surrounded by influences that
were alien and prelatic. The Scottish Privy Council, which
had been the instrument of so many crimes against liberty
and religion, but which, since the Revolution, had been the
friendly coadjutor of the Church, existed no longer. The
Privy Council in London was too remote and too exalted
a body to be readily accessible to the applications of the
Church courts, and was coldly neglectful of requests that
it should confirm, with the authority of the State, the fasts
and other appointments of the Church.

Remonstrances and explanations, made in letters, or
addresses, or by lukewarm political adherents in London,
had little effect; and the Church had to resort to the plan of
sending to the metropolis deputations of her leading ministers, in order to force her representations upon the attention
of the Administration and the Legislature. Among the
minor grievances troubling the minds of Churchmen at this
time were, notably, the difficulties encountered in appointing
those fasts, through which the Church delighted to "testify"
against the errors of the day. There was also the growing
audacity of outrage in the North, where the Episcopalians,
elated by the Greenshields' decision (which, apart from all
liturgical questions, was welcome to them as a blow
inflicted on the Church), were resisting, with triumphant
insolence and violence,* the settlement of Presbyterian

---

* 'Analecta,' vol. i. p. 329. Correspondence, vol. i. p. 195, et seq.
Lockhart, p. 548, et seq. McCormick, p. 776, et seq.

incumbents. But looming most darkly in the future, and obscuring the whole horizon, rose the twin shadows of toleration and of patronage.

> " Nox atra polum bigis subvecta tenebat."

The Church must have a direct and trustworthy representative at headquarters; and a deputation, conducted by Carstares, was authorized to proceed to London.

Carstares spent most of the summer of this year in England, partly at Bath and partly in the metropolis; and there, in November, he was joined by his fellow-deputies—Blackwell, one of the professors at Aberdeen, and Baillie, minister of Inverness. They lost no time in addressing themselves to Lord Oxford, the Prime Minister, by whom they were received in a very friendly way, and who was always particularly kind to Carstares.

On sundry minor points, such as the appointment of a fast, "his lordship granted all that could be expected;" * but over the greater questions of toleration and of patronage, the deputies found they could exercise but little control. The Lord Treasurer was always cordial and polite, ready to promise, but unable or unwilling to fulfil. A Bill to " prevent the disturbing those of the Episcopal Communion, in that part of Great Britain called Scotland," was brought into the House of Commons. "Since Monday last," writes the anxious Blackwell, on the 24th of January 1712, "Mr. Carstares and I have been running amongst the members in all parts of the city, endeavouring to show the unaccountableness of the same; and this day we have been with the Lord Treasurer, who hath promised that some of the most effectual means shall be used towards accomplishing our desire." †

The House of Commons, however, refused even to receive a petition against the Bill presented by Carstares. He then

---

* Blackwell's Letters. ‘Miscellany of Spalding Club,’ vol. i. p. 198.
† Ibid. p. 207.

approached Her Majesty, and laid before her a humble representation from the Church—"obtesting Her Majesty, by the same mercy of God that restored that Church and raised Her Majesty to the throne. to interpose for the relief of that Church, and the maintenance of the present establishment against such a manifest and ruining encroachment." Carstares added a few words of his own, in support of the representation, and received "a very gracious answer from Her Majesty;" * but this appeal to the Throne had no effect in arresting the progress of the Bill.

This letter from the deputies to a correspondent in Edinburgh records their efforts and disappointments :—

"London, Jan. 29, 1712.

"Rev. and dear Brother,—The Bill for a Toleration, not only for Scots Episcopal ministers as such, but also for the use of the English liturgy in Scotland, hath now been twice read in the House of Commons; and this day the said House went into a committee and hath gone through much of the half of the Bill, and hath resolved to proceed into the remaining part upon Saturday next. By the next post you may come to receive a double of the Bill, as here you have enclosed a true copy of the petition which we were advised by counsel to give in to the House of Commons; which accordingly we did this day—but upon the first motion of it, it was rejected and not allowed a reading. We are heartily sorry for the Bill, and so much the more that we conceive not only the discipline of our Church is much stricken at by it, but also that it is like to open a door to great corruption both in doctrine and worship. What entertainment this Bill may get from the House of Lords is more than we know, neither are we to enlarge upon the vexation of spirit and fatiguing measures we have been obliged unto in this affair. Only we are at a great loss in a matter of such consequence to know proper measures, it being a most intricate and perplexing juncture as possibly men could be trysted with. In the meantime we are resolved to do what we can so far as there shall be any access towards the preventing of such a heavy stroke, though withal we have too much ground to fear but little success.

* 'Annals of Queen Anne,' vol. x. p. 330.

Hoping you'll pardon this short note, we rest, reverend and dear brother,

> "Your most affectionate brethren and servants,
>
> "W. CARSTARES,
> "THO. BLACKWELL,
> "R. BAILLIE.

"To the Very Rev. Mr. William Mitchell,
　　Minister of the Gospel at Edinburgh." *

The personal goodwill and moderation of Lord Oxford could not withstand the tide of Toryism in England and Jacobitism in Scotland, which was setting strongly against the Church. The toleration of Episcopalians and the restoration of patronage were both advocated by the party to which Oxford owed his power; and advocated for the sole purpose of regaining their lost ascendency to the Episcopalians and Jacobites of Scotland.† A strong and united Presbyterian Church was the foe which they most dreaded; and their efforts were therefore bent to such measures as, they hoped, would weaken it and split it into factions. The knowledge of these designs, and of their real bearing, lay at the root of the strenuous opposition offered by Carstares and his friends to the Toleration and Patronage Acts. The Toleration, which came first in order, was in itself an equitable redress of an undoubted grievance; but as the true Liberals of 1687 had resisted King James's toleration then, because they knew that it was advanced for the behoof of the enemies of rational liberty and religion, so now, the true Liberals in the Scottish Church withstood a kindred measure proposed with a kindred aim. The religious and political interests were again inextricably interwoven; and behind the shield of toleration of Episcopal worship, the bigotry and monarchical fanaticism of the Jacobites strove to inflict a fatal wound on the rights secured to Scotland by the Revolution.

Carstares saw this plainly, and did his best to arrest the

---

* In the possession of David Laing, Esq.
† Lockhart, pp. 378 and 418. Burnet, vol. vi. p. 106.

treacherous Act. The discussions which it occasioned raised a cloud of anonymous pamphlets, in more than one of which his hand is traceable. In one especially, 'The Scottish Toleration Argued,' * he condenses all the arguments against the Bill which could be openly alleged; but the real argument was one which it was difficult to maintain in public; though it was obviously not less difficult for a liberal politician and tolerant Churchman to make much of those that were overtly avowed.

He rehearses all the laws relating to the establishment of the Scottish Church, from the Reformation onwards; which it is hard to imagine he did not see to be practically irrelevant, as the establishment of one Church could not be fairly held, unless under a tyranny like that of the Stuarts, to exclude the right of celebrating other worship than that of the Establishment. He ought also to have understood that the right of " visitation " and " expurgation," which he claims to have been conferred on the Church by the 5th Act of the 2nd Session of William and Mary, could not be deemed a perpetual right, but was intended to be exercised only until the Church should be properly reconstructed; nor should he have overlooked the difference between bringing Episcopacy into the Church, and simply tolerating the public worship of Episcopalians, who stood aloof from the Church, and did not seek to be reconciled to its communion. One of his chief arguments is that this toleration, by exempting Episcopalians from the censures of the Church, will undo the bonds of discipline. "How," he asks, " can any subject of this country be exempted from the censures of the Church ? Those people will be under no Church government, and so become freebooters both in religion and morals." This plea was one which seemed to Carstares very potent. He was thoroughly " Erastian " (as that phrase is understood in Scotland), and could not recognise any authority to censure or govern as belonging to the Church, except in so far as agreed to and ratified by the State.

* Advocates' Library : Pamphlets, vol. 600.

He adopted the same argument at a conference at which he and the other deputies, along with Lord Ilay, met some of the Scotch Tory members of Parliament, and an account of which is preserved by Lockhart.*

" Mr. Carstares," says Lockhart, who, it must be remembered, was an unscrupulous Jacobite, " had too much sense to offer any reasons against the Bill in general in the present situation of affairs ; so far otherwise he appeared very humble, pretending that the brethren were not for persecution ; and as the Dissenters were tolerated in England, there was much to say why the like favour should be showed to the Church party in Scotland ; but he thought the clause which stood part of the Bill with respect to the power of ecclesiastical judicatories, would be prejudicial to the interests of religion, virtue, and morality—seeing all who were not of the Presbyterian communion were by it exempt from being subject to their judicatories ; and as there could be no Church judicatories but those of the Church established by law, this clause would afford an occasion to evade all Church censures, when even inflicted on the most scandalous persons ; and he humbly submitted if it was not to be believed that the Episcopal ministers themselves would rather desire that the power of Church censures stood vested in the Presbyterian clergy, than that vice and immorality should pass altogether unpunished. Some of the gentlemen there present seemed averse to make any alterations to please the brethren, and on that account would not yield a bit to Mr. Carstares. I happened to be of another opinion, and told them I believed Mr. Carstares had another reason than he expressed against this clause, viz. that by it all the scandalous fellows in the country, when they committed any crime which exposed them to the Church judicatories, would declare themselves Episcopalians, and thereby escape being punished ; but at the same time prove a great reflection on that party and set of men who screened such offenders and coveted to add them to the number of their communion ; that this I took to be

* Lockhart, p. 379.

Mr. Carstares's secret reason against the clause, though for certain reasons he did not think fit to own it; and, for my own part, I agreed heartily with him in it. He smiled, and said he would leave me to make what judgment I pleased of his secret reasons, provided he could thereby make a convert of me against the clause. After some further arguing on this subject, it was agreed to drop this clause, and another should be inserted in its room, viz. that the civil magistrates should not interpose to compel any man, by their authority, to submit to the sentences of the Church judicatories; and it was thought that this clause would leave the Presbyterians sufficient power over those of their own communion, seeing they thought themselves in conscience bound to give obedience to their sentences, and it was absolutely necessary with respect to other people, because the Presbyterian ministers often harassed and plagued many innocent people on groundless pretences and false accusations, whilst the real reason was that they were not good Presbyterians; neither could this clause prove any encouragement to immorality, seeing the Presbyterians might pronounce what sentences they pleased, and the civil punishments might still be inflicted by the civil magistrate against all offenders of whatever persuasion, and nothing was to hinder the pastors of Episcopal congregations from publicly rebuking such as were guilty of scandal. Mr. Carstares was obliged to accept of this change, as the best that he could make of it; and, in consideration thereof, did promise that his own, and such of his party's friends that he had interest with, should not propose the abjuration or any other amendment to the Bill, reserving nevertheless full liberty to oppose the Bill in gross by all the methods they thought proper."

Lockhart complains, subsequently, that the promise regarding the abjuration oath was evaded by Carstares, who, he alleges, procured the insertion of an oath virtually the same as the abjuration, when the Bill came to the House of Lords. The fact was, however, that such a promise, if ever regularly made, was practically untenable. The Whig

party, unable — and probably unwilling — to defeat the
Toleration, were yet determined that it should not be
made the shelter of sedition. They therefore secured the
addition to the Bill of the abjuration oath, as well as of
an injunction that prayers should be regularly offered for
the Queen and " the most excellent Princess Sophia."
The Tories, on their part, no less determined to irritate
the Presbyterians, contrived that the oath and the injunction should be framed in a shape most offensive to Presbyterian prejudices and principles. Obliterating the distinction
between a Church established and a Church tolerated,* they
prescribed the oath in the same haughty terms to the Established clergy and to the deposed and vagrant Episcopalians,
and made the formula, thus offensively prescribed, to embody
the condition (necessarily obnoxious to the Scots clergy) that
the successor to the throne must be a member of the Anglican
Church.† The imposition of this new test exasperated the
Presbyterians more even than the clauses of the Toleration.
These, no doubt, enjoined all magistrates and judges to
protect the Episcopal meeting-houses with all the sanctions
of the law, and virtually gave an official recognition to Episcopal orders, whether conferred by an Anglican prelate, or
by an " exanctorate " member of the hated Scottish hierarchy;
but even this was an offence less personally insulting and
humiliating than the obligation to take an oath, which had
been originally devised by the English Parliament before the
Union, and to the terms of which they had the strongest

* " To be tolerated is no more than to receive the compassion of the law,
without the least share of power, encouragement, or approbation. To be
established is to receive the approbation, judgment, and the whole will of
the law; and a Church established is actually assumed into a share of the
constitution of the Government, with such a share of its power as is proper
to administer its own discipline."—Fletcher (of Saltoun) 'On the Union
of States.' Dalrymple, vol. iii. Appendix, p. 65.

† " The oaths were thrown in by the Whigs to bar the Toleration to the
Episcopals; the October Club, they to put the thorn in the foot of the
Presbyterian ministers, did throw out the amendment in the oath made in
our favours; and both parties let it pass on different designs."—'Analecta,'
vol. ii. p. 194.

political and religious objections.* A protest was drawn up, on the especial ground that to force such a test upon the clergy now in the Church, and to lay it down as a condition of entrance in all time coming, was an infringement of the Treaty of Union, which protected every Scottish subject from any oath or test inconsistent with the Presbyterian Church Establishment. "This plea," says Mr. Hill Burton,† who lucidly exhibits these somewhat complicated affairs in their progress and in their various relations, "was likely to go much farther in England than any general antipathy to oaths, which might be sneered at as fanaticism."

" When required to state their case, the clergy made it out thus:—The abjuration oath bound the juror to support the Protestant heirs to the Crown. But the line of heirs was referred to as indicated by the English Act of Settlement; and when that Act was examined, it was found that one of the conditions of the succession, as there laid down, was that the monarch be a member of the Church of England. An oath making this the qualification for the throne was maintained, and with justice, to be such a test (inconsistent with the Presbyterian Church Establishment) as the subjects of Scotland were protected from by the conditions of the Union. This incident in the form of the oath, probably overlooked by the framers of the Act, had much influence in strengthening the Nonjuring party in Scotland, who gave it the name of the 'logical lie.' Carstares, to whose acuteness the discovery of the anomaly may be attributed, made an attempt, which a person of more violent opinions would not have made, by a little diplomatic movement to extract from the oath the offensive connection with the English Church, without injuring its efficacy. The abjuration oath was made to refer to the succession 'as the same is and stands settled by an Act,' referring to the Act of Limitation. It was proposed that this should be changed, and that the form of reference should be to the succession *which* is, and stands settled. Thus, it was said that the juror who would not

* Burton, from 1688, vol. ii. p. 45, et seq.   † Ibid. vol. ii. p. 48.

swear allegiance to the heir *as* settled by conditions which required that he must belong to the Church of England, would yet have no objection to swear fealty to that line of succession which the Act pointed out. This alteration was made in the Bill as it stood in the House of Lords; but it appears to have been looked on as an engrosser's blunder, or some other result of carelessness, and the previous phraseology was restored, as a matter of routine, without any explanation."

All these finessings ended in the imposition of the obnoxious oath; and the part which Carstares took did not escape the blame which, in excited times, is commonly attached to a cautious policy;* but the more intelligent of his countrymen did him the justice of acknowledging he had acted for the best. He had warned his constituents, when he proceeded to London, that he did not expect to succeed in his opposition to the Toleration, and that while the Tory element was so highly in the ascendant both in the Court and the Government, resistance—avowedly based on the reactionary character of the measure—would only exasperate its promoters: †—

" I had this day your kind letter," he writes on 16th February to Stirling: "I call it so, because you let me know a part of what is said with you of my conduct here, which is friendly; and I am glad that it is acknowledged that I have done better of late than formerly. All I shall say, till it please God to give us a meeting, is, that I have neither changed my party nor my principles, but have endeavoured to manage myself in this perplexing juncture as inoffensively as I could, as I was stated; and indeed I cannot think that I have great reason to be concerned at what talking may be of me. I hope I have been, and shall always be, concerned for our contemned Church. The Toleration Bill is sent down again to the Commons with the abjuration tacked to it; but as for our taking it, it is explained, as I hear, as we desired it; but our Episcopalians are to take it as it is taken here—which some think will make the Bill be dropt, at which I should greatly rejoice, for it still—with all the amendments made to it—is, in my opinion, a breach of the

* ' Analecta,' vol. ii. p. 104.   † McCormick, p. 80.

Union, and ruins our discipline. . . . . My sight is still out of order, but better, I bless the Lord, than it was."

The Toleration Act received the Royal assent on the 3rd of March. The first woe was past, but the second woe came quickly; for the Act for the restoration of patronages was introduced to the House of Commons only ten days later.

The Church had, even long before the Union, dreaded that those who sought to undermine her would make a joint attack, through Toleration and the restoration of patronage ;* nor did the Episcopal and Jacobite party pretend to hide their designs of undoing that portion of the treaty, which solemnly secured the perpetual establishment of the Presbyterian Church.† The Government, however, had been understood to lend no countenance to these designs. In May 1711, Lord Oxford had written to Carstares, assuring him that "the Queen, and all who have the honour to have credit with Her Majesty, are not only resolved to maintain the Union in all its parts, both religious and civil, but there will be no attention given to any proposals which may justly alarm your friends ; and particularly as to that affair of patronages, it was never entertained, and was really an invention suggested by two rash persons, with a design to create jealousies ; but it was never in the least countenanced or entertained."‡ Yet within ten months the Toleration had passed, and the Patronage Act was before the House. The Church might well take alarm, not so much at this measure itself, as at the general policy of which it was an ugly indication. The Act which it proposed to abolish was that which, after the Revolution, had conferred the patronage of a parish church on the Kirk Session and the Protestant heritors. For this it substituted the exercise of patronage by the ancient patrons. The change was not a very great

* See sermon preached before the General Assembly of 1703 by George Meldrum. Adv. Libr. : Pamphlets, vol. 323.
† Lockhart, p. 418.
‡ McCormick, p. 82. Correspondence, vol. i. p. 228.

or vital one. Patronage, exercised by two or three elders and heritors, was in an extremely slight degree a more "popular" right than patronage exercised by the Crown, the town council, the University, or the private patron. But the object of the change was wicked. It was a blow aimed at the Protestantism and Presbyterianism of the Church, in the interests of a superstitious religion and a tyrannical policy. It was a political injury wrought for political ends, and as such, Carstares recognised and withstood it; as he had withstood the Toleration, and as he was ready to withstand every infringement, however trivial, of established usage and prerogative in Scotland, which seemed to promise a transference of the balance of power from the party whose civil and religious principles had won a dear-bought triumph at the Revolution, to the party which had then sunk under obloquy and defeat. He writes, on the 13th of March, to his friend Stirling :—

"I know Mr. Blackwell will acquaint you with the melancholy things that occur here as to our poor Church—as a Bill to be brought in for a Christmas vacation to civil judicatures, and a vacation also upon the 30th of January. Whether they will meddle with a religious observation of those days or not I cannot tell till the Bill be brought in. Another Bill also is allowed to be brought in for restoring patronages. These are heavy blows. I am to make no comment upon this procedure. I hope we shall not be so unwise as to gratify the expectation and desire of our enemies in being the beginners of disorders." *

The Christmas holidays—the old " Yule vacance " of the Court of Session—must have been, in themselves, an affair of very small moment to a man of the world, like Carstares, entirely devoid of all superstitious bias, either for or against the Christian anniversary ; but Christmas holidays, and commemorations of 30th of January and the " royal martyr," and introduction of English liturgy in Scotland, and patronage restored to Tory and Jacobite patrons—were all counts

* Glasgow MSS., ' Lett. Eng.'

in the great indictment of treachery to the Revolution and
its liberties, of which he held the party now in the ascendant
to be guilty.

The Earl of Oxford tried to make good his assurances to
Carstares by opposing the Patronage Act;[*] but, as in the
case of the Toleration, his opposition, if sincere, was fruitless,
and the Bill was rapidly pushed on. In neither House was
much said or done to retard its progress,[†] although Burnet
had promised Carstares—who with his colleagues waited on
the bishop—that he should speak against it. "I resolve,"
said he, "to speak some very free things in the House on
that subject; and I will tell them I noticed the King of
France to proceed just in this way in revoking the Edict
of Nantes; and piece by piece he wore in, and at length
took it away and turned persecutor."[‡]

The first step taken by the deputies of the Church was
to wait upon the Queen, with whom they "used great plainness as to the affair of patronages." Her Majesty made
the cold, but constitutional, reply that "it was a Parliament
business."[§] This was on the 18th of March; and so quickly
was the Bill pressed that it passed the House of Commons
on the 7th of April.

Carstares and his friends then approached the House of
Lords; but their application to be heard at the bar, by
counsel, was, at first, defeated through their own mis-
management. They addressed their petition to "the most
Honourable the Peers of Great Britain," and not, as they
ought to have addressed it, to "the Lords Spiritual and
Temporal." This mode of address was irregular and unconstitutional. The Duke of Buckingham proposed that the
petitioners should be taken into custody, but was pacified by
the withdrawal of the petition, and an apology for his
countrymen's (supposed) ignorance of the forms of the

---

[*] Lockhart, p. 385.   [†] Burnet, vol. vi. p. 108.

[‡] 'Analecta,' vol. ii. p. 174.

[§] Blackwell. 'Spalding Miscell.' vol. i. p. 215.

Z

House, offered by Lord Loudoun.* A fresh petition, on
being presented with the proper address " to the Lords
Spiritual and Temporal," was duly accepted by their
Lordships.†

The indisposition to use the title of " Lords Spiritual "
was, no doubt, owing to the petitioners' knowledge of the
vehement dislike to prelacy which filled the heart of Presbyterian Scotland, as well as to their reluctance to acknowledge
the authority of English bishops in legislation affecting the
Scottish Church. Even Carstares appears to have been unwilling, in his capacity of Scottish Churchman, to admit this
prelatic jurisdiction ; and when, afterwards, Wodrow tried to
get from him the history of the change made in the petition
he waived the subject, and would tell him no more than that
what was done " was not done in the name of the Church,
and was the deed of particular persons." ‡ The principles of
the Church were not to be compromised by a phraseology
adopted, for convenience sake and under pressure, by her
temporary representatives. §

The petition, which was understood to have been drafted
by Carstares, ran as follows :—

" To the Right Honourable the Lords Spiritual and Temporal in
    Parliament assembled, the humble representation of William
    Carstares, Thomas Blackwell, and Robert Baillie, Ministers of

------

* Correspondence, vol. i. p. 307. Letter and note.

† It is odd that Blackwell says nothing of all this in any of his letters.
See 'Spalding Miscell.' vol. i. p. 217, et seq.

‡ Correspondence, vol. i. p. 307. Note.

§ The accounts of this affair are not very distinct. Blackwell says
nothing of it, and no letter of Carstares bears on it. Wodrow states that
a previous petition " to the Peers in Parliament " had been received without
demur (vol. i. p. 307); while Lockhart says, " Mr. Carstares and his
brethren sometime earlier petitioned the Lords Spiritual and Temporal "
against the Toleration Bill. Lockhart, p. 383.

In the ' Analecta,' vol. ii. p. 48, Wodrow confesses that he had failed to
get to the bottom of this business. " I have not been able to get a distinct
accompt of the presenting the representation anent patronages. Mr. C. and
Mr. B. waived answering questions anent it."

the Church of Scotland, concerning the Bill for Restoring Patronages, now depending before your Lordships.

" It is with all humble duty and submission represented unto your Lordships that this depending bill seems to be contrary to the present constitution of our church, so well secured by the late treaty of union and solemnly ratified by the acts of parliaments in both kingdoms : That this may be more clear, it is to be observed, that from the first reformation from popery the church of Scotland hath always reckoned patronages a grievance and burden, as is declared by the first and second books of discipline, published soon after the said reformation, since which time they were still judged a grievance, till at length they came by law to be abolished.

" These patronages having been restored with episcopacy, in the years 1661 and 1662, did continue to the year (1690) that episcopacy was abolished and presbyterian government again established ; and though the act of parliament 1690, resettling presbyterian church government, was founded upon the act of parliament 1592, which bears a relation unto patronages ; yet the said act of parliament 1690 doth expressly except that part of the old act, and refer patronages to be thereafter considered, which accordingly was considered in the same parliament 1690, whereby it is plain that the abolition of patronages was made a part of our church constitution enacted by the act 1690 ; and that this act 1690, with all other acts relative thereto, being expressly ratified and for ever confirmed by the act for securing the protestant religion and presbyterian government, and engrossed as an essential condition of the ratifications of the treaty of union past in the parliaments of both kingdoms ; the said act abolishing patronages must be understood to be a part of our presbyterian constitution, secured to us by the treaty of union for ever.

" Yet it is to be particularly considered that the same parliament 1690 was so tender of the civil rights of patrons and so sincerely desirous only to restore the church to its just and primitive liberty of calling ministers in a way agreeable to the word of God, that they only discharged the patron's power of presenting ministers to vacant churches ; but as to anything of their civil rights, did make the condition of patrons better than before, not only by reserving unto them the right of disposal of vacant stipends for pious uses within the parish, but also for giving unto them the heritable rights of the tythes, restricting the minister, who formerly had the said right to stipends, much below the value of the said tythes: Notwithstanding which advantageous concession to the patrons by the parliament, this bill takes back from the church the power of presentation of ministers, without restoring the tythes, which formerly belonged to her; by which the patrons came to enjoy both the purchase and the price. This being the true account of our legal settlement as to this matter, it appears to be evident that the restitution of patronages, as to the point of presentation, can only gratify a few; while, on the other hand, it must necessarily disoblige a far greater number, that are now freed of that imposition: And, indeed, it cannot but seem strange that this bill should be so much insisted upon when there are so many patrons, and those too of the most considerable in Scotland, that are against such a restitution. It is also apparent that presbyteries must come under many difficulties and hardships as to their compliance with this innovation, and that many contests, disorders, and differences, will probably ensue betwixt patrons, presbyteries, heritors, and people, besides the known abuses wherewith patronages have been attended, even in their most settled condition; whereof many instances might be given; especially, that thereby a foundation was laid for Simoniacal factions betwixt patrons and those presented by them; and likewise ministers were imposed upon parishes by patrons who were utterly strangers to their circumstances, having neither property nor residence therein.

"It is therefore, with all submission, expected from your Lordships' justice and mature deliberation, that a bill, as we humbly conceive, so nearly affecting the late treaty of union in one of its most fundamental and essential articles, respecting the preservation of the rights and privileges which our church at that time was possessed of by law; for the security of which the parliament of Scotland was so much concerned as not to allow their commissioners to make it any part of their treaty, but reserved it as a thing unalterable by any judicature deriving its constitution from the said treaty, shall not be approved by your Lordships, especially, while the nature of the treaty itself shows it to be a reciprocal transaction between the two nations.

" W. CARSTARES.
"THO. BLACKWELL.
" RO. BAILLIE."

In spite of all remonstrance the Bill was carried. It passed the House of Lords by a majority of fifty-one to twenty-nine, and received the Royal assent on the 22nd of May. It was only by the tenacity of the Duke of Argyll, that a clause, enacting that the presentee to a parish must be a Presbyterian, was inserted in the Bill, which had left the House of Commons without any such proviso.*

The Act (10 Queen Anne, c. 12) thus hurriedly passed, under the stress of a Tory and Jacobite reaction, is still upon the Statute Book, after having been the indirect cause of more dispeace and ill-will in the Church than even the Five Articles of Perth, and the pretext of more than one disastrous secession.

Whether the system of patronage vested in heritors and elders, which it displaced, would have worked better, can only be conjectured. Purely popular election to the office of parish minister had never been known in Scotland; and the system thought to come nearest to it,—election by the Kirk Session, subject to the approval of the congregation, which was enacted by the General Assembly of 1649 and abolished at the Restoration, had not existed long enough to establish itself as incontestably the best.†

Great as has been the outcry against the Act of 1712, it may be observed that it left untouched the presbytery's right to examine and reject a presentee, and the congregation's right to express, and give effect to, their wishes in the matter, by their " call," or their " objections." It may be questioned if the mere transference of the initial act of presentation, or rather of recommendation, to a benefice, from a small number of parochial patrons to one patron, would have wrought the damage in the Church which has been ascribed to it, had the Church courts (with which lay the immense power of keeping unworthy candidates out of the Church altogether, and of giving due effect to the reasonable objections of the people) administered the law and used their power with wisdom, equity, and moderation.

* Correspondence, vol. i. p. 304. Cunningham, vol. ii. p. 360. Burton, from 1688, vol. ii. p. 50, et seq.

† See Dunlop's ' Law of Patronage, 1833,' pp. 11-15.

There were rumours of farther assaults upon the Church—
"the air was full of noises." "Some of the Church's
enemies," says McCormick, "who were then in administration,
had proposed that her annual assemblies should be discon-
tinued, as the source of all the opposition to the measures
then pursued by the court. Others were of opinion that
they ought to be permitted to meet, but should be prorogued by Her Majesty's authority so soon as they were
constituted. And, to take away the only pretext for holding
assemblies for the future, or their sitting for any time, a
Bill was proposed, obliging presbyteries, under certain
penalties, to settle upon a presentation, every man to whom
the Church had given a licence to preach, without any
further trial or form.

"Mr. Carstares saw very well that, however prejudicial
these regulations might be deemed to the Church of
Scotland, yet, in the present temper of the Parliament, they
would meet with little opposition, if proposed or supported
by the court. He was willing therefore to compound
matters with the Administration; and upon condition that
he was authorized to assure his brethren that no attempts
would be made to introduce any alterations in the government or discipline of the Church, he undertook to use all
his influence in order to allay those ferments which the late
proceedings in Parliament had occasioned. Accordingly,
upon his return to Scotland we find him exerting his utmost
endeavours in calming the spirits of such of the clergy
as, from a misguided zeal, were disposed to inflame the minds
of the people and disturb the peace of the country."

Carstares left London on the 17th of April, and travelled
down to Edinburgh, where he had to open the General
Assembly, which was about to meet. "Mr. Baillie went off
yesterday and Mr. Carstares to-day," writes Blackwell,
pensively, on the 17th, "though I daresay none of them
loves home better than myself. . . . . I must say that there
hath been much of providence in Mr. Carstares and Mr.
Baillie being here, who have truly acted a most conscientious

and active part. . . . . Our joints have been almost pulled sundry with driving in hackney ccaches through all corners amongst our great men for some weeks; to be free of which, at other times I have often walked till I was scarce able to step farther, so that they have allowed no English beef to grow upon my bones." *

The deputies might well be tired of their laborious mission and its many disappointments. Their solace was to know that they had been faithful to their trust and, though defeated, had fought a good fight and done their best. If they, with the veteran Carstares at their head, had not succeeded, success was hopeless.

> "Si Pergama dextrâ
> Defendi possent, etiam hac defensa fuissent."

* 'Spalding Miscell.' vol. i. p. 220.

CHAPTER XIX.

ON Carstares, as Moderator of the last General Assembly,
devolved the duty of opening the Assembly of 1712.   He
too, "*consulque non unius anni*"—was expected as usual to
regulate the proceedings of his brethren, and "to give all
the light in matters which might otherwise prove very
intricate." *   His sermon in St. Giles', before the Lord High
Commissioner and the assembled clergy, on the 1st of May,
was on the text (Proverbs xxiii. 23),—"Buy the truth,
and sell it not," and struck a keynote of calmness and
moderation, by touching but lightly on the recent political
transactions.†

The Government had looked forward with some nervous-
ness to this meeting.   They knew that the forbearance of
the Scotch clergy had been severely tried.   "I hope in
God," wrote Lord Oxford to Carstares, on the 4th of May,
"that the Assembly will end, so as not to give any occasion
of reproach to those who watch for their halting.   Lord
Dartmouth sends to his grace, the Lord Commissioner, an
instruction in such terms as, I hope, will be very satisfactory." ‡   The Queen's letter showed the same uneasiness
and apprehension, and referred to "late occurrences," which
might have "possessed some of you with fears and jealousies,"§

---

* Blackwell.   'Spalding Miscell.' vol. i. p. 219.
† Correspondence, vol. i. p. 275.
‡ Murray Dunlop MSS.
§ Acts of Assembly, 1712.

but under the judicious management of Carstares, the dreaded occasion passed over quietly. The reply to Her Majesty's letter admitted that the recent occurrences had engendered fears and jealousies, as Her Majesty had surmised, but expressed the hope that the wrongs which the Church had suffered, might come, " in due time and manner, to be redressed." *

The proceedings of the Commission of the Assembly and their deputies in opposing the Toleration and Patronage Acts were approved of in strong terms, and ordered to be engrossed in the minutes ; the worthy minister who preached before the Commissioner on the first Sunday of the Assembly, inveighed against the notion that liberty of conscience " could be a blessing to any people, or person," and enlarged " upon the sinfulness of the Toleration ;" † and with these protests the dangerous position was passed and the risk of a wide-spread clerical disaffection evaded. The fact was that Carstares and his friends knew well that the recent Acts had been carried by the enemies of the Church, whose treacherous ends they would but serve if they allowed themselves to be provoked into hostility to the Crown, or disunion among themselves. The hope of the Presbyterians was in the Protestant succession. The triumph of Jacobitism and the reaction towards Episcopacy would not long survive the accession of the House of Hanover, and if the Church remained united and peaceable, the day of that accession was sure to dawn.

A serious embarrassment remained, however, unaffected by the conciliatory tone of the Government and the temperate demeanour of the Assembly. In an enumeration of " the grounds and causes of the Lord's wrath with Scotland," ‡ in the unhappy year 1712, after naming many, such as " our deep security and stupidity under our sin and dangerous

* Acts of Assembly, 1712.

† Correspondence, vol. i. p. 281.

‡ A manifesto issued under this title by the disorderly Hepburn's party, in 1712.

horrid unthankfulness," the writer comes to his climax, with "the late sinful Union, the boundless Toleration, the restoring of Patronages, and the *Oath of Abjuration*." In every representation of Presbyterian wrongs this hated oath was "the head and front of the offending." It was a more searching and unbearable grievance than either Patronage or Toleration.

The Assembly voted an address to the Queen, in which it was plainly hinted that Her Majesty might find that some of her most faithful subjects among the clergy would not take the Abjuration.* Royal interposition, however, could not be constitutionally invoked to relieve any class of Her Majesty's lieges from the operation of an Act of Parliament; and the only grace that was extended to the remonstrants was the postponement of the day appointed for taking the oath, from the 1st of August to the 28th of October.†

During this interval, Carstares did his best to soothe the scruples of those who were inclined to refuse submission. He argued on this ground—that the Abjuration Oath, as originally framed by the English Parliament of 1701, was simply designed for the security of the Protestant religion in general, and not as a safeguard of the Church of England or of Episcopacy in particular; nay, a proposal to add a clause to it, directly in favour of the Established Church and the Episcopal Communion, was negatived in the House of Commons of that date. ‡ Hence it was to be inferred that the Legislature never intended the oath to be understood in

* They pray that "such of us as may remain unclear as to the taking of the said oath, may yet be favourably regarded by your Majesty as your most loyal and dutiful subjects."—Acts of Assembly, 1712.

† Not the 1st of November, as stated by Mr. Hill Burton.   See Correspondence, vol. i. p. 321.

‡ To the engagement, "I will to the extent of my power support, maintain, and defend the Constitution and Government of this realm, in King, Lords, and Commons," it was proposed to add "and the Church of England as by law established, with liberty of conscience as it is tolerated by law." The committee divided: for the clause as amended, 155; against, 173.

such a sense as to bind the jurant to affirm anything inconsistent with Presbyterianism; Presbyterians therefore might, with a safe conscience, and according to the mind of those who framed and first imposed the oath, take it, and explain it in a way perfectly agreeable to their own principles. This original scope and intention of the oath must overrule any subsequent intention, which a particular party might have in imposing it anew. Carstares received an anonymous letter, in which the facts about the passage of the oath through the House of Commons were detailed. He appears to have attributed great importance to this communication, and to have circulated copies of it among his friends.* Writing in reference to it, to Principal Stirling, on the 14th of June, he says: "I am sorry our scruples about the Abjuration should have made such noise, and shall be more so if they continue." In his efforts to remove these scruples, he had all the aid that the crafty sagacity of old Sir James Steuart could give him. "The advocate," says the admiring Wodrow, who was not himself "clear" (as the phrase went) about swearing, "seems to be preserved for such a time as this is." †

At last the prayers, conferences, fasts, communings, and testifyings, of the brethren drew to a conclusion. The 28th of October, *dies nefastus*, came. Of the Established Clergy the majority took the oath. Among those who refused were a few of the older and more intolerant representatives of the rigid Covenanters, and they now became the nucleus of a sect of nonjurors and dissenters, whose lineal descendants still exist, and are known as the " Reformed Presbyterians." ‡

Of the Episcopalians, those who were in English orders took the oaths. The Scotch Jacobite "curates" almost all refused, and went henceforth by the name of the Nonjurors.

---

* Glasgow MSS. ' Lett. Scot.' It is alluded to more than once by Wodrow.

† Ibid. ' Analecta,' vol. ii. p. 41.

‡ One of the smallest of Scotch sects, numbering forty-two congregations.

Carstares of course complied. At the head of a large body of the clergy and through an enormous crowd, some of whom hooted and reviled the ministers as they passed, he made his way to the chamber where the justices were sitting.[*] There he took the oath, and then repeated a declaration which had been prepared with the advice of the Lord Advocate [†] and subscribed by all the clergy present, and which bore that they would have " carefully avoided taking the said oath, if they were not persuaded that the scruples moved by some about it, as if it were inconsistent with the known principles of the Church, are groundless, and that it cannot be extended to the hierarchy or ceremonies of the Church of England, or anything inconsistent with the doctrine, worship, discipline, or government of the Church established by law." Lockhart of Carnwath, who was present as one of the justices, objected to any declaration or explanation being offered. Carstares replied that he knew the oath was to be taken in its literal sense and without any explanation, but he protested, in his own name and in that of his brethren, that the sense of it which he had now expressed was the true one, and the one in which they took it; and handing in a copy of the " declaration," he " took instruments " in the hands of a notary. [‡]

The general acquiescence in the oath induced the Government to deal leniently with those who forbore to take it; and the Church did not consider itself called to interfere

---

[*] Correspondence, vol. i. p. 322.

[†] See his letters in Glasgow MSS.,' Lett. Scot.'

[‡] Correspondence, vol. i. p. 321. Lockhart's account of this transaction is tinged with the spitefulness which disfigures much of his narrative. He was, as has been stated, present, and says, " After the brethren of the Presbytery of Edinburgh (and I was told they followed the same method in most other places) had sworn and signed the oath, which to them was administered by a full meeting of the justices of peace, they retired to a corner of the court, where Mr. Carstares repeated, or rather whispered over, the aforesaid explanation, in his own and his brethren's name ; and thereupon he took instruments in the hands of a public nottar, brought thither by him for that effect. This jesuitical way of doing business," &c.— Lockhart, p. 384.

with them.* The more zealous, both of the Jurants and
Nonjurants (or "Nons," as they were familiarly called),
would have pushed the question in dispute to an open
rupture. The Jurants would have proceeded, in the Church
courts, against the Nonjurants; the Nonjurants would have
broken off all ministerial communion with the Jurants.
The policy of Carstares, however, who maintained that the
taking or refusing of the oath was a matter for the civil,
and not for the ecclesiastical, courts to deal with, prevailed.
Nor would he admit that any divergences of opinion or
action, occasioned by the imposition of the Abjuration, were
sufficient warrants for divisions within the Church. The
principles and practice, which he inculcated, received
adequate expression and the formal sanction of the Church
in an Act of the General Assembly of 1713.

No Assembly ever passed an Act more wise and charitable
than this one, "for maintaining the unity and peace of this
Church." "The General Assembly .... most seriously
obtest all ministers and people, in the bowels of our Lord
Jesus Christ, charging them, as they regard His honour and
the peace and quiet of this Church, that they abstain from
all divisive courses upon occasion of different sentiments
and practices about the said oath; and that they would, notwithstanding thereof, live in love and Christian communion
together. .... And that all judge charitably one of another,
as having acted according to the light of their conscience in
this matter—and therefore that they carefully abstain from
reproaching one another on account of the said different
sentiments and practices."†

"Both the Queen and her Ministry," says McCormick,‡
"were astonished at the placable temper of the next

---

* Not long after the Hanoverian succession the oath was altered, so as
to be deprived of its objectionable features. The bitter feeling about it
quickly died away; but the schismatic body which had quitted the
Church because of it, preserved its separate existence. To remove the
cause of a schism seldom, if ever, removes the schism itself.

† Act vi.: Assembly, 1713.

‡ McCormick, p. 83.

General Assembly which sat after these Acts of Parliament were passed, and by a variety of letters which he [Carstares] received at that time, testified their approbation of his prudent management, to which they ascribed it.

"Not only so, but by a letter from the Lord High Treasurer, the Earl of Oxford, before the sitting down of the Assembly in the year 1713, Mr. Carstares is desired to name the Commissioner to that Assembly, and to send up a copy of such instructions as he judged seasonable in that juncture.

'Sir,—I received by the last post a letter from Lord Advocate, taking notice of the near approach of the day for the meeting of the General Assembly. I send this to you, by a flying packet, to desire your opinion freely (which shall not be made use of to your disadvantage) whom you would choose to be Her Majesty's Commissioner; and that you would send any particulars you think fit to be added to the standing instructions, and what you judge proper to be inserted in Her Majesty's letter to that venerable Assembly. I hope the last Commissioner gave you satisfaction. I shall have occasion to write further to you in a little time, upon many particulars relating to the repose of the Church, which I know you have much at heart, and therefore shall add no more at present, but that I am, with very great respect,

'Your most faithful and most humble servant,
'Oxford.'

"Mr. Carstares, in return to this letter, recommended the Duke of Atholl as the most proper person for Commissioner, and sent up a draught of the Queen's letter, with the instructions to be given by Her Majesty to the Commissioner. And by another letter, which he received from Lord Oxford, he is acquainted 'that the Queen—in consequence of his recommendation—had sent down the Duke of Atholl.'"

The peaceable close of this Assembly of 1713 was the end of the crisis through which the Church had passed, and which is rendered memorable by the Toleration, the Patronage Act, and the Abjuration.

Each of these had been devised by the enemies of the Church, and with the same malign intention of splitting it into factions, or driving it into an attitude of hostility to the State. In none, however, had the design succeeded. The restoration of patronage was indeed fated to work much mischief in the future ; but its immediate results were insignificant. The Toleration was a recognition of the principles of religious liberty, which, though inimical to the Church at the time, because of its political bearings, was in itself just, and could not have been long delayed under any equitable Government.* To have been provoked by it into obstinate hostility would have been fatal to the stability of the Church. The Abjuration was an unnecessary infliction. An obnoxious oath, which seemed, at least, to recognise the supremacy of the Anglican Church, and which originally was the device of a foreign Parliament, came more home to the business and bosom of the Presbyterian minister, than the general toleration of a liturgical worship, or the possible abuses of the right of patronage. But even the Abjuration would have been a sorry cause of quarrel with the State, or of such internal discords as would have put their strongest weapon into the hands of those political enemies of the Establishment, who knew that if they could upset the Church of Scotland, they could, in all probability, bring in King James the Eighth. Through all intervening trouble, Carstares and his party kept their eye steadily fixed upon the Star of Brunswick. It was not a brilliant orb, and was encircled by no halo of romance ; but, above an atmosphere of corruption and chaotic change, it shone with a certain steady light of liberty and order.

---

* This toleration of Queen Anne's, "protecting and allowing" those of the Episcopal persuasion to celebrate their worship with the use of the English liturgy in Scotland, has been grasped at by modern Scotch Episcopalians as giving a *quasi* legal establishment to their communion and recognition to its titular dignitaries. The intention of the Act, however, is plain. It was passed for the avowed benefit of the English Episcopalians in Scotland, whose present representatives are those Episcopal congregations, which do not own the authority of the Scotch bishops. The Scotch Episcopalians of 1712 welcomed the Act as a blow to the Established Church ; but as a body they disliked and held aloof from the introduction of the " liturgy and ceremonies," which the Act was intended to protect, if not to encourage. No fact in their history is plainer than this.

The Elector, waiting hopefully at Hanover for his kins-woman's demise, spoke of the Presbyterians of Scotland as his "best friends," and did not fail, on occasion, to encourage their great leader by the expression of his approval and goodwill. The Commission of the Assembly of 1713, at its meeting in August, had issued a "seasonable warning" against Popery, and had exhorted the people to combine, with loyalty to the reigning sovereign, a firmness to the Protestant succession in the illustrious House of Hanover, and "a just aversion to the Pretender;" * and in due course Carstares received the following letter from the Elector's secretary :—

"Hanover, le 3 Octobre 1713.

"MONSIEUR,—Comme je compte trop sur nostre ancienne amitié, pour craindre que vous m'ayez tout a fait oublié, je me donne l'honneur de vous informer de l'extreme satisfaction avec laquelle Mad. l'Electrice et Aug. l'Electeur ont lié cet advertissement si chrestien et si salutaire des commissaires de l'assemblie generale du clergé presbyterien d'Ecosse.

"Comme leurs Altesses sont persuadées, que vous avez puissa-ment contribué a une oeuvre si salutaire, elles m'ont ordonné, Mon-sieur, de vous en remercier de leur part, et de vous dire, que vous les obligerez fort, si vous voulez bien assurer les personnes que vous jugerez à propos de la reconnoissance qu'ont leur Altesses de cet que le dit advertissement contient pour elles, et pour la succession. A quoi elles repondront de leur costé, en faissant redresser les griefs de la nation Ecossoise aussistot quelles en auront le pouvoir.

"On ne doit pas croire que, par raport a ces griefs, et meme par raport a dissolution de l'union, les Ecossais pourroient obtenir d'avantage du pretendant que de leurs Altesses, dans la suc-cession des quelles (outre le redressement de leurs griefs) ils trouveront la sureté de leur religion, loix, biens, et libertés. Il nous importe fort que la nation soit bien persuadée de cette verité. Nous vous prions d'y vouloir travailler; et moy je demeure tou-jours, avec respect, Monsieur, votre tres humble serviteur,

"F. ROBETHON." †

During these years of ecclesiastical alarm and turmoil, we have but scant records of the private life of Carstares.

* Acts of Assembly of 1714. Act ix. † McCormick, p. 87.

He appears to have generally gone to England in the summer or autumn, and we hear of him visiting at such times Bath and Scarborough.

In the winter he lived, as his office required, in Edinburgh; although even then, as we have seen, the affairs of the Church occasionally demanded a prolonged sojourn in London. He brought his nephew William Dunlop to live with him, while studying for the Church;* and along with Dunlop another young man, Charles Macky, resided in the house, and pursued the study of the law under the Principal's direction. In the few letters extant there is not much of special interest. He writes, in May 1712, to Alexander Dunlop, congratulating him on the birth of a daughter. "Give little Will a kiss for me," he says, after many kind good wishes; "he is just such a name-son to me as your little Bettie is a name-daughter to my wife." Writing to Mrs. Dunlop, in October of the same year, he says :—

"MY DEAREST SISTER,—Do not think I either forget you or cease to love dearly you and yours. I assure you I do not. I thought we should have seen you here ere now; pray come in before winter, for you shall not be sooner here than you shall have a hearty welcome from my dear wife as well as me. My dear love to my nephews Alexander and William. I forget not the grand-children. My wife and I, having been visited by the common distemper, are now, in the goodness of God, pretty well recovered. Dear sister, yours in entire affection.

"W. CARSTARES."

There was soon a break in the young family circle of Dunlops, at Glasgow, and he writes to his nephew and niece, in April 1713, condoling with them on the loss of more than one of their children :—

* Sarah Carstares had three sons—the eldest was Alexander Dunlop, who was made Professor of Greek at Glasgow; next, John, who died early; and William, who became a clergyman, and thereafter Professor of Divinity and Church History at Edinburgh. His life, full of excellent promise, was cut short at the age of twenty-eight, in October 1720. Macky was, in 1719, appointed Professor of Civil History in the same University.

"God thinks fit in His infinite wisdom," he says, "to begin early with you, in teaching you resignation to His pleasure and submission to His holy will, and to bring you to sit loose to earthly comforts. I pray you seriously to consider the ground that you have to hope that the children, whom God hath thought fit to take from you, are in an inconceivably better state than possibly they could have been in here; while I doubt not but you did both sincerely devote them to God in baptism, an ordinance to which they were entitled through your being believing parents; and that it was your earnest prayer that they might be within the bond of the covenant, all the promises whereof are yea and amen in Christ. . . . . My dear love to my sister. Tell her that next week there is a coach goes from hence with Mr. Finlason and others. I would be glad she would come hither in it, for I long to see her, as doth my wife too, who affectionately remembers you all."

In a letter to Principal Stirling, of date April 22, 1713, we have the last regretful mention of his old friend and early comrade in the battle of civil and religious liberty— Sir James Steuart, whom he had helped long ago to write the 'Accompt of the Grievances of Scotland,' and for whom, amid all divergences of opinion and policy, he had always maintained a constant friendship. "The honest old advocate," he says, "seems to be a-dying, and longs to be at home. He will make a great gap, and we shall miss him greatly." *

Sir James died on the 1st of May : "a very inexpressible loss," says Wodrow,† who records his unwearied services to the Church. "In the affair of the Toleration and Patronages, and I must say generally since the Revolution, most of the public papers of this Church are his draught. . . . . He was a great Christian, an able statesman, one of the greatest lawyers ever Scotland bred, of universal learning, of vast reading, great and long experience in public business. He was a kind and fast friend, particularly obliging, and very compassionate and charitable; and in his last sickness, and at his death, one of the brightest instances of pure and

* Glasgow MSS., 'Lett. Scot.'   † 'Analecta,' vol. ii. p. 202.

undefiled religion under affluence of riches, a fixed reputation, and a hurry of business that I have ever been witness to." The General Assembly was in session at the time of his funeral, and " all the clergy were asked, and so great was the crowd, that the magistrates were at the grave, in the Greyfriars Churchyard, before the corpse was taken out of the house at the foot of the Advocates' Close." *

In April 1713, the Peace of Utrecht, which closed the war of the Spanish Succession, was effected.† The peace, though welcome to the mass of the English people, was unpopular with the Liberal party, who believed that Marlborough's victories should have won terms more favourable to the policy of Britain. Like most of the measures of the Tory Ministry, it found little favour with the Presbyterians of Scotland.

In the Assembly of 1713, the Commissioner had used every argument to procure the insertion, in the address to the Queen, of a clause approving of the peace ; and had only desisted after he had received a declaration signed by Carstares and three other leading clergymen, to the effect that they were convinced that any such clause would create much animosity in its discussion, and on a division would be rejected.‡ The Government, however, were determined to secure the form, at least, of public approval of their policy, in Scotland, and orders were sent down that a day of thanksgiving for the peace should be observed by the Church. The order was generally disregarded.§

Carstares, as usual, advised a wise and conciliatory course. Although his colleague refused to take his proper share in the observance of the day set apart for the thanksgiving, Carstares, on the previous Sunday, holding the Royal proclamation in his hand, but not reading it, intimated the day

* 'Coltness Collections,' p. 368.
† And gave to Britain Gibraltar, Nova Scotia, Newfoundland, and Hudson's Bay.
‡ 'Analecta,' vol. ii. p. 195.
§ Correspondence, vol. i. p. 477.

appointed, and made a speech upon the peace. He confessed that the country might have had much better terms, but there were at the same time " some good things " in the treaty that were matter of thanksgiving. He announced that he would accordingly preach upon the Tuesday, which happened to be the ordinary day of week-day's service— which he did.*

This " mangled " way of observing the thanksgiving was reported at London, and caused much surprise to his political friends there;† but no official notice seems to have been taken of it.

Two months after this incident he went to Scarborough. On his return he was for some days seriously ill at Newcastle; but by the time he returned to Edinburgh — in October — he had regained his health; " and I have at present," he writes to Stirling, " a better temper of body than I have had of a long time." Stirling was then in London, and he adds, " It were too great presumption in me to give my most humble duty to my Lord Treasurer; but I never forget the obligations I am under to him for the many favours he hath honoured me with."

The last, but one, of his letters in the Glasgow collection is written to Stirling on the 28th of January 1714, and is full of characteristic touches :—

" I have yours just now, and shall do all in the affair of Mr. M'Kie I can. . . . . As for the other affair of the presbytery of Paisley . . . . I have reason to be persuaded that such public

---

* Correspondence, vol. i. p. 478. The " good things " Carstares referred to were, no doubt, the full recognition by France of the Hanoverian succession, and her disowning of the heir of the House of Stuart. He probably refrained from reading the proclamation for reasons akin to those indicated by Wodrow as operative in his own case. " I would be difficulted to read the King of France ' the most Christian king ' to my people, when, it may be, in my prayer before they have been joining with me in praying against him, as the main pillar of Antichrist and a bloody persecutor of our brethren. What follows is yet more choking,—' the conclusion of a just and honourable peace.' " Ibid, vol. i. p. 464.

† ' Analecta,' vol. i. p. 221.

fasts, at this juncture, will be looked upon as an alarming the country, and filling the people with jealousies of the Government, as if Papists were countenanced, and the bringing home the Pretender designed. And, besides, these fasts, joined with the noise that there is of arming the country, will certainly be jealoused by the Government. And therefore, while affairs seem to be coming to a crisis and a Parliament is at hand, I think it is fit for us to be quiet, and to give no umbrage to those in power, where plain duty is not concerned, as I judge it is not in the present case; though we have many causes of sorrow and lamentation before God."

Towards the crisis which Carstares apprehended, various dangerous elements seemed to be working, both in Church and State. In the Church, the Jurants and Nonjurants were still standing suspiciously on the verge of hostilities. Outside the Church, it was alleged that Popery was rapidly increasing; and it was certain that the Episcopalians were growing bolder, and, especially in their strongholds in the North-East, more aggressive. In the House of Commons a Bill was introduced to resume all grants out of the Bishops' Rents, and to devote these to the support of the Episcopal clergy. The extension of the English malt-tax to Scotland was exciting a furious discontent, and enmity against the British Legislature. In the House of Lords the dissolution of the Union was gravely debated, and only negatived by the bare majority of three. Every courier from the Continent brought tidings of the Pretender's designs and preparations for coming over to claim the throne, which, it was shrewdly surmised, his sister desired to bequeath to him; the Jacobites were furbishing their arms to be ready against his coming, and the sturdy Protestants of the South and West were thinking it time that they should do the same. But ere these various elements of civil discord were ready for explosion, their force was quenched. The Queen had been for months in failing health, but the end came before it was expected. She died on the 1st of August 1714. On the 5th the Elector of Hanover was proclaimed at Edinburgh, amidst profuse demonstrations of popular loyalty and

rejoicing. The Jacobites were disconcerted and dismayed.
The Presbyterian friends of the Protestant succession ex-
ulted. They seemed, to themselves, to emerge from an
atmosphere of suspicion and insecurity—to have now less
cause to dread their opponents and less excuse for dissensions within their own communion. There were health and
hope in the new *régime*.

"Adspice venturo lætantur ut omnia sæclo."

The Commission of the General Assembly lost no time in
meeting, and despatching a deputation to London to offer
the Church's homage and congratulations to King George.
Carstares was, of course, the chief deputy: and along with
him were Mitchell, one of the ministers of Edinburgh and
Moderator of the last General Assembly; Hart, who had
been the colleague of Carstares, in the Greyfriars Church;
Lining, the minister of Lesmahago; and Ramsay, the minister of Kelso. Hart has left "a journal, by way of diary," *
of this visit to the great metropolis, which affords some
amusing glimpses of the travellers' adventures—their apprehensions of the way, their difficulties as to finding proper
opportunities for orthodox public worship, their experience
of London and the Court.

Hart, Lining, and Ramsay arranged to meet Carstares
and Mitchell at Newcastle, on the 5th of October. In pur-
suance of this arrangement, Hart left Edinburgh on the 30th
of September, at eleven in the forenoon, accompanied, on
horseback, by nearly forty ministers and other gentlemen
as far as Dalkeith. At the "Burrough Loch," he took leave
of his "dear wife and distressed children;" at Dalkeith
he bade adieu to his convoy of friends "all in tears" (after
dinner), "being at that time under strong apprehensions that
we might never all meet together again." † The journey,
however, was most prosperous. At Morpeth, where the tra-

* 'Journal of Mr. James Hart.' Printed at Edinburgh, 1833. Edited
by Principal Lee.
† Hart's Journal, p. 2.

vellers dined, between eleven and one o'clock, Mr. Carstares arrived "in a coach," and stopped at the posthouse, where they called on him. They then rode, and he drove, to Newcastle, in the afternoon, and "we all waited upon him," says Hart, with a tone of unmistakable deference, that night. They proceeded by way of Durham, Darlington, and Thirsk, to York, where the journalist was much confirmed in his Presbyterianism by witnessing the service in the Minster:—"There is so much of man and so little of God in it, and so much carnality and so little spirituality." Carstares, and Hart's party, consisting of Messrs. Lining and Ramsay, and "Mr. Lining's man Adams," seem to have separated after this, and we hear no more of the former until the deputies are all assembled in London. They were presented at Court soon after their arrival, and Carstares, as their spokesman, made three speeches, to the King, the Prince of Wales, and the Princess respectively.

These speeches were speedily printed and sent down to Scotland. Those who thought the first duty of the deputies was to "testify" to the new monarch against the Toleration, the Patronage Act, and the Abjuration, were not satisfied with them. "Some allege," writes Wodrow, on November 18th, "there is too much of compliment and the courtier, and too little of the minister in that to the King." *

The deputies remained for several weeks after this in London, and spent much of their time in trying — with but little success—to interest the Government, which had succeeded to Oxford's discredited Administration, in the "grievances" of the Scottish Church. Nothing, however, could be done (as Parliament was not sitting), and but little even could be promised, to correct the alleged evil effects of recent legislation; but the representatives of the Church were gratified by the sympathetic language of those whom they addressed, and by the personal favours bestowed upon

* Correspondence, vol. i. p. 622.

themselves, of which a present from the King of 100*l.* to each of them, was not the least acceptable.* On the 21st of December they were again introduced at Court by the Duke of Montrose, in order to pay their farewell respects. "We had our audience in public," is Hart's report, "the King coming out to the Bedchamber of State, where there were a great deal of noblemen and gentlemen present. Mr. Carstares made a short speech in English, in which he expressed the grateful sense we had of his royal goodness, and that we would endeavour, more than by words, to express our loyalty and faithfulness to His Majesty's person and Government ; and that we would, in our stations, endeavour to promote what would be for the honour and quiet of his Government. After which we made a low bow and retired. The King bowed to us with a pleasant, smiling countenance."

They afterwards had an audience of the Prince and of the Princess of Wales, to each of whom Carstares made a farewell speech. The Princess replied " pleasantly," when he had addressed her ; " I desire your good prayers for me and the royal family, and I shall be glad of every opportunity to show my sincere concern for the good and welfare of the Church of Scotland." As they left the royal presence, they were followed by the Duke of Montrose, who was commissioned by the King to tell Carstares and Mitchell that he continued to them both the office of Royal Chaplain, which they had held at the death of Queen Anne.†

The day before Christmas all the deputies, except Carstares, left London. Lining, who had sided with the Nonjurants, and who evidently regarded the courtly and politic Principal with some slight jealousy and suspicion, writes to Wodrow : " We have all provided horses but Mr. Carstares, who hath his own business to wait upon, and says he will follow us shortly. I fear our old friends prove our old burden still, and that we are not all steel to the back. I have discovered something of private counteracting of our public

<hr>

* Hart, p. 62.
† Ibid. Preface xi. McCormick, p. 88.

concerts, even when we seemed to be unanimous—and that amongst five."*

Carstares writes from London, on 13th January 1715, to his nephew William Dunlop: "I am like to have you for a colleague in the college; for this day the D. of Montrose did give orders for drawing your gift: and I pray God may make you serviceable in that station† which seems to be suited to your genius,—and I am glad that I have had an opportunity of showing any kindness to your father's son. Tell Mr. Scott that I have been far from forgetting him; and I hope he is convinced of it, ere now, by a letter to him under the D. of Montrose's own hand."‡ Then follows a number of messages to friends, whose interests had been committed to him, and for whom he had been expending much time and trouble at Whitehall and Kensington. "My affectionate service to Professor Hamilton. Tell him that Mr. Mitchell—to whom, by the bye, you are under very singular obligations—will tell him anything that I have to say. My dear love to my sisters, and to our honest cousin Mr. Wm. Mure, who must not take pet at my silence, for I will be friends with him, whether he will or not. I heartily salute all my colleagues. I know you will not forget any of my commissions mentioned above. I shall be glad to find the stair and my closet such as you give me hope of.§ Heartily adieu." This is the last of his letters in the Graham Dunlop collection.

The Nestor of the Church, who had been chosen to preside in her chief court at its first meeting after the Union of the Legislature, was again raised to the same honour in the first Assembly which met after the accession of the House of Hanover. His friend Mitchell, on resigning the chair to him, adopted the unusual course of formally addressing him

* Hart. Preface xi.
† As Professor at Edinburgh.
‡ On Mar's dismissal Montrose became Secretary of State.
§ The Town Council had undertaken to repair his house this winter. Council Records, vol. xli. p. 564.

in a short speech, in which he assured Carstares that in choosing him, by an almost unanimous vote, to be Moderator, after an event in the national history so momentous as a change of dynasty, the Church had expressed in the strongest way her confidence in his ability to serve her. After the Commissioner had delivered the King's letter and made the customary address to the Assembly, Carstares spoke at considerable length. He adverted to the happy succession of the Protestant house, and the "surprising Providence" which had brought it peaceably to pass. With an implicit rebuke to those zealots who seemed to expect that King George should assume the "dispensing power" for the sake of repealing the Toleration and the Abjuration oath, he declared, "There are indeed some grievances that we groan under, to which our Sovereign alone cannot give a redress, which yet we hope in good time we may, through his Majesty's kind interposition, be eased of." His own increasing years, he feared, might hinder his proper discharge of the duties they had entrusted to him, but he would try to do his part with all candour and fairness; and he took their choice of him as a proof of moderation, and of their disregard of the reproaches which his maligners had cast on him, and of their confidence in his honest desire to promote the true interests of the Church.*

His control is visible in the action of the Church at this rather critical time. The irritating legislation of the last eight years had disgusted the Scotch people with the Union; and the Church, injured by the Toleration, and insulted by the Oath of Abjuration, had been disposed to look with moody indifference, if not approval, on the manifestations of popular dislike of the treaty of 1707.

But when the flames of Jacobite rebellion were beginning to kindle in the North, and the Whigs and Presbyterians to find that Tories and Episcopalians were much keener for repeal than themselves, the Church could not safely remain

---

* MS. Records, Glasgow. Correspondence, vol. ii. p. 29.

passive. The Assembly, under Carstares's guidance, gave forth no uncertain sound. Calmly repressing all irregular or unnecessary agitation about its own special causes of complaint, it recalled the whole country to a just sense of the danger attending any policy which should seek to repeal the Union, by an exhibition of its righteous zeal for the Protestant dynasty, which owed its accession to that Union.

Two ministers in Aberdeenshire had refused to keep the day appointed for thanksgiving for the accession of King George, and had never prayed for him since he assumed the crown. Their case was brought before the Assembly. Carstares had always advocated a policy of forbearance and comprehension, where vital interests were not at stake; but in this instance he felt that the Church's sense of the evil of disaffection to the reigning house could not be too firmly marked. The decision of the Assembly was that the two ministers should be deposed; and after the Moderator had addressed them very pathetically, and had pointed out the magnitude of their offence against Church and State, he pronounced the solemn sentence which cut them off from the ministry.*

The proceedings of the Assembly were otherwise uneventful, and terminated on the 17th of May. It was the custom then, as it is now, to sing a psalm before the closing benediction is pronounced by the Moderator. The psalm which Carstares chose was the 124th, that song of exultant faith, which had always in Scotland been associated with the triumph of the "Good Cause." †   As he looked back upon

---

* Correspondence, vol. ii. p. 33.

† Acts of Assembly, 1714.

When, in 1582, John Durie, the banished minister, returned from his exile, and came up from Leith to Edinburgh, 200 men met him at the Gallow Green, and, their number ever increasing, followed him within the Nether Bow. "There they began to sing the 124th Psalm, ' Now Israel may say,' &c., and sang in four parts, known to most of the people. They came up the street till they came to the Great Kirk, singing thus all the way. . . . . . The Duke [Lennox] was astonished, and more affrayed at that sight than at anything he had ever seen before in Scotland, and rave his beard for anger."—Calderwood's Hist. iii. 646 (Wodrow Soc. edition.).

his father's and his kindred's sufferings, and his own years of exile and imprisonment—on the hazards of the Revolution, and the struggle with the wounded hydra of political prelacy—on the Union, and the subsequent encroachments on rights and claims that the Church had long held indisputable—on the perilous discontents and disaffections which had ensued, and which he had often found it difficult to hold in check—on the covert intrigues and undisguised hostilities which, but a few months ago, had been encouraged in high places, and seemed not unlikely to prevail against the cause of liberty and justice; and as he now saw the principles for which, since his boyhood, he had wrought and suffered, at last firmly established, the absolutist and persecuting house of Stuart finally renounced, and the security of the national Church confirmed under a new and distinctively Protestant dynasty—he well might invite his friends and brethren to join in praising God in the ancient strain, never more appropriate,—

> " Even as a bird
>   Out of the fowler's snare
> Escapes away, so is our soul set free ;
>   Broke are their nets, and thus escaped we.
> Therefore our help
>   Is in the Lord's great name,
> Who heaven and earth
>   By his great power did frame."

Carstares's last official act, of which we have a record, was the writing of a letter to the Scottish Consistory at Rotterdam, intimating that the Assembly had loosed from his charge in Scotland the minister who had been chosen by the Church in that city.

"I persuade myself," he adds, after the official statement, "that none of you will doubt my having always been heartily concerned for your interest, for I look upon myself as under special obligations to be so, and to have more than *common* interest in you. However what is above, is, at the appointment of the General

Assembly, signified to you by him, who is to you all, yours in true affection to love and serve,

" WILLIAM CARSTARES, Moderator." *

During the summer of 1715 Carstares was still active, and engaged in all his usual work. But in the month of August he was seized with an apoplectic fit. It gave a violent shock to his constitution, and though it yielded to medical treatment, left him with faculties somewhat impaired, and oppressed by a lethargy which he could not shake off.† He recovered, however, so far as to be able to write; and one of his latest occupations was the preparation of an account of his arrest, imprisonment, trial, and torture, in 1684 and 1685, which Wodrow had asked him to contribute to the history of the " Sufferings."‡

In December his malady returned, and it was evident that the end drew near. He awaited it in "great peace and serenity." A little while before his death those who watched beside him heard him say, " I have peace with God through our Lord Jesus Christ."

He died on Wednesday, the 28th December 1715, in the 67th year of his age.§

On Monday the 2nd of January he was carried to a grave beside his father's, in that historic churchyard of the Grey-friars, which, since the Reformation, had received the ashes of many of the most illustrious of his countrymen. There lay George Buchanan, the sagest and most learned of Scots. There, too, rested from his labours Alexander Henderson, the great leader of the Scottish Church in her conflict with the absolutism of Charles I. Thither, to be interred hard

---

* Steven., p. 149.   † McCormick, p. 88.

‡ Correspondence, vol. ii. p. 41. History, vol. iv. p. 96.

§ ' Analecta,' vol. ii. p. 311. McCormick, p. 88. " On Wednesday last Mr. William Carstares, principal of our college and one of the ministers of the New Church, departed this life, and is very much lamented, being a man of great worth, piety, and learning, and very charitable to the poor."— *Scots Courant* of December 30, 1715.

by the graves of martyrs whose blood he had shed, his friends had carried the body of Sir George Mackenzie.* To the same sacred enclosure a vast throng had followed the bier of his great rival Sir James Steuart.

The place where John Carstares had been buried, and which was now chosen for the burial of his illustrious son, was next to that of the other great Churchman,† whose tomb still bore marks of the bullets with which the soldiers of Charles II. had tried to efface the name of Henderson, and the legend "libertatis et disciplinæ ecclesiasticæ propugnator fuit acerrimus." "When his body was laid in the dust, two men were observed to turn aside from the rest of the company, and bursting into tears bewail their mutual loss. Upon inquiry it was found that they were two Nonjurant clergymen (Episcopal), whose families for a considerable time had been supported by his benefactions." ‡

---

* "When I stand in that historic cemetery, before the tombs of the ancient Covenanters, my heart glows with respect for honourable though mistaken adversaries. When I seek for the grave of Carstares, or gaze on the tomb of Robertson, I delight in the thought that spirits so noble and so generous as theirs were fellow-workers and forerunners in the mission which I, and those with whom I labour, delight to honour. But when I turn to the monument of the Bloody Mackenzie, it is with the bitter thought that I see there the memorial of a valued friend who has betrayed and disgraced a noble cause, and given occasion, it may be, to the enemies of freedom, charity, and truth, to blaspheme those holy names."—Dean Stanley, 'Church of Scotland,' p. 133.

† Mrs. Carstares died in 1724, and was buried beside her husband, "betwixt Henderson's tomb and the wall." In 1726, Sarah Carstares (Mrs. Dunlop) petitions the Town Council for permission to erect a monument "close by the wall, behind Mr. Henderson's tomb," where she states her father, John Carstares, had been buried, and, beside him, her brother and her son, William Dunlop, "late Regius Professor of Divinity and Church History."—'Greyfriars Epitaphs and Monumental Inscriptions :' Introduction, p. lxxxi.

‡ McCormick, p. 91. McCormick says the Latin inscription on Carstares's monument was already beginning to fade in 1793. It has now entirely faded. The monument itself still remains, though the friable stone has suffered much damage from the weather. It stands against the wall, and right opposite the tomb of Henderson. The likeness prefixed to this volume is from the small original painting, in the possession of Mr.

Thus "having served his generation," he passed away. His name is not one that should be forgotten by his countrymen. The gratitude for liberties vindicated and rights secured, which should never die out of the memory of a free people, is due to all those who, "fallen on evil tongues and evil days, with darkness and with dangers compassed round," have been faithful to the cause of civil and religious liberty.

Among those who were the heroes and martyrs of that cause, in times when to be a "leading Liberal" in Scotland had a meaning somewhat more dignified and earnest than now attaches to the term,—who laid the broad foundations of all that is soundest in our national welfare, by helping to overthrow a worthless dynasty and an unrighteous Church, no one is entitled to higher honour than he whose career I have tried to sketch. Ardent yet cautious, diplomatic yet incorruptible, he watched and waited and suffered, during the night of oppression and misrule. After helping to prepare the way of the deliverer, and doing his devoir with perfect courage and address in the contest which overthrew the corrupt system, civil and ecclesiastical, under which his native land groaned, he, when the brunt of the battle was over, was as forbearing and conciliatory as he had been resolute and brave,—a practical exponent of the gospel of charity and peace.

A courtier, he never used the royal favour for his private ends. A Churchman, he never sought to separate the interests of his order from the interests of the nation. A statesman of rare sagacity and knowledge of statecraft, yet forbidden to enter in person the arena of public politics, he stood by without jealousy, ill-will, or intrigue, content if, through his private influence, he could impart to the policy of others a character that should be just, tolerant, and liberal. His principles and his action were free from all harshness

Graham Dunlop (artist unknown). There is a larger portrait in the senate hall of the University of Edinburgh, by Aikman (1682–1731), which was engraved by Cooper. The engraving is very scarce.

For two Elegies on Carstares, see Appendix iv.

and violence of extremes. A Presbyterian, bred in an age
of prelatic persecution and sacerdotal arrogance, he was
indulgent to differences of religious opinion, government, and
ritual. A Liberal, in days when political parties gave no
quarter in their embittered strife, his Liberalism was calm
with the wisdom of experience, pure from all passion of the
mob, large in its scope, constructive and conservative even in
the midst of reform and revolution.

That the "Revolution Settlement," in Church and State,
was firmly established in Scotland; that the Union was
peaceably effected; that the Church, instead of splitting into
a number of hostile and fanatical sects, gradually accommodated itself to that relation with the State which at once
guaranteed its constitutional freedom, and equipped it most
efficiently for its sacred work,—was mainly owing to Carstares.
Men who wield the sword and die in battle, and men who,
with flaming zeal and quenchless energy, lead stormy factions
in days of popular excitement, stamp their names in deeper
impress upon the common memory than those who do the
more quiet, thoughtful, and laborious work of controlling
the impatient and inexperienced, and guiding the general
intelligence and action. But when the havoc of the more
hasty and passionate work has swept past, the result of the
more quiet and orderly abides, although the names of the
workers may be forgotten. For one Scotsman who has
heard the name of Carstares, thousands are familiar with
that of Dundee, though the actual life's work of the one is
woven into the very framework of our national being and
political constitution, and that of the other has been long
since cast into the limbo of unremembered vanities. The
verdict of History ought to redress the injustices of popular
opinion and ignorant caprice, and raise the statues of the
real heroes to their pedestals. To it the memory of Carstares
appeals; and I believe it will accord him, as he deserves, a
place among the best and highest in the long and splendid
roll of those Scotchmen, who have deserved well of the
republic.

APPENDIX.

No. I.

Carstares's deposition, as published by the Privy Council, was as follows :—

" Edinburgh Castle, Sept. 8, 1684.

" Mr. William Carstares, being examined upon oath conform to the condescension given in by him, and on the terms therein mentioned, deposes that, about November or December 1682, James Steuart, brother to the Laird of Coltness, wrote a letter to him from Holland, importing that if any considerable sum of money could be procured from England, something of importance might be done in Scotland. The which letter he had an inclination to inform Shepherd in Abchurch Lane, merchant in London, of; but before he could do it, he wrote to Mr. Steuart above named, to know from him if he might do it; and Mr. Steuart having consented, he communicated the said letter to Mr. Shepherd, who told the Deponent that he would communicate the contents of it to some persons in England, but did at that time name nobody, as the Deponent thinks. Some time thereafter, Mr. Shepherd told the Deponent that he had communicated the contents of the letter above named to Colonel Sidney, and that Colonel Danvers was present, and told the Deponent that Colonel Sidney was averse from employing the Earl of Argyle, or meddling with him, judging him a man too much affected to the Royal Family and inclined to the present Church government; yet Mr. Shepherd, being put upon it by the Deponent, still urged that one might be sent to the Earl of Argyle, but as Mr. Shepherd told him, he was suspected upon the account of his urging so much, yet afterwards he pressed, without the Deponent's knowledge, that the Deponent being to go to Holland however, might have some commission to the Earl of Argyle; which he having informed the Deponent of, the Deponent told him that he himself would not be concerned,

2 B

but if they would send another, he would introduce him; but nothing of this was done, upon which the Deponent went over, without any commission from anybody, to Holland, never meeting with James Steuart above named. He was introduced to the Earl of Argyle, with whom he had never before conversed, and did there discuss what had passed betwixt Mr. Shepherd and him, and particularly about remitting of money to the said Earl from England; of which the said Mr. Steuart had written to the Deponent, namely of £30,000 sterling, and of the raising of 1000 horse and dragoons, and the securing the Castle of Edinburgh, as a matter of the greatest importance. The method of doing this was proposed by the Deponent to be one hour, or thereby, after the relieving of the guards; but the Earl did not relish this proposition, as dangerous; and that the Castle would fall of consequence, after the work abroad was done. James Steuart was of the Deponent's opinion for seizing the Castle, because it would secure Edinburgh, the magazines, and arms. As to the 1000 horse and dragoons, my Lord Argyle was of opinion that without them nothing was to be done, and that if that number were raised in England to the said Earl, he would come into Scotland with them, and that there being so few horse and dragoons to meet them, he judged he might get the country without trouble, having such a standing body for their friends to rendezvous to; and the said Earl said he could show the Deponent the convenient places for landing if he understood, and as the Deponent remembers, where the ships could attend. The Deponent remembers not the names of the places. The Deponent spoke to the Lord Stair; but cannot be positive that he named the affair to him, but found him shy; but the Earl of Argyle told him he thought Stair might be gained to them, and that the Earl of Loudoun being a man of good reason and disobliged, would have great influence upon the country; and recommended the Deponent to Major Holms, with whom the Deponent had some acquaintance before, and had brought over a letter from him to the Earl of Argyle, but the Deponent had not then communicated anything to the said Holms. James Steuart laid down a way of correspondence by cyphers and false names, and sent them over to Holms and the Deponent for their use (which names and cyphers are now in the hands of Her Majesty's officers as the Deponent supposes), and did desire the Deponent earnestly to propose the £30,000 sterling above named, to the party in England, and did not propose any less; for as the Earl told the Deponent, he had particularly calculated the expense for arms, ammunition, &c.

But James Steuart said, that if some less could be had, the Earl
would content himself, if better might not be ; but the Earl always
said, that there was nothing to be done without the body of horse
and dragoons above mentioned. During the time of the Deponent
his abode in Holland, though he had several letters from Shepherd,
yet there was no satisfactory account, till some time after the
Deponent parted from the Earl of Argyle and was making for
a ship at Rotterdam to transport himself to England. James
Steuart wrote to him that there was hopes of the money. The next
day after the Deponent came to England he met with Sir John
Cochran, who, with Commissar Monro and Jerviswood, was at
London before he came over; and deposes, that he knows not the
account of their coming, more than for the perfecting the transaction about Carolina : and having acquainted Sir John Cochran
with the Earl's demands of the £30,000 sterling and the 1000
horse and dragoons, Sir John carried him to the Lord Russell, to
whom the Deponent proposed the affair, but being an absolute
stranger to the Deponent, had no return from him at that time ;
but afterwards having met him accidentally at Mr. Shepherd's
house, where he, the Lord Russell, had come to speak to Shepherd
about the money above named, as Mr. Shepherd told the Deponent.
The Deponent (when they were done speaking) desired to speak to
the Lord Russell, which the Lord Russell did, and having reiterated
the former proposition for the £30.000 sterling and the 1000
horse and dragoons, he, the Lord Russell, told the Deponent they
could not get so much raised at the time, but if they had £10,000
to begin, that would draw people in. And when they were once
in, they would soon be brought to more ; but as for the 1000
horse and dragoons, he would say nothing at the present, for that
behoved to be concerted upon the Borders. The Deponent made
the same proposal to Mr. Ferguson, who was much concerned in
the affair, and zealous for the promoting of it. This Mr.
Ferguson had in October or November before, as the Deponent
remembers in a conversation with the Deponent in Cheapside, or
the street somewhere thereabout—said, that for the saving of
innocent blood, it would be necessary to cut off a few, insinuating
the King and Duke, but cannot be positive whether he named them
or not, to which the Deponent said, That's work for our wild
people in Scotland : my conscience does not serve me for such
things. After which the Deponent had never any particular
discourse with Ferguson, as to that matter ; but as to the other
affair, Ferguson told the Deponent that he was doing what he

could to get it effectuate. As particularly that he spoke to one
Major Wildman, who is not of the Deponent his acquaintance.
Ferguson blamed always Sidney, as driving designs of his own.
The Deponent met twice or thrice with the Lord Melvil, Sir
John Cochran, Jerviswood, Commissar Monro, the two Cessnocks,
Mongomery of Langshaw, and one, Mr. Veitch, where they discoursed of money to be sent to Argyle, in order to carrying on
the affair, and though he cannot be positive the affair was named,
yet it was understood by himself, and as he conceives by all
present, to be for rising in arms, for rectifying the Government.
Commissar Monro, Lord Melvil, and the two Cessnocks, were
against meddling with the English, because they judged them
men that would talk, and would not do, but were more inclined to
do something by themselves, if it could be done. The Lord
Melvil thought everything hazardous, and therefore the Deponent
cannot say he was positive in anything, but was most inclined to
have the Duke of Monmouth to head them in Scotland, of which no
particular method was laid down. Jerviswood, the Deponent, and
Mr. Veitch, were for taking money at one of these meetings. It
was resolved, that Mr. Martin, late Clerk to the Justice Court,
should be sent to Scotland, to desire their friends to hinder the
country from rising or taking rash resolutions upon the account of
the Council, till they should see how matters went in England.
The said Martin did go at the charges of the gentlemen of the
meeting, and was directed to the Laird of Polwart and Torwoodlie,
who sent back word that it would not be found so easy a matter to
get the gentry of Scotland to concur. But afterwards in a letter
to Commissar Monro, Polwart wrote that the country was readier
to concur than they had imagined, or something to that purpose
The Deponent, as above said, having brought over a key from
Holland to serve himself and Major Holms, he remembers not that
ever he had an exact copy of it, but that sometimes the one, sometimes the other, keeped it, and so it chanced to be in his custody
when a letter from the Earl of Argyle came to Major Holms,
intimating that he would join with the Duke of Monmouth, and
follow his measures, or obey his directions. This Mr. Veitch
thought fit to communicate to the Duke of Monmouth, and for the
understanding of it was brought to the Deponent, and he gave the
key to Mr. Veitch, who as the Deponent was informed, was to give
it and the letter to Mr. Ferguson, and he to show it to the Duke
of Monmouth ; but what was done in it, the Deponent knows not.
The Deponent heard the design of killing the King and Duke,

from Mr. Shepherd, who told the Deponent seme were full upon it. The Deponent heard that Aaron Smith was sent by those in England to call Sir John Cochran, on the account of Carolina, but that he does not know Aaron Smith, nor any more of that matter, not being concerned in it. Shepherd named young Hampden frequently as concerned in those matters.

"Signed at Edinburgh Castle, the 8th of September, 1684, and renewed the 18th of the same month.

" WILLIAM CARSTARES.

Perth Cancell. I. P. D."

—

No. II.

LATTER WILL AND TESTAMENT OF MR. JOHN CARSTARES.

At Quarrelltown, Apryle 24, 1664.

I Mr. John Carstares, an unworthie minister of the Gospell, being putt, in the holie and good providence of God not for my sin nor any iniquitie found in my hand by men (thoughe there be alone verie muche for whiche he may most justlie charge me, for the pardone wherof I desyre to flee to Jesus Christ the propitiatione for the sins of the electe world) but for bearing witnesse to a faithfull testimony given by my disseast brother-in-law Mr. James Wood on his deathbed to Presbyterian Government, and because of my not being free in my conscience to appear before the High Commission without a testimony against the constitution of it, whiche thronghe the malice of some Churchmen armed with the power of the civil sword could not have been without eminent hazard of my lyfe. Being put, I say, to flie for my own preservatione according to the Lord's warrant, Matt 10. v. 23, and to wander (tell thou my wanderings O Lord) I know not well whither: And not knowing in this case how soon I may by a violent or naturall death be removed, desyring in well doing to committ the keeping of my soul unto God as unto a faithfull Creator and cordiallie to take him for a portione to my selfe to my wyfe (who hath alonge all this hour of tentatione bein no tentatione to me but a most faithfull companion in my tribulatione and (if I have anay interest there) in the kingdome and patience of Jesus Chryst) and to the children which he hath graciouslie given unto us, I have thought fitt being for present in health of bodie and ordinarie soundnesse of mynd to setle my small affaires the best way I can by making my latter will and testament thus :—The litle estate I have comes to about nyntein thousand merkes, fyve wherof is in my wnckle Sir John Carstares of Kilconwher his hand, tuo in the Laird of Ralystoun his hand, tuo in the young Laird of Duchall his hand (nou in William Hamiltoun of Wishaw his hand), tuo in Sir William Mure of Rowallan his hand, one in William Hammiltown of Barnes his hand. I reckon my duelling house in Glasgow to be at least worth tuo thousand merkes, for I gave six and tuentie hundred merkes for it, besyde nigh three hundred merkes I expended on it since I bought it, whiche I desyre may be sold with the first convenience. In all whiche sumes, coming to fourteen thousand merkes, my wyfe Jonet Mure was lyferented, but some of the bonds have been changed since and drauen at a distance wherin she is not mentioned as lyferenter, therfore that she may sustain no prejudice I doe hereby declare that it is my will and doe accordinglie expresselie appoynt that the said Jonet Mure, my verie loving spowse, shall have after my desscasse during all the tyme of hir life the yearlie interest of the forsaid severall sumes amounting in whole to fourteen thousand merkes, and allowes and appoynts if it be necessarie that the severall bonds be reneued wherein hir lyferent is not specified that the said clause may be insert in them. There is further of the forsaid nynteen thousand merkes fyve thousand in the noble lord my lord Marquesse of Argyle his hand, with four yeares interest at Candlemesse or Lambesse last bypast. Out of all which sumes I doe provyde my children as followeth : I doe provyde for and appoynt unto my eldest son, William, the sum of fyve thousand merkes; to my second son, Alexander, tuo thousand and fyve hundred merkes; to my third son, James, tuo thousand merkes; to my eldest daughter, Sarah, three thousand merkes; to my second daughter, Katharine, tuo thousand and fyve hundred merkes; to my third daughter, Ursula, tuo thousand merkes, and to the chyld wherwith my wyfe presentlie is, whither son or daughter, if the Lord shall think fit to bring it safe to the world, tuo thousand merkes. And if any of the forsaid sumes due to me, by the forsaid persons conforme to the tenure of their bonds granted to me thereanent (whiche are all in my wyfe's custodie, excepte my Lord of Argyle's bonds that is in Wishawe's custodie) with the rights of the duelling house in Glasgow, shall proove ineffectuall for the provision of my children then and in that case I give full and absolute pouer to my beloved spouse Jonet Mure, uith the other worthie friends nominated afterward for the oversight of my children and their affaires, to proportion the losse amongst all the children as their severall provisions may best bear the same, so that if it may be they that have least may have a thousand pounds. And I doe hereby declaire and appoynt that this their deed shall be as valid as to all effectes whatsoever, as if I my selfe had actuallie done it in myne own tyme. And if anay of the children shall presume to gainsay, then in that case I declare and appoynt that anay provision I have made to them by this my Latter Will shall be utterlie null and voyd as to their behoofe and advantage, as if it had never bein made by me, ordaining withall that the provision of such shall be divyded amongst the rest equallie. And if it shall please the Lord to remove anay of the children by death before they come to the yeares that will by the law capacitat them to dispose upon their own portions, then and in that case I appoynt the one-halfe or third part, as their mother and friends after nominated shall think most fitt, to come to my eldest son William, and the other halfe in tuo parts to be equallie divyded amongst the rest of my children. I leave my loving and faithfull spouse Jonet Mure my sole executrix, to intromett with my goods and gear, such as my housholde stuffe and plenishing, reserving the airscape, my books, which will be well worth a thousand merkes thoughe the third part of the pryce be given down and all bygone interests of whatsoever principall summes due to me, and out of these I appoynt hir to pay anay litle thinge I am owing whiche she knows. And I allow no persons in the world whether my children or anay others whatsoever to make anay question or doubt of what she shall give up as debts owing by me nor to call hir to ane account but as she shall please for the particular fore-mentioned books, household stuffe, and by-run interests; and this trust I dar confidentlie putt into hir, being well assured that she will be faithfullie answerable to it. And I nominat and appoynt my verie loving spowse Jonet Mure, the Lairds of Ralstown elder and younger, the Lairds of Halleraige elder and younger, James Mure of Bellibregage in Irland, William Porterfield of Quarreltown, Mr. Alexander Dunlop minister at Pasely, William Hammiltown of Wishaw, Sir John Carstares my unckle, and William Sandilands my brother, when they may be had, for they tuo live at a great distance, tutors to my children and to take as in my rowm and place the oversight of them all, whither under tutorie or not, and of all their affaires and to doe in the premissis, and what else shall be found by them or anay tuo or three of them for the reall good of my children by chairging and renewing of bonds, selling and disposing of houses, transferring and uplifting of sumes, and giving such proportions to such of the children as shall apply themselves to anay calling requyring the same, and all other things as fullie and uncontrollablie as I myselfe could have done. And I doe hereby requyre and solemnlie charge all my children to yeald up themselves as to be disposed upon in all their concernments by them and to be obedient to them, acquiescing as to all things in their determination as they wolde have done in myne as they wolde not displease God and crosse their father's Latter Will. As to them all so I doe more particularlie seriouslie recommend and committ their Christian and ingenuous educatione to my faithfull spowse their mother, willing, exhorting, and obtesting them all to carie towards hir uith that love, respecte, and obedience that becomes. I hope she will keep them with hir selfe (but when its otherwayes necessarie for their good) so longe as she shall after my disscasse live wnmarried, all whiche tyme and till they be otherwayes disposed upon, I doe allow hir to uplift and make use of as she shall think fitt the yearlie interest of the whole nynteen thousand merkes. And if she shall think meet to change hir conditione of lyfe after my disscasse and to mary, wherein I doe heartilie leave hir to hir own libertie, I hope she will for my cause be kind to the children, and consider, since they have so little besyde (and it may come to lesse then no thinge), what she may let goe of hir joynture, wherin also I can with much quyetnesse of mynd lippen to hir, having found hir alwayes tender of me and them. I desyre she may, when she can convenientlie, and that out of the forsaid moveables, give to M. James Blair, or any other fitt person, fiftie merkes Scotts for the use of the poor of Cathcart. Finallie I recommend my loving spowse, my children, and thar overseers to take advyce when need is from Judge Ker, my honoured, worthie, and faithfull friend. And this I allow to stand in force as my Latter Will and Testament. In witnesse wherof I have wreatten and subscrybed thir presents with myne oun hand at Quarreltown the twentie-four day of Apryle, j^m vj^c threescore and four yeares ; befor thir witnesses William Porterfield of Quarreltown and Mr. James Stirline minister at Pasely

(Signed)   Mr. J. Carstares
"   W. Porterfield, witnes
"   Mr. J. Stirling, witnes.

No. III.

Catalogus Librorum Gul. Carstares.   April 9.   Londini 1685.

1. Eylsemii conciones sacræ comæ applicatæ, sive piæ animæ deliciæ.
2. Clopenburgii compendium Socinianismi confutatum.
3. Voetii oratio funebris in obitum Schotani.
4. Hoornbecki examen bullæ papalis.
5. Flockenii opera theologica.
6. Dallæi Vindiciæ.
7. Dauhaneri Jura, &c.
8. Essenii triumphus crucis.
9. Pauli Voet theologia naturalis, et disquisitio de anima separata.
10. Kirchwajeri Nepos illustratus.
11. Althusii Politica.   Editio 5ta.
12. Junii et Tremollii Bibl. latina.
13. Leusdeni Biblia Hebraica.
14. Voetii select. disp. pars 5ta.
15. Spanhemii Vindiciæ biblicæ.
16. Altingii theologia Historica.
17. Altingii theologia problem.
18. Introduction à la langue Françoise.
19. Sept Sermons par Durant.
20. Itinerarium Benjaminis.
21. Institutiones juris civilis.
22. The Bishop of Dunblain's Accommodation examined.
23. Essenii system. theol. tom. 2^{dus}.
24. Scaliger de subtilitate, contra Cardanum.
25. Fernelii Medicina.
26. Triglandii trina dei gratia.
27. Stegmanni Plotinianismus.
28. Compendiosa methodus discendi linguam Germanicam, Gallicam, et Italicam.
29.* Rhetorfortis examen Armin. 2 vol.
30. Gentiletus contra Macchiavellum.
31. Voetii confraternitas Mariana.
32. Confessio et Catechesis eccles. Belgicarum.
33. Berkringeri Dissertatio de Conciliis.
34. Voetii Bibliotheca.

Rutherford.

35. Omphalii Rhetorica.
36. Wendelini Theologia Christiana ed. 3^{tia}.
37. Leusdeni Clavis græca novi Testamenti.
38. Carninii Apparatus bellicus contra Libertinos.
39. Grammatica Gallica de la Grue.
40. Testamentum Græcum.
41. Justini historia.
42. Trelcatii loci communes.
43. Taciti Annales.
44. Pauli Voet Jurisprud. sacra.
45. Beza de repudiis.
46. Leusdeni manuale hebraicum et chaldaicum.
47. The covenant between God and man.
48. Rhetorfortis Exercit. Apologet.
49. Voet. de Idololatria Indirecta.
50. Herebordii Ethica, et Maccovii Metaphysica.
51. Rosæi Virgilius triumphans.
52. Revii Cartesiomania, vol. 2.
53. Voet. de cœlo Beatorum, et bismortuis.
54. Wolzogivus de Scripturarum interprete.
55. Thaddæi Conciliatorium Biblicum.
56. Leusdeni Philologus Hebræus.
57. Turretinus de Satisfactione.
58. Scharpii Symphonia.
59. Valerius Maximus.
60. Yarrow's soveraign Comforts.
61. Dan. Voet. Meletem. philos.
62. Compendium philosoph. manuscriptum.
63. Paul. Voet. de duellis.
64. Hornii dissert. politicæ.
65. Suffragium Theologorum Magnæ Britanniæ de 5 Articulis
66. Horatii poemata.
67. Dan. Voet. Pneumatica.
68. Whitakerus de Scriptura.
69. Juelli Apologia.
70. Ovidii Epistolæ.
71. Synopsis physica.
72. The Monk unveiled.
73. The Countess of Kent's manual.
74. Bovet of Witchcraft.

No. IV.

In Obitum Desideratissimi

Gulielmi Carstarii,

Academiæ *JACOBI* Regis *Edinburgenæ* Gymnasiarchæ,

ELEGIA.

MOLLI Membra Toro stratus cum mane jacerem,
  Et premeret Somnus, talia visa mihi.
Astitit ante Oculos Vultus suffusa nitentes
  EDINUM Luctu ; tristis, Acerba gemens.
ALMAque flens MATER, riguos urgebat Ocellos :
    Vixque sinunt Lachrymæ hæc tristia Dicta dare.
  "Consilio qui nos, Meritis qui sæpe juvabat
    "Occidit : Huic quis par repperiendus erit ?
  "Temperet a Lachrymis quis ferreus ? ipse maderet
    "*DEMOCRITUS* Fletu, tristia Fata sciat.
Et pallere mihi visa est ECCLESIA, obortas
  Extincto Tenebras Lumine questa sibi.
Orbatamque suo Fulcro titubasse putavi :
  Hos & lugubres hausimus Aure Sonos.
  "Raptus abest is cui Veri Rectique tenaci
    "Dulce solum PATRIÆ vertere Dulce fuit.
  "In PATRIAMque Redux qui effulsit Lumine miro
    "Nostri semper Honos Ordinis atque Decus.
  "Lilia marcescunt, perit heu ! Flos sæpe Rosarum,
  "Infelix Lolium dum dominatur Agris.
Latius hinc planctum Serpentem gliscere vidi :
  Regia Mærore & tangitur ipsa Domus.
Rus fremit, Urbs plangit, deflentes Lumine cassum :
  Ipsas PIERIDES ingemuisse putes.
Excussus Somno, Lachrymis exclamo profusis,
    "*CARSTARIUS* Magnus, proh Dolor ! occubuit.
  "ALMA Ducem MATER gemit hunc, hunc *SCOTIA* Civem
    "Luget : Et hinc Planctus visus adesse mihi.
  "Hujus ad Exemplum instituant Homines modo Vitam,
    "Aurea tu nasci denuo Sæcla putes.
  "Tunc iterum colerent PAX & CONCORDIA Terras,
    "His ASTRÆA Comes linqueret ipsa Polum.
  "Non ita distraherent infesta infaustaque CLERUM
    "Schismata : Non Fratrum Gratia rara foret."   *J. K.*

In Obitum Desideratissimi
Gulielmi Carstarii, S.S.T.D.
Academiæ *Edinburgenæ* Gymnasiarchæ,
ELEGIA.

SCOTIA SE tanti Matrem miratur Alumni !
    Et TE sublatum Terra *BRITANNA* gemit.
ALMA Ducem MATER dolet HUNC, ECCLESIA Patrem,
    Atque HOMINES Civem ex nobiliore Luto.
SCOTIA TE raptum dolet, immedicabile Vulnus !
    TE *MECÆNATEM* CASTALIDUMque Chorus.
Et Domus *AUGUSTI* felix TE luget ademptum,
    Nam sibi devinctum vix habet illa PAREM.
Libera Gens *BATAVUM* plangit, CUI, Gloria Secli !
    NASSOVIUM fuerat non cecinisse Nefas :
Hospitio excepere suo, post mille Labores
    Sacratos PATRIO, cum PIETATE, Solo.
LUGDUNI postquam libasset Numinis Aræ,
    Tunc redit in PATRIAM, *NASSOVIO*que Comes,
Cujus & Auspiciis, ob Res feliciter actas,
    Astrixit PATRIAM, FANAque, TEMPLA sibi.
Et sub Vexillo REGIS, Labaroque *GEORGI*,
    Sustinuit puræ RELLIGIONIS Onus.

                                   D. D.

INDEX.

BY THE SAME AUTHOR.

———◆———

ROBERT STORY, OF ROSNEATH: a Memoir, including Passages of Scottish Religious and Ecclesiastical History during the Second Quarter of the Present Century. Crown 8vo. 7s. 6d.

MACMILLAN AND CO.

CHRIST THE CONSOLER. 12mo. 3s. 6d.

EDMONSTON AND DOUGLAS.

LIFE AND REMAINS OF ROBERT LEE, D.D. 2 vols. 8vo. 30s.

HURST AND BLACKETT.

www.ingramcontent.com/pod-product-compliance
Lightning Source LLC
Chambersburg PA
CBHW032144110726
47902CB00003B/685